Love Finds You™

in Victory Heights

WASHINGTON

Love Finds You™ in Victory Heights WASHINGTON

BY TRICIA GOYER
AND OCIEANNA FLEISS

summerside
PRESS™

Summerside Press™
Minneapolis 55438
www.summersidepress.com

Love Finds You in Victory Heights, Washington
© 2010 by Tricia Goyer and Ocieanna Fleiss

ISBN 978-1-60936-000-9

Unless otherwise noted, all Scripture quotations are from the Holy Bible,
King James Version.

The town depicted in this book is a real place, but all characters are
fictional. Any resemblances to actual people or events are purely
coincidental.

Cover design by Chris Gilbert | www.studiogearbox.com.

Interior design by Müllerhaus Publishing Group | www.mullerhaus.net.

Vintage photos of the Seattle Boeing plant and factory workers are
from the U.S. government archives and are public domain. Photo
of modern-day Victory Heights provided by the authors.

Author photo of Ocieanna Fleiss © 2010 by Jessica McCollam |
Jessica's Visions Photography.

Author photo of Tricia Goyer © 2010 by Jessica McCollam |
Jessica's Visions Photography.

*Summerside Press™ is an inspirational publisher offering fresh,
irresistible books to uplift the heart and engage the mind.*

Printed in USA.

Dedication

....

To my grandma, Dolores Coulter,
whose loving guidance pointed me to Jesus.
Tricia Goyer

To the Rosie the Riveters of World War II,
who left the comfort of their homes
to brave strenuous and unfamiliar jobs
in the national pursuit of victory.
Your strong arms played a mighty role
in preserving the freedom we now enjoy.
Ocieanna Fleiss

Acknowledgments

To my Michael, whose love and support carry me through each day. Without his help with the kids, the house, and his own career, this book wouldn't have happened.

To the best kids in the world—Ben, Gabrielle, Christian, and Abigail. Thanks for being on my team!

To Tricia, for laboring over edit after edit and making it shine.

A huge thank you to the real-life Rosies, who generously gave their time and stories to Tricia and me on a cool October afternoon: Georgie Kunkel, Anita Lusk, Chris Holm, Margaret Seis, and Rowena Tobias. Also, to my dear friend Jan, who shared photographs and stories about her mom, Iris, the first female auto parts deliverer in Seattle.

Thank you to my McCritters: Annette Irby, Dawn Kinzer, and Veronica McCann, for their great plotting advice; and to Kathy Jones, for her expert critiques. Many thanks go to Vicki Stiles from the Shoreline Historical Museum, who poured out her wealth of information about the Victory Heights area as well as Playland. To my mother-in-law, Nellie Fleiss, for research help, and my sister-in-law, Poppy Tackett, for being a first reader. Sharon Chastain at the Maple Valley Library also answered my panicked requests for research help.

I can't adequately express my gratitude for Emmanuel Ortho-dox Presbyterian Church, which faithfully preaches and teaches the Word of God, and especially to a group of ladies who inspired me with a Rosie-inspired OCIEANNA CAN DO IT T-shirt. Love it!

I'm also always thinking of my mom, who supported any

dream I wanted to pursue and shared stories of her life as a little girl during the War.

And most of all, to my faithful Savior, Jesus Christ, who fully paid for all my sins with His precious blood.

Ocieanna Fleiss

Acknowledgments

....

Words cannot express the gratitude I have for those who pour into my life to make these books possible. Topping the list: my awesome coauthor, Ocieanna Fleiss, who must have Rosie biceps now for the many ways she carries me!

I will forever be thankful for my family and friends: My husband, John. My kids—Cory, Leslie, Nathan. My grandma, whose prayers lift me up every morning. My numerous friends at Easthaven Baptist Church, who lift me with their prayers. My small group friends: the Dittmers, Waltmans, Griffins, Callans, and Klundts. Also, much appreciation goes to my friend Jim Thompson for his wonderful insights and edits.

Tricia Goyer

And last but not least, we want to thank those who have so prayerfully and diligently worked to make this book possible, including our agent, Janet Grant. A special thanks to Carlton Garborg, our editors—Rachel Meisel and Ramona Tucker—our publisher, Summerside Press, and so many of their staff. We couldn't have done this without you! We hope you will always know how much we appreciate you.

Tricia Goyer and Ocieanna Fleiss

*Not unto us, O L*ord,
not unto us,
but unto thy name give glory.
PSALM 115:1

NAMED FOR VICTORY HIGHWAY, which had celebrated the triumphant end of World War I, Victory Heights is a neighborhood in north Seattle, Washington. The damp streets and cedar-clustered hillsides paint a portrait of down-home America. During the Second World War, stars hung from windows representing sons at war—and those who had fallen. Hopeful workers lugged their belongings into the small homes of Victory Heights, and its women rose to action, hefting the load while their men fought for freedom overseas.

Seattle brimmed with life during the War. Its West Coast location made it the perfect launching ground for military missions to the Pacific Theater. For the area's protection, brownouts, barrage balloons, and anti-aircraft missile sites were set up. Some you can still visit today. Despite Seattle's commitment to victory, folks in the Northwest also knew how to have fun. Restaurants (such as the odd-shaped Igloo), dance clubs, and the famous Playland served as fun escapes for the hard-working population. Not only did many celebrities, such as Bob Hope and Lana Turner, make stops at Seattle's Victory Square, but dignitaries such as President Franklin D. Roosevelt and First Lady Eleanor Roosevelt also celebrated Seattle as a great contributor to the War effort. Researching the Northwest's rich World War II history gave us great admiration for the area.

Tricia Goyer and Ocieanna Fleiss

Prologue

....

May 3, 1942
Seattle

The cool, misty air caused Rosalie Madison to pull her arms tight against her as she focused on the twenty bombers that lined the runway, wingtip to wingtip. They were a forest of gray metal except for one bright spot, a splash of color on the nose of Vic's B-17. It was the painting of a young woman's face—*her face*—the word *Rosalie* scripted beneath it.

Her hands covered her mouth. Wide-eyed, she turned to Vic. "I'm there. I mean, that's me. My face is on that bomber!"

Vic beamed like a child presenting a birthday gift. "They usually paint the nose-art—and name the planes—overseas, but since I'm flying this one all the way down to the South Pacific, they gave me the honor of having it done."

"I can't believe you did that for me. I've never had anyone give me such a special gift." She couldn't get her eyes off the image. She could tell from her painted, playful smile that whoever drew it copied the photograph she and Vic had taken last summer to announce their engagement.

"It's partly selfish." Vic grinned. "Nothing could be more inspiring than to see your smiling face before every mission. To remember, more than anything, who I'm fighting for."

"You're a good catch, you know." She playfully punched his shoulder.

"I know that." He cocked an eyebrow. "Do you?"

A twinge of sadness struck her heart at his question. Her smile faded. "Yes, of course. How could you even ask?"

Since she was a young girl, the one thing she'd wanted more than anything was to find a good man to spend her life with—to grow old together, to raise children, to pursue dreams side by side. Then, one day, she saw the caring guy she'd grown up with in a whole new way. Who better than a best friend for a fiancé? She had good hopes for their future together, but now—in this moment—she needed his strength.

Vic led her across the freshly mown airfield, toward the flight line, and Rosalie savored the assurance of his hand pressed against the small of her back. Vic was the steady one, the brave man she relied on to plan, lead, and support her. But did she love him as more than a friend? A knot tightened in her stomach. If they'd followed his plans, they'd be married now.

Did I make a mistake? Will I regret not saying "I do"?

Rosalie's heartbeat quickened as the bomber grew larger in her sight. Taking in the immense machine, her chest constricted with pride, knowing her work played a part in crafting these great gray beasts. She was also proud of Vic—proud he was going. If she couldn't fight the Japanese herself, at least she could send her man.

Anger filled Rosalie's mind at the thought of that morning last December when everything had changed. She'd been lying in bed, reminiscing about the fun time she and Vic had the previous night, jitterbugging at the Harbor Room, when her mother knocked on her bedroom door. The horror on her mother's face should have prepared her for anything. But not for the news of the attack. From the first moment she heard of Pearl Harbor's bombing, Rosalie worried about her brother, Rod, who was stationed on the USS *Arizona*, one of the ships pummeled by enemy fire during the attack.

Then the horrible reality struck home. Rod's remains were never recovered but were still trapped inside, along with his crewmates', in an underwater tomb. Rosalie wondered if those bodies would ever be removed. She also had a feeling that Vic, a pilot, would be one of the first to sign up for the fight. She was right. They'd lost her brother, and now Vic was leaving too.

Sadness and fear swelled, but she quickly shoved it down. She'd pull those emotions out later—during her work at the factory when her muscles throbbed and her heart ached with thoughts of Vic fighting so far away. Fighting to save life, as they knew it, against some foreigners' greed for land and power.

Hand in hand, Rosalie and Vic hurried through a sea of McChord Field's best ground crew, engaged in orderly chaos. The mechanics were diligently checking and rechecking the bombers' massive radial engines, hydraulics, control cables, and airframe. Large tanker trucks rumbled by on their way to fuel the aircraft. The only things missing were the bombs that would be loaded into the specially designed compartments. No bombs here. Not yet.

Rosalie tucked her pocketbook more firmly under her arm. Until Vic returned, she had a job to do. In addition to her work at the plant, she was determined to stay strong. Strong for Vic—and for herself. In the midst of their time apart, she'd make a decision about her future. About *theirs*.

Her pumps squished through the cold, wet grass, chilling her feet.

"I understand you wanting to wait until I get back, you know, to tie the knot," Vic said, sensing her thoughts as usual. "I'll be home on leave next spring. You'll love an April wedding. Your tulips will be in bloom." His lips curved in a reassuring smile.

She leaned her head against Vic's shoulder as they neared the bomber. "Yes," she said simply. "April's a beautiful month." But what would Vic think if he knew her hesitation had more to do with her own doubts than the great big war that consumed everyone's thoughts these days?

He tugged her toward his B-17 and patted its belly. "Rosalie, this is Rosalie. She'll keep me safe while I'm away."

His mention of being kept safe sent a surge of anxiety through her. "She better," Rosalie mumbled while studying Vic's eyes. Worry eclipsed the joy of a moment ago.

"Rosalie, I want to say—"

The light May rain abruptly transformed into a waterfall of water pounding noisily on the plane's thin, sheet-aluminum-covered wings and fuselage. Rosalie and Vic dashed under the wing for shelter.

She forced a mask of cheerfulness, not wanting to hear Vic's words, his heart. Lightening the mood, she deepened her voice like a Hollywood actress. "Don't worry about me, flyboy. I can take care of myself."

Vic grinned. "Oh, you can, can you?"

"You bet." She put a hand on her hip and brandished a wagging finger. "You just promise to do the same."

"Oh, I will." He tugged her to himself and gently stroked her curls. "Watch yourself." Tenderness dripped from his voice. "Don't overdo it at the plant. I need my strong girl waiting—someone I can come home to." Vic's voice turned serious, but Rosalie recognized the hint of teasing. "Remember, you're *just* a girl."

Rosalie whacked his arm. "Just a girl? You wouldn't even have a plane to fly if it weren't for me."

"Weren't for you? Just you?" His mouth formed that crooked grin.

"I know I'm one of many, but—" She reached over his shoulder and fingered a rivet on the fuselage. "I think I remember this one. I named him Rivie." Then she stepped back and held her hands up as if holding an invisible rivet gun. "Yep, I'm sure of it. I made this plane."

"Sir?" a man's voice interrupted.

Rosalie spun around, feeling as if their private party had been crashed.

A young airman raced across the airstrip and joined them under the wing. "Sorry to, uh, interrupt." A hint of red colored his cheeks. "Control tower says you have five minutes." Then he disappeared as quietly as he'd come.

"Five minutes?" Rosalie felt her brave façade crumble. She clutched Vic, stealing one last measure of strength.

"Where's my independent Rosie?" He gently thumbed away a tear. "Where's the Boeing girl who'll win the war all by herself?"

Boots stomping through the rain grew louder.

"I swore I wasn't going to cry like those other girls."

"But you're *my* girl." Vic touched her chin, then leaned his cheek against hers. "I love you, Rosalie. I'll be back soon."

Rosalie opened her mouth, but she couldn't return his loving words—not when uncertainty still filled her heart. "You're a wonderful man," she managed to say.

Nine crewmen approached to board the plane. Vic kept his eyes on her as he grabbed the cockpit ladder and stooped under the plane's belly. "You keep saving the world, will ya?"

She waved back. "I will. You too!"

As he poked his head into the hatch, her resolve faltered. *Save the world?* She couldn't even save her own feelings.

Alone, Rosalie walked back to the gate, hoping to enjoy one last glimpse of her flyboy before he taxied out, but the sky's reflection on the Plexiglas wind screen prevented it. She had to be satisfied with watching the plane taxi to the runway, wait its turn, and depart with its engines' deep-throated roar. One by one the planes departed and, second to last, the *Rosalie* lifted, then vanished into the clouds.

"Okay, girl," Rosalie whispered to herself. "Pull it together. This is your life now."

In the parking lot, she slid into the front seat of Vic's 1938 Ford. Vic had told her to sell it to help the war effort, but she knew she wouldn't be able to. He loved this car. The least she could do was care for his "baby." Then she'd surprise him with it when he got home. It wasn't exactly what Vic had planned, but life didn't always work out as in one's dreams.

Chapter One

....

June 7, 1943
Seattle

Rosalie Madison's lips always curled into a smile at her roommate Birdie Phibbs's high-pitched giggles. Even on hard days. Even on *this* day.

The salty tang of ocean air, subtly mixed with diesel exhaust fumes, wafted through the open windows, past Rosalie and a squad of other female factory workers. Loose coins in the fare box jingled as the Seattle city bus jounced through potholes en route to the Boeing plant. There they would join an army of other women who lovingly welded, riveted, and pounded out B-17 bombers to win the war and bring their boys back home.

Rosalie fixed her gaze on a middle-aged couple walking shoulder to shoulder down the sidewalk.

Look away, she told herself, noting their easy gaits. *Don't. Don't imagine the warm sensation of your hand wrapped gently in a large, strong one.* If she could have anything at this moment, it would be that peaceful joy of being close to someone she loved, instead of the burden of loneliness that had become her constant companion. Added to that, the heavy weight of guilt caused her shoulders to slump and her eyelids to droop, even at the beginning of her workday.

As the bus passed the couple, the man placed a soft kiss on top of the woman's head, causing laughter to spill from her lips. Rosalie sucked in a cool breath, but it felt like lead in her chest. Her fists balled on her lap, and her lips pressed into a tight line.

Why did she do this to herself? Why couldn't she simply look away? It should make her feel better that the war hadn't changed everything—that bits of happiness could still be found in the world—but it didn't.

Birdie chatted with the woman in the seat across the aisle, but Rosalie focused on the florist shop, the bank, and the small café outside her window. The bus driver's voice broke through her thoughts. "University Street and Fourth!"

Rosalie turned back to Birdie. "Oh no! This is where I need to get off." She stood.

"What are you doing, girlie?" Birdie tilted her head, flaxen curls brushing her petite shoulder. "Aren't you coming to work today?" Her lips puckered. "If you're not there, who'll be my partner? More than that, what will our boss say? You'll be in big trouble for sure!"

The bus whined to a stop amidst exhaust fumes and the screech of air brakes. Rosalie grabbed her satchel and eyed her roommate. "It's Vic. I have to go to the square."

"It's today—?" Birdie's smile softened, her eyes narrowing in compassion.

Rosalie nodded. "A year."

"I understand," Birdie murmured and touched Rosalie's forearm with her dainty, yet strong, hand.

"You comin' or what? Get the lead out, lady." The driver held the bus's door open for her, frowning at her in the large rearview mirror.

Rosalie gave Birdie a quick hug. "I'll just be a few minutes. Won't take long." Then she shuffled past Birdie's knees and jogged down the aisle. "I should make it before the whistle," she called over her shoulder.

"You better, or the boss'll be off his lid!"

Rosalie bounded down the steep steps, hitting the pavement with her sturdy shoes. She again breathed in the cool gusts sweeping down from the cloud-splotched blue sky. As she hurried forward, the stabbing guilt she'd carried since Vic had asked her to marry him pierced her heart. *If I'd only married Vic before he left, like he wanted....*

Turning the corner, Rosalie spotted her destination: Victory Square. The city had blocked off a section of the Seattle downtown district for war bond rallies, starting in May and going until Labor Day. The day before he left, she and Vic had seen Bob Hope perform the square's dedication show. Rosalie's pace slowed, and she eyed the stage. A work crew scurried around for the daily noon performance.

Pain drilled a hole into her heart as she remembered Bob Hope's voice calling over the crowd, his finger pointing straight at Vic. "Hey, lovebirds! You two married yet?"

When Vic said no, Mr. Hope had joked, "Well, what are you waiting for, flyboy? A war?"

Rosalie and Vic had laughed, but the laughter only pierced her heart, especially as Vic gently massaged her neck, his comforting touch beneath her bobbed, brunette hair.

But that was then. Today he was here with her too, in a different way.

She hurried across the bustling square, past the Olympic Hotel and the large podium, crafted as a replica of Thomas Jefferson's Monticello.

A group of sailors tried to get her attention as she passed, but she lifted her chin and ignored their calls. Another painful memory surfaced, but she pushed it down. She couldn't think of that—not today. One painful memory was enough to carry.

Rosalie hurried her steps toward the 75-foot-high replica of the Washington Monument, looming like a sentry from the other side. Reaching it, she slid her fingertips over the names etched into one of the wooden walls, feeling each indentation. The edges of the newer ones were sharper, slightly jagged. There were so many rows, so many names of the men from King County who'd died in the war.

EDWARD C MESCHER
JAMES M MESERVEY
LEWIS T MESHISHNEK
DOUGLAS L METCALF

She didn't rush past the names of these men who had sacrificed their lives for freedom but whispered a wish—a hope—for those living with the crushing emptiness of grief. For those left behind, who stirred up impossible strength and faithfully bought war bonds, planted victory gardens, donated silk, scrap metal, tires—and did their greatest duty by offering up more sons.

As Rosalie progressed through the names, the clamor in the street amplified, and she noticed small clusters of city dwellers on lunch break filling the empty spaces on the block.

Remembering her limited time, Rosalie returned her focus to the engraved names, still fingering each one. Finally, she stopped.

VICTOR MICHAELS

A gravel-gray cloud drifted across the sun, shading the square with a swathe of gloom. A shiver trailed down Rosalie's arms as she traced the letters: V-I-C...

A year ago today. She thought back, remembering how one call had changed everything.

She'd almost missed it. Rushing out the door of her and Birdie's apartment for her swing shift, Rosalie had stopped to enjoy Birdie mimicking Jimmy Durante. Even now she had to smile, thinking of Birdie shaking her head as if she possessed a magnificent schnoz, pretending to hold a cigar, and singing in her most scratchy voice, "*Ink a dinka do, a dinka dee...*"

Rosalie had been bent over laughing when the phone rang, but hearing Mrs. Michaels' tense silence on the phone ended all that.

The older widow's voice sounded tight, shaky, and Rosalie's breathless laughter caught in her throat as dread, panic, and disbelief pounded home in her mind. Before Mrs. Michaels even spoke the words, Rosalie knew Vic was gone.

His mother had received the official visit, the officer trying hard to sound compassionate after hundreds of such visits. As Rosalie wasn't Vic's wife, she wouldn't get the official visit. No, Mrs. Michaels had to endure that.

The *Rosalie* was shot down in a battle at a place called Midway Island. His bomber had been hit, yet Vic stayed at the controls until the rest of the crew made it out. He died a hero. Because they buried Vic in Hawaii, the family wasn't allowed to go to the funeral—not with Jap subs lurking along the West Coast.

The dark torrent of grief, normally bolted behind an inner dam, renewed itself with vengeance on this anniversary of her fiancé's death. With a trembling hand, Rosalie drew Vic's OCS graduation photograph from the pocket of her red-checkered work shirt.

"You were only supposed to be gone eleven months," she whispered to the captured image of the handsome airman. "A spring wedding, remember?" Rosalie blinked back tears. One managed to escape, and she swiped it away. "I would've married you." She tightened the muscles in her face, cocking her jaw and refusing to crumble under the emotions, while also attempting to hide the shameful truth.

Fact was, she didn't know if she would've walked the aisle with the man who loved her. She cared for him, always had, but their time apart had crystalized the reality of her heart. She didn't love him like a wife should love a husband. She knew back then she couldn't marry him, not under the guise of being in love. So rather than planning a spring wedding, she'd intended to gaze into Vic's trusting eyes and place the ring back in his hand—breaking his heart once and for all.

Then he was dead. Gone. And Rosalie lived amidst the shambles of heartbreak and guilt. *I should've been grateful that you loved me. I should've freely given you my heart—you deserved it.* Rosalie fingered the empty place on her finger where she used to wear Vic's diamond ring. "But I didn't," she whispered.

She kissed the Kodacolor photograph and put it back in her pocket, then palmed his etched name. "I'm sorry, Vic." She'd make it up to him the only way she could. She'd rivet those planes till no other girl's man had to die. She'd rally the folks at home to salvage and save and work—all for the war. To end the war. "I'll make you proud, Vic. You'll see."

A glance at her wristwatch made Rosalie's head jolt upright. She'd have to hurry to catch the next bus. The gray clouds had again swept aside, allowing sharp sunlight to illuminate the sea of bodies that now filled the square. So absorbed in her thoughts, Rosalie hadn't noticed the lunch crowd had expanded to a rally sized throng, with more people spilling in. She hurried toward the podium and paused, trying to eye the best route through the crowd to the other side.

A band was assembling on the stage, and Rosalie recognized the bass player, Nick, who had recently started playing at the Igloo, her and Birdie's favorite hangout. On Rosalie's left an army jeep was parked. In the passenger's seat sat a pretty brunette—probably a celebrity brought in for the rally. Rosalie didn't have time to figure out which star had graced them with her presence. She rushed in the direction of Fourth Street, struggling to weave through the ever-tightening crowd. She needed to get away. She needed to think.

While other riveters complained that their job was too noisy— they couldn't talk or joke as they riveted—Rosalie enjoyed it. It gave her time to ponder life, dream, escape into her own thoughts.

Before she took ten steps, a tall man zigzagging the other direction shot out in front of her, and she smacked into him. Her chest hit his elbow, and a sharp pain pulsed through Rosalie's ribcage. As she stumbled backward, she spotted the man's camera, which must've jabbed into her side.

Emotions flared when she saw the camera. *Figures.* Guys like him couldn't be trusted to get a story right, tell the truth—and now, obviously, watch where they were going.

With no room to hit the asphalt, Rosalie stumbled against a stout army guy with sergeant stripes, sipping a Coca-Cola. The drink flipped from his stocky hand, and dark, syrupy fluid spilled over his wool uniform jacket, splashing onto Rosalie.

"Watch it, Toots!" the soldier boomed as he helped straighten her. "That was my first Coke in three months. You owe me a cola ration."

Rosalie swiped off the droplets of soda collected in the folds of her pleated slacks. "Sorry, mister, but it wasn't my fault."

She glared at the light brown-haired sap who fiddled with his camera lens. He paid no attention to her or the soldier.

And then she was there again—five years old, lonely, and confused. She'd learned to never trust a man who paid more attention to his camera, his story, than her.

* * * *

"My camera!" Kenny Davenport barked without looking at the woman who had just barged into him. He checked the lens of his Speed Graphic for scratches, then examined the bed brace and the track to make sure they weren't bent.

"Man," he muttered, "if this camera's broken—"

Kenny's boss, Mr. Bixby, had been crystal clear. "Get a shot of Miss Turner the moment—the very second—she walks on stage."

Bixby demanded Kenny's photographs capture the star's "electric-icity," whatever that was. The newspaper man, ironically, had a habit of fumbling his spoken words. What Mr. Bixby most likely meant was the "electricity" performers exude at the crowd's first cheers.

Along with taking photos, Kenny's job was to write a sparkling story about the occasion, highlighting the details—the brightness of the performer's eyes, the smiles of the crowd, the zippy tunes of the band. Kenny let out a rolling groan. Despite his camera's moniker of *Speed* Graphic, it took several seconds to reload the film. As he was reloading, he looked to the stage, hoping the star didn't step into the spotlight before he was ready.

This type of story was not why he'd become a reporter. But with the hot water he'd recently gotten into—sneaking behind the boss's back to nab a "real" story about a corrupt union boss—Kenny knew he had to nail this one, no matter how fluffy. And the next one too, and the one after that. Otherwise he was out on his can.

Relieved his camera wasn't broken, Kenny aimed it toward the podium, where Lana Turner was about to appear under President Jefferson's dome. He was focusing the lens when a hand thrust his arm down.

"What's the deal?" Kenny barked, his fist gripping the camera to keep it from dropping. This was important, expensive equipment. Didn't people realize that? He turned to find himself looking into the face of the woman who'd slammed into him.

The woman's brown eyes glared at him. "Hey! Don't you see what you did to us? How can you just go on and act like nothing happened, mister?"

"What I did? You barged into me—" He glanced at the woman, noticing some type of drink had spilled down the front of her shirt and onto her slacks. He also noticed a tall sergeant standing beside her with beefy arms crossed. Coke dripped from the man's shirt.

Kenny stepped toward the woman. Her hands gripped her side

as if she was injured, and her angry face faded into a pained look. Seeing that she was hurt, he was no longer as concerned about the star about to mount the stage. "I'm so sorry. I didn't mean to, Miss—" He lifted his fedora slightly, with his apology.

"My Coke!" the tall man piped in with a gristly voice. "That's what I care about."

Kenny eyed the man, hoping he wasn't going to swing his ample fist and throw punches. "Yes, you're right, of course, but can you give me just a second here?"

Kenny shifted his gaze back to the woman who glowered at him with fierce intensity. Instead of repelling him, her powerful reaction intrigued him. He was used to females twittering around him, posing for photos, and acting like his camera and position at the paper made him a star in his own right. Yet her dark, curly hair, high cheekbones, and flawless neck attracted his eyes like a magnet.

"I—I have to cover Miss Turner," he finally finished, then glanced toward the podium. "I need a photo for the morning edition." He pulled a card from his gray suit pocket and offered it to her. "My name's Kenny Davenport. I work at *The Seattle Tribune*. I'll gladly pay for your cleaning, but I really have to get this shot."

"Well, I 'really have to' go pound rivets into a Flying Fortress. I'm already going to be late." She swept her hand across herself, displaying her Coke-splattered clothes. "How can I show up for work covered with Coke?"

The sergeant sidled a step closer to the woman, as if backing up her words.

The woman's scolding reminded Kenny of the way his older sisters used to bawl him out, like the time his sister Bernice caught him painting a mustache on her boyfriend's photograph. Kenny knew if this woman was anything like Bernice, any sign he was enjoying this would only make her angrier. He struggled to suppress the laugh.

She apparently caught on. "Are you amused, Mr. Davenport? I should march to your office and tell your boss how you almost trampled a riveter and a"—she glanced up at the sergeant—"a fella with a soda!"

The hard-boiled soldier's balding head lowered. "And what you gonna do 'bout that cola of mine?" By the sergeant's accusing gaze, Kenny would've thought his crime was spying for the Nazis rather than spilling a Coke.

"I have an extra ration book at home. I was saving it for my sister, but—" He slipped another business card from the pocket of his slacks and handed it to the man. "I'll bring it to the office tomorrow. You can get it then."

"Fine. I'll be there."

The tune to "I Remember You" filled the air as the band kicked into its first number. Even though no one sang out loud, the lyrics played through Kenny's mind. *"I remember you…you're the one who made my dreams come true."*

Kenny eyed the stage and spotted his friend Nick. It was his buddy's first big rally, and he'd been hoping to get some shots of Nick in action too. The musician's fingers plunked the thick strings on his stand-up bass, and his head bobbed along. Kenny noticed that all Nick's weight was on his left leg—his good leg. But most people would never guess the guy had been injured overseas and was finally on the mend—or at least as good as he could get, considering his injuries.

Kenny knew the music meant Miss Turner would be on stage momentarily.

"Look, miss." He spoke politely, yet firmly. "I said I'll pay for the cleaning. I really am sorry about your clothes—"

The crowd erupted in cheers, and in an instant, Kenny centered his camera on the brunette beauty who strode onto stage, her delicate hand waving to the crowd. "Hi-de-ho, Seattle!"

Rowdy cheers exploded in the square, and Kenny scrambled to grab the "electric" images that would preserve his job—filmplate-flashbulb-click...filmplate-flashbulb-click...filmplate-flashbulb-click. His hands did their job automatically.

The crowd quieted, and Kenny sighed in relief. "I got a few good ones." Then he turned back to the woman and shot her a smile. She really did intrigue him. His mind scurried to think about an excuse to see her again—something more interesting than paying for her cleaning. Maybe Mr. Bixby would be interested in a story about a riveter, but what would be the hook?

As he pondered this, the woman frowned. "Just forget it." She pivoted to leave, but then paused, tilting her head back over her shoulder. "Next time, pal, be a little more considerate."

Kenny blinked, shocked. Hadn't he been more than contrite? "You know, Miss Riveter, my mother could teach you a lesson or two about manners. I apologized," he called after her. "I offered to pay for cleaning—all of which I really didn't need to do since it was you who bumped into me."

"What? No. You popped out of nowhere." She turned to where the sergeant had stood a moment before, but the soldier was already gone.

Kenny stepped closer to her, wanting to prove his point and justify himself. He wanted her to stick around for just a moment longer, even if it meant she was angry with him. "I don't think so. I was headed for the stage when you slammed into me, then ricocheted into the poor sergeant. *You* should be the one to offer extra rations."

Up on stage, Lana Turner was saying something to the crowd, but Kenny wasn't focused on her words. This woman in front of him was more interesting—more beautiful—than any star he'd ever met.

"I can't believe you think that!" The woman stamped her foot. "Why, I've never met such a—a—swell-headed individual!"

Without warning, the crowd around them fell silent, and all gazes turned toward the two of them sparring.

"Well?" Miss Turner said. This time her words came through loud and clear. "Are you two lovebirds coming up here or what?"

Chapter Two

. . . .

What seemed like a thousand unrelenting voices—along with a few yanks and pulls—urged Rosalie toward the black platform. What they didn't know was her reluctance to go on stage wasn't a cute simpering. Sweat poured from Rosalie's hands. Since childhood, Rosalie's greatest fear—her high school counselor had dubbed it a *phobia*—was being in front of a crowd.

A woman in a gray suit tugged on her elbow. "Go ahead. Lana Turner wants you up there."

"Wait! I need to get to work. I'm going to be late," Rosalie protested, but her voice was lost in the cheers. Before her, the crowd parted like the Red Sea before Moses. Hundreds of heads turned her direction. A cold chill traveled up her arms and pinched her neck. The faces in front of her faded slightly, and she told herself not to faint. The voices of the crowd muted, then grew louder again, and she knew she wasn't going to get out of this. The only way to escape was to go up there and let Lana Turner say a few jokes at her expense. Then, and only then, could she leave the crowd behind and hurry to work.

The crowd delivered Rosalie to the four-foot-high stage and she briefly wondered how she'd climb over the edge without losing her dignity, but the same hands that had pushed her there seemed to levitate her to Miss Turner's level. She simply stepped forward and her foot landed on the stage as Lana Turner gripped her elbow.

The movie star was even more beautiful in person than in the pictures—with flawless skin, shoulder-length brown hair, and a figure curved in all the right places. Rosalie hunkered down, feeling like the ugly duckling standing next to a beautiful swan. She glanced down at her checkered shirt and jean slacks, then patted her pinned-up hair, feeling heat rise to her cheeks.

"C'mon, honey." The actress smiled directly at Rosalie with what seemed like genuine warmth. "I don't bite."

Rosalie met the woman's gaze, and her stomach tossed like the waves of Puget Sound. Her knees softened slightly, and she leaned into the woman's touch. *This is Lana Turner. Lana Turner's hand is touching my elbow.*

An overwhelming impulse to blurt out praise gathered behind her lips. "I love your pictures, Miss Turner. You were fantastic in *Somewhere I'll Find You.*" Instead, Rosalie pressed her lips tighter, refusing to let the words escape. She'd never live it down if news got back to Birdie that she was swooning. After all, Rosalie had always been the one to say she didn't care about Hollywood "stars." Just yesterday, when Birdie was cooing over Clark Gable, Rosalie boasted that if she ever met a famous actor, she'd treat him or her like anyone else. But now, with Lana Turner smiling and touching her, Rosalie felt like a starstruck schoolgirl.

Lana guided her to center stage, then turned Rosalie to face the roaring crowd. So many eyes—mostly GIs ready to ship out—ogled her. Rosalie's muscles tightened in fear, and her stare fixed on the masses, who again blurred in her vision.

Miss Turner placed a hand on Rosalie's back, and Rosalie let out a soft breath. "Wave and smile, hon," Lana Turner said, doing the same.

Rosalie's arm felt weak as she lifted it, and for the first time she saw Mr. Davenport had followed her onto the stage and was now standing beside her. One shiny black wingtip tapped along with the music. Her eyes moved from his shoe to his face, and she noticed his cool blue eyes sent a quick glare behind them toward the grinning, red-headed bass player.

One thing she knew was that Mr. Davenport was enjoying this. Reporters always acted as if they were there to capture events, but they enjoyed being a part of them even more. To feel important by hounding important people. Not her—she'd rather shoot rivets. Gathering her breath, Rosalie remembered she had to get to work. The hollering crowd died down, and she leaned toward the slender star and spoke in her ear. "Miss Turner, it's an honor to meet you, but I really have to get to work. I'm going to miss my bus." Rosalie gazed past the throng of enthralled GIs jammed into the seemingly never-ending square. The idea of forging her way through all those people in time to catch the bus seemed impossible.

The actress touched Rosalie's shoulder and spoke away from the microphone. "Oh, honey, of course. Doing your part in the war effort—are you a welder?"

"No, a riveter. I work on Flying Fortresses."

Lana smiled. "Good for you. I'll keep it short." Then, sending a gleaming smile back to the crowd, Miss Turner wrapped her manicured hand around the mic stand. With that one motion the crowd quieted.

"So, how long have you two been an item?" Lana's voice carried through the speakers and over the crowd. She winked at the handsome photographer. Then she looked to Rosalie, her eyes sparkling with fun.

Rosalie shook her head. "Why would you think that? I—we're not—"

Miss Turner wouldn't let her finish. She tilted her head. "The way you two were bickering, I'm guessing you've been together a *long* time."

Rosalie caught a flash of the reporter's grin as the crowd exploded in laughter. Mr. Davenport leaned back with his hands in his pockets, reminiscent of Clark Gable, chuckling. His chin tilted Rosalie's direction, his eyes grabbing and holding hers. Unexpected warmth rushed to Rosalie's cheeks, and she touched one of them with her palm. They heated up even more when he threw her a dangerously flirtatious wink.

"You mean you've never met each other before?" Miss Turner prodded Mr. Davenport closer toward Rosalie.

Rosalie grasped her hands behind her, hoping to hide her sweaty palms. The crowd she could get used to. The star was just a woman like her. But that wink—her heartbeat quickened. Small butterflies in her stomach fluttered and flipped.

"No, uh," she muttered, inching sideways. She needed to get away, to get to work. Couldn't they see that? *I need to get away from…him*, she thought and took one more sideways step.

The platform disappeared beneath her right heel.

She teetered, arms flailing, sure she would topple into the crowd. Then a hand caught her arm. A strong hand, pulling Rosalie away from the edge. Like a yo-yo on a string, she coiled toward Mr. Davenport and landed against his chest. He smelled of soap and cologne.

Before she could mutter a thanks or apology, he removed his grasp and stepped back, putting distance between them again.

Acting as if nothing had happened, Mr. Davenport shifted to Miss Turner. "I accidentally caused a Coke to spill all over her work clothes, and we were arguing." His eyebrows angled into an upside-down V, and his head tipped back. "We've never met."

"Well, it's high time you did," Miss Turner said with a nod. "What's your name, sir?"

Rather than answering Miss Turner, he stuck out his hand to Rosalie. "Kenny. Kenny Davenport."

Rosalie bit her lip, wishing she could take back her tantrum from a few moments earlier. *How childish I was.* She placed a hand over her stomach, now churning with regret. *The poor guy didn't mean to bump me.* She sent Kenny Davenport what she hoped was a grateful and apologetic smile and grasped his warm hand. "Rosalie Madison. It's nice to meet you."

An *"Aww"* fluttered through the crowd.

Miss Turner patted Kenny's back. "That's the way, boy. And you never know—this could be 'the beginning of a beautiful friendship.'"

Laughter resounded again at Miss Turner's Humphrey Bogart impression. Then she announced, "Let's hear it for Kenny and Rosalie!"

Cheers erupted.

The actress stretched out a hand to shush the crowd. "Listen up, folks." She put an arm around Rosalie. "Rosalie here's gotta get back to work making those Flying Fortresses for our boys! She's a hero, I'd say!"

The patriotic crowd cheered louder than ever. *"Vic-tor-y! Vic-tor-y! Vic-tor-y!"*

Miss Turner joined in the chant, and Rosalie did too, but when she glanced over at Kenny Davenport, the smile on his face faded. His fingers tightened on his camera. If Rosalie didn't know any better, she'd think he was embarrassed. And then, as the blanket of seriousness caused him to look older, a new thought came to her. *Why isn't he overseas?*

Righteous thoughts rose up in her. *Who does this guy think he is? Is he too good to fight?* Vic sacrificed his life. Rod too. Did this Kenny Davenport think he was too good to answer Uncle Sam's call? Rosalie looked away, disappointed.

Miss Turner motioned for the crowd to quiet, then neared the microphone once again. "This gal's got a bus to catch way over there across the square. Do you all think you could make a path so my driver can give her a ride to the bus stop?"

"Anything for you, Lana!" one young sailor called.

Miss Turner eyed Rosalie. "I'm sorry my driver can't give you a ride all the way to work. I have a flight to catch right after this."

With one last wave to the crowd, Rosalie shook Lana Turner's hand. "No problem. I'll be fine. Thank you. This was—a highlight. You've added a bit of brightness to my day, that's for certain."

Miss Turner's eyes squinted slightly as she smiled. "Anytime. Hey, look me up if you ever need anything."

Rosalie nodded, surprised by the actress's generosity. She moved toward the Jeep, where the army driver waited for her.

As she descended the steps, Kenny offered his arm. She tentatively took it, and he led her down the steps and to the Jeep. He seemed like a nice guy, and she felt bad for assuming he was like other reporters she knew. Or, rather, *one* other reporter—someone she still refused to talk to or even acknowledge.

She climbed in and turned to her escort. "Thank you, Mr. Davenport," she said, trying to be polite. "I'm sorry I was so rude. It was just a rough morning, a rough day." The fierce pain she'd felt earlier returned and grew in intensity, wrapping around her heart like barbed wire. She ignored the pain and forced a smile.

"Hey, I was no saint either. Can I make it up to you? Buy you a burger sometime?"

"I'm sorry, I don't think—"

"Aw, come on, miss," the driver interrupted. "Let him have your number. Give the guy a chance!"

"You got someone else waiting for you at home?" Kenny asked.

"No, but I…" How could she explain to this stranger what she still felt about Vic? Her guilt that she hadn't loved him enough to marry him when he wanted, sending him off instead to be killed?

The Jeep's engine started with a rumble. Kenny's sincere eyes almost made her change her mind. After all, Vic wasn't here. It was Kenny who stood before her, wearing a big grin. And she hadn't been on a date recently. Or at least a real date that didn't involve her friends setting her up or sneaking away during a picture show—leaving her alone with some soldier who "just happened" to be seeing the same movie at the same time.

Kenny's eyes searched Rosalie's face. "If you don't want to give me your number, can we meet somewhere?"

He seemed so nice—a guy she'd like to have a conversation with.

"There's a place I go with my friends." She dug in her pocket for a slip of paper so he could write down the address, but then her fingers touched Vic's photograph.

Even if she only wanted to be friends with this guy, he could eventually want more than that. She shook her head, curls bouncing. She couldn't risk her heart. Not again.

"I mean, I'm sorry, Mr. Davenport. I—I have to go to work." She forced herself to look away. She didn't have time to explain.

"Sir," she said, tapping the driver on the shoulder, "I'm ready to go now."

"Yes, ma'am." The young GI threw Kenny a look of sympathy, as if to say, "Hey, bud, that's the pits."

The Jeep slowly edged through the crowd toward the bus stop.

"But, Rosalie!" Kenny called after her.

Rosalie folded her hands in her lap, refusing to look back.

I did the right thing. I'm not ready for romance. Not until I've done all I can to make my failures up to Vic. Not until I rivet a million rivets—or at least prove myself to him. Prove that I'm worth loving... and dying for.

Chapter Three

....

Kenny stood alone beside the platform's steps, following the Jeep's slow progress past the old-style stone Metropolitan Theatre, onward to the model of Monticello, and out of sight. He took in a breath. Rosalie's perfume, light and flowery—like roses—still lingered in the air. The soft scent contrasted with her strong, independent demeanor. Yet, the sincerity in her eyes when she apologized revealed a gentleness she obviously tried to hide. Kenny blinked, instructing himself to stop attempting to solve the riddle of Rosalie Madison—a girl clearly not interested in him.

Behind him, *ha cha cha chas* and drum rim shots sounded from the stage as Lana Turner and a local actor performed a comedy bit. The crowd guffawed. Apparently the almost-romance between Kenny and Rosalie was already forgotten. Kenny scratched the back of his neck and tried to rein in his emotions. Then he remembered his assignment for today: to find a story.

As the lunch hour ended, the music stopped and Kenny heard a snicker. Then he felt a hand on his shoulder.

"Hey, buddy." Nick's broad smile greeted Kenny as the bassist limped off the last step from the stage and hung his arm around Kenny's shoulder. His friend was only a few inches taller, but Nick's colorful personality made him larger than life.

Kenny frowned. "Did you tell her to do that?"

Nick planted his fists on his hips, backing away from his long-time friend. "Who, me?" Nick placed an index finger on his chin. "What're you talkin' about?"

"Lana Turner! That famous Hollywood star a few yards behind you. You told her to bring us on stage, didn't you?"

Nick's shoulders scrunched up as he shook his head. "Naw, not really."

"Not really?" Kenny returned, feigning—well, half-feigning—anger. He'd truly been embarrassed. "You love making a fool out of me, don't you?"

"What d'ya mean? Nobody thought you were a fool."

"C'mon, I looked like a desperate loser—not overseas at war *and* not getting the girl."

"Aw, think about how much joy you brought to so many people today." Nick swept his arm toward the lingering crowd.

Kenny zeroed in on his friend's eyes. "How could you, after all I've done for you? I took you in like a lost puppy; shared my mother's care packages."

Nick lifted his palms upward, like Spanky from *The Little Rascals,* trying to look innocent. "Maybe I gave her a hint, but think of it this way. You're here to write a story, aren't you? I gave you one."

Kenny groaned. "You could have just introduced me to Miss Turner after the show."

Remembering he still needed some more good shots, Kenny took a few photographs of the pinup girl signing autographs for the crowd. Then he set his camera on one of the steps, shook his head slowly, and unleashed a surprise attack, grabbing Nick in a head-lock and punching him lightly in the gut. "You have way too much fun embarrassing me. It's gotta stop, ya hear me?"

"Okay, okay, okay." Nick pushed away from Kenny and moaned as if in pain, but Kenny could see the twinkle in his eye. "You gonna injure your poor, crippled friend?" He held his thigh, where shrapnel remained lodged from his run-in with the Germans.

"Fine." Kenny backed off. He readjusted his hat, then picked up his camera again, looping the strap over his head. "Use that excuse. Tops anything I have."

Nick grinned. They retreated to the other side of the steps and leaned against the platform.

"So…" Nick's gaze followed a pretty blond in a swooshing skirt who walked by. "You get that riveter's phone number?"

Kenny shrugged, remembering again the feel of Rosalie's hand in his as he helped her down the platform steps. "I tried."

"You gonna try again?"

"Nah." Kenny glanced at the tiny brown splatter decorating the right top of his black wingtip. It was probably from the spilled Coke. "She's not interested in me. Plus, Bixby's on my back to bring in more softball stories."

"Softball stories?"

"You know, simple, easy to hit—I mean, print. But after the Lana Turner piece, I don't know what I'm gonna write about. I'm sure it'll be something equally uninteresting and unimportant."

"You have to admit, though, the riveter was a looker." Nick's brain didn't seem to register how a good-looking girl wouldn't be worth pursuing or why Kenny was trying to change the subject.

Who was he to argue? She was beautiful—an image of her was seared into his mind—intelligent, yet vulnerable. Dark eyes, a slender waist accentuated by slacks and a checkered shirt. A burst of affection mixed with curiosity welled up within him, but he pushed it away.

"Yeah, she was pretty, but not really my type." Kenny tried to shrug it off.

The trumpet player from the band approached and tapped Nick's shoulder, indicating he needed to get back to work.

"I'm playing at the Igloo tonight if you wanna come watch your old friend," Nick told Kenny, limping back up the stairs.

"Tonight? I was going to mow my aunt's yard. The grass has to be a foot high by now."

"Is that what you call fun? I'm sure it won't hurt the grass to grow for another day. One foot and one inch. Besides, the Igloo is a cool place. You *really* should come. Maybe it'll get your mind off that girl who's 'not your type.'" Nick winked.

Kenny lifted a hand and turned away.

Weaving through the crowd, Kenny crossed the square to the sidewalk on Fourth Street. The odors of vehicle exhaust and garbage, the noise and bustle—the city's ambiance—smacked his senses as he turned and headed toward Seneca. He figured he'd develop the photographs of Miss Turner and then write the story.

What a difference I'm making in the world. He rubbed his tightening forehead, trying to keep at bay the headache fogging his brain. *If it wasn't for that promise…*

It had seemed like the right thing at the time. He'd promised his father, an army chaplain serving in the South Pacific, that he wouldn't join the military on one condition—*if* someone would hire him as a newspaperman in a big city, and *if* he'd be able to use journalism to "make a difference."

Since listening to Bible stories while perched on his father's knee as child, Kenny had grown up realizing the power of story. The right words could stir emotion. They could unite and excite people, and help bring important causes to light. Yet, as the months passed, Kenny came to realize he was simply wasting time in Seattle. He wasn't writing about things that mattered—not when his boss rejected every serious story. He felt disrespected too. Every other healthy guy his age was off at war. He saw the curious look in folks' eyes—like that riveter—wondering why he wasn't off fighting, assuming he was a coward.

Worse than that. After being on a naval vessel attacked by the Japs, his father had been injured—pretty bad from what his letter had said. While his dad was recouping in Hawaii, here he was, snapping shots of famous actresses. It didn't seem right.

Turning the corner, Kenny paused, gazing down at the sparkling Elliot Bay. He breathed in the scent of ocean air and thought about what it would be like to be on a ship, sailing off to fight the Japanese or even flying over the Atlantic to battle the Germans. Beyond the water, in the distance, the white, jagged Olympic Mountains jutted into the sapphire sky. So different from Eastern Idaho where he grew up. No mountains there—no waterways, either.

Continuing his downhill trek toward his office, he walked past the U.S. Navy recruiter's office, as he did every day. The new poster this week showed a shadowy sailor with his fist raised. *Avenge December 7* was written in blood-red ink, with a ship sinking in the lower corner of the poster. As usual, Kenny dispelled an urge to go in.

Lord, are You sure You don't want me to fight the Japs or maybe the Nazis? This is the plan? He sighed, remembering his promise. He just wished he could do something more meaningful than piffle celebrity stories.

Twenty minutes later, Kenny reached Alaskan Way where his office was located. The roar of an engine approached, and a woman's voice called his name.

"Kenny! Kenny Davenport!"

A motorcycle driven by a brown-haired woman wearing a jump-suit pulled up beside him. "Hey, Kenny, I need to talk to you. Meet me over there." Iris pointed a red-tipped finger toward a side street, then zoomed ahead.

What can she want? Kenny wondered as he set off in that direction. Iris delivered auto parts when the newspaper's truck broke down. Was she in trouble? Maybe she needed help from a man of the press....

Kenny jogged to where she waited. With the bike parked, her legs barely reached the ground. It still seemed strange to him to see a woman on such a big machine. "Everything all right?"

Iris's cherry red lips stretched wide in a smile. She reached in her pocket and pulled out a paper, folded in fourths. "For you." She winked, straightened her leather helmet, then vroomed away.

Kenny unfolded it and frowned, not recognizing the handwriting. His eyes skimmed to the bottom of the page for a signature. When he saw it, his heart bounded into his throat: *Rosalie—the girl Lana Turner introduced you to.*

Chapter Four

....

Tying her yellow, Boeing-mandated bandanna in place, Rosalie ignored the less-than-ladylike odors of cutting oil, grinding dust, and welding flux as she entered the front doors of the Boeing plant and quickened her pace toward the women's locker room.

All in a girl's work, she thought as she peered up at a wall poster of Rosie the Riveter. Rosalie admired the icon's strapping arm posed like a body builder. Riveting the skins onto B-17s eight hours a day for the last year and a half had given her ample biceps herself.

She eyed Rosie's intense message, WE CAN DO IT!

"Sorry, honey," Rosalie spoke to the lady on the poster, "I'm not 'doing it' so well today."

Thank goodness for Iris, at least. Her friend had probably saved her job by giving her a quick lift on her motorcycle.

Rosalie smoothed her slacks where the cola had spilt. Still sticky. The thought of the handsome reporter sent a cool tingle to her neck. Probably because Iris had gibed about her and Kenny's "moony" introduction all the way to the plant.

"Give the guy a chance," Iris had said. Thankfully her friend and neighbor had seen the show and come to Rosalie's rescue. "Who else do you know that's been introduced on stage by Lana Turner?"

The auto parts deliverer—the first woman in Seattle to do the job—even thought up a plan. "Write him a note," Iris had ordered. "Apologize, and give him your number. I'll deliver it." Rosalie had crumbled to her friend's demands, and now her thoughts ping-ponged back and forth, wondering if she'd done the right thing.

If I see him again, I can apologize.

He'll most likely never call anyway.

What if he calls? What will I say?

He probably thinks I'm a floozy. The nerve of sending my number!

Then again, he did seem like a nice guy. Maybe he's not like other reporters.

But she didn't have time to worry about those things now. She had a job to do.

Factory sounds filled the air, and Rosalie had to admit she felt useful here, important. A part of something. Once a woman entered the plant doors, it didn't matter if she was single or married, a mother, or even a grandmother. At work, she was judged by the job she accomplished, not by who was waiting for her back home or dreaming about her from far away.

She admitted—if only to herself—she was lonely without Vic. He'd been her best friend for so long, and despite the way she'd sent him off, she missed him. But who was she to whine? She was merely one in a world of women who'd lost their men to the war.

A part of her heart longed for love—she wasn't afraid to confess that. Moreover, in quiet moments, she even admitted to twinges of curiosity about others' "head over heels" experiences—like Birdie's with her husband, John.

As Vic had done, John flew the B-17 bombers Rosalie and Birdie riveted. While he was deployed, John sent Birdie the most romantic V-mail messages. And they weren't just mushy nonsense. The parts Birdie shared conveyed deep honesty and even vulnerability. John always encouraged Birdie to trust in God, to stay cheerful, and he regularly signed off with an instruction: *Keep laughing.*

Birdie certainly knew how to laugh. When she'd asked Rosalie if she was interested in rooming together while their men were gone, Rosalie hadn't hesitated. After Vic died, Rosalie's bubbly friend's laugh lifted her out of the dark hours. Her patient, listening ear enwrapped Rosalie with the comfort of not treading alone along the isolated path of grief.

The letters Vic wrote while away at training had been filled with encouragement for Rosalie too, but they'd lacked passion. Sometimes Rosalie wondered if this elusive phenomenon—romance, passion, true love—would ever find her. Maybe someday, but romance was not for her now. Even if Kenny did call, she'd make up for her sour attitude, but she wouldn't let it go any further.

Rosalie shoved a stray strand of hair inside her bandanna as she slinked past the boss's office. His large window overlooked the floor, and she could see her boss inside, scribbling something on the ledger in front of him. Light reflected off the top of his balding head, and she hoped he wouldn't look up to see her late arrival.

Rosalie opened the door to the hallway that led to both the locker room and the production floor. The mechanical din rumbling through one of the world's largest buildings grew in volume, and the unsettling thoughts of love dissipated. She breathed in the plant's metallic smell, welcoming the sense of calm determination that settled over her. *This is what's important.*

A high-pitched squeal blasted as she approached the locker room door. "Rosalie! There you are." Birdie raced to the open door and grabbed her arm. "Where've you been?"

Before Rosalie could answer, booted footsteps sounded behind her, and she turned to find her boss striding up to them. His chin was tucked against his chest, making his forehead seem abnormally large.

"Bullhorn" Hawkins' eyes peered into Rosalie's face. "You're late." His voice was low, scratchy, firm. Bullhorn's vocal cords had been damaged in the Great War, or so the rumor went. He never yelled, but Rosalie had heard that when he was younger, his voice boomed so forcefully that other commanders used him to shout to their troops when their own voices faded. Now he spoke low, yet the officer's authority had remained. So had the nickname.

Rosalie had never been late before—not even one minute. Her molars clenched together, and her eyes focused on Bullhorn's shined boots. She wanted to apologize but knew better than to speak. Birdie stood beside her, silent. Rosalie finally dared to look into his face.

"You know how tight the schedule is?" Bullhorn's eyes narrowed.

"Yes, sir."

"Even if you're late on the floor, you still have to rivet the normal quota. And if you stay longer, there's no overtime pay—for you or your partner." He pointed to Birdie, and the side of his lip lifted in a snarl. "Understand?"

Rosalie closed her eyes, queasiness sprouting in her gut. "Yes, sir."

"Don't let it happen again." Bullhorn swiveled, then his boots clanged up the scaffolding, where he could watch everything from a bird's-eye view.

Rosalie cocked her head toward Birdie. "I'm so sorry."

The shift whistle split the air.

"It's all right, sweetie." Birdie patted her arm. "The others are just heading out. Throw your things in the locker, and we'll join them." Birdie grinned, and Rosalie gave her a hug, grateful for her understanding friend.

"I was worried about you," Birdie said as they hurried into the locker room. "What happened?"

The last hour's events roiled through Rosalie's mind like a Bendix automatic washer, and she puffed out a breath. Where to begin?

They hurried into the locker room, and Rosalie linked arms with her friend. "Tell you what. Come with me tonight to the Igloo, where I'll not only tell you all about it, I'll also buy you a malt for getting you into trouble."

At the sink, Rosalie grabbed the bar of white Dove soap, then splashed cold water over her calloused hands. Hurrying to her locker, she pulled Vic's photo from her pocket and lodged it in the door's seam.

Another memory flashed into her mind, and her lips arced in an involuntary smile. Before he'd go home for the night, Vic would lock her windows, and she'd walk him to the door. A sweet, simple kiss, and then he'd leave, warning her to bolt the latch behind him. After he'd walk out, Vic would always pause and check. If the door was locked, he'd teasingly say, "That's my good girl." They called it their Good Night Safety Check.

Rosalie let out a breath, recalling how she'd sometimes leave the door unlocked just to rile him, just to hear his mock scolding. *Vic, you were so good to me. Why could I not love you?*

Rosalie grabbed her gloves and work boots, putting them on in a hurry in order to catch up with the other women who were already dressed and shuffling out to the floor. Clara, tall and lanky with dusty blond hair, was already dressed in her big, heavy welder's suit. Rosalie wondered how she could move in such a getup.

As Rosalie tucked her civilian clothes in the locker and slammed the door shut, Clara patted Rosalie's shoulder. "How you doin', honey? You look a little blue."

Rosalie shrugged. "I'm okay. Just a rough morning."

"This war can get to ya." Clara glanced at the ceiling with a wistful look, and Rosalie knew she was thinking of her own husband, who'd left for basic training two months ago.

"I'm missin' my Pete like nobody's business," Clara said as they walked together toward the floor. "Hey, how'd that date go the other night? What was that airman's name?"

Rosalie shrugged. "Jack."

"Now that boy's got one of those chiseled jaws, and those dimples make women swoon. If I were single—"

"The *date* went fine. And I appreciate you girls trying to set me up—even though you tricked me into it," she scolded.

"Oh, sweetie," Eunice piped in, slowing her pace to walk beside them. Nearly half Clara's size, Eunice's job was to climb into the smaller spaces of the plane to work on wiring. "We just thought you needed some fun."

"And sneaking out of the movie, leaving me alone with Humphrey Bogart, Madeleine LeBeau, and Jack—whose idea was that?

Poor Airman Jack had to suffer through all my tears." Rosalie grasped Eunice's shoulder. "That's your idea of fun?"

"Ain't it yours?" Eunice smirked.

"It was *very* kind of you all." Rosalie gave a swat to Eunice's rear. "Jack was very nice, but he's shipping out this week. I'm just not interested in those army boys. You know how it is."

Birdie sidled up and looped her arm around Rosalie's neck. "Then we'll have to find you a civilian. Some unsuspecting sap."

A united chortle arose from the ladies.

"Good luck with that one," Rosalie bantered. Her mind carried her back to Kenny Davenport, but she pushed his smiling face from her memory.

"Don't you worry. If there's a worthy non-flyboy or jughead in Seattle, I'll be the one to find him for you!" Birdie's bouncy blond hair jiggled as her contagious laugh splashed through the line.

They passed another Rosie the Riveter poster, and Birdie paused. "Hey, you know what?" Birdie gave Rosalie a once-over. "That girl kinda looks like you."

Rosalie laughed. "Not with those muscles."

"No, I think she's right," Eunice added. "Rosalie the Riveter. How about that?"

"C'mon." Birdie curled her arm like Rosie on the poster. "Do it with me."

A chuckle sneaked past Rosalie's lips. "Oh, all right." She posed, even tilting her chin for emphasis. "I can do it."

The pack of ladies clapped, and Rosalie smiled at her friends' support, grateful for them. And grateful for her rivet gun's ability to shoot away her worries.

"Uh-oh, ladies, look at the clock," Clara warned. "We'd better light a fire under it."

Entering the production line, Rosalie took in the sight that never ceased to impress her. A hundred B-17 bomber cockpits were lined up in rows on the plant floor. Sunshine beamed through the ten-story-high windows, and a whole world seemed to swirl in the heights of the scaffoldings. The din of mechanical sounds—rivet guns, saws, hammers, and more—blended together, producing the resonant hum that both comforted and excited Rosalie.

Rosalie and Birdie tromped toward the tool crib, where Ralph waited. His cocoa-colored face wore a grumpy expression, but he always made sure Rosalie and Birdie got the best tools.

A stocky, middle-aged male riveter swaggered away from the gate. "Twenty-seven hundred rivets in one shift," Bill Anderson stepped in Rosalie's path, cutting her off. The arms of his shirt had been rolled up to display his bulging muscles, and his cocky demeanor caused Rosalie's stomach to turn. "Which makes us only four hundred short of the national record."

His eighteen-year-old son, George, skulked beside him.

"A woman could never come close to that," Bill continued, leering at Rosalie. "Could you, sweetheart?" His bald head reflected the overhead lights, making him look like a polka-dotted monster from a Saturday flick at the Fifth Avenue Theatre.

Birdie's hands shot to her hips. "Real funny, Bill."

Rosalie stepped around Bill and tugged on Birdie's sleeve, urging her forward. "Not today, Birdie." Rosalie leaned close to her friend's ear. "C'mon."

"Listen to your friend, Tweety-bird. Time to fly off to work." Bill flapped his arms.

A snicker burst from George, who was also deemed unfit for military service, for whatever reason.

Birdie brushed off Rosalie's hand. "Ha, ha. You think you're funny?" She stepped forward, stretching her thin, short frame to make herself appear larger.

Rosalie's heart pounded. She'd worked with Birdie enough to anticipate her next words. "Bird—"

"Me and Rosalie could beat that record," Birdie interrupted. "Hands down." Then her eyes widened, as if realizing she may have to substantiate the claim. She tugged Rosalie's arm. "Let's go."

But the challenge was out. Rosalie knew they'd never hear the end of it. She tried to move past Bill, but he blocked her once again.

"I'd like to see it," Bill scoffed. "Everyone knows you girls aren't gonna make it here. Women will be out of the plants and factories before Christmas. I'd rather have my ten-year-old boy work at the plant than some woman!"

Most of the men at the plant respected and supported the women, but a few—like Bill and George—never missed a chance to degrade a woman working hard to support her country. Well, he'd picked a bad day to bully Rosalie. For her, this was round two. She straightened her shoulders and lifted her chin, looking Bill directly in the eyes. "What's the national record?"

It was now Birdie tugging on Rosalie's sleeve, but she stood her ground like a soldier protecting territory.

"What does it matter? Little thing like you—you'll have no chance of reaching it." Bill smirked.

Movement from the corner of her eye made Rosalie pause. A group of women had gathered to watch. Suddenly Rosalie knew what she had to do. This would be for them—her friends. It would give them all a boost.

"I asked you about the national record, Bill." She cocked her chin. "What—is—it?"

"Thirty-one hundred rivets in one shift, Rosalie," one of the gals cut in. "A team back East did it last week."

Rosalie's heart kicked against her chest. "That's a lot of rivets," she muttered to Birdie. Bill and George began to snicker, and Rosalie's glare narrowed back to Bill. She sucked in a breath. All she wanted to do was lose herself in the rhythm of the riveting gun, to forget about everything—the anniversary of Vic's death, a new attraction that wouldn't let her thoughts go, even a silly riveting record. But, perhaps for those very reasons, today was the best day to go for it.

She stepped toward Bill and wiped any joking from her face. "You watch us. It'll be done, tonight. By Birdie and me."

Bill's face drooped. His eyes gleamed a trace of fear.

Rosalie and Birdie turned to go, but George, silent till now, called out in his young voice, "What's in it for us? What do we get if you don't do it?"

"I didn't say anything about a wager." Rosalie crossed her arms, hoping they wouldn't notice her trembling hands.

"What are you, scared?" George lifted an eyebrow.

"I didn't say that."

"A small wager then." Bill reentered the conversation. "Just shine my boots." He pointed to the scaffolding looming above. "Up there, so everyone can see."

Rosalie scanned his filthy boots and swallowed hard.

George grinned at Birdie. "And the blond'll do mine. Spit-shined, like the army boys."

Rosalie's heart sank. The humiliation would be awful—and so disgusting. But she was in it now, too far to back out. "Okay, you're on, Bill. But if we *do* win, you have to apologize to everyone in this plant for the way you've been treating them." She swept her arm, motioning to all the women workers.

"If you think—"

"Oh, and one more thing. The magic number doesn't include fixing your shoddy work."

Bill's face darkened as he took a step closer. "Why, I oughta…"

George grabbed his father's upper arm.

Rosalie refused to back off. "You and what gang of brutes?"

Then she turned her back and took two steps before glancing over her shoulder. "Start working on your apology, *Bill*. I want it to sound sincere."

From there she picked up her pace, and Birdie walked double time to keep up with her. Between running late and their verbal sparring, they were already ten minutes behind getting started, which meant ten minutes less of rivets, making the national record even more out of reach.

Once out of Bill's earshot, Birdie grasped Rosalie's arm. "Do you really think we can do it? It would be hard enough on a normal shift, but we're getting a late start."

The other women followed, circling them again.

"Rosalie, what were you thinking?" Eunice strode beside her. "I've never even come close to that number. Boy, you're gonna hate spit-shining those boots."

Rosalie clenched her fists. Her shoulders tensed. Her mind raced. If Vic could become a top pilot in the Army Air Corps, she could fire off a few little rivets. What was that number—3,100?

"C'mon, Birdie. Let's show 'em what we're made of."

Chapter Five

....

Kenny clutched the folded piece of torn-off paper as he strode into *The Seattle Tribune*'s waterfront building. He opened the door and hiked to his office on the third floor. The newspaper, more than anyplace else, was a man's world. Even though many of their windows faced the water, most guys sat in hard, wooden chairs turned toward the center of the room. Their heads were down, and their fingers moved in sync with their thoughts as they pounded on the keyboards. Cigar smoke filled the space, giving it a hazy feel.

One phone hung on the wall and more were scattered around the room on desktops. Every few minutes the phone's sharp ringing pierced the air and caused the reporters' heads to lift—just slightly— until someone broke away from his flow of words to answer it. Once answered, the pounding on the keyboards started up anew.

Sitting at his desk, Kenny eyed the handwritten note again.

> *Sorry I was rude.*
> *Hope we can get together so I can make it up to you. Call me.*
> *Rosalie—the girl Lana Turner introduced you to.*

Following her name was her telephone number.

What a roller coaster of responses from this girl. First, her smoky brown eyes piqued his anger. Then, up on stage, her lower lip had puckered in remorse. And when he had walked her to the Jeep, he could have sworn she was flirting with him. He'd thought for sure she'd say yes to dinner.

Kenny tossed his fedora toward the hat rack near his desk. The hat teetered on the hook. "She acted like she was about to, but then no," he mumbled. *Flomp*. The hat tumbled to the floor.

"What're you muttering about?" Charlie Hudson, the boss's number-one newsman, sauntered to Kenny's desk and sat on it, crushing a stack of notes. Charlie's icy blue eyes shifted toward the phone number and name scribbled on the paper, then angled toward Kenny. "Rosalie, huh? Got some skirt's phone number, did ya? Weren't you supposed to be covering Lana Turner?"

"I did," Kenny said brightly, ignoring Charlie's attempt to irk him.

Kenny scanned the feminine handwriting once more before crumpling the note. He'd never call her. Someone that indecisive equaled too much work. His steady girl in college was like that— feisty, bordering on fierce, but always second-guessing herself. Kenny had spent his freshman year jumping through hoops like a dancing dog at the circus. He'd decided back then he needed a grounded woman. Someone who loved the Lord and cared about the important issues of this world. Someone kind. Not someone who enjoyed making a guy feel like a fool.

"Just a lead." Kenny tossed the crumpled paper in the trash can. "Didn't pan out."

Charlie's eyebrows shot upward. "Are you sure that's what you want to do? I know you haven't been around here long…"

Charlie always treated Kenny like a stupid kid—as if the great Charlie was the journalistic top cat. Kenny knew his five years writing front-page news in Boise were small potatoes to these bigshots. Seattle was the *real* market—especially since President Roosevelt's son-in-law took over.

Still, what did it matter what they thought? Kenny knew fair-haired-boy Charlie would be handed all the best stories until Kenny redeemed himself for digging up dirt without permission. So much for taking the initiative.

At the time, Kenny believed once the boss heard the story—how people were being swindled and hung out to dry—Mr. Bixby would want to fight for justice. But he was wrong. Kenny now realized he shouldn't have conducted interviews for the piece without Bixby's approval. It was disrespectful and presumptuous, plus the political connection put everyone on edge.

But now Kenny had the perfect story. Not the Lana Turner one. He'd write that too, but a new idea had come to him as he'd walked back to work from the rally.

Kenny ignored the puffed-up, big-talker Charlie and rolled a sheet of paper into the typewriter.

Charlie wasn't one to be ignored. "You're throwing a lead in the trash can?" He spoke loud enough for anyone around to hear.

"What?" Their boss Mr. Bixby's voice blared from his office, followed by footsteps. "You never throw out a lead." Bixby, round and short, waddled to Kenny's desk.

Charlie squinted at Kenny. His mouth hinted at a sneer as if implying, *I knew that was a bad idea.*

"Well, Davenport?" Bixby boomed. "What's this number you trashed? Don't you know better than that? Even a useless lead can be useful later, for a *skilled* reporter. Boy, are you *blue* or what?"

Don't you mean green? Kenny didn't dare correct the boss openly. He smothered a chuckle and glanced at Charlie.

Charlie only frowned.

Despite his boss's blunder, Kenny's heart rate pulsed. Something about this bulldog made him nervous.

"Sure, boss, I know." Kenny pulled the paper from the trash can and flattened it. "But I have a great story for you. A friend of mine is having a problem with—"

"Don't tell me he's having a problem with the unions," Bixby said, "because I don't want to hear about it. Only an indigent would pitch that story again."

Kenny shook his head without answering. Bixby meant "idiot." The chief's hard-as-nails attitude made up for his lack of a functional knowledge of the English language—at least in the spoken word.

The sun coursing in through the green-tinged window heated Kenny's shoulders. He balled his fists at his side, his frustration mounting. Sucking in a breath, he then slowly released it, remembering how his father had always told him to respect his superiors, no matter what.

"It's not about the unions this time, sir. It's about brave men who serve overseas as ambulance drivers, come back wounded, and are denied help by the Department of Veteran Affairs."

A flash of interest formed in Charlie's eyes before it was replaced by disapproval. Kenny's gut dropped like a bomb.

"Hey, don't you remember?" Charlie piped up, his greased-back hair gleaming. "The boss asked you about that lead." He winked at Bixby. "I don't think it's a lead at all. Most likely a bird's number he picked up while working the Lana Turner story." He tilted his head toward Kenny as he uttered a derisive chuckle. "A real newsbreaker."

Bixby's brow folded as his eyes narrowed. "You franchising on company time?"

"No, I'm not *fraternizing* on company time," Kenny silently corrected, but this time he didn't find it funny.

He glared at Charlie. Why'd that guy have to bust his chops all the time? Yet, Kenny shouldn't have fibbed about the number being a lead. *Could* he make it into a piece? She was a riveter. He could do a story about her and how she dealt with doing a man's job. The only problem was, a lot of other ladies in town were also riveters. What made her so special?

Of course, he could just tell the truth and say it wasn't a story, and the girl had given him the number for a date. Kenny's chest constricted. *Lord, if I tell the truth, they'll think I was fraternizing, and I wasn't.*

Well, I guess I was—a little.

The two men waited, and Kenny's conscience gave him no choice but to turn the fib into a truth.

"The number was from a girl who works at the Boeing plant." *That's the truth.* "She's a riveter. It, uh, might be interesting to do a story on her." He shook his head. "I know, I know, it's been done before. So I scrapped the idea."

The phone on the desk next to Kenny's rang, and Charlie lunged to answer, spoke a few words, then hung up.

"That was a *real* lead." Charlie's voice sounded triumphant. "A source called to say construction began today on the United States' first nuclear reactor. They're building it somewhere in one of the southern states. I'm gonna head over to the university and get the opinions of some of the scientists there to see if this thing is for real." Charlie grabbed his coat and hat. "Be back in a couple hours."

"Good work, Charlie. Be the first. It's gonna go national."

Charlie took off out of the press room, and Bixby walked away while Kenny sat, discouraged. The emotions in his chest churned in frustration. If Charlie got a real story—a big story like this—and Kenny didn't end up with anything newsworthy, he'd slip even farther down the pecking order. The only thing that topped a big, national story was a local one that stirred everyone's patriotism in a new way.

"Mr. Bixby," Kenny called. Bixby paused at the threshold of his office. "Let me do the piece about the ambulance drivers. It's a good story, with a local tie. It could bring the guys' plight to the people's attention and maybe help a lot of our boys."

Bixby drew a pack of Marlboros from his shirt pocket. The ink from his fingers left faint smudges on the white fabric. He lit a cigarette as he returned to Kenny's desk, shaking his head.

"That's not a bad story." He leaned on Kenny's desk. "But Kenny, I need to be able to trust you. Son, you really went over the line with that union piece. I know you want a big story, and I respect your reasoning. But everyone has to pay their dues."

"I want to pay my dues, Mr. Bixby, I do, but—"

Bixby straightened. "Then do the riveter story," he challenged.

The riveter story I didn't mean to pitch?

"Find a Seattle hook. Make our readers love her. Give that girl a jingle. See what you can dig up."

Another corny story about a pretty girl. Lord, will I ever get the chance to prove myself?

Kenny closed his eyes and nodded. "Yes, sir."

Chapter Six

·····················

Polishing off the last of his Igloo Burger, Kenny leaned back in his puffy, white-cushioned chair and sipped his Dr Pepper. He swiped a fry through the puddle of ketchup on his plastic plate as he ran through the possibilities for turning the lady riveter story into something newsworthy. Sure, similar stories had been told many times, but maybe he could come up with a fresh angle.

It means I'll have to call Rosalie.

He'd picked up the phone a least a dozen times that afternoon, then put down the receiver again. Problem was, he needed just the right words, and he needed to get over the lump in his throat that rose every time he thought of her pretty face.

Like a cold Seattle rain, he was doused with misgivings. *She'll think I want a date. But even if I wanted to date her now, I can't. The boss would flip his cap.*

Kenny allowed his attention to wander to the ice-blue stage, where Nick jigged and be-bopped with his bass fiddle, an echo of the lighthearted bloke he was before the war.

Drop-diving into his music was how Nick maintained his carefree disposition—away from his war memories and his wound. Away from the fact that the country he served wouldn't pay for his medical bills. All because he'd served in a contracted ambulance unit rather than the U.S. military.

Kenny let out a lingering breath. Whether with an official U.S. Army unit or not, Nick had still worked on the front lines in France. He'd risked his life transporting not only French soldiers fighting against the Nazis, but also women and children.

How many people had Nick risked his life to rescue?

He'd sacrificed plenty, long before the United States was even in the war. At a time when most Americans agreed that staying neutral was their best option, Nick had shipped off overseas to make a difference. And he'd paid a heavy price for his convictions. He'd never walk again without a limp. He'd never run. Never live without pain.

Which was why Kenny wanted—needed—to write that story. If only his boss would let him. Kenny sighed as Nick's band, The Jaybirds, closed their set with, "I'll Never Smile Again," by Tommy Dorsey.

"*I'll never smile again until I smile at you*," Kenny sang along, under his breath.

The lead singer, a Dorothy Lamour look-alike with a sultry voice and swaying hips, rasped the last verse as if her vocal cords were scraping over asphalt. Kenny wondered if she'd make it through another set.

The song finished. Nick set his bass on its stand and ambled to the mic. "Back in fifteen, folks." Then he whispered something to the vocalist before stepping off the stage.

A waitress wearing a blue and white polka-dotted apron over a short, puffy skirt popped over to Kenny's table. Her bare legs caused him to blush. Now Kenny knew why Nick liked working at this place.

"Done with that, mister?" she asked.

"Oh, he's done all right." Flipping a chair around, Nick straddled it, giving the waitress a grin. "Thanks, sweetheart."

Rolling her eyes, the waitress picked up his plate. "Aw, Nick, you're flappin' your gums again." A flattered smile turned up her rubied lips, and a blush tinted her neck. Kenny had seen this before— the Nick Effect. A "hi, sweetheart" was all it took to send some girls tripping over their feet.

"Bring me the usual, will ya, sweetcakes?" Nick winked.

She nodded and flashed a smile. "You got it," she said, sashaying to the kitchen.

Kenny folded his arms and waited for Nick to finish ogling the waitress's legs.

Catching sight of Kenny's teasing scorn, he raised an innocent palm. "What? What'd I do?"

"Must you *always* be fishing?"

"Always." Nick nodded decisively. "Nice gams on that doll."

"I suppose." Kenny shrugged. "But Mama taught me that a girl's good looks soon fade, while what's in her heart just keeps getting more beautiful." He grinned, knowing Nick would probably tease him for talking about his mama.

Nick tossed his head back in a hearty laugh. "Gotta love your sweet mother's advice."

"Pay attention. She's got some good things to say. You might learn something."

"Probably more than I ever learned from my own mama." Nick's gaze dropped to his hands. "Yours was more of a mother to me than mine ever was. I listened to everything she told me about Jesus."

Kenny's heart rate jumped at his friend's unexpected mention of Christ. Was Nick finally ready to talk about this? Kenny had been praying for him, especially ever since Nick had lived with him after returning from Europe. He didn't want to push his friend, but he hoped Nick was paying attention. Did he see Kenny reading the Word and going to church? Did Nick wonder about the strength he saw in Kenny? The peace only God could give? It was hard to know if any of it seeped in.

"I know she's right, and"—Nick's eyes reflected thoughtfulness— "I might change someday. You know, follow the straight and narrow. But I'm just not ready now. I'm having too much fun."

Then, in a flash, Nick's serious moment blew away, and the sunny Nick returned. "Enough about me, for pete's sake." Nick slapped Kenny's arm. "I'm glad you're here. I've kept this place from you long enough." Laughter tumbled from Nick's throat. "Let me buy you another Dr

Pepper, and we'll talk about that feisty little dolly-bird who spurned you today." He emphasized *spurned* as if relishing Kenny's rejection.

Kenny smiled, yet inside he wished Nick had lingered on spiritual matters a bit longer. Still, Kenny knew the worst thing he could do was press the issue. He determined to follow his friend's lead and talk when the time was right. But he'd also continue praying...most definitely praying.

Kenny took a sip from his soda, then shook his head. "Spurned? I don't know what you mean. But you'll never believe it. One of her friends—or at least I guess it was her friend—rode up on a motorcycle and gave me Rosalie's number. I'm considering doing a story on her, but I don't want to date her."

Nick's gaze shifted past Kenny toward the door. "Oh, really?" A knowing smile creased his face. "Well, here's your chance to tell her that."

The welcoming bells on the door jingled, and girlish laughter flowed into the Igloo. Kenny looked over his shoulder, following Nick's gaze. A cluster of ladies from the Boeing plant exploded through the front entrance, their voices resounding through the room.

> *"All the day long,*
> *whether rain or shine,*
> *she's a part of the assembly line.*
> *She's making history,*
> *working for victory,*
> *Rosie the Riveter."*

Nick hobbled to the stage, as if inspired by their song, and Kenny turned in his seat toward the singing.

Smiling and laughing, the brown-haired lioness from this afternoon, surrounded by her gaggle of friends, strolled past Kenny's table.

"Rosalie," he whispered.

"Gee, Rosalie," one of them said, "I think you should get some type a reward for your big achievement. How 'bout it, girls? Who wants to pitch in for Rosalie's favorite—a double cheeseburger with fries? And Birdie too—Rosalie couldn't have done it without Birdie! Waitress, can you put in that order for us?"

"Hey, don't be calling her Rosalie. She's Rosie from here on out! Rosie the Riveter," a petite woman called out.

"Add a chocolate malt to Birdie and *Rosie's* order," a tall woman added. "It's not every day something like this happens to one of our own."

Kenny's heart slammed against his ribs. Until now, seeing her praised by these women, he hadn't realized how impressive she really was. Suddenly, he wanted to talk to her. *Really* talk to her. He lifted the paper with her number from his pocket.

Chapter Seven

....

"Whoopee ding, girlie! We did it!" Birdie wrapped an arm around Rosalie's neck. A flock of their coworkers, just as keyed up as they were, circled around them.

"We did, didn't we?" Rosalie planted an exuberant kiss on the top of her petite friend's head. "Where's the music? It's time to celebrate!"

Rosalie's right arm ached, her feet throbbed, her ears buzzed from the never-ending *bam!* of her gun, but she didn't care. For once she intended to forget her responsibilities—her guilt—and celebrate at her favorite hangout. It seemed right, in a way, that she and Birdie had broken the record on this day. Vic had always been proud of her, but today, for the first time, she felt worthy of his pride.

Ever since she'd started at the plant, breaking the record had always niggled at her—as if reaching that goal would somehow prove her worthy of Vic's love. Well, now she and Birdie had pounded more rivets than Bill and George, or anyone at the plant. Or anyone anywhere. The success of breaking that record energized her. She'd forgotten how good it felt to be happy. Her cheeks hurt from smiling.

Thronging the dance floor, the ladies burst out in another verse of "Rosie the Riveter," and Rosalie laughed. "That's not what I had in mind when I asked for music, girls!"

The meaty aroma of grilled burgers and french fries filled the place, making her stomach growl. She wanted to dance, but she needed something to eat first. The ladies charged to the dance floor, nearly trampling the waitress and her tray of food bound for Rosalie and Birdie. In a second, the woman workers were be-bopping with the GIs who'd found their way into the place. Rosalie hung back, diving in to the hamburger and fries, voracious, while trying not to look like it. Birdie's food sat there, getting cold, but Rosalie knew Birdie was having too much fun to care.

Rosalie's heart lightened once again as the delicious food hit her stomach. She hadn't realized until now how much energy the high-speed riveting had taken from her.

When she finished, she considered skedaddling to catch the next bus, but then she thought of what waited for her at home. An empty apartment. More memories of Vic. Birdie and Clara caught her eye as they danced a fast jig together. Laughter bubbled from Rosalie's lips.

Maybe she could stick around a *little* longer.

Iris, the auto parts delivery girl, entered the restaurant and looked around in wide-eyed surprise. Clara rushed over to her, no doubt filling Iris in on the cause of the celebration.

Without hesitation, Iris traipsed to the bass player and whispered something in his ear. Rosalie's smile wobbled. It was the second time she'd seen Nick that day. Her cheeks warmed as she remembered how foolish she'd felt earlier in Victory Square. She just hoped Nick wouldn't bring it up.

Flashing the bass player two thumbs-up, Iris rushed back to the group, and the band swung into a jazzy rendition of "Rosie the Riveter." Rosalie wondered where the vocalist was and then noticed Nora, sitting at a table sipping a hot drink. Nora's free hand cupped her throat. *Poor gal must've lost her voice.* They didn't need her voice for this song, though. The gals ramped up the volume. Though the sun was finally setting outside, her heart felt warm and light.

Birdie's face was red from dancing when she hurried to the table. "We did it," Birdie squeaked again over the music, as if freshly realizing their feat. "I can't believe it!"

She grasped Rosalie by both hands, pulling her to her feet and toward the dance floor. They found an open spot, and Birdie swung in a circle. Rosalie had no choice but to follow. Soon the upbeat jazz filled her with its rhythm.

Iris bopped over to them, her arm draped across the shoulders of a girl Rosalie didn't know.

"This is Lanie!" Iris's voice lifted above the music.

Lanie, whose golden hair flowed over her shoulders, smiled. "Nice to make yer acquaintance," she drawled with Southern sweetness.

"Lanie Thomas is my new roommate." Iris's tough-as-steel body swayed as the band launched into a Benny Goodman tune. "She starts at the plant tomorrow with you gals."

Rosalie shook the girl's slender hand. "You nervous?"

"What?" Lanie leaned in, cupping her hand around her ear.

Rosalie came closer. "I asked, are you nervous?"

"Oh yes, I sure am." Lanie grasped Rosalie's hand. "I'm so amazed that you broke that record. I'll be plumb happy to squeeze one little rivet into the right spot."

"You'll do fine, hon." Birdie grabbed Rosalie's other hand, flinging Rosalie into an Around the Pole, pulling her away from Lanie's grasp.

Swinging back around to Lanie, Rosalie remembered how nervous she'd been before her first day. "You'll do great; don't you worry. By the time you're done with training, you'll be yearning to plug in those rivets."

Disbelief garnished Lanie's eyes, but Rosalie knew it was true. Women came to the plant from all different worlds—timid young gals, like Lanie, to middle-aged housewives. And, somehow, stepping out of their skirts and into work slacks released strong, bold, dedicated women. Women who were like a secret weapon, ready to jump into action when needed. Women who'd produced over one hundred B-17s in the last year alone—enough to give the Allies an edge.

The song, "Kiss the Boys Goodbye," wound down with a zipping trumpet solo, and then Nick limped to the mic. Rosalie couldn't imagine anyone pulling off a limp with more style—even dreamy Frank Sinatra.

"I hear history's been made today!" Nick announced. The crowd roared their cheers. "Will the two ladies who broke the record come on up?"

For the second time that day, Rosalie found herself onstage. She surveyed the beaming faces of her friends. As much as she hated the spotlight, the thrill of the day's victory trumped her reluctance. Birdie grabbed Rosalie's hand and lifted it up as if she were a boxer who'd won the title. The crowd cheered as Nick wrapped his arms around their shoulders and leaned into the microphone.

"So tell me, ladies, what exactly did you accomplish today?"

"They broke the national record!" Iris's strong voice bellowed from somewhere in the audience.

Rosalie scanned the room for her, but instead her gaze tripped on a familiar face. A man's face. *That reporter—Kenny.* He was talking to the oh-so-cute Lanie but seemed distracted. His eyes darted past the new girl toward the stage. The way he looked at her made her stomach flip. His focus seemed stronger than it had been this morning—more caring too. His smile was becoming. But instead of making her eager to talk to him, the emotions stirring within made her want to escape.

Without warning, the reporter's eyes locked with Rosalie's. And then he winked. Rosalie placed a hand over her stomach, surprised by the unexpected butterflies. He totally unnerved her—for the second time that day.

Oh no. Smoldering heat rose from her neck to her face. *Why did I let Iris talk me into giving him my number?* She turned her head, glancing toward the crowd of her friends again, but it was too late. She knew he'd seen her blush.

The anxiety of being onstage resurfaced. The euphoria over winning the contest and the anticipated satisfaction of making Bill and George grovel in apology tomorrow faded as she struggled to come up with an escape plan. Could she manage to do it without Kenny noticing? Maybe if she simply avoided eye contact, he'd lose interest and she could slip away.

Birdie's slim fingers tugged on her arm, and her voice filtered through the din. Birdie was saying something about needing help from men to break the record—or not needing them.... Birdie tugged on her arm, smiling. "Do you think so, Rosalie?"

"What?" She tried to refocus. What had Birdie been saying?

"Did we need help for what we did this afternoon?"

Rosalie turned her attention back to the crowd and faked confidence she didn't feel. "Nope, Birdie, we didn't need any help!"

The room hushed, and numerous pairs of eyes focused on her—a mix of surprise and pain.

Birdie's eyebrows scrunched; then she rose on her tiptoes to whisper in Rosalie's ear. "Uh, Rosalie, maybe you heard me wrong. I asked you if we could've done it without the help of our sisters."

Rosalie gasped, embarrassed heat flooding her cheeks. She scanned the faces, seeing their confusion, wishing she could take her words back. She leaned toward the microphone. "I'm sorry. I didn't mean—" She couldn't help but look at Kenny, to see his response. A sympathetic grin filled his face.

"That's all right, sweetie!" Iris called out. "We knew what you meant. You're our Rosie the Riveter!"

Kenny clapped along with the others, then coiled his fingers into his mouth to release a shrill whistle.

Rosalie leaned in toward Birdie. "This is why I hate being in front of people. Never turns out good," she mumbled.

Birdie squeezed Rosalie's hand as the cheers followed them from the stage. "It's okay, sweets," Birdie said. "They knew what you meant."

Rosalie slinked through the crowd of ladies, also trying to find a place to hide from Kenny.

"Rosie, come and sit with us!" Clara called to her from the booth she shared with two other women.

Rosalie eyed the booth, then the door, then the booth where

Clara was saving her a seat. She couldn't leave now, after what she'd accidentally said. They'd think badly of her for sure. She hurried over and slid into the booth next to Clara.

Nick took the mic again. "We know all you ladies are tops when it comes to building airplanes, but I have an extra-special request. Our lead singer's out of voice."

Nora waved apologetically from her table.

"Any of you riveters own a smooth set of pipes?" Nick glanced around the room. "C'mon, this could be your big break."

"Lanie'll do it!" Iris pushed the girl away from Kenny and toward the stage. "She's got a great voice."

Lanie blushed and dithered, but the spark in her eye told Rosalie she relished the chance to take the limelight. It didn't take much persuasion to get her behind the mic.

Nick gaped at her for a moment of awkward silence before stepping away to make room for her. As he reached for his bass, he fumbled over the microphone's cord, almost tripping. So unlike the usually suave Nick.

Finally, he seemed to pull himself together, whispering something to Lanie just before the band started up with the newest hit: "The Boogie Woogie Bugle Boy."

Rosalie remained at her table, content to watch the others dance until enough time had passed that she could leave without hurting anyone's feelings. But as she rose to head toward the door, she felt the electrifying presence of someone behind her.

Kenny's voice sounded in her ear. "She's got some pipes, don't you think, Rosalie?"

Rosalie whipped around in surprise, almost upsetting the soda he was holding.

With one quick motion, he swooped it out of the way to avoid spilling it. Then Kenny chuckled. "We're not having much luck with Cokes today, are we?"

Chapter Eight

....

Kenny led Rosalie over to a small, round table next to the dance floor. He set down his Coke and offered Rosalie his best smile.

They'd started off on the wrong foot this morning. Did she regret their inauspicious beginning as much as he did? She did send her phone number via courier, so that was a good sign. Maybe she'd just had a hard morning.

Tonight her piercing brown eyes didn't seem flighty, and neither did the fact that she'd broken the national record for setting rivets in a shift. Only a focused, decisive woman could do that.

He wiped his palms on his slacks, tipped up his chin, and offered his elbow. "Wanna?"

She shook her head. "I don't think…" Her gaze slid to her friends, who bobbed their heads in wide-eyed encouragement. One of them even flashed a thumbs-up, causing Rosalie to flush pink. A very becoming pink.

"C'mon—just one dance?" He knew she wanted to. She would have already blasted him with a resounding no—just like this morning—if she didn't.

Kenny dared to reach out and take her hands. They were small but strong. He pulled slightly, and she followed as he led her to the dance floor.

He turned to face her and couldn't help but see excitement in her gaze. Was it excitement over him or over being able to dance? He wasn't sure, but it didn't matter. At least she wasn't mad or stomping away.

Kenny swung her hands from side to side in time to the music before easing her into a smooth three-step, silently thanking his sister for all the times she'd forced him to be her practice partner.

Rosalie's eyelashes swept up as she dared a look into his eyes, and her lips parted as if she wanted to say something but didn't quite know what. He swung her around, and she seemed both surprised and pleased by the comfortable way he moved on the dance floor.

He pulled her around to face him again, pulling her closer to his chest than he usually did with his dance partners. "I'm not gonna tell you how much I enjoyed seeing you onstage. And I promise: no probing questions—at least not till later," he teased.

Her perfect red lips spread into a grin. "You could ask, but that doesn't mean I'd answer them, *reporter.*"

Lanie belted out "Shoo Shoo Baby" like she was one of the Andrews Sisters, and Kenny promenaded Rosalie into the center of the dance floor. Easing her into a Sugar Push, he pulled her to him, then unwound her gently back out, like a yo-yo on a string. She followed effortlessly, her hands gripping his lightly.

After a few more easy steps, like the Skip Up, Kenny thought he'd try the Lindy hop with Charleston variation. From the regular Charleston, Kenny continued holding her hand and then turned clockwise to come around in an outside turn, so he was in front.

Then on the first kick move he waited, wondering if she'd be able to follow. As if she'd been dancing with him her whole life, Rosalie did her own clockwise turn and spun around so she was in front, and they kicked their right legs in unison. Cheers rose up from her friends who were watching, and she only glanced over to them for a moment before turning her attention back to him.

Kenny squeezed her hand tighter as they continued the move two more times.

As the song wound down, Rosalie spun to face him. Her eyebrows flicked upward. "Is that all ya got?" She smirked.

Laughter burst from his lips at her unexpected challenge. Noting the determination of her chin, he imagined she had the same expression as she riveted, especially today as she had worked toward the record. The music kicked up again in a fast number.

"You want more?" he called over the tune. "I'll show you more."

He pulled her to him, dipped his shoulder, and turned. He expected to surprise her, but she rolled over his back with grace.

"Whew!" she hooted as she landed.

Without a pause, Kenny swung her into a sidecar, her legs kicking first to his left, then right. "You wanna flip?"

Without bothering to reply, Rosalie hurled herself forward, coiling around his arm. She landed on both feet with a *Well, hotshot, what else have you got?* glimmer in her eyes.

"Now that's what I'm talking about." Rosalie's cheeks were flushed, and her eyes gleamed. "You're not so bad."

Kenny rolled her to him, their bodies tight as their feet shuffled in rhythm beneath them. For an instant, he felt dizzy from all their spinning and twirling. Or was it the scent of her perfume?

As they glided past the stage, he caught a glimpse of Nick's amused grin, and Kenny knew his friend was relishing the prospect of razzing his smooth dance moves.

Kenny tried to think of something witty to say. He wanted to tease Rosalie—to joke in the easy way Nick would. But his mind couldn't get beyond the joy of just dancing with her.

Together, Kenny and Rosalie swung, jumped, and flew around the dance floor until the music wound down once again. Kenny glanced at his watch. To his astonishment, an hour had passed. The woman was tireless, and he loved every minute of it.

Finally, the band left the stage for their break. The other couples who'd been dancing moved toward the tables and booths, but Kenny remained, trying to catch his breath. He leaned over, hands to knees, panting.

"Uncle!" he managed to say between breaths.

"That's what I like to hear," she said, fanning her flushed face with her hand.

He gazed up at Rosalie, and it was more than the stage lights haloing her head that convinced him he needed to spend more time with her. Someone put a nickel in the jukebox, and "Hello Young Lovers" wound itself around the room as the lights dimmed.

Rosalie leaned over him, moving her face closer and chuckling as he again tried to catch his breath. "Worn out, huh?"

Kenny nodded as he straightened, noticing Nick leading Lanie by the hand onto the dance floor, where he cautiously pulled her into a slow dance.

"Me too." Rosalie let out a slow breath.

"How 'bout a drink?"

"Just so long as it's not a Coke." Her lips turned up once more in a smile at their private joke.

A man could get lost in that smile.

"Uh, yeah, sure," he mumbled.

Nice, Kenny, you write for a living, and that's the best you can do?

Rosalie glanced over to Nick and Lanie, and a thoughtful look passed over her face. "Actually, I'm more tired than I thought." She let out a slow breath, and he noticed her shoulders slump. "Maybe I should go."

"Just one soda? I can't send you home thirsty."

"Okay, as long as it doesn't take too long."

The refreshment line was long, filled with other winded dancers who had the same idea. Yet in her presence, he hardly noticed the passage of time. It seemed like mere minutes until he was guiding her to an outside table. Rain scented the air, and he prayed the clouds would hold their moisture for a little longer.

One block away, a stream of headlights flowed down Victory Highway. The Igloo was nestled just off the busy highway and the small shops. In the distance twinkled the lights of Victory Heights, a name that fit a neighborhood where many war-production workers lived.

"So." Kenny swigged his Orangeade, savoring the cool refreshment on his parched tongue. "Now can I ask you a question?"

He caught Rosalie mid-sip. Her eyes took on a wariness as her lips parted from the straw. "Uh, it's not about a certain friend of mine, who delivers brazen notes by motorcycle, is it?"

"No." Kenny set his glass bottle on the tabletop.

"Good, because I'm not the kind of girl who—" she stammered, the vale between her eyebrows crinkling.

Kenny fought to hide a grin, enjoying her discomfort.

"I don't know why I let Iris give you my number." She exhaled.

"My question is not about the girl on the motorcycle." Kenny sipped his drink, his eyes never leaving her face. "It's about the girl who sent the note. I—"

"Actually, why don't we try this," she interrupted before he could finish. "Why don't I ask you a question first? Then you can ask me one."

Kenny fingered the neck of his bottle. He knew she was trying to get him off topic, but he wasn't afraid to play along. "Okay, shoot."

She tapped her temple, as if trying to come up with something on the spot. "So how do you know Nick?"

"Well," he started, "we grew up together. He sat behind me in third grade and always drove me crazy with his humming in class. I didn't like him for years—ignored him mostly—until we were paired up in track for the relay race. With his speed and my endurance we won nearly every race in high school."

"Really? I can't imagine Nick being on a relay team. You can't help but notice his limp. I assume he hurt it in the military?"

"Yes, he was injured, but he wasn't in the military." Kenny went on to explain Nick's role as a contracted ambulance driver in France. "He was overseas even before Pearl Harbor, but his service doesn't seem to matter."

"I don't understand. Why not?"

He explained about the fighting in France and Nick's role in helping evacuate towns where the Germans wrested control, leaving destruction in their wake.

"More than that, there's a problem within the Veterans Administration," he added. "They don't want to help Nick because he wasn't officially with the military."

"That doesn't seem right. Let me know if there's anything I can do to help." She shrugged. "I'm not sure what that would be, though."

Kenny nodded. "Thanks for the offer. I'll remember that. I agree that it's not right at all, and I want to write a story about it someday."

"You should. I think the citizens of Seattle need to hear about it. If it happened to Nick, I'm sure there are others out there who—"

The door swung open, and a few of Rosalie's friends scampered out, encircling their table, interrupting her words.

The slight blond with curly hair sidled up to Rosalie. "Sorry, Rosie, we don't want to cut your fun, but we're all pooped. Thought we'd catch the midnight bus."

Rosalie scooted her chair back, and Kenny's heart sank. It pleased him that she cared about Nick and agreed with him that something needed to be done about it. He wanted to hear what she'd been saying before she was cut off. More than that, the conversation hadn't returned to her. He had numerous questions about this intriguing riveter, but her answer to even one—giving him a glimpse into her heart—would be enough to hold him until he could see her again.

"Sorry, Birdie. It's the second time today I owe you an apology." Rosalie stood. "It's later than I thought. I didn't mean to keep you."

"It's okay. I'll tell the others you're coming." The small blond walked toward the others who were waiting for the bus.

Kenny stood and dared to touch his hand to her elbow. She was wearing the same red-and-white-checkered shirt she had in the morning, but tonight his whole perception of her had changed. He wanted to do more than just touch her arm. He wanted to sit beside her, shoulder to shoulder, and talk into the night. Did she care deeply about all the unfair practices, all the people in need of a voice, who also concerned him? He had a feeling she did.

His mind raced, attempting to figure out a way to see her again.

"Thanks for the dance, Kenny." Rosalie's voice softened almost to a whisper. "I had a nice time."

Then she waited—this strong, beautiful woman standing before him waited for him to say something. Anything.

He grasped her hands. "I really want to see you again," he blurted. *Great. A regular old silver tongue.*

"I'd like that." She tipped her head, her gaze lingering. "Do you work tomorrow?"

Work. How was he going to face Mr. Bixby tomorrow without any leads as he'd promised? Then, with a quick breath, he remembered the riveter story he needed to nail down. Rosalie had broken the national record. Why hadn't he thought of it before?

He studied her face, noticing she seemed open to him—maybe even open enough for an interview. "Rosalie, I have a question for you," he started. "I do have to work, but I was thinking we could get together tomorrow. If you're available for an interview—"

"Interview?" Her smile faltered, and she pulled her hands away.

It was only one word, but her pained expression told him everything.

"Listen, Rosie—I mean, Rosalie. I mentioned you to my boss and he said—"

She squared her shoulders. "Know what, Kenny? I mean, Mr. Davenport. I don't want to hear it. It seems that from the first moment we met you've been intent on making sure you got *your news*. The news is, buddy, it's not all about the words on the page. The people you write about are real people—not mere stepping-stones to your goal." She lowered her gaze, and Kenny was sure he saw hurt more than anger. "No thanks, bub. Nice dancing with ya."

The bus approached the curb, and most of Rosalie's friends waited to board.

The petite blond waved. "C'mon, Rosie! You're gonna miss the bus!" The blond's smile faded; she must have noticed her friend was upset.

Rosalie looked once more into Kenny's eyes, then turned away and hurried to catch up with her friends.

Kenny thought about running after her, but what was the point? What could he say or do to undo the damage he'd just done? More than anything he wanted to see her again, and not for the story, either. Now he worried he never would.

Rosalie disappeared in the throng of other women climbing onto the bus steps. A few more plant workers lingered at the other outdoor tables, despite the nippy air, chatting with GIs who didn't want the night to end.

Kenny was surprised to see Rosalie's sidekick and a few others hanging back. She was a tiny little thing, Birdie—yes, that was her name. It fit her. She looked at the bus, then back to him, frowning, and to the bus again.

She watched as the bus doors closed and the loud vehicle rumbled into the night. Then she turned to him, approaching with quick steps that told him this woman meant business. "Hiya, Mr. Davenport. Can we talk?"

Chapter Nine

....

Ａмерica Begins Second Half-Year of War with Victory Certain, the newspaper headline read.

I sure hope so, Rosalie thought as she read about American battles in places she hadn't heard about, hadn't cared about before.

The black tea—weak but comforting—warmed Rosalie as she scanned the paper. A pink petal from a cherry tree fluttered onto her arm as she cozied into the soft round chair she'd pushed out to the small apartment balcony with a view of the other quaint buildings along Queen Anne Hill. The slightest warm breeze ruffled the hem of her skirt, tickling her legs.

Drinking in the floral spring scent, she inspected the range of quaint, turn-of-the-century apartment buildings—their white-rimmed bay windows lining Kinnear Park. She yawned as her gaze traveled along the park all the way to Elliot Bay, where the sun danced on the calm waters. Then she turned back to the paper.

Czechs Told to Mourn for Hangman; Heydrich's Body Borne Through Crowds on Way to Berlin Funeral. U.S. Fleet Still Pouring Steel Vengeance on Japs. Nazi Generals in Canada among Thousands of War Prisoners.

She closed her eyes, allowing the morning sunlight to warm her tense muscles. With a twist and stretch of her neck, she peeked at Birdie sitting not far from her, also reveling in the quiet moment, reading her Bible and writing in a journal.

After reading all the way through the front section, Rosalie flipped to the local page. *Wonder what's going on in our fair city today. Another scrap-metal drive? A street fair?* She skimmed through a quaint story about a kindergarten class collecting dimes to buy war stamps, which took her to the next article accompanied by a photograph. She slapped her hand over it and gasped. "That's me!"

It was her all right, dressed like a man ready for work, looking like a frump beside the elegant Lana Turner on the stage at Victory Square. There was Kenny too, even handsomer than she remembered. Without thinking, she allowed her fingers to brush his face. Then she slouched. *As if being shoved in front of all those people yesterday wasn't enough, now I'm displayed for the whole Puget Sound area to see? That'll teach me to trust a reporter!*

"What's wrong?" Birdie asked, and Rosalie looked up to find her friend's eyes on her.

Rosalie folded the page over so Birdie could see. "I'm in the *Tribune*."

Birdie grinned. "Is that all? Good heavens, the way you gasped, I thought maybe the Allies had surrendered or something. Let me see."

Rosalie handed her the paper. Birdie read aloud: Local Love-birds Meet Lana Turner, by Kenny Davenport." She looked up at Rosalie, eyebrows arched.

"How could he?" Rosalie gasped. "We're not lovebirds. I hardly even know the man!"

"Really?" A knowing smile quirked Birdie's mouth. "Way you two were looking at each other on that dance floor last night, I'd say you know each other better than you think."

Rosalie peered at the picture again. "How'd he get that shot? He was on the stage with me."

"Must have had a buddy in the crowd."

Remembering, Rosalie's hands grew damp, envisioning again the stares of all those strangers. In a small voice, she asked, "What does the article say?"

"Let's see." Birdie closed the Bible and journal and set them on the little round table next to Rosalie. She ran a finger over the grainy black-and-white mug of Kenny. "He sure seems like a nice guy. He's got a pleasing smile, doesn't he?"

"Pleasing smile? Is that what you call it? The guy spilled Coke all over me; plus, if it wasn't for him, I never would have ended up onstage."

"Did you know he'd be at the Igloo last night?" Birdie asked.

"Gracious, no!"

"Hmm, 'cause the way you were dancing, it seemed like you were made for each other."

"You've been reading too many Hollywood magazines," Rosalie muttered, hoping Birdie wouldn't read past her words to the truth: that she had enjoyed dancing with him more than she'd enjoyed anything since…well, since Vic.

Kenny was fun to talk to, laughed at her jokes, even played along with her sarcasm. She touched her neck with the pads of her fingers. But he was a *reporter*—and he'd just proven he was not to be trusted. She tightened her lips.

"I think he's friends with Nick. I bet Nick told Kenny you'd be there," Birdie said, then turned her attention back to the paper. "It doesn't sound too bad. Listen to this."

Rosalie buried her head in her hands, prepared to be humiliated.

It is never a reporter's job to write about himself, but yesterday, it was I who took center stage at Victory Square. Fortunately, I was not alone. A lovely riveter named Rosalie (Seattle's very own Rosie the Riveter?) joined me. Mistakenly hailed by the one and only Lana Turner as lovebirds, the swell riveter and I were herded onstage in front of thousands of giddy onlookers. Alas, Miss Rosalie and I are not an item; in fact, we'd never met until that moment! When the kind

Miss Turner heard this, she put that to rights by introducing us front and center....

Rosalie lifted her head. She planted her elbows on her knees and cupped her face in her palms. Birdie continued reading. The article described everything that happened until they left the stage. It concluded with this:

> *So all in a day's work—this lowly journalist was lucky enough to meet the famous and fabulous Lana Turner. But as for me, I'm even more blessed to have made the acquaintance of a strong, driven member of the Army at Home— dedicated to her patriotic work. Although I have no desire to ever write another article about myself, I'd love to write more about beautiful Rosalie. So, Seattle's own Rosie the Riveter, if you read this, look me up over at* The Seattle Tribune. *I'm sure you already have a following of dedicated fans.*

Birdie lowered the paper. "Rosalie!" Her eyes rounded like gumballs.

A flattered grin formed, unbidden. "Could've been worse, I guess."

Truth was, Rosalie had expected *much* worse, but Kenny was a perfect gentleman. So much the gentleman, in fact, that it cast what happened last night in a whole new light. Her heart picked up speed as she remembered his hands around her as they danced, the joy in his eyes.

Maybe he's not like I anticipated. Maybe I shouldn't compare him with other reporters.

"He called you beautiful." Birdie's shoulders hunched up around her neck in excitement. "He really likes you."

She could hardly admit to Birdie what she was barely able to acknowledge to herself: that she craved this feeling. The knowledge of being wanted, liked, appreciated—*pursued*. And her reaction was equally surprising. *Admit it, girl, you like him too.* The attraction she felt for Kenny was not only irresistible; it was something she'd not felt for a very long time. If ever.

But could she really trust this guy? Weren't reporters known for pumping up the charm to make you talk to them? Just like in that movie, *His Girl Friday*? But Kenny didn't seem like Cary Grant. Not really suave, but genuine, and kind. Was it all a façade?

Plus, Rosalie had another reason to distrust reporters. Rosalie had seen it all before, up close and personal.

Pops.

Her father was a reporter for *The Tacoma Herald*. She remembered the smell of cigarettes and whiskey—"Old Jack," he called it—wafting through the house when he'd come home at all hours of the night. He'd be wound up about some "big scoop" he nabbed and didn't care that the children were sleeping.

But the worst part about Pops was his broken promises. How many times had he promised to take her to the park, or fishing in the Wenatchee River, or to let Mom enroll her in a cooking class at the Y? But only when he wanted something from her, like helping him make it up to "the old lady." That's when he'd pile on the charm and say pretty much anything to get his way. Once he got it, he'd forget all about whatever promises he'd made.

She hadn't fully understood what was happening when he took a position as a foreign correspondent. After that, he hardly ever came home.

Then, when Rosalie was fourteen, he left for Europe and never returned. She still got letters from him now and then, but she never opened them anymore. She'd gotten tired of reading about the latest story he was chasing. He never asked about her—or the rest of the family. It was always the story. The story reigned supreme, like the Kaiser, or Mussolini.

She breathed in the early summer air, allowing it to dissipate her pained thoughts. No need to rehash ancient history. She and Mom had spent hours talking about it, exorcising those demons. And, of course, there was Uncle Albert. Thankfulness whispered through Rosalie. He'd been more of a father to her than anyone.

Her uncle was currently training female pilots in Sweetwater, Texas, and his letters always made her laugh. They also spoke of his love for her. He longed to see her turn to God, return to church. Rosalie studied her hands. Not yet. Not now.

"Sweets, are you with me?" Birdie waved her hands in front of Rosalie's face. "Hi-de-ho."

"Sorry." Rosalie managed a smile. "Just thinking."

"Trying to find reasons to not like Kenny?"

Rosalie coughed. "Would I do that?"

"Well, yeah, you would." Birdie chuckled. "But I also think it's a losing battle. Maybe you should just trust…"

Birdie's voice seemed to fade as another thought filled Rosalie's mind. The Scripture verse Uncle Albert always included at the bottom of each letter: *Trust in the Lord with all thine heart; and lean not unto thine own understanding.* Rosalie liked how that sounded, but she didn't understand what that could mean. Besides, it was easier to think about trusting God than some guy she had just met. She didn't know much about Kenny Davenport.

"Birdie?"

"Hmm?" Birdie rose, walked through the balcony door, and replaced her Bible on the small bookcase.

Rosalie set the newspaper on the table and followed her friend inside. "Why do you suppose he isn't overseas?"

Birdie folded her arms. "There could be a hundred legitimate reasons he's not fighting." She took their mugs to the small kitchen.

"Not really. Just two. Either he's a coward, or there's something wrong with him."

Birdie's face grew stern. "That's not nice. Listen. I talked to him last night—"

Rosalie grabbed Birdie's arm. "You did? When?"

Birdie tipped up her chin, daring Rosalie to challenge her. "Look, I'm willing to look out for you, even if you aren't. Partly I stuck around last night so the other girls wouldn't have to ride home alone—like I told you when I came in. Partly I stayed to talk to Kenny. He's a swell guy. Honorable, nice, and funny." Birdie rinsed out the dishes and left them in the sink. Then she hurried into the small living area, sitting on the sofa to put on her shoes.

Rosalie trailed after her again, wondering what made her friend so anxious this morning. After putting on her shoes, Birdie started straightening up the living room as if she had a bee in her britches.

"You learned all that last night?" Rosalie didn't know whether to thank Birdie or be horrified. But what if Kenny thought she put Birdie up to it? Her toes curled just thinking about it.

On the other hand, she felt a rush of gratitude toward her friend. Her mother always said that moms and friends could see the truth better than you could. You could count on them to determine if a guy was a bad apple or a good one.

"Yes, Kenny was a good sport." Birdie clasped her hands together, a mischievous grin curving her lips. "He let me ask the questions. I knew I didn't have much time, so I sort of drilled him. He was really nice about it." She preened a little. "Even told me you were a lucky woman to have a good friend like me."

"He's right." Rosalie reached over to squeeze Birdie's hand.

"But to answer your question, I don't know why he's not fighting, but I do know that rather than jumping to conclusions, you should find out for yourself." Birdie patted Rosalie's hand, then hurried back to the balcony. She grabbed the newspaper left on the table, then entered and closed the door, locking it.

Rosalie appreciated her friend's concern, but nothing Birdie said changed the fact that he was a reporter. Besides, Rosalie had already given him a chance, and he had proved that he only wanted her for a story.

"I just don't know if I can trust a guy like that, Birdie." She silently pleaded with her friend to believe her—if not, her yearning for love might triumph over common sense. In the end, she'd only get hurt. "Last night, I fell for his line. But obviously he just wanted me for a story."

Birdie sighed, shaking her head. Then she clapped her hands together twice. "Hey, why aren't you hurrying? We're due at breakfast in twenty minutes!"

"Breakfast?"

Then, as if remembering a dream, she recalled Birdie coming in late last night and suggesting they go out for breakfast as she crawled into bed.

"Breakfast. Right." Rosalie rubbed her brow. "But does it have to be this morning? I'm not sure I'd enjoy it. I have a lot on my mind."

"Yes, it has to be today. We have to celebrate, uh—" Birdie lifted the newspaper in her hand. "It's not every day that you make the paper." Birdie held it up for her.

Rosalie didn't want to disappoint her friend, so she put on her shoes. She was about to comment that Birdie hadn't even known about the news story when she invited her to breakfast, but Birdie's small gasp caused Rosalie's gaze to dart to her friend. "What is it?" Rosalie hurried to her side.

Birdie's thin hands concealed her face. The open newspaper lay at her feet.

Rosalie picked it up, noticing a small story that she'd missed the first time.

U.S. FLIERS RAID FOE IN INDO-CHINA;
HONGAI IS TARGET FOR BOMBERS ESCORTED BY FIGHTERS—
BIG FIRES ARE STARTED

CHUNGKING, China, June 9 (U.P.)—The Fourteenth United States Air Force, switching its operations against the Japanese in Indo-China after helping the Chinese win their greatest victory of the war in Central China, yesterday attacked Hongai, coal mining and shipping center....

Birdie's husband, John, was in the Fourteenth.

Rosalie lifted her head. "Oh, Birdie."

Birdie's eyes filled with tears. It wasn't that this news was any different from the numerous other stories reported every day. The difference was that it was *personal*.

"He'll be all right. He's the best pilot...." She patted Birdie's back, trying to provide the same kind of comfort her friend gave her, but her words felt hollow, empty. But what else could she say? Ever since Vic had left, she'd heard all the platitudes. She'd been assured and encouraged. But none of it really helped. In the end, all the good thoughts and warm wishes never helped Vic—or eased her guilt.

From the apartment above came the patter of light footsteps across the floor, with heavier footsteps following. As with most of the tenants in their building, their upstairs neighbor Betty's husband was off fighting, leaving her to raise their child alone. Then came a loud crash, as if Danny had run into something, followed by the toddler's cry.

Birdie walked blindly to the sofa and dropped onto it as if her legs could no longer bear her weight. Rosalie remembered the swirling thoughts that worry brought to the surface. Birdie probably saw visions of John in his flight suit, the newsreel images of Japanese zero fighters' missiles whistling through the air. Rosalie experienced it each and every time the newspapers reported a new mission in the Pacific—where Vic was. And then her fears were realized.

The child's crying stilled, and a door opened and slammed as Betty left the apartment to drop off Danny at her sister's house before heading for work. Betty was one of the lucky few who had family close by to help her.

Birdie's chest rose and fell as she fingered the arm of the sofa. "Y'know," she spoke without looking at Rosalie, "just a few minutes ago God was reminding me in His Word about His faithfulness." A silent hope shined in her eyes beneath the worry. "God's with John, watching over him. He promised."

A crank turned in Rosalie's stomach, cinching it tight. Vic's mom had claimed that same promise—and where had it gotten her son? "Tell you what. Let's stay home for breakfast this morning. We have a little sugar ration left. I can whip up some of my famous apple-cinnamon muffins."

But Birdie shook her head, as if trying to shake free from the worried thoughts. "No, I still want to go out. Besides, I've invited Lanie and Iris to join us." Birdie tried to make her voice perky, but it didn't work. Instead she squeaked like Mickey—or, rather, Minnie—Mouse.

"You sure?" Rosalie smoothed her skirt. "If you'd rather do it another day…"

"No, really." Birdie wrapped her hand around Rosalie's arm. "I need something to keep my mind occupied, and a big stack of pancakes is just the thing. I've heard the place is great."

Chapter Ten
....

The persistent trill of an alarm clock penetrated Kenny's dreams, jarring him from an exhausted slumber. As he rolled onto his back, he felt every spring and lump of the thin mattress. From the room's other twin bed, Nick snored away—despite the clock's continuing frantic vibrations. *C'mon, Mr. Schwarz, shut the blasted thing off.* Seven o'clock today had arrived much too soon.

Finally, the slap of a hand on metal, and then blessed silence. Kenny squinted open bleary eyes and found morning sunlight sifting through the slits of the threadbare curtains.

The run-down tenement's thin walls allowed tenants on surrounding floors to share Mr. Schwarz's rise-and-shine schedule. The elderly Jewish gentleman, resettled from the Netherlands, retained exclusive, decisive control of the alarm, and negotiating was not allowed. But since a fellow had no way to get his hands on a new alarm clock these days—or toaster, fork, bicycle, or anything metal for that matter—Kenny thanked Mr. Schwarz for being an early riser.

Kenny yawned and sat up, then groaned as his body ached in protest. Ugh, he hadn't jitterbugged like that since—well, since the last time Nick dragged him out. He massaged his stiff calf while his awakening mind ran on ahead. He had a cargo hold of plans for the day, and first on his list was breakfast at The Golden Nugget—with Rosalie.

A sparrow sang outside his window, and Kenny felt like singing along. Last night, Kenny's spirits had soared to the moon when Rosalie's friend Birdie had bounced back from the bus. They'd talked for quite a while, then she'd told him point-blank that she wanted to know how she could help Kenny and Rosalie get together again. He suggested The Golden Nugget—his home turf—and she promised to have Rosalie there at eight o'clock sharp. Aside from the question of whether she'd actually go out on a date with him, he needed that riveter story. And maybe, just maybe, as they spent time together, she'd see that he really was a good guy.

"Thank you, Birdie!" he exclaimed as he bounded out of bed.

"Huh? What?" Nick mumbled.

"Nothing. Go back to sleep."

Kenny showered in the bathroom down the hall, then settled at the rickety, folding card table to read and pray. The scent of freshly brewed coffee made Kenny's mouth water, and he wondered who in this rundown complex, a block from the old Skid Row, had managed to get his hands on that precious commodity.

Kenny finished his morning Bible study with 1 Corinthians 1:25: "Because the foolishness of God is wiser than men; and the weakness of God is stronger than men."

Thank You, Lord, he prayed, but his mind whirled too much to concentrate. He usually found thoughts most clear in these morning times, when he was able to forget about deadlines, the daily commute, and even about the war. But today, no matter how much he tried, he couldn't forget about Rosalie.

He eyed his grandfather's watch. *7:36. Time to go.* Nick snored on from the bedroom as Kenny donned his black fedora and headed out the door. But at the top of the shabby stairway, his neighbor and landlady, Mrs. Rosetti, called to him.

"Kenny! Kenny! Kenny!"

Inwardly, he groaned. Not Mrs. Rosetti. Mrs. Rosetti was notorious for buttonholing unsuspecting tenants in the hallway, trapping them into listening to her interminable ramblings—only half of which anyone could understand through her thick Sicilian accent.

Reluctantly, he turned. "Yes, Mrs. Rosetti?" He looked at his watch again, impatient.

She thrust a scrap of paper into his hand. "Phone. Message for you." And to his immense relief, she departed back into her cave.

But his relief was short-lived as the import of what she said hit him. Phone messages and telegrams—these days, neither of them meant good news.

With trepidation, he unfolded the thin slip of paper, and his heart slammed against his ribs when he saw who had called.

Mom.

He picked up the black receiver and held it to his ear, hoping he could get through. Those on the homefront were asked to only use long-distance calls for emergencies and to keep even those brief. Often phone calls were delayed because the metals needed to build extra phone circuits were being used to fight the war. He said a silent prayer that this call would connect.

"Number please?" came the operator's bored voice.

"Wallingford, 554. Collect." Kenny leaned against the paneled wall and stared at the dusty stairwell.

"One moment please, sir."

The electric light hanging down buzzed as he waited, tapping an impatient foot. He didn't want to miss Rosalie, but—

A fresh slap of worry hit his gut.

Finally, his mother picked up. "Hello?" she said, and he knew from her slow, muted tone that something was very wrong.

"I have a call for you from Seattle, ma'am, from a Mr.—" The operator waited, and Kenny neared his mouth to the receiver. "Kenny Davenport. This is a collect call. The charges will be billed to..."

Kenny closed his eyes as the operator seemed to speak to his mother like a recording on slow speed. On his end, the noisy rush of tenants headed for work faded, and his throat thickened with fear. *Is it Dad? What else could it be?*

He imagined the rough touch of his father's hard-edged hands as he embraced him as a child. His father's hands covered with grease as he and Kenny spent Saturday afternoons under their Model T. His hands embracing Kenny's when he graduated from college. *Is he with You now, God? Are You holding his hand now?*

The operator continued, finally asking, "Will you take the call, ma'am?"

"Yes," his mother said.

"Go ahead." The operator hung up.

"It's your dad, honey."

Kenny waited, numb.

"He's okay. Well, mostly."

The muscles stretching from Kenny's back and shoulders relaxed as a wave of relief cascaded through him. He wasn't gone.

Since Dad had shipped out to the South Pacific, Kenny grasped that there was a possibility he and his mom and sisters could join the somber fellowship of families who lost their sons, brothers, and fathers. Just like everyone else, the prospect always loomed. His father's letters had implored them to take heart if he did lose his life, knowing he served the Lord and the sailors under his spiritual care to the end.

Six months ago, when they'd received word his father had been injured, they were not overly concerned, because Dad's letter told them he was recovering in Hawaii and would be home soon. They'd been a little worried when the letters stopped after that, but a call into Veterans Affairs confirmed he was well and still recovering. Now Kenny wondered if there was more to the silence.

He blew out a slow breath. He couldn't imagine building a future without Dad's advice, prayers, and guidance. When he was a child, he'd always climb on his father's lap when he got home from work. His dad would listen to Kenny's discoveries of the day and answer Kenny's questions—like how to make a prop plane from sticks and a rubber band, and why the ants down by the creek didn't like to swim. Kenny smiled, remembering those days.

Even after his dad had left for the open seas, Kenny couldn't stop sharing the high points of his day with him, but now he put his thoughts into letters. Every night he wrote to Dad, laying out everything that happened, trying to make the mundane details sound fascinating or funny, and wishing he had something more heroic to tell.

"Kenny, are you there?" In the background he could hear his sister talking to someone—maybe one of his aunts or a neighbor. Homesickness rushed over him, surprising him, and he longed for her presence. To see the peace in her eyes and to claim some for himself.

"I'm here." He gripped the phone. "Mom, what's wrong? What happened?"

From the stairs came the uneven *click-click* of Mr. Schwarz's cane, preceded by a cloud of cigar smoke.

"Yesterday in the mail was a bundle of letters. You know how long it takes them to get through. They must have had quite a trip from Hawaii to take so long—"

"And the letters, Mom, what did they say?" he interrupted.

"There was a lot of news. A few months' worth, but in them your father explained the accident and his injuries. He happened to be in the section of the ship hit by the torpedo. So many men weren't as lucky. Many didn't survive."

"And Dad? What happened?"

"His leg was crushed, Kenny. It—it's amazing he survived, but they had to remove his leg. His left leg." Her voice caught. "I'd known he'd been injured, but, well, I didn't expect it was something so life-changing."

Kenny envisioned Dad's faith-filled eyes. Even though his father's strong back could carry any burden, like Christian in *Pilgrim's Progress*, he also knew how to lay his burdens before the Lord.

Kenny leaned his shoulder against the wallpapered wall, water-stained and peeling. "Did it say when he's coming home?"

"Your dad said he was recovering well—or as well as could be expected. He was hoping to leave soon. At least that's what he said in the last letter that was dated over a month ago. Oh, I wish it didn't take so long to get the mail. But, Kenny, he sounded good. His faith is strong, but…" She faltered. "For a man like him to lose a leg—"

Kenny heard the operator pick up.

"I'm sorry, but prepare to hang up. You have one minute. You are about to lose your circuit."

"Mom, is there anything I can do?" he hurriedly said.

"Just pray, hon. Pray for your dad."

"I already am, Mom." His throat tightened and suddenly he wanted nothing more than to be with his mom, to hold her and his sisters. "Mom, do you want me to come home?"

"No, no. Don't even think about it. You've got important work to do. You know, finding a good woman and, oh, that reporting thing you do too." She chuckled. "Just teasing, honey. You know I'm very proud of what you do."

"I know," Kenny responded, grateful that, even now, his mom retained her sense of humor. "I love you. Let me know when you hear anything."

"I will. I love you—"

The phone clicked, and a dial tone buzzed.

Kenny hung up and stared at the receiver. His father had lost his leg. Impossible for him to grasp. Memories flooded his mind: football games in the fallen leaves after Thanksgiving dinner. All the living room furniture pushed back to make room for his dad and his sisters, falling over themselves laughing while trying—and failing—to teach him to jitterbug.

Kenny swallowed hard, and his heart felt heavy. How often had he written a story without understanding the emotion behind it? He was good at focusing on the facts. But the emotion—*that's* where the real story lay. It was more than just battles and dates to him now. Much more.

He breathed in and looked at his watch. *7:54.* Less than fifteen minutes had passed since the last time he'd checked, yet everything had changed. He'd be late now for meeting Rosalie, but suddenly, that didn't seem so important anymore. Maybe he'd axe it and visit the Veterans Hospital instead. Write a story about the men who sacrificed and continued to suffer. He thought of Nick slumbering down the hall. He still longed to tell Nick's story—now more than ever. If only he could get Bixby to sign off on it.

Something clicked. *Let's say I did get a fix on the Rosie the Riveter story. If Bixby liked it well enough, couldn't it open the door to more?*

Rosalie was the key to opening that door.

One more glance at his grandfather's watch told him that if he really hustled, he might still make his date.

Chapter Eleven

A light breeze off Elliot Bay ruffled the burgundy awning of their apartment complex. Two large flowerpots overflowing with fuchsias and petunias welcomed visitors and residents to The Queen's Garden.

Pausing beneath the awning, Rosalie tossed a smile to their neighbors, Lanie and Iris, who called their names as she strode up the sidewalk. Iris wore a sporty blouse beneath a pale mint knit cardigan—almost identical to Rosalie and Birdie's. When she and Birdie weren't working, they often chose the femininity of a soft sweater and skirt, although many ladies wore slacks even when not at work.

Lanie wore perfectly clean and pressed work clothes—jeans and a blue shirt like the one from the Rosie the Riveter poster. A bandanna tightly covered Lanie's shiny blond hair.

Rosalie grinned. "Aren't you the eager beaver this morning?" she teased Lanie.

Lanie nodded and shrugged.

Then Rosalie looked at Iris. "Birdie said you were meeting us to walk to this *sublime* greasy spoon she heard about, but it looks as if you two were already out and about." She strove for a light tone, for Birdie's sake.

"Well, I was hoping the fresh air would do me good," Iris said, wriggling between Rosalie and Birdie in order to chain elbows with them. Together they tromped past the small businesses lined up on Queen Anne Avenue. "Didn't have the best night last night, to tell the truth, so Lanie and me decided to go for a morning stroll. That's when we saw the notice."

"Notice?" Rosalie echoed.

"We're all getting kicked out."

Birdie halted. "Honestly? Kicked out?"

Birdie, already pale as she processed the reality of her husband flying a dangerous mission, now looked as if she might cry. Rosalie unhooked her arm from Iris's and wrapped it around her friend.

"When?" Birdie asked.

"One month. Pretty big of 'em, eh? Giving us a whole month to find a new place to live?" Seeing Birdie's lower lip tremble, Iris added, "Now, now, don't you worry. That's plenty of time to ask around. We'll find something for sure."

Still, Birdie's shoulders slumped, and Iris pulled her into a hug, then kept an arm over her shoulders as they continued down the hill.

Trailing Iris and Birdie, Rosalie kept step with a quiet Lanie and wished she could be as positive as Iris. But Rosalie knew that, despite Iris's confidence, finding a new place wouldn't be easy. New laborers arrived in the city every day, and each of them needed a place to live.

Only 7:40, and already the red transit buses, filled with mostly female laborers, rumbled by, one after another. Rosalie covered her nose as a gust of warm exhaust wafted over her. Then she fixed her gaze on the city spread before them, wondering if someplace out there they'd find a new home.

From here the view of the downtown area was breathtaking. No wonder people chose to build such beautiful homes in this location. Rosalie had long ago resigned herself to never living in a fancy home like that. A roof over her head was fine by her.

Would she have even that a month from now?

Her friends were quiet, apparently lost in similar worries. Their landlord had warned them months ago of this possibility. Rosalie had hoped it wouldn't happen quite so soon. Hard to believe their building would be torn down—the cozy, inviting apartment she and Birdie had created along with it.

Burying her worries, at least for now, she quickened her pace until she drew alongside Iris. "You said you didn't have a good night," she said. "Why? What happened? You seemed your normal electric self when we flew the coop last night."

Before Iris could answer, an aging soldier from the Great War, lounging on a nearby bench, hooted, startling them all.

"That's her!" he exclaimed. "That there's Rosie the Riveter!" He elbowed his companion and pointed at Rosalie.

His friend looked up and a broad smile creased his leathered old face. "Sure as shootin', it *is* her!"

The old veteran rose and shook the *Tribune*'s morning edition at Rosalie. "Miss! Will you autograph this for me?" he asked, shoving his paper at her.

Rosalie's cheeks warmed. "My name's not Rosie, sir."

Birdie poked Rosalie's back with her finger, nudging her forward.

"Ain't this your picture?" the veteran asked, holding up the paper.

Iris lifted the *Tribune* from his liver-spotted hand, glanced over the image the man pointed to, then handed it to Rosalie. "You're right. That's her, sir." She threw the old guy a wink. "Don't worry. She'll sign it for ya."

The man's companion fumbled at his shirt pocket. "Hold up, now. I'm sure my Bonnie stuck a pencil in my pocket so's I could do my crossword puzzles. Hold up." He patted his pants, front and back, before reaching again into his right shirt pocket, then finally the left. "Aha! It was in my left pocket. The left pocket! What was that woman thinking? Fifty years she tucks it in the right side, and today the left."

"Aw, shut your trap, will ya?" his friend grumped. "I've never seen it in any pocket but the left one."

"I'm not sure," Rosalie faltered. "It's not like I'm a star."

"You're a star to them," Lanie said sweetly. "Just look at their faces."

"And what's one small signature?" Birdie cooed. "It'll make their day."

"Fine," she mumbled. She glanced at the gentlemen, whose faces brightened at her attention. Then she signed the bottom right-hand corner of the picture before handing it back to the man whose face shone with the same awe and gratitude fans had given Lana Turner.

Rosalie turned away and joined her friends as they continued past the bus stop but paused as the old veteran called after her, "And make sure you give that Kenny Davenport the chance to write more about you!" He gave Rosalie a droll wink. "I kinda think he likes ya."

Rosalie huffed and spun on her heel. She glowered at Birdie. "See! Now do you understand why I don't want that *reporter* writing any more articles about me? He's already embarrassed me enough." Just the thought of people recognizing her on the street—asking for autographs—made her want to run home and throw her grand-mother's quilt over her head.

Her father used to do that to people too. He'd find some poor unsuspecting sap to shove in the public eye. It'd start small—maybe just a single article, and then if the readership responded well, he'd write more, more, until before he knew it, the poor guy would be attending grand openings of new stores and presenting lame awards, anything to get folks to buy more papers. Rosalie's hands began to sweat. "Reporters don't care about anyone but themselves."

Birdie tossed her hair, shaking her head. "Quit painting every-body with your broad brush, Rosalie. Not all of them are like your father. Kenny's not."

"How can you say that? You see what he's done—"

"I just know, that's all. Same way I knew John was the man for me, I know Kenny's a good guy."

Rosalie's gritted her teeth and took a deep breath, counting to ten so as not to wring her trusting friend's naïve little neck. "Listen, Bird, I know. Never trust reporters. They're snakes."

Birdie forced a smile. "Well, I disagree."

Iris changed the topic to the latest movie coming out at the Paramount, and the girls chatted while Rosalie brooded. She, of all people, did not deserve these kinds of accolades. She hid too many secrets. Hurt the man who loved her. Hurt him in more ways than she wanted to think about.

At the corner of Queen Anne Avenue and Mercer, Birdie directed them left and urged them to quicken their pace. Iris drew alongside Rosalie. "To get back to your question, Rosie—"

Rosalie thwacked Iris's arm. "Ros-*alie*."

"Touchy, touchy." Iris smirked. "Anyway, Jake was home when we got there last night."

"He was?" Overhearing this, Birdie caught up to them. "That's good, isn't it? Was he sent home on furlough?"

Iris nodded. "He wanted to surprise me. Said he got home around eight, loaded down with gifts from the South Pacific. Said he waited and waited, and when I never came home, he decided he deserved as good of a time as I was having, and went out and had a few drinks. When I finally got home, he was already there, drunk as a skunk. And whatever he'd brought home for me, he lost somewhere along the way."

Rosalie rubbed her friend's back.

"But how were you to know he was going to show up last night? That's hardly fair."

A tight breeze dashed up from the bay, and Iris shivered. "He says I shouldn't be out spending our hard-earned money on partyin' with the ladies."

"But it's your money too. And it was only a burger—" Rosalie caught herself before she stuck her nose into business where it didn't belong. "Are you okay?"

"Oh yeah, I'm fine."

Lanie leaned in. "He said some pretty mean things, like—"

Iris shook her head and grabbed Lanie's arm. "He was just upset, but we worked it out."

Lanie frowned. "He was none too happy to see me there."

Iris brushed a lock of brown hair from her cheek. "We made up. That's all that matters."

Rosalie wanted to argue this point, but who was she to offer marriage advice?

They strolled past a Japanese tea shop, where Birdie used to drag Rosalie for her favorite green tea with their ration books in hand. CLOSED read a sign on the door, and Rosalie knew the owners had been relocated to internment camps in Idaho. A week after "evacuation" announcements were posted on telephone poles and bulletin boards, she'd watched Mr. and Mrs. Fukushima and their daughters board the bus headed twenty-five miles south of Seattle to Puyallup, Washington. Their son, Adam, born in America, was serving in the U.S. Army. Rosalie missed their welcoming smiles and their tea— the best tea in Seattle. She wondered if they'd get their shop back after the war.

"Jake doesn't understand," Iris went on. "Sometimes I need to get out, you know? I don't know how to build a marriage when he's gone so much. And then when he does come home, he has all these expectations, and I have no idea how to meet them, so we end up fighting. I feel like a terrible wife."

Rosalie stared down at her wedge sandals as she tromped along. Once upon a time, she was going to marry Vic when he came home for his first furlough.

"Hey, Rosie the Riveter!" a man's voice yelled.

Rosalie's head jolted up as a bus zoomed by. A GI hung out a window with a big grin on his face, throwing kisses at her. "You gonna be on a poster too? Seattle loves you!"

A couple of his buddies joined him.

"Marry me, Rosie!" one called.

Rosalie's cheeks blazed. She was happy when the bus turned the corner and continued out of sight. With each step, she realized she could thank one person for all of this embarrassment: that reporter, Kenny Davenport.

"You're famous, Rosalie." Birdie opened the door of The Golden Nugget and held it for Rosalie. Her eyebrows slanted in sympathy. "Just what you didn't want, huh?"

Rosalie nodded, grateful that Birdie understood. Keeping her eyes down, Rosalie slunk into the squishy vinyl booth in the back corner, her back to the door. Iris slid in next to her, and Birdie and Lanie scooted into the other side.

Rosalie scanned the small establishment, wondering why they hadn't found this place before. It was small and clean, with booths along the outer walls ringing the red-cloth-covered tables in the middle. A fresh flower in a jelly jar graced each table, and a corner jukebox played Benny Goodman.

A colored older woman with a friendly smile handed them menus and filled their glasses with water. "How you ladies doin' today?" Her name tag said she was Miss Tilly.

Rosalie noticed the morning edition of the paper resting on the broad, marbleized counter where the woman had been standing. If Miss Tilly recognized Rosalie, she didn't say anything.

"Been better," Iris replied. "We're getting evicted. Can you believe it?"

At this, something sparked in Miss Tilly's close-set brown eyes, but she didn't comment. Instead, she nodded at Lanie in Boeing-approved attire. "You work at the plant, hon?"

"I start today," Lanie said. She gestured at the rest of the table. "The rest of them work there too. Well, except for Iris, here. She delivers auto parts all over Seattle on her motorcycle."

Miss Tilly smiled, her cheekbones forming jolly orbs beneath her lashes. "Is that a fact?" She touched Iris's shoulder. "My dear old Earl used to take me on motorcycle rides all over the Idaho hills. You may not believe this, but he delivered parts too."

A strange longing, close to jealousy, tiptoed through Rosalie as Iris and Miss Tilly shared a common experience. Even though she didn't know the woman, Miss Tilly's grandmotherly kindness appealed to Rosalie. She hadn't seen her own family in so long— didn't even write letters much anymore. What a relief it would be to share her secret aches with someone who seemed wise, kind, and impartial like Miss Tilly. Maybe she could make sense of the chaos that always churned beneath the surface.

She swept off the uninvited sentiment. *Sheesh, Rosalie, you're so emotional today.* Probably all the extra attention, stirring her up. Rosalie sucked in a breath and shifted a pleasant face toward the others.

"Well, let me know," Iris continued, "and I'll give you a ride any time." Iris grinned.

Miss Tilly reached up and patted her hair, as if remembering the feel of wind streaming through it. "I may take you up on that; don't think I won't." Miss Tilly leaned back with an easy smile. "I'll be back in a minute to take your orders." She ambled off.

After they settled on what they'd have for breakfast, Rosalie zeroed in on the issue most on their minds. "How are we going to find a place to live?" She scanned her friends' faces. "Not just us, either. What about all the other ladies at the plant who live in our complex?"

Just then a girl of about fourteen and her mother exited the ladies' room, situated near their table. Her glance fell casually on the tableful of ladies, moved on, then swung back in a double take.

"Mom, look! It's Rosie the Riveter." She clapped her hands together, then scurried to Rosalie's table. Other patrons in the restaurant turned to stare.

Rosalie felt like she was going to be sick. When Birdie's tiny elbow jabbed her ribs, she knew she needed to do something. She managed to smile at the girl and her mother, then held the menu up in front of her face.

"I'm gonna kill that Kenny," Rosalie muttered to Birdie through clenched teeth. "If I ever see him again."

The bell above the door jingled, and Birdie threw Rosalie a nervous grin before waving at the new arrival. Rosalie turned, expecting to invite one of their coworkers to join them. Instead, her jaw dropped as Kenny Davenport paused in the entryway. Seeing Birdie, a winsome smile stretched across his chiseled features.

Without any acknowledgment of her presence, he sauntered to the counter, where Miss Tilly promptly poured him a cup of coffee.

Rosalie looked down at her hands clenched in her lap. *How dare he?* she seethed. *How dare he plaster my face all over Seattle and then not even say hello!*

Chapter Twelve

....

Bacon. Fried eggs. Toast. Coffee. Kenny breathed the scents in. *Ah, smells like home.* Yet today, instead of it being a purely pleasant smell, the aroma caused an ache in his heart. Even when his dad made it back, things would never be the same. Home would never be like it was.

The bells on the door jingled as it closed behind him, and the jukebox played "Don't Sit Under the Apple Tree" as Kenny meandered into The Golden Nugget. Spotting a group of women at the far table, Kenny recognized Birdie, who seemed excited to see him, waving and shaking her head. His heart skipped a beat even though the only thing he could see of Rosalie was her brunette curls over the back of the booth. He'd talk to them, especially Rosalie, but not yet. First he needed a smile from an old friend.

He expected to be greeted by the call of Aunt Tilly's voice. Didn't feel right entering without it.

And, sure enough: "Kenny, boy, is that you sneakin' in here on this bright morning?" Tilly pulled him to her in a tight embrace, and the sweet scent of her hair lotion transported him back to childhood. She moved around the counter, pouring him a cup of steaming coffee before setting it before him on the Formica counter. Her smile lit her face as she wiped her hands on her pink frilly apron.

"C'mere, darlin'. Haven't seen you in a few days." She stood no taller than his shoulder, but Tilly's personality filled the room. Tight gray ringlets covered her head, reminding him of a halo. If anyone should wear a halo, it was Tilly.

Tilly and her late husband, Earl Wilson, had worked a farm near Kenny's parents' spread in Idaho. In God's providence, Aunt Tilly had never had children—she'd lost two in childbirth—so the

Wilsons had practically adopted Kenny and his sisters. Kenny was just as much at home at their house as his own. The caring couple had even littered their backyard with tire swings, bicycles, a slide that dropped into the creek. His lips curled up slightly remembering that innocent time—before he had to worry about writing the perfect story. Before this war.

Aunt Tilly held him in an affectionate gaze as she straightened the napkin holders. "The usual?"

"Bacon and eggs, just like Mama used to make."

"Adam and Eve on a raft!" Aunt Tilly called to the cook, then returned her gaze to Kenny. "Your mama is the best cook in all of Idaho. At least that's what your daddy used to say, and I agree with him."

Kenny followed her and clutched the metal-rimmed counter. The memory of the conversation with his mom stabbed him again. It didn't seem real. It hadn't sunk in yet. In his mind's eye he pictured his dad's athletic build and strong gait.

Lord, help Dad. He'd whispered the same simple prayer at least fifty times since he hung up from his telephone call with Mom thirty minutes ago.

"Son, is everything all right?" Tilly approached him again.

"Only a rancher thinks he's man enough to buck hay himself—and he's wrong." He could almost hear his dad's voice in his head. *"It's more efficient to ask for help. No room for pride during harvesting season. Many hands make light work."*

His dad had many illustrations, but most of them had to do with farming. Even when Kenny's heart was broken by Alicia Harcourt his senior year, Dad used the farming lesson as a picture of spiritual things. *"Don't let your heart grow hard. Water it with thankfulness to God. In our Maker's perfect time He'll plant a seed and make it grow."*

"Kenny boy, don't you want to tell me what's wrong?" Concern dripped from Tilly's voice. "I can take a break—find someone to cover."

"I will fill you in." He sighed. "But not now. I—I'd like to come back later, if that's okay." Kenny scratched his chin, knowing he'd share his burden with Tilly when they could sit down, really talk, and pray—maybe later today, after the ladies left.

She patted his cheek. "You don't even need to ask. I'm available anytime."

"Thanks." Kenny's heart lightened just knowing he'd share the load with Tilly. He gave a smile. "I'd have to say, though," he said, returning to the previous conversation, "Mom would argue that she's the best cook. Don't you remember? Neither of you would ever accept the blue ribbon for apple pies at the fair. 'Give it to Shirley,'" Kenny mocked. "'No, no, no! Tilly deserves the prize.'" He pinched her cheek slightly, just as she used to do to him when he was a child.

Laughter spilled from Tilly, dancing around the room. "Now, now, you grab a seat, and I'll bring that order to you in a few minutes." She glanced at the table of ladies. "Maybe you want to introduce yourself. I promised your mom I'd find you a wife in the city. There are a whole slew of fine prospects, ripe for the picking!" She wiped her hands off on her apron.

"Aunt Tilly," Kenny said in a loud whisper, then folded his arms against his chest, pressing his thin navy blue tie against his white dress shirt, "will you and Mom ever let up about finding me a wife?"

"I doubt it, dear."

"Well then, I guess I'd better introduce myself."

"You will? You really will?" Then her eyes narrowed. "What are you up to?"

Kenny merely grinned at her before sauntering over to the corner booth. He tried to ignore the way his stomach flipped. Was it his attraction for Rosalie, or fear of being rejected a third time?

He only hoped she'd read this morning's article. When he returned to his apartment last night, Kenny couldn't bear knowing he'd upset her—even though her only accusation was that he was a reporter. He stayed up late rewriting his article, hoping a flattering, yet honest story might make everything right with her. He'd rushed it to the midnight crew—despite the chill of the night air and the downpour—and his typesetter buddy Al had pushed it through for him. Yet another favor he owed Al.

Rosalie leaned against the window, pointing at something outside. Giggles escaped her smooth lips, and her nose crinkled. The other ladies pressed in behind her, and Kenny tipped his head so he could see what they saw. A kitten on the sidewalk batted a feather that was whipping around in the wind.

"You should grab that feather, Rose," Birdie said, settling back in her seat. "Put it in your war effort bin."

"Or maybe I should rescue the kitten and give it to Mrs. Sorrenson," Rosalie said. "Ward off her loneliness with all her boys gone. That reminds me. I have letters for them. Did you all remember to write to our boys? It's not that hard to write a short letter, and the USO gals tell me it really lifts their spirits." She swiveled toward Lanie, sitting next to her. "If you want to write, I'd be happy to mail it for—"

Seeing Kenny, her smile faded. No more crinkled nose.

Kenny palmed the back of his hair. *Boy, oh boy.* He'd said she was beautiful in the article, but the word barely described her loveliness. The sunshine gleaming through the window showcased her beauty, bringing a sparkle to her eyes and a shine to her dark brown hair.

But why the frown? Surely she couldn't still be angry with him. Could she?

"Hiya ladies," Kenny said, raising his voice to be heard over the Louis Armstrong song coming from the jukebox. "*I'm in the mood for love simply because you're near me,*" old Satchmo sang. Kenny looked at Rosalie, who fixed her gaze resolutely on her friends.

"What's buzzin', cousin?" Iris said. "Have a seat."

Kenny pulled a curved-backed chair from the next table and

swung his legs around it, sitting backwards and scooting up to the booth.

Rosalie still refused to look at him. "So, ladies, as we were saying," she said coldly, businesslike, "where are we going to live?"

Kenny glanced at Birdie, who smiled apologetically and shrugged.

"So, Kenny"—Lanie tipped her head and flashed a smile—"what brings you here this morning?"

Kenny's feet rocked from ball to heel. "Well," he said, looking cautiously at Rosalie, "I was just wondering if you—"

She gave not even a glimmer of acknowledgment that he was there.

He continued, "If you all read my article this morning?"

"Oh no." Birdie covered her cheeks with her palms and shook her head.

This time Rosalie acknowledged him, her eyes blazing in fury. "I did, actually," she snapped. "Thank you very much!"

"You're, ah, welcome?"

"I've never been so humiliated in my life!"

He drew back, alarmed. What was wrong with this girl? He pushed his chair back, but there was no escaping her seething words.

"How could you write an article about me—print a photograph—without asking?"

"I'm sorry, Rosalie. It's not policy to—"

"I don't care about your policy. Or that it was just a short article. Or that you were in the picture too, if that's what you were going to say."

Kenny scratched his chin. They actually were good points. Points he would have used. All at once, he felt like he was trapped in a bad movie. The dialogue was all wrong, and the soundtrack too overbearing.

He opened his mouth to defend himself, but she steamrollered over him. "Because of you," she spat, "first I'm thrust on stage in front of multitudes. And then you're all smooth and nice at the Igloo, just to lure me in." Her eyebrows arched like a comic-book villain. "And then you have the nerve to plaster me all over the front page?"

Kenny fought for calm. He tried to put himself in this woman's shoes and ignore her friends' shocked expressions. "It wasn't, actually, the front page," he mumbled.

"All I want to do is work at the plant and keep to myself. I'll collect scraps, silk, rubber for the war effort. I'll plant victory gardens in every neighborhood in Seattle. I'll even go door to door asking people to buy war bonds, but let the Lana Turners of the world bask in the attention."

Kenny's mind sped like a stock car as he attempted to keep up with her arguments. "You did break the national record, Miss Madison." Kenny's rational mind attempted to reason with her. "You had to expect some interest from the media."

She lowered her chin, her cheeks flushed. "I didn't break the record to win some kind of fame. Me and Birdie here"—she grabbed Birdie's hands—"we did it for our own satisfaction, right, Birdie?"

Birdie pursed her lips. "Well," her high-pitched voice squeaked, "I think it'd be kinda fun to be in the paper." Her eyebrows perked up. "And there was the bet—"

Rosalie yanked her hands away and glowered at her friend.

"What?" Birdie lifted her palms in innocence. "I'm just telling him what I think."

"But he's a reporter!"

Birdie's eyebrows narrowed. "You know, I wasn't going to say anything, Rosalie, because I know you didn't mean to be offensive. And I know you're really only so angry because you're attracted to this guy."

Electricity bolted through Kenny at her words.

"But sweets," Birdie continued, her voice shaky, "my brother was a reporter before he left for war. I happen to think it's an honorable profession."

Rosalie sat back in her chair as if she'd been slapped. An awkward silence sifted around them.

Lanie was the first to crack the stillness. "I don't have a problem with reporters." Her pink lips lifted in a slight smile. "I thought your story was real nice."

Kenny took in Lanie—beautiful, sweet, soft-spoken. *Why can't I fall for a girl like her?*

Were it not for Nick's obvious interest, he'd ask Lanie for a date right now. Heck, maybe he should make his next story about her. Southern crooner comes to the big city, joins the workforce, all the while holding out for her dream of a career in music. It could work.

The farther away he could get from Rosalie, the better.

Rosalie cleared her throat. "I didn't mean it that way, Birdie," she said softly.

For the first time, Kenny wondered who had hurt her so badly that she'd react like this. The way she snipped and snarled reminded him of the stray dog that hung around his home when he was a child. The dog tried to bite anyone who wanted to help or even bring him food. His mother told him it was because someone hurt him—and the poor pooch was reacting to that, trying to scare away even those who wished to be a friend.

Kenny could tell Rosalie was trying to make things better with Birdie, but he'd never met a more opinionated and frustrating woman.

"Rosalie." Birdie's hands trembled. "You need to think about others' feelings. Your words can hurt. I don't always say anything, but when you're talking about my brother, I needed to speak up. Being frustrated with Kenny, for who knows what reason, doesn't give you the right to bash all reporters."

Rosalie reached out her hands toward Birdie's, but Birdie pulled them under the table. Rosalie looked as if she might cry.

Kenny scooted his chair back and stood. If he'd come here

looking for a break from a stressful morning, he sure hadn't found it. He only hoped Aunt Tilly was too busy with the other customers to be paying attention to all this. Tilly had a way of standing up for injustice—in a loving but firm way, of course.

He rotated his chair and put it back at its spot at the other table. Again he glanced at Rosalie. "I apologize, miss, if the article upset you. I truly only wanted to let folks know about the talented and hard-working riveters at our Boeing plant. You and Birdie deserve accolades. My intentions were honorable. I hope you believe that."

Rosalie kept her gaze downcast, refusing to meet his eye.

"I had a wonderful time dancing with you," Kenny said. "But I won't be bothering you again." He turned toward Lanie. "Come back to the Igloo soon. Nick would love for you to sing with them again." He tipped his head and smiled at the group. "Good day, ladies."

The song "Miss You" sang from the jukebox as he rambled toward the door.

Aunt Tilly intercepted him with a plate of food. "Kenny, your order's ready, honey."

"Sorry, Aunt Tilly, I'm not hungry anymore." He put two quarters on the counter to cover his bill. "Talk to you later, okay?"

"All right, darlin'." And from her wistful look, Kenny knew she'd heard every word of the exchange at the corner booth.

Chapter Thirteen
....

Rosalie barely tasted her eggs and bacon, though the eggs were cooked to perfection and the bacon crisp, the way bacon was meant to be. From the corner of her eye, she saw Birdie picking at her food as well, though Iris and Lanie consumed their breakfasts as though they hadn't seen food in a month, chatting amiably all the while.

Now the four plodded back up the Queen Anne Hill, retracing their path toward home. The gleaming sunshine from their earlier walk hid behind a small bank of gray clouds. Rosalie glanced behind her toward Mt. Rainier—the majestic mountain that reigned over Seattle like a king. Beyond the moveable clouds she spotted sun glistening over the snow-blanketed peak. Soon the gray would shift and permit sunlight to soak the city's streets again, but at this moment, Seattle was bathed in a dingy bleakness.

The frustration that had festered and swelled since the moment Rosalie saw the local page continued to gnaw at her stomach. Iris and Lanie chatted, but Rosalie kept her lips pressed tight.

It didn't seem fair that she hadn't done anything wrong and it had come to this. It had been Kenny who ran into her at the square. Kenny who got her on stage with Lana Turner. Kenny who tried to weasel in when her defenses were down and ask for an interview. The list went on. Yet *she* was the one Birdie was mad at!

She ventured a peek at Birdie, who stormed alongside. Birdie's eyes focused straight ahead. Rosalie hadn't meant to hurt Birdie. She hadn't meant to make her day worse than it already was. Her friend should've understood that Rosalie was referring to the reporters she knew—mainly Pops—and not Birdie's brother. Even though Rosalie tried to explain what she meant, Birdie wouldn't listen. Besides, it was really Birdie who had slighted her.

Why didn't she back me up? She knew how upset I was about that ridiculous photo and even more ludicrous story. "Lovebirds!"

As friends, roommates, and work partners, they usually dealt with hurt feelings quickly—both sides admitting her part in the conflict and releasing the tension with a good laughing spell. But this time Birdie was being stubborn. A friend was supposed to support you and not take things personally. Birdie should've known what she'd meant.

I can't believe she thought I was talking about her brother too.

They marched past the S&M Market, and a gush of cool wind sent shivers up Rosalie's legs under her skirt. Her lips ached from the dry wind, and she reached for her lipstick from her satchel.

"Shoot!" she grumbled. "I forgot my pocketbook."

"You better go on back and get it," Iris suggested. "I bet it's still tucked under the table."

Rosalie pivoted around without looking at her roommate. "Does anyone want to walk back with me?"

No one answered, but she was past the point of caring. "Okay, then. I'll see you ladies later. I should be able to join up with you to catch the bus to work."

"Sounds good." Iris offered a smile.

Lanie waved. "See you then."

Birdie simply tromped on.

Rosalie inspected her sandals, now dirty from the walk. She again shivered at the brisk breeze on her legs. If she'd worn slacks, she could've run back. Not that she was in a hurry. She had three hours before her shift. Maybe the walk would be good for her. Maybe it would give her time to clear her head—to figure out how her world had turned upside down in just a few days.

She arrived at The Golden Nugget a few minutes later, the rushing breeze following her in, rustling the *Life* magazines lined up in a rack.

"There you are, honey." Miss Tilly's hand disappeared under the counter and reappeared with Rosalie's satchel. "I figured you'd come back for this. If I knew where you lived, I could have delivered it after work. Then again, you most likely would have been at the plant by then." A soft chuckle bounced from the older woman's mouth.

Rosalie sighed in relief as she received it. "Thank you, ma'am, I—"

"Call me Miss Tilly." She patted Rosalie's hand. "My friends do."

The kindness in the woman's maternal smile smoothed Rosalie's rumpled spirit.

"Actually, I'm glad you came back," Miss Tilly said. "There's something I wanted to ask you, but you left so sudden, I didn't get the chance. C'mere." She motioned Rosalie behind the counter.

Rosalie paused. "Back there?"

"Come on." Her eyes shimmered. "Don't be shy. I want to show you something."

"Okay." Rosalie skirted the counter, and Miss Tilly grabbed her hand like she was a child before leading her through the swinging kitchen door.

The smell of bleach immediately hit Rosalie, along with a splatter of water on her legs from a mop splashing into a bucket. A slim man with white-blond hair and ruddy cheeks peered up at them, his frosty blue eyes unimpressed.

"Hans, honey," Miss Tilly patted the man's back but didn't stop walking, "I'm takin' a break. Lydia'll be here in a minute."

"Ya sure," Hans answered in a Scandinavian accent.

Miss Tilly practically skipped as she tugged Rosalie through the tiled kitchen and out the back door. Glinting light washed over

Rosalie. Glancing at the sky, Rosalie pondered that any clouds had ever darkened that crisp blue sky. "Guess the wind blew those clouds away," she mumbled as she walked. When Miss Tilly stopped short, Rosalie stumbled, nearly bumping into her.

"What are we doing, Miss Tilly?"

The older woman didn't answer, and an aroma, strong and sweeter than perfume, tickled Rosalie's senses. She could almost taste it. Rosalie took in the sight of a back alley, small, probably only ten by ten, but overflowing with potted flowers. Bright pink, yellow, purple, red—even colors Rosalie didn't know the names of—transformed the dingy alley into a true queen's garden.

"It's beautiful," she breathed, frustration and anger seeping away like stagnant water down a drain. "Did you do this?"

"Well, some of it." Tilly led Rosalie down a narrow path through the middle of the lush garden of potted plants, the only evidence of the cement beneath the foliage. "When I started working at this place a few years back, I discovered that a flower garden once flourished back here, but only there, along the wall." She strolled to a row of pots blooming with pansies and creeping ferns.

Rosalie fingered a pansy's velvety petals.

"I thought we should have a victory garden, so I planted that."

Rosalie followed her hostess's eyes to a raised bed striped with rows of cabbage, lettuce, carrots, and peas.

"I come out here during my breaks to tend to the plants. It seems no matter how full the place is, I always find another spot for a flower pot. When that happens, I use an old bucket and fill it with soil from my garden at home. Then I either take a seed from home or borrow a neighbor's clipping and plant it." She chuckled. "You should have seen the looks I first got on the bus—me in my Golden Nugget uniform, carryin' an old bucket of dirt on with me." She shrugged. "Now the regulars, they know me. Mr. Potterfield—that's the bus driver—he's the first to ask what I'm gonna be plantin' this time."

"It's very pretty." Rosalie closed her eyes and took a deep breath. She let it out again and felt some of the tension from the morning release with it. "You should be proud of all your hard work."

Miss Tilly squeezed her hand. "Oh, it's not just me, honey. Soon folks from the other businesses started addin' pots, buckets, baskets." She pointed up at a window imbedded in the brick wall overlooking the garden. "Mrs. Patterson who's ninety-one and her seventy-year-old daughter planted that window box. They keep it up real nice too—when they're not assemblin' part kits for Boeing in their apartment, that is. I love how hard everyone works to support the war. And Mr. McCluskey, from the cobbler shop across the way there, started the ivy growin'. It's like our own secret garden back here."

Secret Garden.

Rosalie had read that book for the first time to her little sister, Sue, when she was fourteen and Sue was five. She relished the pleasant memory. She wondered how Sue was doing these days. Last she'd heard, Sue was working as a nursing assistant, caring for soldiers injured overseas.

Rosalie cupped a lovely pink rose in her hands. "You went to so much trouble. Most people's minds are too focused on all the hardships and struggles to put time into something that's simply pretty to look at."

Miss Tilly waved away the compliment. "Yes, well, while I agree that we need to give as much time as we can to growin' our own food and supportin' the war effort, there's another element people often overlook. Just as our troops need to be supplied, and our families fed, our souls need to be nourished too. Like my ol' car needs fuel, my soul needs to be filled up, and that's what this garden's all about. Not just for me, but my friends too."

Miss Tilly's light blue skirt fluttered in the breeze as she led Rosalie to a bench in the middle of the garden. "Let's sit a spell." Tilly held her back as she eased herself down on the bench and stroked the spot next to her. "If you'd like, I can tell you more about my garden. But first, there's something else I need to ask you."

Chapter Fourteen
....

Tromping up the steps to the second-story newsroom, Kenny's hand gripped the cherry-wood railing. As much as he tried to put his heart into the mundane stories Bixby made him write, he doubted he'd be able to concentrate today. First, the news about his father—it was hard to comprehend that his dad would never walk again. Maybe it would sink in after he actually saw Dad. He tried to picture that— seeing his father on crutches or maybe in a wheelchair. Seeing his pant leg hanging empty. Did he experience a lot of pain? Was there any chance of complications in the future?

And, of course, the other matter. Kenny hadn't felt a strong attraction for a woman in years—not since Alicia, his high school sweetheart. Rosalie seemed like a strong woman, and she certainly was, but he also detected a tender, compassionate heart. He reached the landing and drew in a breath. *Obviously not.*

Aunt Tilly had reminded him this morning that she and Kenny's mom had been praying for him to find a good Christian wife. And Kenny wouldn't want to marry someone who didn't love God with her whole heart.

I suppose I should've found out if she was a Christian. Not that Christian women are perfect. Alicia, his girlfriend in high school, attended church and claimed to serve God, but she was as manipulative and backstabbing as any Hollywood vixen.

Still, he couldn't shake that riveter's dazzling mug. He couldn't forget the way they'd danced and laughed together last night, and even her concern for Nick during the conversation they'd had at the Igloo. When she offered to help the wounded contracted workers, Kenny visualized them working side by side. And maybe when Nick and others like him received the help they needed, he and Rosalie could move on to other causes. He pictured her, chin determined, organizing supply drives, rallying folks to write letters and buy war bonds—and him writing about it. To be married to someone you not only loved and cherished, but who went all out for the same mission—that would be ideal. A blessing more than he could fathom.

Planting his scuffed stomper on the final step, Kenny straightened his suit coat. Of course, he shouldn't let ideas about working side by side with Rosalie take up even one speck of space in his mind. She made it clear he was lower than a Seattle slug to her. Besides, he had plenty of other things to keep his mind occupied. No point carrying a torch for her. No gorgeous eyes and perfect dance moves were worth the abuse she dished out.

The real problem now was finding a story. Ironic that Bixby demanded a story that Kenny would love to write, but one in which no leads were panning out. It was too bad Rosalie had turned out to be such a pill. He wanted to ask about her work. Her relationship with her friends. Her family. Her—true love?

A thought crossed his mind, one Kenny hadn't considered before. Did she have a guy overseas thinking of her? His shoulders tightened as he considered that. *Nah.* Surely, Rosalie's friends wouldn't have encouraged his interest if she was already set on another guy, yet he didn't doubt there were plenty of other guys—like him—who'd been interested.

After this morning he wouldn't touch that story with a ten-foot pole. Maybe the Lanie idea would work. If only he could do the piece about Nick and the other guys who'd been spurned. *That's a real story.*

Maybe he *should* just focus on Lanie. She seemed kind, gentle. Maybe he could follow Lanie through her first day at the job. Kenny's mind tried to get excited about that as he entered the smoke-filled newsroom and placed his hat on the coat rack.

"Davenport!" Bixby's gruff voice greeted Kenny as he entered the large newsroom. "That you?"

"Yes sir, I just got here. I'm not late, am I?" He turned to see Bixby striding through the door of his office. Kenny paused, then took a step back, surprised. Instead of the typical scowl, Bixby's lips turned up in a hint of a smile. It was only a hint, but it matched the excitement flashing from Bixby's eyes. Kenny knew something good was going on.

"No time for chitchat, boy. Your Rosie the Riveter article's going through the roof, ya hear? Phone's been ringing off the hook all morning. I even got a telegram from Russell W. Young asking about you."

Kenny shoved his hands into his pockets. "Seriously, sir? It was just a simple article." Even as he said the words, a tingling pleasure danced in his chest. Ever since he'd started working for Bixby, he'd hoped for a response like this. He was merely surprised that this story—of all things—was the one to get it.

"Just a simple article? Did I hear those words come out of your mouth? That's where you're wrong, my boy." He slapped Kenny's upper arm. "You were brilliant. Brilliant!"

"What do you mean, sir?"

"It's the romance. Romance sells papers! The calls we're getting all say the same thing. Thousands of people saw you two at Victory Square yesterday. They watched Lana Turner introduce you as lovebirds. Then what did they see when they opened their *Seattle Tribune* this morning? 'Lovebirds Introduced by Lana Turner!' They're head over heels for your story, my boy!" He pulled a stogie from his pocket, as if he were celebrating the birth of a baby, lit it up, then offered another to Kenny. Kenny waved his hand no, but Bixby stuck one in Kenny's mouth anyway.

"So here's what you get to do." Bixby pulled up a chair next to Kenny's desk and plopped down. "Take a seat, son. Take a seat."

Kenny removed the cigar from his mouth and stuck it in his

coat pocket. He cautiously sat, not leaning back, not allowing his body to settle in. Bixby was up to something, and he had to stay on guard.

"You, my boy, not only get to do a series of stories about that handy-dandy little riveter of yours, all Seattle is going to follow along as you romance the girl! Take them with you as you stroll beside her and gaze into the bay, or as you wait for her outside the Boeing plant with fresh flowers. Most guys are off at war, but that doesn't mean women readers don't want to hear about someone else getting swept off her feet." Bixby took off his hat and fingered it in his hands, as if trying to work out the nervous energy coursing through him. "I've been getting pressure from the big chief for more feel-good stories for months, and now you've delivered it. This is exactly what Mr. Young was hoping for."

Tension started in his feet and crept up his legs. Russell W. Young knew Kenny's name—was excited about his story. How in the world would Kenny tell the owner of the paper that he couldn't deliver?

He rose and circled behind his chair, then paced back and forth between the desks on either side of his. Even though his coworkers typed with their heads down, he could tell by the slow pace of their pounded words that they were listening. What did they think of this? Were they jealous of the attention? Or, like him, were they horrified by what Bixby was suggesting? It was a crack in the wall that separated personal and professional. No, more than that. It was a wrecking ball, smashing it completely.

"You want me to write articles about my private life, sir? Romance a girl just to sell newspapers? What about the no fraternizing rule?" Kenny's chest constricted. He knew writing about his personal life wasn't the biggest problem. Rosalie would never go for it. She hated reporters and despised him for the story—the innocent, non-threatening story he'd already written.

The sharpness of her words still stung. The anger he'd witnessed in her eyes caused his gut to ache. His shoulders tightened just with the idea of seeing her again. There was no way, absolutely no way, she'd agree to let him write about their dates—putting them on public display. More than that, she most likely wouldn't even accept a date!

"I'm sorry, sir." He let out a low breath with his words. "I won't write about my romancing a girl just to sell papers."

Bixby folded his arms over his barrel chest, resting them on top of his belly, and chortled. "No, no. Of course not. You think I'd do that? What kind of newspaperman do you think I am?"

The doom of a moment before lifted, slightly. "You had me worried, sir." Kenny brushed his hair back from his forehead.

"You're not going to write the romance part. That'd be ridiculous. One of that Roosevelt girl's lady reporters'll do that. You just write a week in the life of Rosie the Riveter story. Then take the opportunity to romance her. You know, lay it on thick—flowers, candlelit dinners, dancing. And a gal from the Women's Page desk will put legs on that part." He puffed the cigar, then pulled it out of his mouth and tapped the ashes into an ashtray on the desk. "Brilliant!" he repeated.

Kenny's abdomen tightened. He was glad now that he hadn't eaten Tilly's breakfast. He'd disliked some of his assignments before. He'd thought most of them to be a waste of time. But he'd never been physically ill over them. Not only did Bixby want him to spend a week following around a girl he hoped to never see again—that would've been torture enough—Bixby also wanted him to throw romance into the equation and have another broad write about it. He could see the headline now: SEATTLE REPORTER, WHO HAS NO GOOD REASON FOR STAYING HOME FROM WAR, LOSES AT LOVE TOO.

He swallowed down the bile rising in his throat.

The fat cat rose from his chair, still puffing his cigar. The smile was much more than a hint now, and Bixby glanced around the newsroom, as if wondering if the other reporters were also taking note of his brilliance.

"I'm sorry, Mr. Bixby. I can't do it. I won't." Kenny spoke as forcefully as he could, hoping Bixby would grasp his earnestness and drop the whole matter.

"What?" Mr. Bixby took a step back, and his foot connected with the leg of Kenny's desk. Before Kenny could reach out, the older man slid backwards, landing with a thump on the floor.

The clicking of typewriter keys around him stopped, and Kenny rushed to help his boss. Curses flew from the seasoned man's mouth.

"Mr. Bixby, let me help you."

With a *humph* Mr. Bixby grasped Kenny's hand. Kenny pulled with all his might, expecting to hear the words, "You're fired, Davenport," explode from the editor's mouth.

Instead, Bixby leaned forward, peering up into Kenny's eyes. His brown, bushy eyebrows formed a V, and sweat dripped from his receding hairline. "I'm sure you didn't say what I thought I heard. Please tell me you did *not* just refuse to do this story," Bixby demanded, his cigar breath and spit droplets assaulting Kenny.

Shaking his head, Kenny attempted to look apologetic. "I won't do it, sir. It's not right."

Kenny expected Bixby to explode. Instead, he sat back down, planted an elbow on the desk, and leaned his head against his hand. Kenny crossed his arms and waited. The other reporters waited too, but after thirty seconds the clicking on the typewriter keys began again. Obviously Bixby was taking his time, and time was a valued commodity around the newsroom.

"Listen, Davenport, I know you want a big story, right?" Bixby finally said. "Well, I'm telling you, I've got one."

Kenny lifted his hands, as if defending himself from the words to come. "Actually—"

"Stop acting like a scared sissy, son. Not *this* riveter story. I'm talking about one that you *really* want. The one about the VA Hospital not providing care to the contracted workers." He slanted his head and squinted, his eyes disappearing in the chubby cheek flesh. "Don't you have a friend in some predicament?"

Kenny's heartbeat spun like a propeller. He could feel it winding up in his chest.

"I didn't tell you," Bixby continued, "but I thought it was a great story. I ran it by the big wheels upstairs. They liked it too. Told me to give it to Charlie."

Kenny's fingers coiled into fists. "But that was *my* story."

Bixby nodded. "You haven't even heard the whole of it. They want to send him overseas to see firsthand how those contracted workers serve on the front lines."

Kenny's jaw dropped. This was the kind of story he'd been waiting for. The one that would make his job as reporter worthwhile. Dad would be proud. Nick would be helped. And Kenny wouldn't have to be ashamed anymore. Charlie couldn't have the story. How could they do that?

"Mr. Bixby, you know this was my idea. I'm the one whose heart is in it. I'm the one who can make it shine. You have to give it to me. No one is going to care as much as I do."

Bixby grinned, nodding. "It's yours."

"Really?" Kenny sank down into his chair. "Why thank you, sir. I don't know what to say."

"Just do the Rosie the Riveter series first. You do it, and you'll get the ambulance driver story too. You don't do it, Charlie gets the story, and you'll have to find a new paper to write for." He clicked his tongue. "But you're a bright boy. I'm sure you'll find something."

Kenny placed his face in his hands. If he could, he'd will his chair to sink through the floor and escape the newsroom altogether. Here he was a professional man, with five years of lead reporting experience, and Bixby was playing with him like a toy puppet on a string.

Kenny's heart sank. He knew pleading with Bixby wouldn't work. He glanced out the window at a cloud bank. As he watched, an airplane emerged, preparing to veer south to land at McChord Field, no doubt returning from some foreign mission. He thought about Nick, who'd returned on an airplane like that one. He thought about the pain his friend suffered every day. If taking this Rosie the Riveter story meant Kenny could help his friend, wouldn't it be worth it?

Bixby sat before him, waiting. The chief obviously grasped the prize he offered Kenny—like a precious pearl in Bixby's fat hand. All Kenny had to do was nail one story and then his life's striving would suddenly mean something. But how could he? First of all, Rosalie hated him. Second, she'd be right in her belief that he was just a scoundrel reporter who'd do anything for a big scoop. But more than that, he'd be toying with someone's feelings. Lying.

Of course, Bixby wasn't giving him any alternative. If he didn't do it, he'd have to start all over in another newsroom in another city. And then Nick wouldn't get the help he needed—at least not for a while.

Still, as much as he wanted to bolster his career and help Nick, this was not the way. Couldn't be. He had to be trustworthy, even if it meant giving up everything to start again.

"I'm sorry, sir." For a second Kenny could hardly believe he'd said it. The other typewriters stilled again, their eyes focused on him. Kenny rose, grabbed his briefcase, then strode across the room to retrieve his hat.

"Oh horsefeathers!" Bixby shot to his feet, followed, and grabbed Kenny's arm, stopping him. "You're as stubborn as I am. Listen, Davenport, what if you just do the week in a life part? Forget the romance."

Kenny eyed his almost-former boss. "Really, sir? I thought the romance was the part you liked best."

"Well, I'm sure all the dames out there would love it, but I'm a newsman. Just the facts. We can leave romance for the gossip papers."

Kenny studied Bixby's face. Bixby always drove a hard bargain. Why was he willing to compromise?

"Don't give me that look, son. I give you my word. Only the riveter story. It'll save your job. It's the only thing that will." He reached out his hand. "Wouldn't want to lose a fine reporter like you, Davenport."

Kenny would've never thought his boss would change his mind on something like that. And this quickly. Of course he'd do the Rosie the Riveter story if it meant he'd keep his job. Even though Rosalie was definitely not the person he wanted to spend a week with, he could trudge through. What was a week, after all?

About to accept, he paused. "And the VA story? That's mine too, right?"

"Don't push it, Davenport." Bixby's eyes bore down on him, and just when Kenny was about to insist, the older man winked. "Do a good job on that riveter piece, and you'll be on the first plane over."

Kenny stuck out his hand, and they shook.

Now to figure out how to convince Rosalie.

Chapter Fifteen

. . . .

Maybe it was the flourishing array of flowers encircling her—or just being in the presence of this older woman's warmth—but a sense of acceptance and peace blanketed Rosalie. It was more comforting than her grandmother's quilt, and she lowered herself onto the wooden ornamented bench.

Miss Tilly scooted toward Rosalie. She crossed her legs and a bony knee protruded from beneath her skirt. She draped the fabric into place, but her smiling eyes stayed fixed. "You work at the plant, Rosalie, right?"

"Yes."

"And you said you and those other ladies need a place to live?"

Rosalie nodded. What was Miss Tilly leading up to?

"We only have one month to find a place."

"That's just terrible. You ladies need a good comfortable haven to rest your heads." She held Rosalie's hand, her rough skin reminding Rosalie of her grandmother's. "You work so hard for our men over there."

"Thank you," Rosalie said, rubbing the thoughtful woman's hand. "I'm sure we'll find something."

A broad grin expanded over Miss Tilly's face. "I've been prayin' about this ever since you left, and do you know what? The good Lord brought to mind a Scripture for me. Isn't He good, honey? Listen to this: 'Come to me all ye who are weary and heavy-laden, and I will give you rest.' Honey, is that for you, or what?"

Rosalie rubbed her neck. Glancing up, she saw an old woman's face peeking out her window from the apartment above the diner. "We are weary after work." She didn't mention how often they stayed out past midnight dancing. That might play a part in their weariness too.

"Well, I have a place for you to rest." Tilly clapped her hand on Rosalie's, then scooted back in her seat as if to say, *There. I said it. Isn't this exciting?*

But Rosalie was confused. "You have a place?"

"Yes. A beautiful, giant house. It's lovely with gables and bay windows and so many rooms. It's what you call a house of character, honey. A story lingerin' in every room. And a huge backyard with a tire swing. The kids in the neighborhood play baseball back there. I bring them cookies every now and then. Oh my." She released a breath as if imparting her joyful feelings onto Rosalie. "Earl and I inherited it from my grandma Ellie. We had lots of plans for that old place. We lived in it when we first moved here, but then my dear husband passed, and I couldn't keep it up. For the past twenty years it's been sittin' empty except for the repairs my nephew does. I'd love to offer it to you ladies."

Rosalie pressed her cool palms against her cheeks. "It's amazing. But why would you do this for us? Such a gift. I mean, we'd pay rent, of course, but still—"

Polka music drifted out the door from the diner, and Rosalie turned her head. She could see Hans, through the doorway, doing a bit of polka himself.

"Oh, no no, I won't charge rent. But there is one little matter. It's pretty run down, and, well, I've been told that if it's not fixed up in one month," Tilly's eyes narrowed, "the city's goin' to tear it down." She clasped her hands together. "Poor old Gus at the city hall has been tryin' to hold it off for me, but he can't anymore. I was goin' to have to say good-bye to the old place. Then came the news of you ladies and your plight. I'm sure if you can put together those large airplanes, you can fix anything. You ladies could make it livable. If you want to take the time and energy, that is."

Rosalie couldn't believe the woman's kindness. A house? A cramped trailer in the lot behind the plant, or a dingy apartment, at best a room in a boardinghouse—those options she'd contemplated, but a big, quaint, wonderful home?

Many of the ladies in the apartments had children. Some, like Betty, had help with child care, but many didn't. Rosalie cringed, thinking of the unkempt little rascals wandering the halls of a boardinghouse unsupervised. She didn't blame their mothers who were off working to support the war, but how much better to bat a ball around a yard than play doorbell ditch 'em on old lonely ladies at The Queen's Garden?

"Miss Tilly, I'll have to talk to the gang, of course, but I'm sure a large crew of us would be thrilled to move in to your precious home. And you're right. We've got carpenters, plumbers, electricians, and, of course, the menial labor like me."

Joy painted Miss Tilly's demeanor. "Wonderful, honey. Thank the good Lord. Oh, but did I mention it's in Victory Heights? I know that's far, but the bus runs there. That'll be okay, won't it?"

"I'm sure it will." In her mind's eye Rosalie pictured the path. It wouldn't add more than ten extra minutes to their bus ride.

"Even though all the repairs are too much for my nephew, I'm sure he'd help too. He knows the place better than anyone."

"That'd be great. I'm sure we'll need all the help we can get."

A glance at her wristwatch told Rosalie she should start her trek up the hill toward home. She wanted to share the amazing news with the girls before work. She couldn't wait to see their reaction, especially Birdie's. Maybe this would brighten Birdie's day and patch things up between them.

Yet something held her on the bench. An uneasy sense that if she left this spot—and the presence of the woman sitting next to her—the bright joy she swam in for the last fifteen minutes would give way to her usual murky sadness. Like a child clinging to a mother's hand, Rosalie didn't want to let go of Miss Tilly and this rare contented feeling.

The breeze awakened, and a gentle shower of a cottonwood tree's white fluffs floated over them, like a whispering snowfall. A new thought seemed to accompany them.

"Miss Tilly," she said, brushing cotton from her hair, "I know you probably have to get back to work, but would you tell me a little about this garden? If you have time."

Miss Tilly patted her lap. "Of course, honey. They can get along without me until the lunch rush." She gazed at Rosalie in sympathy and understanding, rubbing a bit of cotton between her fingers.

"I love telling the story of this garden," she began, her voice animated again. "During the Great War, this diner was owned by a New York entrepreneur, Charlie Whalen, who came here for the big World's Fair exposition back in '09." She tapped Rosalie's hand. "He saw our lovely city and had to become a part of it. That's how the diner got its name, by the way, The Golden Nugget. You know, because that exposition—"

"The Alaska-Yukon-Pacific Exposition?" Rosalie asked. "My grandma took my mother to the A-Y-P. She loved the Hawaii room. My dad always promised to take us to Hawaii." Rosalie sniffed sardonically. How silly she'd been to believe his promise.

"My, wouldn't that be nice? Anyway, they made quite a hullaba-loo about the gold rush at the exposition, or so I'm told. I guess the gold rush is what helped make Seattle a bona fide city. But I've gotten off the point, haven't I?" She chuckled at herself. "What I wanted to tell you was that Mr. Whalen didn't fall in love with our city only. A young lady recently arrived with her brother from Norway also tickled his fancy—and won his heart. Soon the two were married."

"And she's the one who planted the garden?"

"That's right. Savea—that was her name. What a lovely girl. There's a photograph of her in the office. She had a cheerful smile, and even from the picture you can also tell she had shining blond hair and fair eyes. She planted the flower garden and lovingly tended to it.

"When the Great War broke out and Mr. Whalen left for the trenches, Savea had to take care of the diner all by herself. Then he died over there." Tilly placed an aged hand on her chest. "Of course I didn't know him, but I've heard all about him from Hans. You saw him, the one mopping the floor. He's Savea's brother. She died a few years after the Great War. Typhoid."

"It's a lovely story," Rosalie said. "Sad but lovely."

The sound of an airplane, probably an army transport from McChord Field, boomed overhead, breaking the peaceful silence.

"Yes, but Hans also shared a dark side to it."

Rosalie leaned closer.

"Apparently after Charlie's death, Savea became bitter. At first she tried to stay positive, but the pain got too heavy to carry. It was as if she let go of the only ropes that clung to happiness and tumbled into a pit of anger and resentment. She stopped tendin' her garden—it all died. And she growled at Hans and any family who'd come to help her. Hans said she acted as if she'd rather be dead. Her heart was dead already." Miss Tilly breathed in a deep breath, then freed it. "I wish I could've shared the Lord's love with her. His grace. I think it was more her own bitterness that killed her, rather than the typhoid."

A hummingbird darted to a hanging basket of geraniums. Its invisibly fast wings whirred, not unlike Rosalie's thoughts. As she'd listened to the older woman's story, many yearnings awakened in Rosalie's soul about love, friendship, and following one's dreams.

"You know," Tilly's voice softened, slowed, "I heard you girls talking earlier."

Rosalie slumped, a ball winding tight in her stomach as she recalled her argument with Birdie. Of course Tilly heard them. They weren't quiet about their quarrel, and Rosalie was the most vehement of all. *Such a temper. Why can't I control it?*

"I'm sorry about that. We were pretty loud. I—I wasn't kind."

"I forgive you. But you know, when you lash out, it reveals more than momentary frustration. I'm guessin' there's a deep hurt that makes you blow up at your loved ones. And, honey, the Bible says the root of all self-centered anger is sin."

A gray cloud blocked out the sun again, leaving the vibrant flowers muted and bowing their heads. Rosalie shivered as the ball in her stomach rose to become an aching mass in her throat. Sin? She knew her temper was a problem, but sin? How could that be when the argument wasn't her fault?

"Miss Tilly, I'm sorry, but you don't know the situation. That no-good reporter, Kenny, splattered my name and identity all over Seattle without asking me."

Silence rained around them. Miss Tilly didn't answer.

And then something stirred—a knowledge in Rosalie's heart that she'd been wrong to condemn Kenny. She thought back to the article, trying to remember exactly what it had said. Kenny had said he'd like to get to know her better. He said he'd enjoyed meeting her even more than Lana Turner. He said—he really hadn't said anything harmful, had he? Sure, she didn't like the attention the news story brought, but if Kenny Davenport purposefully tried to hurt her, he could have done it a dozen ways.

"Oh, Miss Tilly, you're right. I treated Kenny awfully from the first moment I met him. He was so sweet when we danced. In that article he said I was beautiful, but all I could do was think of how I didn't want people to see it—see me." She wasn't sure if Miss Tilly understood what she was referring to, but she needed to get the words out. "Birdie too. I really should apologize. I was wrong to be mad at her." Rosalie breathed out, a hint of relief relaxing her shoulders. But the cloud still covered the sun, and her arms shivered.

Tilly wrapped a warm arm around Rosalie. "Honey, I'm glad you see that you weren't justified in your anger toward your friends, but that's only part of it. Have you ever thought about why you lashed out? Not what *they* did, but what lies within you?"

Rosalie's hands trembled as the word Tilly had used flashed in her mind like a newsreel. *Sin. Sin. Sin.*

Moisture rose to her eyes. "Of course sin is the cause of my anger. I've treated people horribly. I've thought about myself before others. I used to go to church. I remember what the Bible says about sin."

Did she bring me out here to condemn me? Didn't she know I've been trying to make it right ever since Vic died—since before he died? But the guilt, the stress, never lifts.

"I try so hard, Miss Tilly. I know I've failed, but I do try to make it right. It's never enough." She dropped her head into her hands and unbridled tears wet her fingers. "I'm so tired of trying, Miss Tilly. So tired."

As she said the words, a weariness weighed on her chest. It was different from the aching arms and back she felt after work. It was different from the tired feet after a night of dancing. It was deeper and never seemed to lift. Even a good night's sleep, a smile from a friend, and shared laughter didn't help.

"'Come to me all ye who are weary and heavy laden and I will give you rest.' Remember, honey? He will give you rest—not just for your tired bones, but for your exhausted heart."

"But you don't know what I've done. God must hate me for what I've done. How could He ever give me rest?"

"God's Word says to confess our sins to one another. Have you told anyone where you've messed up? Have you let anyone else help you carry the weight?"

"No, how could I? Everyone would hate me." She sniffed and looked at Tilly.

Compassion shone in her eyes, not condemnation. And even though Rosalie had just met her, she saw something special radiating from Miss Tilly's face. She knew this woman would listen, would not judge or accuse, but would tell the truth. Would insist on the truth.

Miss Tilly seemed to read Rosalie's thoughts. "Tell me, honey. And then, together, we'll tell Christ."

With a tearful voice, Rosalie choked out everything: how she was never in love with Vic, how she was afraid to tell him, how she called off the wedding—breaking a noble, loving man's heart. As she spoke, a miracle surprised her. The miracle of a tender touch on her back—Miss Tilly's soft fingers caressing, communicating something Rosalie couldn't fathom. Love, but not Tilly's love. *God's.*

Rosalie'd said this much, so she may as well test this new acceptance with the darkest, ugliest side of herself. "I cheated on Vic too, Miss Tilly. I kissed a sailor I didn't even know and spent the weekend acting like his girl. I was lonely. I was mad that Vic had left and…it was just days after that when I heard he wasn't coming back at all." She expected the woman's hand to stop its gentle touch, but it kept on.

"Everyone, including Vic's family, thinks I was madly in love with Vic. And I've accepted their sympathy for the last year. Even Birdie and the girls. They all feel so sorry that I lost this wonderful man. But I didn't deserve him, and I definitely don't deserve their sympathy. I justified my lies in different ways, but now I see how wrong I was."

All these months, she'd thought verbalizing her guilty deeds would cause her misery to multiply. She assumed the shame would strangle her, leave her devastated like a discarded waif. But instead, a small bud peeked out its newborn head, finding root in her soul. Hope.

She cautiously raised her eyes, and Tilly pulled Rosalie into her time-aged arms. It was hard to believe they'd just met. It was hard to believe she'd confessed all, and still this woman snuggled her close.

The tears came, but with each cry she released, it seemed the wind picked the heartbreak up and carried it away like an old crusty leaf.

Then, when her past lay before her, naked and stark, with no more accusations and regrets, an irresistible urge to pray captured Rosalie.

Vic, Birdie, her family all had spoken the truth of how Jesus took her punishment when He suffered and died on the cross. She'd heard more than one sermon that had proclaimed we simply had to confess our sins, and God would be faithful to forgive them. More than that, He'd also take the punishment too. She didn't understand a love like that, but it was worth trying out.

Take my punishment, Jesus.

Rosalie knew she deserved to be condemned for her sins; she'd always known that. But she thought she could somehow serve the sentence herself by doing good things, working hard, acting perfect. For the first time, she understood that her sin was too heavy for her to carry, too weighty for her to pay off. She needed someone else to carry it for her.

Her mom had sung of Christ's "vast, unmeasured, boundless, free" love, but Rosalie had never thought it was for her. She had too much sin, too much darkness, too much pride. But now she knew His forgiveness belonged to her. And she belonged to Jesus.

"Jesus, thank You for accepting me when I don't deserve it," she whispered. "From this day forward I want to live for You." She closed her eyes, soaking in the sun, which had returned to warm her.

And as she enjoyed the warmth of Tilly's hug, Rosalie pictured Jesus holding her in the same way.

* * * *

Her feet seemed to carry Rosalie up Queen Anne Hill on their own. She felt as if she'd lost a hundred pounds, and she couldn't remember a day so beautiful or an inner peace so comforting.

As she approached their apartment building, Rosalie eyed the structure, no longer feeling the pain of knowing the place would be torn down. Through Tilly, God had provided something better. A new place for her and her friends.

Rosalie strode up the sidewalk, and a dark blue tarp caught her attention. Vic's car had been parked behind the apartment building since he'd left. Before Vic died, she'd taken his "baby" out a few times—even given it a wash and shine. But since she heard he wasn't coming back, she hadn't touched this tangible reminder of her loss.

Rosalie strode around the shady side of The Queen's Garden, through the dew-laden, tall grass toward Vic's Ford. Her fears, so real since Vic died, now seemed distant. She wanted to face her unresolved ache over Vic—the guilt was swept away by Christ's forgiveness—but her wound would take time to heal.

She didn't know why she'd been holding on to the car. Maybe as something to remember Vic by. Maybe because she'd promised to care for it. But as she lifted the tarp and eyed the shiny metal underneath, Rosalie knew what she had to do.

Hurrying around the building, she slipped inside and stepped over to the telephone perched on the wall in the hall. "Tacoma, Jefferson 334," she said into the receiver, wondering what it would be like to hear Vic's mother's voice again.

After the operator connected her, a young woman's voice answered. "Hello?"

"Hello, this is Rosalie Madison. May I speak to Mrs. Michaels, please?"

"I'm sorry," the young woman's voice chirped. "There is no Mrs. Michaels anymore."

A cold tension radiated from Rosalie's heart, pumping through her whole body. *She's gone?* Rosalie pictured the older woman's heart-shaped face, her gentle, almond eyes. Quiet and kind, she'd loved Rosalie like a daughter from the first time they'd met. Rosalie's lower lip quivered. Was it heartbreak over losing her son that killed her?

"Uh—do you have the number of either of her daughters? I'd—" Rosalie brushed away a tear and sucked in a shuddering breath. "I'd like to offer my condolences."

"Your condolences?" The lady laughed. "My dad's a pill sometimes, but not that bad. If you'd like to reach Mrs. *Williams*, though, I have an address. They just bought a house on the beach and don't have a telephone line yet."

"She's married?" Excitement bubbled. "Oh, yes, an address would be fine." Rosalie pulled a notecard from her handbag to jot down the address—one of the ones she used to write to the troops. "I have something that belongs to your stepmother, and I'd like to return it. I think she'll find it to be a wonderful surprise."

Chapter Sixteen
....

"Aunt Tilly, you're going to kill us!" Kenny grasped the leather seat of Aunt Tilly's '29 Model A Ford as she drove them toward her home in Victory Heights. It'd been too long, at least two weeks, since he'd worked on the old place. Since it was condemned, he could barely face saying good-bye. How many late-night hours had he studied in the drafty abode back when majoring in journalism at the University of Washington? That was before the war, of course, when journalism seemed like the best contribution he could make to inspiring people—urging change.

Losing the house felt like letting go of a piece of his past—a warm, happy, secure part. Another example that a lowly reporter no longer seemed to fit within the changes happening in the world around him.

Aunt Tilly slowly angled her head away from the road and toward Kenny, making his already furiously beating heart pound faster. "You worry too much, honey. I was at least a foot away from that army truck."

"Yeah, Kenny," Nick piped in from the backseat. "If you can't handle your aunt's driving, I have an idea for you. A new invention—" The car lurched to the left as Aunt Tilly took a curve too fast. Nick yelped as he bumped against the door.

Kenny scrambled to brace himself, and he was sure the right wheels had abandoned the pavement for a moment as they went around that turn. He imagined the metal box he'd labored to keep polished, shined, and purring like a kitten—all to honor Uncle Earl—scraping across the thoroughfare, with them inside.

Aunt Tilly recovered control, returning the car to the straight and narrow. Kenny took a breath. Then he launched a sarcastic scowl to the backseat. "What were you saying, friend?"

"Watch out, Miss Tilly. Don't hurl me out the window." Nick chuckled and straightened his shirt. "I was saying, they should have some kind of belt to keep you in a car seat. I've heard some of the airplanes have such a thing."

"Mercy! That *was* close." Aunt Tilly laughed nervously. "I'm sorry, boys. I'll lay off the pedal. Just feels like we're going so slow. Cars are passing right and left."

Kenny patted her arm. "This old thing can't take curves like that. You're not driving Uncle Earl's motorcycle, you know."

"I know. I know. But he did love this car."

"Yes, he did."

Kenny gazed ahead. The road looked pretty straight, at least for now. He took in a breath, inhaling the memories embedded in this old jalopy—him and his sisters squirming around in the backseat as kids, off on some adventure with the Wilsons.

Approaching the Aurora Bridge, the bridge's crisscrossed, curved rods created a stunning silhouette against the sky, especially on a sparkling day like today. In the distance he spotted the high arc of the Dipper roller coaster at Playland, Seattle's popular amusement park.

Remembering that, Kenny couldn't help but think of Rosalie. He still hadn't contacted her about the Rosie the Riveter articles—not because he didn't want to. In fact, despite her biting words, the determined gal had dwelled in his thoughts. Rather, he gave himself a few days, hoping she'd calm down—remember his sizzling dance moves and their comfortable conversation, rather than all the ways he messed things up.

Kenny had also taken time to pray. Since that first morning after The Golden Nugget, every time she appeared in his thoughts, he prayed for her. Some prayers were simple: *Lord, help Rosalie.* Others he layered with Scriptures. God knew why she needed the prayers, and the more he prayed, the more his attitude toward her changed from a disappointed romantic to a compassionate friend. A friend from afar, of course. At least for now.

They exited onto Victory Highway. Acres of trees—mostly a blend of cedars and maples—swept out from the concrete pavement, but Kenny knew soon the few Lake City businesses would emerge. The ancient Bartell Drugs, with its famous soda fountain, had to be at least forty years old. And the old speakeasy left over from prohibition, The Jolly Roger, was a popular spot. There was also another place he and his college buddies had loved, the Swing Inn Café. Kenny supposed that, after Tilly's house was torn down, he'd not have much reason to trek to this part of town anymore. And if he didn't get a yes for the riveter articles, maybe he'd be leaving Seattle altogether.

Yet even with all his prayers, Kenny still wasn't sure how he'd convince Rosalie to let him write not just one article, but a whole series about her. *Because she seemed to love the first one I wrote so much*, Kenny thought sarcastically.

He'd not only need permission to write the stories, he'd need to follow her around for a week—at work, home, everywhere. More than once he considered telling Mr. Bixby it wasn't going to happen, but then a peace stirred inside him telling him to wait, to pray. He'd done both, but still couldn't imagine it ever coming to pass.

Kenny hauled in a "go get 'em, boy" breath and glanced at Aunt Tilly. At the risk of distracting her, he decided to ask her a question that had been sticking around his brain like gum to the bottom of his shoe. "Aunt Tilly, you haven't happened to see Rosalie around the diner, have you?"

"Oh now, Kenny," she responded, her eyes lighting up.

"You know who I mean, right?" he interrupted. "The brunette who was there the other morning."

"The one who gave you the what-for, sunny-side up?" Nick asked from the backseat. "Miss Tilly, I couldn't stop laughing when he told me about it. You are one sinister reporter, bub." Nick laughed. "Of course, you've had it for her from the first time you laid eyes on those steamy gams."

Kenny shifted around and eyed Nick. "Put a sock in it, will ya? I seem to remember a little blond who struck *your* fancy."

"Naw." Nick cleared his throat, his tone turning serious. "It's different with Lanie and me."

Kenny'd never seen Nick in love. As much as he'd prayed for his friend to find a good wife, Nick seemed more comfortable flirting with lots of girls rather than settling down to get to know just one. To see his friend vulnerable over a lady made Kenny nervous.

"Okay, buddy. Just be careful with your ol' ticker there. A girl like that could break a fellow's heart."

"Now, Kenny, stop it. That Lanie's a nice girl." Aunt Tilly's wrinkled knuckles arched over the wide steering wheel. "I'm glad you like her, Nick."

"Guess you've seen us in the diner a couple mornings, eh, Miss Tilly?" Nick leaned his face forward, peeking between Kenny and Aunt Tilly.

"Is that where you've been going so early?" Kenny asked.

"They've been occupying one seat in my corner booth every morning at nine o' clock," Tilly said. Then she directed her words to the backseat, still keeping her eyes on the road, much to Kenny's approval. "Nick, Lanie does seem like a sweet girl. You know that Kenny's mom and I have been praying for you too, just as we do for Kenny. I can't wait to tell Shirley, next time we talk," Tilly gushed.

Kenny's stomach churned. He still hadn't talked to Aunt Tilly about Dad. He'd wanted to tell her, but, well, he was having a hard time facing it, believing it.

The car swayed as Aunt Tilly turned right, up the hill to Victory Heights.

"Now honey, there's something I want to tell you." The old woman's coarse hand touched Kenny's arm. "You asked me a question, but then you got all sidetracked with Nick's girlfriend. But I want to tell you that you should've come in to the diner this week."

"I know, Aunt Tilly, I'm sorry. I suppose I've been avoiding you. There's something I need to tell you, and I didn't know how to say it." He cleared his throat.

"Shirley called me, honey. I know about your dad. Didn't want to say anything until you were ready."

"Thanks, Aunt Tilly. I—" He didn't know what to say. Maybe that he was thankful she knew? That he didn't understand why she wasn't overwhelmed by the news as he was?

The white-blossoming shrubs of Tilly's place came into view and a rush of comfort embraced Kenny. This house always felt like home. How could he say good-bye? It was a loss he wasn't ready to deal with.

"I'm real sorry about your dad, but I know our dear Lord will take care of him. I've been keeping him in a lot of prayer too, but right now I need to talk to you about Rosalie. That sweet, sweet girl. I love her so much." Tilly pulled the car into the driveway, and when the engine stilled, children's voices traveled to them.

Kenny's face broadened in a smile. Baseball. They'd want to play. Perhaps playing baseball with the neighbor kids was the real reason he wanted to come to Victory Heights today. That and the fact Aunt Tilly had asked for his help. His guess was she needed him to pack up the last of her things before the city tore the house down.

"We're here already?" Aunt Tilly moaned. "I see I'm not going to have time to tell you everything." She flicked her hand as if brushing away the matter. "Oh well, it'll be a surprise. Yes, a surprise is always nice."

"A surprise—about Rosalie? And what do you mean, 'sweet girl'?" He angled his gaze to her, then climbed from the car.

Aunt Tilly waited in silence for Kenny to come around and open the door for her. Her lips were pressed tight, but her eyes twinkled. He almost didn't want to know what she had up her sleeve.

He opened the door for her, and the three strolled up the azalea-lined path toward the front door. To his surprise, Kenny noticed the condemned sign had been taken down. And, even more shocking, women's voices sounded from inside, intermingled with pounding and sawing. Had Aunt Tilly found a way to save the house?

Before he had a chance to ask, the door flew open, and Lanie stood on the other side. "Oh thank goodness!" She focused her gaze on Kenny. "Rosalie's stuck in the attic. We can't get her down."

Lanie hurried back through the door but not before flashing Nick a flirty smile.

Nick followed her in without questioning what was going on. He just seemed happy to see Lanie.

A little boy Kenny hadn't seen before rushed by with a paint brush in his hand.

"Danny, you come back here this instant," a dark-haired woman called, chasing after him. "I don't think I'd call that helping, young man."

Kenny looked around and noticed drop cloths on the floor. The broken banister was down, and the window with the cracked glass had been replaced. He had questions about those changes, but one question reigned above them all.

Kenny gaped at Aunt Tilly. "Rosalie's here?"

Aunt Tilly nodded, and she removed her jacket with a gentle grace that conflicted with Kenny's revved-up emotions. "That's what I wanted to tell you, son. You better go save her."

Chapter Seventeen

....

"Somebody help!" Trying to stifle her panic, Rosalie focused on what to do next. The upper half of her body struggled to stay perched on the attic floor and not plunge through the ragged hole to the hard wood below. "I'm gonna fall. I'm gonna fall," she muttered beneath her breath.

Her right hand stretched to hold onto the one plank—a supporting beam—not deteriorated by dry rot. The scratchy wood lodged splinters into her palm, and she was sure her fingers' top layer of skin was scraped clean away. Her other arm searched for a spot to hold onto, but every possibility crumbled beneath her grasp. She pinched her lips, fighting off tears of pain and fear.

Her bottom half dangled below. With each moment, she inched closer to hurtling to the floor.

"Can you scoot your legs up?" Rosalie heard Iris's voice call from beneath.

Afraid to move, Rosalie wanted to yell, "No!"

Instead, she took a deep breath and said a quick prayer. "I'll try, but the wood is pretty weak." Her hand ached as she pulled her weight against it. She swung her leg, trying to get a foot up to the attic floorboards. It connected and held.

"Thank you," she whispered. But as she tried to put her weight on it, the floorboards flaked off, tumbling to the ground with a thud, and leaving her with even less to hold onto. Weakening, her hand slipped down the plank another half-inch.

Rosalie bit her lip to keep from crying out. She had to stay strong. She couldn't show her weakness and fear.

She slipped again, and her resolve took a hike. "I'm gonna break a leg, and not in the showbiz way!" she called.

A frustrated laugh burst from her lips, followed by a sob as she imagined slipping and hitting the floor below. Could she work with her leg in a cast? Would they be able to finish that house, or would everyone be too afraid to continue?

"Don't worry, sweets!" Birdie's out-of-breath voice called. "I couldn't find a ladder, but I found Kenny. He's gonna bring one. And Iris just took off to find a mattress."

"Who?"

Was it *the* Kenny? Kenny, the reporter?

That couldn't be possible. How could he have hunted her down in Victory Heights? A headline popped in her head—RIVETER FALLS FOR REPORTER—but she pushed it out of her mind. This was no time for humor.

She'd been praying for an opportunity to apologize to the handsome reporter, but she never imagined it would be today, like this.

God, surely You could have figured out a better way.

A spider crawled over her hand, and she sucked in a breath of mildewed, dusty air. "Tell Kenny to hurry, will ya?"

"I'm here," Kenny called.

Rosalie let out a slow breath. Never had a man's voice stirred such relief. She heard the ladder opening, and Kenny's footsteps scampering up the rungs.

"How are you gonna hold me and stay balanced?" Panic overtook her, and she gripped the plank as hard as she could.

"It's all right; you have to trust me. I can hold on with my legs and lower you down. You'll have to stand on the top of the ladder. Can you do that? Then once you have your balance, you can sit, turn, and then I'll guide you down."

"Wow, is that all I have to do?"

Rosalie's heart raced. She wanted to cry, but she mustered her courage and held it in. "But what if I fall—we fall?"

"That's what the mattress is for."

"Mattress?"

"I sent the ladies to find one, to break your fall, just in case. But we won't fall."

"How do you know that?" She dared to flick her fingers to shoo the spider away. "I can't feel the ladder. All I feel is air."

"I'm right here." His voice was closer.

She tried to crank her neck to get a look at him, but she couldn't. From the sounds of his voice Kenny was right under her—she just wished she could see that fact. She felt his hands on her legs. *I am so glad I wore pants today.*

"See, I told you I'm right here."

"But I still can't feel the ladder." The dust tickled her nose, and she held back a sneeze.

"The ladder doesn't quite reach." Kenny's voice was calm. "I need you to lower yourself down farther. Just think of it as moving from the side of the swimming pool into the water."

"But this is not water. You can float on water. It's just air—and a hard floor after that."

"Just scoot a little bit, Rosalie. Your toes can almost reach."

Even though everything in Rosalie told her to cling to the board, she scooted back a little, sliding her ribcage over the beam, lowering herself down. As she did, she felt Kenny guiding her legs. Then her toe touched something. The top of the ladder.

"Okay, let yourself down a little more," he directed.

She did, until both feet were flat on the top of the ladder. Most of her torso hung in the air, but her hands still gripped the beam. She looked down, and she was on the top of the ladder all right, but facing the wrong way.

"Okay, take another slow step down. One more after that and

you can hold the top of the ladder to help balance yourself. Then you can sit."

"I don't think I can—"

"You need to feel with your foot where the next step is," he interrupted. "It's going to feel awkward to step down like that, but remember, I'm holding you."

Rosalie stretched and did as she was told. Soon she was standing on the second rung with the top rung at the back of her calves. Only her fingertips clung to the beam, and when she looked down, she could see Kenny's face below. He was looking up at her, and he didn't look mad. He looked concerned.

"Now, go ahead and let go. And then sit down on the top of the ladder. Once you're seated I'll help you turn around."

"I can't."

"Yes, you can, Rosalie." His grip tightened on her legs. "I'm not going to let you fall."

"I was awful to you." Rosalie looked down into his dreamy blue eyes. "A few days ago at The Golden Nugget. Really horrid."

"Yes, I know." He offered a soft smile that told her she was forgiven. "But we can talk about this later, can't we? Why don't we focus on the situation at hand?"

"If I let go, I'm going to lose my balance, swing backward, fall to the ground, and crack open my noggin."

"Nope. That's not going to happen." Kenny's grip tightened around her legs. "I'm holding on to you. I'll balance you. You have to trust me."

Did she trust him?

A few days ago she would have said no. But the more she thought about their various interactions, she realized he'd never purposefully tried to hurt her. If anything, he'd attempted to make it clear he cared. The wood dug into her fingers even deeper, and she knew if she didn't let go she'd damage her hands more—maybe even too much to rivet.

"Okay. On the count of three," she called. "One, two, three—"

She slowly uncurled her fingers, and her body slipped down. Rosalie gasped as she waved her hands and tried to hold her balance, but Kenny's hands steadied her. Bending her legs, she plopped her rear on the top of the ladder, grasping its sides with her hands. Kenny took a step up, released his hold on her legs, and reached for her hands. She winced slightly as his hand embraced her wounds. Even though it hurt, she felt safe—or, at least, safer.

She dared to look around and saw her friends and neighbors circling the bottom of the ladder. The fear in their wide-open eyes faded, but only slightly.

"We're not footloose and fancy-free yet." Kenny glanced down, and Rosalie followed his gaze. A pile of decrepit wood, white as if with leprosy, lay in a heap along with old photographs, envelopes, and a baby doll. There was no mattress.

She clung tighter to Kenny's hands.

"I'm sorry, Rosie," Iris spoke up. "I couldn't find a mattress. No one sleeps here anymore."

Rosalie sent a silent plea to Kenny with her eyes.

He smiled with such sympathy it made Rosalie's hands loosen their grip a tiny bit.

"Just breathe," he offered.

Inhaling the manly cologne scent—much better than the stinky-attic aroma—Rosalie soaked in Kenny's good looks. His smile melted her, despite her anxiety.

He rubbed the tops of her hands with his thumbs, comforting her, and she longed to fall forward into his arms and let him carry her to safety. Sizing up the ladder, she could see that plan wouldn't work.

"I'm sorry." She shook her head. "I'm not usually such a sissy." Rosalie had never thought she was scared of heights, but she supposed she'd never been in this type of situation before.

"It's okay. Just relax." His hands held hers. "It's easy as pie. I'm going to step down. Then you can swivel and follow me."

"I'll do my best."

Kenny released his grasp and stepped down but still stayed close enough to steady her if she needed it. Rosalie swiveled, then stretched her right foot and felt it connect with the next rung. She followed it with her left foot, and then did the same again. And when she made it to the bottom, finally standing flat on the floor, she turned to face him.

In his gaze there was no hint of the anger toward her that she expected.

"Kenny, I—" She had something to tell him, but then she looked around at her friends' faces, remembering she had an audience.

Kenny lowered his head, taking a deep breath, and then looked into her eyes again.

Rosalie's muscles, which had been wound tight as a lug nut, relaxed a notch. "Thank you," she said simply. "You're too nice to me." She focused on his eyes and noticed they sparkled with sincerity—not pride.

"You're safe." He released the words in a breath and smiled. The smile sent tingles like butterfly kisses up her spine.

Rosalie longed for a quiet moment to relish being near him again, but instantly her friends huddled around her with hugs and words of relief. She laughed with them and joked about their new attic access point. When she looked up again, Kenny was gone.

* * * *

Kenny's gaze followed the baseball arching over his head, becoming black against the still-bright early evening sky and back down again, landing in left field—almost hitting the rusty motorcycle parked in the gravel driveway.

He'd heard from Aunt Tilly the incredible news that not only were the ladies moving into the old house, they were volunteering their time, skills, and even supplies, to get it up to code. He'd spent the afternoon ditching dry-rot-ruined framework and replacing it with the sturdy new lumber the ladies from the plant had gotten local lumberyards to donate.

But best of all had been the news about Rosalie's relationship with God. Kenny's heart soared, knowing the transformation that had happened inside her. Knowing her eternity was now secured in God's kingdom.

Of course, her relationship with God only drew him more to Rosalie. That's why he'd made a conscious effort through the day to avoid her. Helping her down from the attic, his attraction had been strong, almost painful. He couldn't let futile thoughts of romantic dinners, long walks, and evenings of dancing muddy his thinking. If he got up the nerve to ask her about doing the articles, he'd have to stay professional.

But distracting himself with manual labor hadn't helped. His mind kept racing back to her. So once the work was done, he decided to visit his old friends—who happened to be half his age and younger. Whenever baseball with the VanderLey brood called, he happily answered.

"Gerard, you did it again!" Kenny shouted as the ten-year-old towhead raced around first base and on toward second. "When am I ever going to strike you out?"

"Never, busterboy. Never!" Gerard's thick Dutch accent had almost disappeared since he, his seven siblings, and his mother arrived in the United States three years ago, before Pearl Harbor. Their father didn't make it out of the Netherlands before the Nazis forced him to join their army. Last Kenny'd heard, Mr. VanderLey had defected to France. Gerard's little sister Britt's blond tresses bobbed as she chased after the elusive ball.

"Another home run!" Nick yelled from the catcher's spot. "When're you gonna learn to pitch a strike, eh, Ken?"

"You wanna take the mound, sometime? That boy's—" Movement from the house halted Kenny's words, and he turned to watch.

It was Rosalie, slipping out the back door.

Seeing her, Kenny's breath stuck in his throat like a B-17 without an engine. She smiled and tilted her head. The candle-like quality of the sun dipping in the evening sky created a golden glow on her lovely features.

"Where've you been all day?" she called. "It's like you disappeared."

Thump. Pain shot up Kenny's thigh from a direct hit, catching him off guard. Excited kid laughter resounded through the field.

"Hey, pitcher, keep your eyes on the ball," Nick called.

"Ouch." Kenny rubbed his leg and noticed Rosalie laughing too.

"I think I'm going to sit the next inning out," Kenny called to the kids.

"Aw, Mr. Davenport, do ya hafta go make moon eyes at Miss Madison?" Danny whined, but Nick shushed him and the others who complained by hobbling to Kenny's spot on the mound.

"How 'bout if I let you use my mitt." Kenny handed over his mitt to his new friend Danny and ambled across the grass.

"I didn't disappear," he told her, responding to the question she'd asked. "I helped in the basement. After replacing some of the dry rot, we found a few pipes that needed to be welded. Your friend Clara's a whiz with the welding torch—wouldn't let me help. But when the kids came knocking, I finally put down my tools and headed out." He looked back at the house. "I'm amazed by what you've already accomplished in a few days. It's wonderful what you ladies are doing for Aunt Tilly."

"She's the one doing us a favor. We're being booted from our apartment building. I'm not sure if you've looked around lately, but it's hard to find a decent place to stay these days, with all the war workers coming to town and all."

"I'm well aware of that." He laughed. "You should see the dump where Nick and I live, but I don't mind. It's good to be near my beat—" Kenny halted his words, remembering her aversion to reporters. "Uh, Rosalie, you wanna sit down?" He pointed toward the porch swing. "It squeaks, but it's pretty comfortable. I think the old folks next door—the Hughes—sneak over and use it some evenings."

He followed her across the white-planked porch, thinking how nice it would be to see the paint touched up after so many years of peeling.

Rosalie sat down and palmed the faded, floral cushion. "Comfortable."

"Yeah, Mrs. Hughes sewed that, I expect. You should keep a watch out for the neighbors over there." He pointed toward the side opposite the VanderLeys' house. "Those old-timers, and the other couple that lives next door, are cantankerous at times, and well, they play practical jokes. It can be dangerous."

"Oh dear." Rosalie laughed, and for the first time, Kenny spotted a relaxed, rested look in her eyes.

"I'm sorry I was so awful to you," she said for the second time that day. "I know you must be thinking I'm a bumbleheaded baboon to spend the evening dancing and talking with you at the Igloo, and then switching things up and giving you a verbal knuckle-sandwich the next day."

"Yeah, well, you didn't leave that evening off on too good of a note either. I was hoping my story would make it up to you." He focused his gaze on his feet, pushing off against the planks, rocking them. "That parting at the Igloo was strike two."

"And strike one, I assume, was at Victory Square?"

"Yup, and with The Golden Nugget being strike three, I thought I was out for sure."

She smoothed her navy blue slacks, then tucked a curl behind her ear. "Well, I wanted to apologize for all of it and also wanted to say thanks for saving my neck today. It was quite a fine mess I got myself into."

A royal blue Stellar's jay landed on the cherry tree next to the porch, searching for food in an empty bird feeder.

"Are you doing okay? Your hands looked pretty scraped up."

She examined her hands and laid them on her lap. "Oh, I'm fine and dandy now." Her cheeks curved as she smiled. "Just a couple scrapes. Iris helped dig out the splinters."

Kenny gently touched the abrasions on her fingers, his hand resting on hers. "It looks pretty sore. Why didn't someone bandage that for you?"

He looked up to find Rosalie's shoulders rising and falling with each breath. He wished he knew what she was thinking. At least she wasn't scowling.

"My hands are fine," she finally said. "You're so sweet. I mean, kind, and I simply don't deserve for you to be nice to me." The Stellar's jay squawked, drawing Rosalie's attention.

When it stopped, she sighed peacefully and gazed at Kenny. "Kenny, I'd really like to tell you something. The other day when I met Tilly—"

"Wait, Rosalie. I need to tell you something first." Whatever she would say, Kenny longed to hear it, but first he had to get something out of the way. He was a reporter, and he had to do a story about her, or lose his job—and also lose everything he'd fought so hard to gain. If she wanted to criticize him for that, it would be better to know up front than to expose his feelings and get shot down again.

He removed his hand from hers, speaking with strength. "I'm a reporter, you know, and I want to be friends with you, maybe even more." He hurriedly went on. "But, well, my boss wants me to do a story on you, Rosalie." What a relief to spew out the words.

"And not just one story, but a series of stories. I know how you feel about having your name in the paper, and how you feel about reporters in general, but if I don't do this story, my boss will fire me. But if I do a good job, he said he'll give me an important story. Nick's story. One that will really help a lot of people." He took in a breath, her rose perfume tormenting his senses, and spoke more softly. "I understand if you don't want to do it—help me out—but I hope you will."

Rosalie's eyes, so bright a moment before, now gazed toward the kids still playing baseball with Nick. Her shoulders straightened, her hands folded on her lap. Finally she turned to him. "I, uh…"

"Soup's on!" Lanie called from the door. "Y'all come and eat. I fixed up some real Southern fried chicken."

Rosalie smiled weakly. "Maybe we should talk later."

Chapter Eighteen

....

Unfortunately, the night ended without Rosalie and Kenny having that chat. The group had gobbled down Lanie's grits, perfectly fried chicken, and homemade apple pie—delicious despite the tiny amount of sugar rations she used. And then Miss Tilly said she needed to "rest these old bones," asking Kenny to accompany her home.

By the time Rosalie had returned to her apartment, she also needed to rest her bones—they felt tired and sore too. But it hadn't worked; she hadn't slept much. Instead, she engaged in an imaginary midair dogfight in her weary state. Her attraction to Kenny's warm sincerity, sense of humor, and thought-provoking conversations battled against her preconceived repugnance to reporters.

Even though the sun now beamed through the windows, Rosalie's body felt weary enough to remain in bed for another eight hours. Since that wasn't possible, she stretched, kicking off her wadded-up blankets and sheets, and gazed over at her friend.

Birdie lay curled in a little ball, her back toward Rosalie, and Rosalie wondered if she were awake or still sleeping. They'd mostly made up since their little spat on Queen Anne's Hill. After talking to Tilly—and connecting with God—Rosalie had apologized. Birdie had accepted her apology, and they'd embraced, but ever since that day things hadn't been completely the same. The emotions would take time to simmer down, or at least that's what Tilly said. She'd also suggested Rosalie give Birdie time. "Just like scrapes and scratches don't heal overnight, sometimes hearts take a little time to mend."

Maybe that's what was taking Rosalie so much time to get all her feelings straight concerning Kenny. Her heart still didn't feel healed from all the wounds, mostly self-inflicted, caused by her relation-ship with Vic—even though they were well on their way. She also had the issues with her father and her dislike of being in the center of attention to deal with. Poor Kenny, he had no idea what a hornets' nest he was poking with a stick when he became involved with her.

She thought about their last conversation the previous night. Before Kenny had scooted into the driver's seat—despite Miss Tilly's protests—he'd faced Rosalie for a final good-bye. Kindness perme-ated his gaze as he asked her to come by the newspaper office—second floor, newsroom.

"We'll talk about the possibilities, and whatever else." He'd squeezed her hand.

Rosalie turned to her side, snuggled the pillow under her chin, and smiled. She knew the possibilities he talked about were the arti-cles, but she also wondered if there were other things he wanted to talk to her about. If she could read his gaze, there was.

Still, she didn't want to go there, not yet at least. Even though she was beginning to trust Kenny, she didn't know if she liked the idea of her face—her life—plastered all over the paper.

"Birdie?" Rosalie whispered, wondering if her friend was awake.

"Hmm?" Birdie answered. She rolled to her back and rubbed her eyes.

"I have a million thoughts spinning around my mind, and I need to do something productive that doesn't have to do with swinging a hammer. We have half a day until our shift. Got any ideas?"

"Well," Birdie mumbled, "we could sling bacon and eggs to guys at the USO Club."

Flyboys, soldiers, sailors. She'd never been at the USO Club a time day or night when the club wasn't full of all three. A pin pricked Rosalie's heart, and she realized that's where she'd met Clifford—the sailor she'd danced with, toured the city with, and even kissed, in hopes of taking away her loneliness for even one weekend. In the end, she'd felt more lonely and more depressed.

Rosalie took in a deep breath and let it out slowly. "Sure, I guess we can go there." She knew it would mean a lot to Birdie. Birdie cared for military soldiers, stationed locally, with hopes that other women overseas were volunteering to make bacon and eggs for the man she loved. Even though Birdie still hadn't heard news about the results of her husband's mission overseas, Rosalie knew the reality of John bombing China didn't stray far from Birdie's thoughts.

As they rose and dressed, excitement built over spending time with the appreciative soldiers, serving up food and laughter. And by the time she and Birdie arrived at the USO Club, Rosalie's smiles were genuine.

"Good morning, soldier," Rosalie said as she scooped scrambled eggs onto a GI's plate. She gave him a lingering smile, trying to show, even in a small way, her gratitude for his commitment to freedom.

Glancing at the sofa and armchairs by the fireplace, Rosalie noticed a flyboy reading the *Tribune*. Immediately her thoughts zipped back to Kenny, and the dogfight from her sleepless night resumed. Though she now accepted the truth Birdie brought to light—that all reporters weren't manipulating weasels like Pops—how could she stifle a lifetime of distrust?

More than that, she questioned if a relationship with Kenny was possible. She'd learned from the quick weekend romance with the sailor that she didn't even want to spend time with a handsome fellow unless she believed a serious relationship could result from it. She could tell from being with Kenny that he cared for her, just as she cared for him. Continuing down that thought trail, she wondered where a relationship with him could end up.

The idea of life as a reporter's wife stirred anxiety. She clearly remembered her mom's muffled cries when she crumbled from the exhaustion of raising four kids alone, even though she was married.

And when Pops *was* home, his mind was never really with them. He'd obsess about his next story, then fly the coop as soon as a hot tip came over the wire or a shady character knocked on their door with "the goods." Her mom was more like a widow than a wife.

Rosalie wiped her hands on her apron. Even a good man would surely be pressed with the same demands. *It's not the life I want.*

Also, before she could think about starting any relationship, she needed to consider her newfound faith. Her life with Christ had given balm to her wounded heart, but Tilly explained the aches wouldn't immediately disappear.

Even though relieved of her guilt over hurting Vic and the pain of losing him, the festering wounds about her father needed the intensive care only God's Word could offer. Her journey had only begun. Her worries about people peering into her life and seeing her flaws still gripped her.

The line of soldiers stretched on, and she scooped up another helping of eggs.

"Hey, sugar, are you rationed?" The voice of a fresh-faced sailor, probably nineteen or twenty, stirred Rosalie from her musings.

Another voice followed the sailor's question. "I'd like to know that too."

Rosalie immediately recognized the voice. Kenny peered over the soldier's shoulder. As she gazed at him in his white work shirt and tie, the sleeves rolled up, she felt a smile spread across her face.

"Kenny!" she blurted. "What on earth are you doing here?" As soon as the words were out, she stifled the grin that traitorously displayed her excitement.

"Take your turn, Mac. I was talkin' to the lady." The young soldier in line pushed his plate in front of Rosalie and shouldered Kenny aside. "Well, ya hitched up, or what?"

Rosalie lifted her chin and smiled at the inquisitive GI. "I'm not rationed. Why do you ask, huh, fella? You fishin' or somethin'?" She plopped a scoop of scrambled eggs onto his plate. "You seem like a swell guy, but even though I don't have a sweetheart, I'm not interested today. Thanks for asking."

"Aw, you're all wet." Unfazed, the GI moved toward Birdie and the bacon she offered. "A pretty girl like you's gotta have a beau," he said to Birdie.

Birdie flashed her wedding ring. "One or two slices of bacon, bub?"

"Two please," the soldier said, then his eyes widened as he approached the next young woman down the line. "Hiya sugar, you rationed?" he repeated.

"I'm taken too, but I have pancakes." She put a few on his plate.

Rosalie shook her head as the GI moved on to the gal at the toast station, his grin no longer as bright.

The Joe gone, Rosalie shifted her warm-cheeked face to Kenny. How come just seeing him made her heart smile? "Do you want something to eat? You look like you've been working."

"I already filled up at The Golden Nugget," Kenny said. "I came by before work to help the gals load up the truck with pots and pans they're donating to the metal drive." He unrolled his sleeve, once again hiding his muscular forearm, much to her disappointment.

"I can't stay." He touched Rosalie's arm. "But bumping into you made my morning a lot brighter. That's for sure."

Her hands trembled. Her tongue malfunctioned. "Uh, thanks."

Kenny offered a small chuckle as he let go of her arm and shifted toward the door. Then he grabbed his coat from the rack and slung it over his shoulder. "What's shakin', Birdie?"

"Hiya, Kenny. Have a great day."

The next guy in line cleared his throat, and Kenny stepped out of the way.

"I'll be seeing you, Rosalie. Be at the *Tribune* if you need me." Kenny threw her that deadly wink.

Only half of Rosalie's scoop of eggs made it onto the next guy's plate. The rest tumbled to the floor. Kenny moved toward the door, but Birdie's voice halted his steps.

"Y'know what?" Birdie said. "We were just leaving ourselves. Wanna walk together?"

Rosalie's jaw clenched as she threw Birdie a warning glower. She still hadn't found out what thought emerged victorious from her midnight dogfight.

Kenny ambled back. "Uh, if you're heading out in the next couple minutes, I can wait."

"Sure, I'm all out of bacon anyway." Birdie elbowed Rosalie, whose stomach scrambled like the eggs she served.

A minute later, the food had been replenished to feed the remaining soldiers, and two other bright-eyed young women eagerly took their places, serving up the chow.

Rosalie followed Birdie's lead through the double swinging doors into the kitchen, which smelled of dish soap and hash browns.

"What are you doing?" Rosalie demanded, under her breath. Even though she was trying to be discreet, she noticed a group of older ladies at the kitchen sink, peeling potatoes and tilting their heads as if trying to listen in on the conversation.

Birdie tipped her head playfully as she poured bacon grease into a can. Then she pointed to a poster above the sink. It was a drawn image of a cluster of missiles bursting out of a skillet's grease drippings.

"'Save waste fats for explosives,'" Birdie said, quoting the poster's slogan. "I'm helping the war effort, can't you see?"

"Not that." Rosalie scraped a few dry eggs into a container of compost. "You know I'm not talking about this food or the war effort. I'm talking about Kenny."

A young girl who was mopping stopped the swishing of her mop to listen. Rosalie cast her a glance, and the girl resumed her work.

"Steady, girl." Birdie sidled up beside her and fanned Rosalie. "You should've seen how your face turned three shades of red when you saw Kenny in line. I thought more than eggs was going to drop to the floor.

Rosalie swatted at Birdie with a laugh. "I wasn't going to faint or anything."

"Kinda looked like it." Birdie's lips pursed together, stifling a chuckle. "I gotta tell ya something, sweets. I think you were fibbin' to that poor sappy soldier a minute ago, saying you don't have a sweetheart."

"I do not have a 'sweetheart,'" Rosalie said. "If you're talking about Kenny, we're just friends."

"Okay, Miss 'thu, uh, thank you.'"

Rosalie grabbed a dish towel from a stack and whacked her friend on the shoulder. "We're just friends. That's all."

Soft laughter came from the sink, and Rosalie knew the other ladies were enjoying the show.

Birdie grasped for the towel. "Okay, okay!" she pleaded as Rosalie continued walloping her. "Friends is more than you were a week ago."

Rosalie grinned. "He did save my skin."

"Yeah, he sure did."

Rosalie plunked her egg container in the sink. "Oh Birdie," she moaned. "He's expecting an answer from me about the stories."

"Well, maybe you should set the topic of articles aside for a while—until you get to know him to see if he's worthy of your trust. And how are you going to get to know him if you don't spend time together? That's what did it for John and me." She squeezed Rosalie's shoulders as she pushed her along. "I'll make an excuse to leave you two alone." Birdie reached ahead and opened the swinging door.

"No way, lady." Rosalie tugged Birdie back by her apron strings, and the door almost whacked her friend in the face. "You saw how I swooned like a foolish schoolgirl just from a simple hello. You have to stay, or I'm making an excuse to leave too."

"Aw, I thought you were braver than that." Birdie's lips pinched together in a teasing grin. Then she put her slim arm around Rosalie's shoulder. Finally, Birdie turned and winked at their audience at the sink. "Alrighty, sweets, I promise. I'll stick around."

"You're right, Birdie." Rosalie restrained her nerves and rallied her courage. "I am brave. He's just a guy, right?"

"That's right. C'mon."

Rosalie marched back into the cafeteria, with Birdie behind her, to find Kenny holding two roses. He shot her that melting smile, obliterating her bravery. She froze like a dimwit.

Birdie pushed Rosalie toward him.

"A rose for a Rose." Kenny handed her one, his eyes connecting with hers.

Rosalie received it from his hand. "Thu–thu–thu–thank you, Kenny."

Kenny broke their momentary connection and gazed at Birdie. "And for you."

"Why thank you, sir."

Kenny extended his elbows. "Ladies."

Rosalie and Birdie linked their arms through his, and the three left. As she traipsed out the door, Rosalie noticed the empty vase at the check-in table, and the old woman sitting behind it waving her well wishes.

* * * *

Kenny glanced at Smith Tower—Seattle's oldest and tallest landmark—as they rambled down the street, Elliot Bay glimmering in the distance. Bing Crosby's smooth voice crooned, "Be Careful, It's My Heart," from the radio of a convertible Ford that rumbled by, and Kenny bobbed his head to the music's beat. He considered it good luck that he'd just happened to run into Rosalie today. Saved him the effort of tracking her down.

"You're quite a fella," Rosalie said, twirling her rose in her hand. She quickly glanced at him, then to the bay. "I mean, it's kind of you to help around the USO like that. There aren't too many guys around to help with those big boxes."

He felt his chest constrict slightly at her words, but he could tell by her peaceful expression she didn't mean to accuse. Nick always said that Kenny made a bigger deal about his not fighting than anyone else did. He hoped that was the case.

Walking arm in arm with the girl who, twenty-four hours earlier, he'd thought despised him felt like a dream. *No, more like an answered prayer.* At least she didn't hate him. That was a start.

"Did you hear the other ladies talking?" Rosalie looked to Birdie. "They said the barber at the corner shut down his shop. He was a German, and everyone stopped going to him for haircuts."

"But wasn't he born in America? His parents moved here from Germany long before he came along." Birdie placed a hand on her hip. "That doesn't seem right."

"What do you think about that, Rosalie?" Kenny turned to her.

"I can understand the fear. And I'm sure some people are untrustworthy," Rosalie said, "but it's sad that the innocent ones get hurt in the process. I think that's the nature of war, though. A few people whose minds are bent on taking what they want and on hurting people they hate for whatever reason. The majority of people have to live with the consequences."

"I've never thought about it that way before," Kenny said. "I'd say the three of us are most likely here, walking down the street together because of the war."

Rosalie glanced at him with a curious expression.

"Not that it's a bad thing," he hurriedly added. "I'm thankful I got to meet you."

"I'm thankful too. For the chance to meet you and Birdie. And because of the love and care of my new friend, Tilly, I also have a new relationship with God."

Birdie's squeal pierced Kenny's ear, but he understood her excitement. His heart did a double beat. He'd heard the news from his aunt, but it meant even more coming from Rosalie. As he looked closer, he noticed a peace in Rosalie's eyes that he hadn't seen before.

Rosalie nodded. "I can't believe how everything seems different now. Life—the war—our friendships. I'm more thankful for the way God's love has flowed through the things and people He's brought into my life. And as for the hard stuff, I have more of a peace about those things than I used to. Life is hard, but I'm thankful we have a strong God to turn to."

Kenny kicked at a pebble on the sidewalk, yet it felt as if his feet weren't touching the ground. He'd been praying for a confirmation that Rosalie's change was real. He just didn't realize God would answer so soon.

They continued to talk as they walked, sharing how each of them ended up in Seattle. Kenny talked about staying with Tilly—a good friend of his mom's—while he attended college. Rosalie launched into the story of how she met Birdie the first day of training and how they'd been attached at the hip after that. As the words spilled from Rosalie's mouth, it was clear that she cared for all the women there and that she hated to see them struggle so much in daily life. Hearing her talk reminded Kenny of what Nick had said. Just last night he and Nick had played cards till midnight. When the subject of Rosalie came up, Nick's offhanded comment was a revelation to him. "You can talk to her. She cares about people. She has interesting insights."

Nick was right. When she wasn't assailing him, Rosalie's frankness refreshed him.

He glanced over at her as she walked alongside him.

Rosalie's gaze was focused on the bay. "Isn't it a beautiful sight?"

Kenny nodded, keeping his eyes focused on her. "Yes, very beautiful."

She turned. When she met his eyes, her face glowed in the same way it had that night when they'd danced at the Igloo—before he let the air out of her tires by mentioning the articles.

Kenny really didn't want to break the mood, but he wondered if she'd let him know her thoughts about that. He'd told Bixby he was working on it. Praying hard was work, right? Still, his boss had no idea he hadn't even gotten a *yes* yet. Would she answer his life-altering query today?

He rubbed the back of his neck. If she'd do the story, in a way it meant she accepted his career, or at least she didn't hate it anymore. And that would give him hope. Not assurance of a grand romance or future together, but hope. Yet something inside told him to wait.

Kenny could wrestle for a story as well as any hardboiled reporter, but not this time. Not with Rosalie. He'd leave the Rosie the Riveter series—his job and future—up to God. If God wanted Rosalie to do the stories, He could influence that, right? And if not, well, Kenny had to trust that even if it looked like his world would come crashing down, God would still be there—building something new out of the rubble.

Rosalie's head tilted downward, the sunshine gleaming off her brown curls. Smiling eyes tipped up. "Are you always such a flirt, or is it just when you're trying to unsettle a hardworking USO volunteer?"

"Make that two hardworking volunteers," Birdie put in.

"I'm not one to flirt, actually." Kenny caught Rosalie's eyes. "You bring it out in me."

The wind picked up. Kenny's white shirt ruffled in the breeze as they crossed Pine onto Pike Place. The immense red PUBLIC MARKET

CENTER sign with its yellow and red clock welcomed visitors to the huge, old complex.

"I bring it out in you?" Rosalie placed a hand over her heart and mimicked Scarlett O'Hara. "Whatever could you mean, sir?"

Kenny laughed. Then he patted the hood of a buffed and shined gray Ford, definitely bought before the war since car factories were used only for military production now. His pulse bounded. Was he ready to tell her how much he liked her? *Really* liked her. "I, well, I don't know—"

"A pig!" Birdie pointed excitedly toward a farmer who led a small pig on a rope to the entrance of Pike Place Market, then traipsed down the hill toward it. As she approached, she patted its head. "What a cute little guy. I wish I could buy you and give you a home."

Rosalie shrugged. "She should've been a farmer's wife, the way she goes crazy over farm animals."

"I heard that!" Birdie called. "Me and John are planning on starting a small spread when he gets back—after the war."

"It fits you," Rosalie hollered back.

"Or maybe open our own grocery store. Or maybe get our own fishing vessel and hit the seas. Doesn't matter, as long as we're together."

The farmer eyed Birdie, who was now hunkered down in front of the animal and petting its face, with amusement.

Kenny watched Rosalie bantering with her friend. "What those two have sounds nice. Like something I'd like to have some day."

"There you go, flirting again." She playfully punched his shoulder. "You've got to stop that!"

"Maybe it's your zing that makes me want to fl—" Kenny snagged on the word *flirt*. Not only did the word suddenly seem less than suave, it exposed his interest in her—as if she didn't already know. Still, he wasn't sure if he wanted his affection to sound out like an air-raid siren. "Uh," he fumbled. *Where's Nick when I need him?*

Rosalie silently waited, the corners of her lips tweaked vaguely upward in a contented smile. "What was that? I didn't hear you." She smirked.

It was deliberate torture. He could see that—and respected it in a way. He'd tortured her with his winking earlier, relishing the pink hiking to her cheeks. He probably deserved a little dose of his own castor oil.

Lost for a good comeback, he decided to spill it all. "You think it's funny, watching me sweat, don't you?" They reached Birdie waiting by the pig, but her presence didn't stall Kenny. "Well, fine, I'll admit it. I enjoy flirting with you. You're beautiful, funny, an amazing dancer, and full of life and laughter. I like you. There, I said it."

Kenny crossed his arms and waited for whatever sassy remark she could dish out, but instead Rosalie's cheeks turned the color of her name, and she avoided his eyes. His smile faded. He hoped, more than anything, that he didn't ruin things—didn't drop a bomb onto the fun they were having.

With a brush of his hand and a too-loud laugh, Kenny changed the subject. "Now let's move on to much more important things. So Miss Madison, tell me how you picture your life after the war. When there's no need for bombers—which we all dream about and wait for—what do you hope to do?"

Rosalie's shoulders visibly relaxed, then her eyes flicked up to his. "Okay, Mr. Davenport, I will tell you, but first, I need you to know something. I, uh, like you too."

She didn't wait for his response, but with a skip in her step, she joined Birdie, turning her attention to the pig.

Chapter Nineteen
....

"Are you asking me what I want to do with my life, Mr. Davenport?" Rosalie looked back over her shoulder. A surge of energy, fueled by Kenny's affectionate words, prompted Rosalie's playful side.

"You know, I love to watch the planes taking off and landing. Sometimes I dream about what it would be like to fly. Not a bomber, of course, but something simple, like a Piper Cub. There are other things that interest me too, but I'm not sure where I'll end up after the war. Sometimes I just consider getting in my car and driving to see where the road takes me." As the words built, she wanted to stop them. She hadn't meant to mention Vic's car. Rosalie turned to the row of market stalls. "Uh, yes, as I was saying before, don't you love this market—"

"You have a car?" Kenny interrupted.

"Yes, well, I just sent a letter to the person who really should have it, but for now it's in my care. I don't use it much. Gas rations make public transportation so much easier." She knew she should tell Kenny about Vic, but she couldn't do it.

After her visit with Tilly in the garden, Rosalie had felt many burdens lift off her shoulders. She now knew she'd done the right thing by not marrying Vic, but how could she explain the whole story to Kenny? There was too much going on in her mind and heart to figure out what to say—how to say it. She'd think of a way, but not today.

Birdie had returned, walking alongside them, but remained silent. Rosalie wished she could get some help here, changing the subject, but Birdie seemed too entranced in her own thoughts to help.

Rosalie eyed Kenny, studying him from his work shoe to the top of his fedora. "Where are you from again?"

Kenny's gaze narrowed, and she could tell he wasn't ready to drop the subject, but instead of prodding her, he gave a simple answer. "Idaho."

A handful of ladies, probably on an afternoon excursion to the market, spilled out of a Plymouth, cackling as they strutted past.

"Oh, there's much more for an Idahoan to discover in our market than just a little piggie." She led Kenny and Birdie to Charlie's Fish Market, a small stand with salmon, halibut, buckets of clams, and many more Northwest seafood selections stacked in icy displays.

"Freshest fish in town." She waved to a scruffy man behind the counter. "Right, Harold?"

"Hi, Miss Madison, lookin' for salmon filet today? Reeled in some fine sockeyes this mornin'."

Rosalie sighed, imagining a barbequed salmon swathed in butter for supper. Unfortunately, her butter and fresh meat rations only went so far.

"You like salmon?" she asked Kenny.

"Never had it." Kenny's eyes were focused on a large monkfish, lying on a bed of ice. "This thing gives me the heebie-jeebies. Looks more like a sea monster than a fish."

"You haven't had salmon? And you've been here six months?"

"Actually, I lived here in college too, stayed at Tilly's house, but she's not much of a fish person."

"Hard to imagine living here and not loving fish."

The image flashed to mind of herself in the backyard of Tilly's place, serving Kenny his first Northwest salmon dinner. She'd make rice, green beans, and salad from the victory garden. They'd sit and talk for hours.

"Would you like me to wrap you up a large one, miss?" Harold chose a nice, big salmon from his ice tray.

Rosalie shook her head. "No thanks. Not today." No salmon dinner with Kenny tonight. Not until she decided whether she'd let

Kenny interview her. She wanted to, she really did, but every time she thought of it, her lungs seemed to constrict, making it hard to breathe. It was as if a chain had been looped around her chest and was being tightened link by link. The chain connected her to her father and her past, she knew. She just didn't understand why it was still there.

"I'll be back, don't you worry." She smiled at Harold.

"All right, Miss Madison." Harold returned the salmon to the ice. "But be sure to visit if you change your mind."

"Thank you, I will." They continued strolling down the covered walkway in front of the market stalls. Birdie traipsed ahead of them—far enough away to give them some privacy. Close enough to eavesdrop.

"It's so calm here." Kenny peered down the long, nearly empty market. A group of ladies stood around the lone flower stand, and a few other straggling patrons stopped at the nut stand and the single produce stand.

Birdie slowed her pace, falling in step with them, and then inched next to Rosalie. "You okay if I check out the flower shop?" she whispered. "You won't faint away if I leave you with Kenny, will ya?"

Rosalie patted her hand. "I think I'll be okay. Go ahead."

Birdie trotted away, and Kenny padded next to Rosalie. "I haven't stopped here in a while. I don't remember it being so quiet."

"These days it is." Rosalie led him through the cave-like walkway. "I used to spend many summers up here. My grandma lived in Seattle and we visited her often. When I was growing up, the market was a world of chaos." She pointed to a boarded-up produce shop. "My grandma brought me there nearly every weekend. They had everything. Apples, oranges, cucumbers, broccoli, squash." She wrinkled her nose. "Even zucchini."

"You don't like zucchini?" Kenny's neck poked forward. "Me either. Everyone thinks I'm off my rocker, but I don't care."

"Something in common." She gave him a grin. "An aversion to zucchini."

Kenny's eyes glinted. "I think we have more in common than that."

Rosalie swam in the joy of Kenny's attention, as they continued walking. *Why is he so nice to me, when I was such a pill?*

She resumed the conversation. "Mr. Nakamura had to close down—"

"Ah, of course."

He nodded, and Rosalie knew, as a reporter, he was aware of what had happened to the Japanese citizens of Seattle—and all of the western states—but she appreciated how he listened intently, like he really wanted to hear what she had to say.

"Yeah, he and most of the other farmers were Japanese." She pointed out the other closed stalls. "Mrs. Satou used to scream at us kids all day long. 'You no touch my beans!' But once when I fell and scraped my knee she bandaged me up—and gave me a fistful of snap peas. What a treat. After that we were pals."

They'd footed it all the way through the long hall and now stepped out into the sunlit morning. Landscaped trees and flowers decorated the landing that preceded the next section of the market. Rosalie perched on the back end of a bench, her feet resting on the seat.

"Were you living here when they left?" Kenny asked.

"Oh, yes, it was right before…uh. It was about a year ago." She'd almost talked about Vic again. When he shipped out. When she first saw the *Rosalie*.

Kenny leapt up beside her. Rosalie felt his arm brushing against hers.

"Too bad they had to fork over their businesses," he said.

"And we lost their tasty produce. But I guess I can see why the government did it. I mean, the Japs bombed our boys. Killed our…

men." Rosalie heaved in a breath. "Still are." She sat back down from the bench.

She considered telling him about Rod but didn't know where to start. Her brother was older than her and had moved out when Rosalie started high school. She hadn't heard from him much in recent years, but that didn't make losing him at Pearl Harbor any less painful.

Kenny turned his shoulders toward her. Noticing the sun glaring in Rosalie's eyes, he shifted his head to block it. "But a bundle of those folks were American citizens. They had rights— supposedly 'inalienable' rights to 'life, *liberty*, and the pursuit of happiness.'"

Always keen for a good debate, Rosalie's pulse drummed. So he was going to challenge her, even though he liked her? *Hmm, this could be promising.*

"I feel bad the innocent ones had to suffer too," she said, "but this is our country's existence we're talking about. You heard about the Jap attack on the ship in Oregon. Plus, they actually caught Japanese spies here in Washington. I heard about one on Whidbey Island who held a pilot captive after his plane crashed there. He tried to turn him in to the Japanese. Should we just let them hand over our secrets and do jack-diddly-nothing about it?"

Kenny scooted over on the wooden bench next to her. "So that means your friend who used to work at this market, Mr. Naka-mura, deserved his farm to be plucked from his hands?"

"Actually, Mr. Nakamura *told me* he was proud to go if it meant spies wouldn't be able to hurt America," she explained. "He under-stood everyone's distrust."

Kenny's eyes rounded like Mr. Nakamura's radishes. "I guess I shouldn't be wowed by that. Folks all over the place sacrifice their fortunes and even lives for 'victory.'"

"I'm sure not all the Japanese feel that way, but he did. I'm not saying it's right. I just think the government was trying to protect us."

Kenny's thumb and forefinger rubbed his chin as his mind's cogs seemed to plug away. "I wonder what's happened to their farms? There's got to be a Rockefeller-fortune worth of fertile acres. Bet they're not sitting fallow. Someone's raking in the lettuce," he chuckled at his own pun, "and they're not letting it cook in the bank for when the Japanese come home, either."

"Y'know, I hadn't thought of that. Maybe some reporter somewhere should write a story about it."

Rosalie'd never had a discussion like this with Vic. Kenny not only held his own in a friendly debate, he also listened. Even though he might disagree with her, he evaluated what she had to say. Seemed to value it.

"Speaking of which." Kenny stood and reached for her hand. "I better head to work. Not that my boss notices too much when I come and go, just if I have a good story."

Rosalie's stomach scrunched. *Here it comes.*

But he didn't bring up her articles. Instead, he offered his hand, helping her up. Then they strolled with his hand placed gently on her back into the market, where they joined Birdie.

On the other side of the fish shop, Kenny led the girls down two flights of stairs, their footsteps echoing through the tall stairwell. Reaching the bottom, they ended up on Alaskan Way.

"Well," Kenny pointed to the tall *Tribune* building on the east side of the street, a block down, "I'll be seeing you. And Rosalie, you know where to find me, okay?"

* * * *

"Kenny, help!"

Kenny silenced his whistling rendition of "I'm in the Mood for

Love" and dashed to Lanie, who was plummeting down the wooden stairway inside the *Tribune* building.

He reached her just in time for her to sprawl onto the bottom stair, landing on her side.

She grasped her ankle, tears smearing black mascara on her cheeks.

"Oh, it hurts," she said with shaky breaths. As she sat up, she smoothed her straight pink skirt and white belt.

"What hurts, Lanie?" Kenny said, thinking it strange she worried about her appearance when she'd just toppled down a dozen hardwood steps. "Did you bump your head?"

She applied a palm on her forehead. "I don't feel any lumps." She drew in a breath and exhaled. "It's my ankle that's painin' me."

"Do you want me to check it?"

She nodded, blue eyes pleading as Kenny cautiously removed her white pump.

After a moment of rotating the ankle and gently stroking the sore area, Kenny replaced the shoe. "I think it'll be okay. Just twisted."

The young Southern belle wiped her eyes with manicured fingers, then smoothed her tousled hair. "Are you sure? I'd hate to miss work."

Kenny grasped her elbow, helping her to stand. "Well, I'm not a medic or anything, but my sister broke her ankle once, and it got swollen and bruised real fast."

Clinging to Kenny's hand, Lanie struggled to put pressure on the sore foot. "Oh," she moaned. "It does hurt somethin' fierce, but I think you're right. It's not broken."

"Yeah, when my sister fractured hers, she howled like an alley cat. It swelled really fast too. You should be back to riveting in no time." Kenny assisted her to the glass-paned door.

"What were you doing here, anyway?" he asked as he opened it for her.

"Well, my uncle's a big cheese at the paper here." She twisted a strand of hair. "He's part of the reason I moved to Seattle."

"Really? I had no idea you were related to anybody here."

"Yeah, Uncle Jimmy—"

Kenny tilted closer. "Jim Bixby?"

Lanie squealed. "You know him?"

"Yeah, he's my boss."

She clapped her hands. "Wonderful. You must be grateful to work with such an accomplished journalist." She grabbed his forearm and flashed a smile. "I better get back so I can be ready for work. Today, I'm rivetin' my first real airplane. Hey, did you know I'm gonna be on the radio tonight?"

This girl shot one surprise off after another. "You are? Singing?"

"Yessiree, boy. I'm in the Flying Fortress Quartet. That sweet man of mine, Nick, encouraged me to try out, and I made it." She giggled. "I do like that fella, you know."

"Nick seems happy to be getting to know you."

She giggled again, then offered Kenny her left hand, up toward his face, as if she wanted him to kiss it like in the pictures.

Kenny awkwardly grasped her smooth fingers, pressed his lips to the back of her hand, and then his eyes focused on something that made him jump back as if it were a pin-pulled hand grenade.

A simple solitaire diamond engagement ring. Nick's grandmother's.

"Lanie, are you and Nick—?"

Without answering, she tossed her hair behind her and limped out the door into the sunny morning.

"Wait." He rushed after her, craving an answer, but stopped short of the door. He was already late for work. He'd have to wait till he got home to talk to Nick. *He wouldn't ask a girl to marry him without telling me first.*

This morning, when Nick shuffled to the washroom and back,

his best friend and roommate hadn't mentioned anything about popping the question, not even hinted. Then again, Nick didn't communicate much more than a grunt anytime before eleven a.m.

Kenny gripped the glossy railing and skipped steps up the stairs. He hoped Nick wouldn't act so rash. *I mean, he barely knows the girl.*

Yet Nick didn't always weigh his options before he acted. Kenny paused at the top and gazed out the window, worry for his friend's future gripping him. *Lord, draw Nick to You. Give life to his dead heart, and Lanie's too. Give me wise words. Amen.*

The newsroom bustled with clacking typewriters and men's voices as Kenny moved to his desk. Before he sat down, he spied a Western Union telegram envelope planted on his blotter. His stomach lurched. Had to be about Dad. He reached for it, but before he could open it, Mr. Bixby burst into the room.

"Davenport, Lewis, Dupont, Williams. In my office. Now."

"Yes, Chief," Kenny said, pausing to glance at the sender's name: ANDREW L. DAVENPORT.

Dad.

"Davenport, you fond of making us wait?"

"Coming, sir." Kenny set the telegram down and hurried to the meeting.

Chapter Twenty

....

Rosalie's gaze trailed Kenny until he disappeared inside the towering *Tribune* building.

I have to give him an answer soon, she thought. *But no matter how dreamy he is, I still don't know if I can handle a series of stories.*

She looked at her watch. They still had three hours before it was time to catch the bus. Even though she'd hardly slept, excited energy pulsed through Rosalie. She felt good enough to dish up food for a hundred more guys, or maybe greet a passel of soldiers returning from distant lands.

"Well, Birdie." Rosalie shooed away her confused thoughts and patted her friend's back. "You wanna take a little ramble? I heard the *Kalakala*'s coming in this morning." She pointed to her watch. "There's still time."

Birdie clapped. "*Soitenly*. I keep telling Myrna I'll help greet the boys coming home." She swiveled south, toward the Colman Ferry Terminal. "Oh look, I see it."

A cargo ship lumbered through the bay, heading to Pier 70, and to the south of it, Rosalie spied the *MV Kalakala*—Washington State's world-famous art deco ferry. Its smooth, chrome nose gleamed against the crisp sapphire sky as it cut through the dancing breakers. Puget Sound's "work horse"—she had no doubt—was delivering wearied GIs returning from the Puget Sound Navy Yard on the peninsula.

"Yeah, we better hurry."

They strode along the sidewalk next to Elliot Bay. Passing the huge piers, Rosalie spied the cargo ship slogging to the dock. Its wake pulsed closer until it finally broke on the rocky shoreline.

Rosalie noticed the corner of Birdie's mouth creep up. An impish glint grew in her eyes, and she opened her mouth. "You gonna grill me now?" Rosalie asked.

Birdie's hand flew to her mouth. "What do you mean?"

"I know you. You're going to interrogate me about Kenny. I can read you like a *Little Abner* comic."

"The way you're talking about 'interrogating,' sounds more like *Dick Tracy*. Are you saying I'm a snoop?"

"Nah, not really." Rosalie widened her grin so Birdie could see she was only teasing. "But I know your Cheshire cat curiosity torments you."

Birdie's dainty chin poked out. "Well, since you brought it up. You do seem to like him, and I know he likes you. He said so!"

Rosalie shoulders rose at the joyful memory of his words. "He did, didn't he?"

"Look at you, sweets. You're over the moon."

"He's a really nice guy." Rosalie glanced at the splashing water in the bay below. A school of jellyfish blobbed their iridescent bodies through the dark blue depths. "But what's eating me are the articles. He wants to write a series about me, Birdie. That would mean more attention, more people asking for"—she rubbed her stomach, trying to squelch the nausea—"autographs." She pressed a hand to her cheek. "Why me, Bird?"

"Well, sweets, you did break the national record. That's a pretty big to-do, don't you think?"

"*We* did. Not just me."

"No, Rosalie—Rosie the Riveter—I was just the bucker. You're the one who actually shot those rivets."

"Thanks, Birdie." Rosalie breathed in the salty air. "But I'm *not* Rosie the Riveter. And I'd really rather not have a whole slew of newspaper articles written about me."

They approached the Colman Ferry Terminal, where the *Kalakala* would dock. "Here it comes." Rosalie pointed to the streamlined ferry almost reaching the dock.

They jogged up to the platform and stood against a railing to watch the dock workers secure the ship. Once secure, a gaggle of USO gals skittered past them carrying baskets filled with gift bundles for the GIs. Some of the guys who returned—like Nick—were wounded too badly to be sent back. Others were just envoys headed for a new post.

Myrna, a redhead Rosalie knew from the USO Club, stopped when she spotted them. "Hiya, Birdie! Rosalie!"

"Hi, Myrna!" Rosalie waved.

"Or should I say, Rosie the Riveter?" Myrna laughed, edging up next to her. "When are we gonna read more about your romance?" She sighed and patted her own cheek woefully.

Rosalie's stomach grew queasy again. And the pier seemed to rock under her feet as if she were the one on the ship. "I, uh, don't know. Probably never—about the romance at least." She wanted to throw herself over the dock but compelled herself to chuckle instead. "Do you need some help?"

"Now you're talkin'. C'mon."

Myrna led Rosalie and Birdie across the wooden planks to where the car deck of the *Kalakala* would soon open and unleash a brigade of military men.

Myrna linked arms with Rosalie. "I just loved that article. What a swoony reporter. At least in the photograph." She patted Rosalie's arm, then faced Birdie. "Don't you think so?"

"I do." Birdie's big smile, verging on a mocking laugh, painted her face.

"Just get a loada you, famous girl. You met Lana Turner! Anyway, why don't you two go inside to help the boys in the wheelchairs? We've got it covered out here."

"Sure." *Anything to escape this conversation.*

Myrna pointed to a flight of stairs, climbing up to the passenger entrance. "The guys in wheelchairs are up there on the passenger deck."

Rosalie followed Myrna's gaze, her eyes looking for a ramp, but she didn't see one.

"Okay." Rosalie nodded. "So, how do we, uh—"

"Get them down the stairs?" The light breeze tossed Myrna's hair around her face. She used her hand to push red waves back from her cheeks. "A couple of beefcake soldiers will come and carry them down the inside stairs to the car deck. Then you can wheel them off."

"Sounds good!" Birdie bounced up the stairs, and Rosalie followed.

"So, back to Kenny." Birdie insisted on reviving the subject of her prospective love life as they entered the ship. "You're not off the hook yet, sister." Birdie stuck her hands in her pockets and tilted her head back. "Remember, I'm Dick Tracy." She squinted mysteriously.

"Oh, brother."

Rosalie took in the *Kalakala*'s interior curving yet geometrical design as they crossed the shiny floor. The men in wheelchairs and a nurse waited next to a railing at the far end of the observation deck. "There they are."

"Oh yeah, I see 'em." Birdie eyed Rosalie and slowed her pace. "C'mon, Rosalie, listen. I want to tell you something. Put the article and all that *revolting* publicity aside. Are you carrying a torch for Mr. Kenny Davenport?" She pinched two fingers together, leaving a little gap between them. "Maybe a little?"

Rosalie placed a hand to her chest as Kenny's blue eyes and welcoming smile streamed into her mind's eye. "I do like him," she said with a sigh. "I just wish he wasn't a reporter."

"Sweets, I understand you're scared, but how do you feel? He was super chivalrous to you yesterday, rescuing the fair maiden from the collapsing castle."

"More like a screeching polecat than a tittering princess."

"Aw, you weren't screeching. Just a little, uh, *concerned*."

"*Pathetic*, Bird, that's what I was. But it's okay. I really didn't mind that he helped me down." She snickered. "Kinda liked it."

Birdie slapped Rosalie's arm. "I knew you were sweet on him. Here's what I think."

Before Birdie could bestow her wisdom, a young soldier in the wheelchair whistled. "Here comes our escorts, boys."

Rosalie waved. "Just a minute, fellas." She tugged Birdie's arm, halting her and pulling her behind one of the arched beams. "Tell me, Birdie. I've only been a Christian a week. You've known the Lord nearly your whole life. I've been mulling over this all night. Praying. I need your advice."

Birdie held Rosalie's hand. "It seems pretty simple, Rose. If you like him, these articles seem like a perfect way to get to know him. God's giving you this easy-as-pie opportunity to spend time with a kind, smart, funny, Christian fella—how often do you meet someone like that? And then you can explore your friendship without putting your heart at risk. At least at first. You don't even have to date him. Just let him interview you, follow you around, and then you can decide what he's really like." Birdie took in a breath and released it with a *hmm*. "Seems clear to me."

Seemed clear to Rosalie too, but her heart still gloomed like Seattle in January. "It's a fine plan, Birdie, but you forgot something." She grasped Birdie's shoulders. "I don't want to be in the papers."

"Oh, sweets, you've got this all wrong. Remember, God calls us to put others before ourselves." She gently pushed down Rosalie's arms, holding them to her sides. "It's kind of like being at the plant, Rosalie. When we first started, we didn't think we could make it through the first day, remember?"

"Yeah, I was scared I'd miss a rivet and cause one of our bombers to crash over the Pacific."

"Right. And now you're afraid your heart will crash."

"In spiraling flames!"

"But what if this is the mission God has for you right now? He might use the articles to help someone. Or maybe He has a gift for you on the other end of this. But you won't know until you roll up your sleeves and accept the assignment." Birdie tucked a stray curl behind Rosalie's ear. "And it's even better than that. God's not like the boss who gives you an assignment and then leaves you to do it all by yourself. He's a loving father, who walks you through each step. And if you miss one—forget to pray or lose your way—He's still there, loving you, calling you His child. It's amazing."

Rosalie longed to trust her newfound Savior. She craved His guidance, His love. But prying her fingers off of her own life, and trusting herself to God, pained her. "I'm so used to only having myself to rely on, Birdie. I like being the one to rivet on my own."

"Yeah," Birdie conceded. "It's hard—impossible really—to let go of that on your own. The good news is, sweets, you don't have to. Even the letting go is by His grace alone."

"You're right."

"Of course I am. Because it's the truth of God's Word." Birdie nodded determinedly. "Plus, think of it this way, if nothing else, maybe dozens, or hundreds, or who knows how many ladies will sign up to work at the plant to be just like 'Seattle's Own Rosie the Riveter.'"

Rosalie's shoulders slumped. She was grateful for her friend's honesty, but it wasn't easy to hear. "You had to pull the old *think of others more than yourself* thing on me, didn't ya?"

Birdie's eyebrows arched up. "Works every time."

Rosalie didn't have to be convinced anymore. She knew having Kenny write the articles would be a good decision. She also knew she needed to fill Birdie in on everything.

"There's, uh, something else I didn't tell you about, Bird. Kenny said if he does a good job on my story, his boss will give him another really important assignment that could help people." Rosalie cringed, building a case against herself.

"Really?" Birdie shot her hands to her hips. "Is that all? What else didn't you tell me?"

"If he doesn't do the stories about me, he'll be fired." Rosalie hid her face in her hand.

Birdie gasped. "Rosalie! Why haven't you said yes already?"

Rosalie marched toward the soldiers. "I know. I know," she said, assuming Birdie'd catch up. "I'll let him write about little ol' me." And as she accepted her assignment to become "Rosie the Riveter," a burst of new joy lit in her heart. One that hadn't been there before. Joy in knowing that, no matter what plastering her name—and life story—all over Seattle's papers would bring, Christ was guiding her steps.

She grinned to herself. *And spending time with Kenny might not be so bad, either.*

Chapter Twenty-one

....

"There you are," the pert young soldier in a wheelchair chimed as Rosalie traipsed toward him. "Where've you been all my life?"

"Allan, psst!" A nurse with ebony hair and olive skin nipped her fingers against her thumb, reprimanding the GI. "Leave the girl alone." The nurse's eyes softened as she smiled at Rosalie and Birdie. "He's been like this ever since Bremerton. He's asked me out on a date at least a dozen times." The wrinkles around the woman's eyes deepened as she laughed.

"No problem." Rosalie patted Allan's back. "We know how fresh these kids can be."

"Fresh? Me?" Allan feigned.

Birdie tapped down his hat, pushing it over his eyes. "Yeah you, Cassanova." Then Birdie looked around. "Seems to me our escorts aren't going to be around for a few minutes. Care to stroll the deck?"

Allan nodded. "I'll race you, sweetie." He turned the metal rim on his wheels, rolling into the sunshine.

"Hey, wait up!" Birdie called, quickening her pace.

Rosalie chuckled, then glanced at the other two men and immediately sobered. Both older than average GIs, one guy's hat rested against his broad chest, and his graying hair blended with the ferry's metal walls.

The other's pale blue eyes zeroed in on his clenched hands. Sweat spilt over the deep rivers of his forehead, and his bottom lip was clamped beneath his teeth. A thick wrap of bandages coiled around the man's thigh, and a small red splotch stained the middle.

The name on his uniform read CARLSON.

The nurse must have seen the blood seeping through the bandage the same time as Rosalie. Without hesitation, she turned and grabbed a white metal first aid kit from under a red-cushioned chair, positioned by the ferry's window.

"I thought we got that bleeding stopped." The nurse's voice was tense.

The gray-haired man's attention was focused on Carlson, and he patted his friend's shoulder, the uniform's fabric beneath his hand bearing sergeant's stripes.

"Thank you, Andrew. Thank you for being here," Carlson mumbled.

The lines around the gray-haired man—Andrew's—intense eyes constricted as, without words, he comforted his friend.

The bloodstain on Carlson's leg grew, nearing the edges of the white bandage wrappings, staining his pants.

The nurse hurried to Carlson, carrying a heap of folded cloth compresses. "Here, this should stop the bleeding." Placing them on top of the other bandages, she pressed down firmly with her hand.

Carlson winced as her hand connected with his leg, and a low moan escaped from his lips. Then he grasped onto Andrew's arm.

With her other hand, the nurse felt Carlson's cheek. Her lips pursed slightly, and her eyes filled with worry.

It wasn't until Rosalie leaned down in front of the two men that she noticed Andrew's left pant leg tucked under his knee, where his limb ended. He slipped his hand from Carlson's shoulder and grabbed the man's hand. "Hang on, friend. Mary Ann's waiting for you. Won't be long now."

For the first time, the man's eyes peered up and pushed his lips into a tight smile. "And Lucy," he choked out. "And—" He couldn't finish but winced and clutched the other man's hand.

"When we get you downstairs, we'll give you something for the pain, okay, darlin'?" the nurse said.

"And Tim," Andrew continued. "You'll see Tim as soon as he gets back from serving his country, a hero like his dad. Mary Ann'll give you his letters, though, as soon as you see her. "

"Letters," Carlson rasped.

Rosalie didn't know if it was from loss of blood or perhaps infection, but Carlson's face was a pale gray, and his eyes struggled to stay open.

The nurse left to hurry into a small room and returned with a blanket, covering him. "Where are those marines to take him down?"

Kneeling next to Andrew, Rosalie reached across, covering the two men's fists with her hand. "It'll get harder before it gets easier," she whispered. "You'll be carried downstairs, and I know it won't be comfortable, but I'll pray that God will give you strength."

Lord, ease Carlson's pain, Rosalie prayed, *and help Andrew comfort his friend.*

Thankfulness for the magnitude of these men's sacrifice—for her and the millions who counted on them—surged through her. She longed to break the dam welling up in her heart and flood them with her fathomless gratitude. But how? No words said it all. No action spoke enough. She patted Carlson's hand and continued her silent prayer.

Finally footsteps pounded up the stairs beneath the railing and two marines appeared.

"Okay, who's goin' first?" one of them boomed.

The nurse stood and put her hand on Carlson's back. "This gentleman."

The marines moved to him, then paused as they saw his pain—and his rank. They eyed each other and then, with a respectful formality, advanced to him. "Sir, just put your arms around our shoulders; we'll have you downstairs to the medic double-time."

Cautiously, and far slower than "double-time," they lifted him from his chair.

"I'm right after you, my friend," Andrew called, shifting his wheelchair toward the steps. "Think of Mary Ann. I'll be right there." Andrew waved a thin arm, and when he smiled, Rosalie noticed how gaunt his cheeks appeared.

The marines carried the man down the stairs, his stifled moans echoing through the large steel vessel. The nurse followed with the wheelchair.

"A good man." Andrew gazed at Rosalie, shaking his head. "A squadron commander. He took that shrapnel in his thigh saving a kid from a grenade. He wouldn't let the doctors take his leg, though— even though it would have been the better choice. I just hope his stubbornness doesn't cost him his life."

"I'm sure your friend will be all right," Rosalie said, even though she didn't completely believe her words. "Do you two go way back?"

Birdie was still by the deck's railing, enjoying the sun and talking to the younger guy, Allan.

"No," Andrew answered. "Just met him on the train. Told me all about his life before the pain kicked in. But we're all brothers, you know." He threw her a grin as his eyes sized her up.

Rosalie sent a smile back. "That was real kind of you to comfort him when you've got your own—" She glimpsed his leg and paused, realizing her words could hurt. She eyed him, hoping he saw the apology in her eyes.

"My own injury?" The man palmed the air as if comforting her. "I only wish I could've carried him down those stairs. A prayer and a bit of time, that's easy to give. What he really needs is the Lord's mercy and grace."

Yet even as Andrew said the words, Rosalie saw him shifting in his seat. Sweat beaded up around his shirt collar, and his cheeks flushed. He rubbed his knee just above where his leg ended and forced a smile. Rosalie realized he was in pain too. Yet in his desire to help his friend, Andrew hadn't focused on himself.

Rosalie scanned the man's face. Peace filled his blue eyes, and a cross was pinned to his collar. "You're a chaplain?"

"Willing to serve the Lord anywhere He calls me. It's the end of my military career, though." He pointed to his stump. "Maybe I'll get my own little parish here. Doesn't matter. I will be glad to see my family, though."

Rosalie looked over her shoulder and noticed the marines still weren't coming, and she knew from her work at the USO that the one thing soldiers appreciated the most was someone to talk to. Someone to listen. She scooted a red-cushioned chair next to him. "Tell me about them. Do you have children?"

"Two girls and a boy—all grown, of course. My son lives here in Seattle."

As Rosalie listened, she noticed the name on his shirt for the first time. It had been hidden behind his hat resting on his chest. It read Davenport.

Rosalie racked her brain, trying to remember if Kenny had said anything about his dad being a chaplain. Yet the more she thought about it, she didn't know if he had mentioned his dad at all. Not that he ever had a chance. She was too focused on her own needs, worries, and frets to ask.

Rosalie shot a glance to Birdie, waiting to point out the man's nametag. But she was already walking down the steps with Allan and the two marines Rosalie didn't notice arrive. Rosalie switched her gaze back to the chaplain, who still talked about his son in Seattle.

"I'm mighty proud of that boy. Ever since he was a little boy, he paid attention to things. Took note of the world around him."

"Your son's not Kenny, is he?" she blurted. "Kenny Davenport?" She pointed to the nametag on his jacket. "I noticed your name."

The chaplain's eyes gaped open, and he peered at her. A grin spread his lips. Tears touched his eyes. "That's my boy. He's a reporter—"

"Oh my!" Rosalie's heartbeat rocketed like a missile. She pictured Kenny's face at their reunion. The joy of meeting his father. The sadness of seeing him broken, weak—not the man he was before the war.

"I know him, Reverend Davenport. He's just down the street." Tears blurred her vision. She wiped the tears away, and as she studied the older man's face, she wondered why she hadn't recognized him sooner. Kenny had the same jawline, the same nose, the same thoughtfulness in his eyes as his father.

"You know my Kenny?" Love radiated in his eyes—a father's love and pride over his beloved son. Seeing it caused an ache to rise in Rosalie. She'd never experienced that type of love before.

She bit her lip and realized she shouldn't expect it with her own father, but she did understand it better than she ever had before. Now she had a new, adopted father in God. Would His eyes gleam with a similar adoring look if she could see them now?

"Yes, I know your Kenny," she answered his question. "Not well, really, but I'm getting to know him. He's a great dancer, your son." She winked.

Andrew rolled closer to her and patted her arm. "Make sure he treats you like a lady, okay?"

"Oh, he does, sir. He does. Not that we're an item or anything, but…never mind. Does he know you're here? That you were coming? I left him at his office just a few minutes ago. I'm sure he would've said something, if he knew."

"I sent a telegram, but you never know when those things will arrive." He looked down at his empty pant leg. "I'm not even sure if my family knows the extent of my injuries. From all the letters I've received from my dear wife, and from Kenny, they don't mention it, and I wonder if my letters ever made it to them." A twinkle lit his eye. "Kenny writes me every day, you know. He continues on the same piece of paper and mails it at the end of the week. I've kept every one. And I'm sure if I weren't to arrive home right now, his upcoming letters might even mention you."

An excited determination flushed Rosalie's cheeks. "He'll want to see you." She stood and looked to the stairs. "I'll go get him. I can run." She swung around the railing and dashed down the first steps.

"Hold up there, sweetheart! Come back before you go running off."

Rosalie paused her steps, then turned back. "I'm sorry. It's just that I know he'll want to see you."

"Simmer down, girl. You remind me of my daughter, Bernice. So quick to get fired up."

Rosalie returned and knelt next to his chair. Reverend Davenport enfolded Rosalie's hands in his rough, warm grip, and a sweet peace encompassed her. "I need to be with Carlson, right now." His eyes pierced hers. "I can't tell you how much I'm longing to see that boy of mine, but he doesn't need to rush right over. They're taking me to the naval hospital up in Lake City. It'll take a few hours for me to get settled in. Do you know where that is?"

Rosalie clutched his hands even tighter. "Yes. It's next to Victory Heights. Down the street from where I'm going to live."

"Ah." He tipped his head. "Must be near my friend Tilly's old place."

"Miss Tilly! That's where I'm going to live. Well, we will be living there once we fix it up."

The marines' boots clomped up the steps, on their way to carry Reverend Davenport down the steps.

"I'll see my boy soon, but first I need to ask you a favor."

"Anything."

The hefty marine and his partner reached the top of the stairs, took three giant steps, and were at Reverend Davenport's side. "You ready, Preacher?"

"After they take me downstairs," he said as they lifted him, "don't worry about wheeling me to the train. I can wheel myself. Just go find Kenny and tell him one thing—well, two things. No, make that three."

"I can do that, sir."

"Tell him"—his eyes moistened—"I love him."

"Yes, of course."

He breathed in a breath, releasing it with a smile. "Tell him I'll be at that hospital. He can come see me there."

"Got it."

"And finally, sweetheart"—he threw her a wink, just like Kenny's—"tell him I like his new girl."

Rosalie couldn't help but laugh. The marines lifted Mr. Davenport, and a quiet laughter spilled from his lips too as they steadied him and carried him down the stairs.

"Will you tell him?" he called back. "Promise!"

Rosalie strode to the stairwell, following. "I'll tell him," she said, still amazed that Kenny's father was here—in Seattle—and she'd already met him. "I promise."

Chapter Twenty-two

....

Kenny rolled his eyes as he and the gang of other reporters rambled out of Bixby's office into the cigarette-smoke-clouded newsroom.

"Yes sir, Mr. Bixby. I'll take care of that story. You can count on me," Kenny said, unable to stifle his sarcasm.

"Hoopty-doo, Kenny boy." Charlie slapped Kenny's back. "You must be tucked in Mr. Bixby's pocket to nab a story like that."

"Go suck an egg." Kenny pivoted toward his desk, not in the mood for a skirmish with Charlie. At the meeting, Bixby handed out the newest assignments to his "top" reporters.

Kenny's assignment? Interview a Seattle macaroni manufacturer, Mr. Merlino, about his son and nephew. Kenny could barely believe Bixby was serious. The son, a GI stationed at the POW prison in Texas, stumbled across his cousin, Mr. Merlino's nephew, at the facility. The nephew, recruited into the Italian Army, was captured by the Allies. The two cousins were in the same family but facing each other across the barbed wire.

"What are the odds, Kenny," Bixby had said, "that two cousins on opposite sides would meet up in Texas?"

Kenny sat in the chair at his desk and looked over the notes Bixby had related. He'd jotted down the uncle's name, address, and the "facts" of the story, including the interesting note of how the boy from Italy liked the American prison so much he hoped to stay in the States after the war. *Is this why I'm not fighting with our troops? Is this gonna make one lick of difference?*

Charlie followed him, sitting on Kenny's stack of papers on top of his desk. With a toothy grin, he flaunted his manila envelope in Kenny's face. Inside were airplane tickets to the other Washington—DC. "Congrats on your big break, pal. I wonder if the macaroni man will make you up some pasta. It's a story and a meal." Charlie shook his finger. "Such things shouldn't be taken lightly these days."

"Hey thanks, pal." Kenny lobbed the disdain back at him and sat back in his chair, tapping his pencil on the edge of his desk. "Tell the president I said hello."

"Oh, I'm sure we won't have time for pleasantries. I'll be unearthing FDR's reaction to the Germans' threat of poison gas." He shuffled his weight, messing up Kenny's papers even more. "I might get some lunch at the White House. Hope I'm not too disappointed if it's not macaroni."

"Give it a rest, will ya? Go hound out your presidential assignment and leave the macaroni man to me."

"Well, if you insist." Charlie hopped up from Kenny's desk, grabbed his coat from the rack, and strutted out the door like a regular hero. The other reporters paused their typing as they watched him go, deferring to his greatness.

Kenny puffed out a breath. Rubbing the back of his neck, he then rested his head back on the top of his wood chair. If only Rosalie would agree to the Rosie the Riveter articles. When those raked in the sales, then at least Bixby would give him the one break he needed—he'd go overseas, interview those contractors, write it up, help Nick. *And then I'd be cookin' with gas. Who knows? Maybe he'd assign me as a foreign correspondent.*

Not that he needed the big scoops to boost his ego, like Charlie. When he became a reporter, he envisioned his role as helping the war effort, carrying the cause of the helpless, and—

He leaned forward, elbows on the desk, again remembering the telegram. He slipped it from his blotter and ran his finger over his father's name.

And make Dad proud.

He slid his finger down the side of the envelope to open it. Tension built within him, and he hoped it wasn't bad news.

"Davenport, why aren't you following up on that macaroni story?" Bixby's bark near his ear caused Kenny to jump. "That fella's not gonna hang around all day!"

"Yes sir." Kenny shoved the telegram in his coat pocket, rose, hurried to the coat rack, then donned his fedora. "Okay, Mr. Macaroni, uh, Merlino, I'm on my way."

Ten minutes later, Kenny was hunkered down at the bus stop half a block away from his office, waiting for the bus to take him uptown. People hurried up and down the street, their collars lifted, as a cold wind blew up from Elliot Bay. The traffic hummed as it zoomed by, and dock workers' shouts echoed from the waterfront. He lifted his own collar, wondering if it would rain. Looking at the gathering gray clouds, it was hard to believe this morning had held sunshine.

He closed his eyes as he pictured this morning's sunlight dancing in Rosalie's eyes. He glanced at his watch, realizing she should be getting ready for work now. Then he opened his eyes again and retrieved the telegram from his pocket and stared at it.

It probably just said his dad would be arriving soon, but Kenny's gut gnawed at him.

What if it was something else? What if his leg got infected or his transport ship was torpedoed? He reached his fingers to open it, then paused. The anxiety in his chest roiled too deeply, and he asked himself what his father would do. Pray, of course.

Lord, I need Your peace. No matter what the telegram says, help me to trust You.

He opened it.

COMING TO SEATTLE STOP
WILL BE THERE SOON STOP
WILL CALL STOP
LOVE YOU SON STOP
DAD STOP

"Kenny!" a woman's voice hollered from the street.

Kenny jolted to his feet and poked his head outside the covered bus stop. Rosalie sprinted like Jessie Owens toward him. Her smile brought with her shards of sunshine, beaming through his gloomy mood.

"Oh, Kenny." She huffed in air as she completed her sprint, then planted her hands on her knees. "I'm glad I caught you."

* * * *

Rosalie's chest ached, and her cheeks burned, only this time not because of Kenny's deadly wink. "A guy in your office said you'd be here, on your way to a 'macaroni story'? I have no idea what that means, but there's something I have to tell you." She battled to catch her breath.

His dad was here. The kind man whose eyes deepened with delight when she mentioned his son. The man Kenny wrote daily letters to. Rosalie's heart soared when she imagined Kenny's comfort and joy over hearing that his father was only a short drive away. Today, in a few hours, they could sit together in Reverend Davenport's hospital room. They'd talk face to face after so many months, sharing a cup of joe, and filling each other's hearts with a joy Rosalie had never experienced with her own father. She was happy for him, grateful he'd receive this blessing. *And I get to deliver the news.*

She glanced up from wheezing to see Kenny leaning back with his hands in his pockets, Clark Gable-like, as he had on the Victory Square stage the first day Rosalie met him. A dimple decorated his amused grin, and she wondered if it was her frazzled appearance he was laughing at.

She stretched her fingers through her curls, framing them around her cheeks. Then she smoothed her lemon-colored work shirt and trousers.

When her eyes tripped back to him, familiar butterflies returned, fluttering to her stomach. She wiped moisture from under her eyes, hoping her mascara hadn't smeared down to her chin. If only Kenny's blue eyes weren't so sparkly. If only his crooked grin didn't communicate such character. If only...

"Kenny, why do you have to be so handsome?" The words slipped out before she could harness them. And then, in a reckless rush, more followed. "If you weren't, it wouldn't be so humiliating for me to be out of breath and looking a mess."

Kenny's countenance brightened with a surprised, but jovial, smile. His cheeks flushed, and Rosalie suddenly didn't mind her rash words. *Let him squirm, for once.*

Rosalie's compliment shut his mouth, as he seemed to search for a comeback.

"Well," Kenny's chin perked up, apparently finding the words he sought, "if you weren't so beautiful, I'd be able to get my work done and not think about you all the time." His eyebrows rose triumphantly.

Rosalie's knees melted like brown sugar on oatmeal, his swoony looks and heartfelt words overwhelming her lonely heart. "You're a rascal." She placed a hand on his forearms and the feel of his muscles made her wilt even more.

Kenny laughed and patted her hand. "Maybe I am, but you still haven't told me your important news. You didn't sprint all the way here just to brighten my afternoon, did you?"

An expectancy shone in his eyes, and Rosalie realized he probably thought she wanted to give him an answer about the Rosie the Riveter articles. *Yes, that too.*

Her stomach writhed, despite her determination to go through with them. But first—Reverend Davenport's peace-filled gaze came to mind.

She grabbed both of his hands, squeezing them. "Kenny, your dad's here in Seattle." She blew out a relieved breath. "Isn't it amazing?"

Kenny gazed at her, but instead of joyful excitement, the smile lines around his eyes disappeared and his grinning lips uncurled. "My father? He's already here?" his voice rasped softly.

Rosalie studied his face. She could see anxiety in his eyes. At first she didn't understand. She'd expected joy, excitement. That was all everyone ever talked about—when their love ones returned home.

He lowered his gaze, looking to his hands in hers. Then he released his grasp and placed his hands on his thighs, letting out a low breath, as if coming to terms with a great loss.

Then she remembered. Kenny *was* experiencing a loss. His father lost his leg. He was not returning the same man as he left. Of course Kenny would be apprehensive. Kenny, probably for the first time, would see him weak, relying on others. Broken. Why hadn't she thought of that before?

Rosalie patted his hand and noticed the yellow envelope peeking out from Kenny's pocket. Reverend Davenport's telegram. Kenny already got it. He knew his father was on the way. He was most likely already trying to work through all the varied emotions when she'd shown up.

But Rosalie understood something Kenny didn't. She'd seen how strong Reverend Davenport was, despite his condition. He'd encouraged her with his kindness to his friend. He'd inspired her with his faith, even in the few hasty minutes they shared. Kenny needed to know that. Perhaps it would help dispel some of his fears.

"Kenny."

Kenny's eyes retained their wistfulness as he lifted his hand and stroked her arm. Then he shifted her toward the bench. "Why don't you tell me how you found out, Rosalie? Did you see him? Is that how you know?" He glanced at his watch. "The bus seems to be late."

Late? Rosalie looked at her watch. It was only an hour until her shift started. If she left now she could get home, change, and get to work on time. But how could she leave Kenny?

She sucked in a deep breath and let it out slowly. "Okay, this is gonna be quick."

* * * *

Kenny had known since that call from Mom that Dad would be coming to Seattle, but when he'd read the telegram, fear gripped him. He hadn't wanted to face Dad, not yet. His dad had something to show for his dedication and sacrifice. What did Kenny have to show for it?

"You got a telegram, didn't you?" Rosalie's sincere voice encouraged Kenny.

He looked at her and realized he'd never felt so comfortable around a woman.

"Yeah, it just came." He slid the heavy paper out of its holder. "The telegram says he's coming soon, but that's all. You saw him?"

"Yes!" Rosalie explained how she and Birdie were helping the USO girls welcome the troops at the Colman Ferry Terminal. "I was talking to your father for a while before I realized it was him. He was caring for a friend—putting someone else's needs before his own."

Kenny nodded. "That sounds like my dad. He's always taking care of everyone. He's always been so strong. He'd walk around like—" Kenny paused, his eyes getting misty. He shook his head. "He's always acted like he was put on this earth to care for others." Emotion built in his throat, but he swallowed it down.

"You must be nervous to see him." Her eyes filled with compassion. "He's strong, though. Even without—even with his injury."

"I know. He lost his leg." Kenny's eyes closed, and in the blackness he strove to imagine his father's muscular arms reaching down to roll a wheelchair. His one leg—normal, strong; his other gone at the knee. From now on, people would always be helping him reach things, drive places, get around. He'd never be able to walk hand-in-hand with Mom, dance with his sisters, tackle Kenny at football. Kenny opened his eyes, trying to accept reality.

He tried, but he couldn't see his father as anything but the stout, powerful man he'd always known. Rosalie's words didn't surprise him. "Of course he's strong. His strength comes from the Lord."

"I could feel that. He encouraged me."

A soft chuckle escaped Kenny's lips. "He has a way of encouraging folks, even when he's in trouble." A memory floated to Kenny's mind like a nostalgic breeze. "There was this one time—"

Rosalie leaned closer, hand under chin, eyes engaged.

"He was plowing the potato field. The tires got stuck in a sloggish mud puddle leftover from a storm. Dad got out, thinking he'd locate a board to shove under it, give it some traction. That's when he got stuck." Kenny rested his back against the bench, his thoughts far away.

"The way he tells it, first he lost a boot, then another, then his balance. Before he knew it, sticky muck trapped him up to his knees. With all his strength, he couldn't pull himself out."

"Oh no." Rosalie's forehead wrinkled. "I just can't imagine your father stuck in mud like that."

"Well, guess who happened along?"

"You?"

"Yes, ma'am. I was probably four or five, and my pet frog had just died. I was out looking for my papa, hoping for a hug."

"I bet you were a cute little guy." Rosalie's eyes danced.

"I'll have to show you photographs sometime, so you can judge for yourself. Anyway, somehow I managed to stay out of the mud. I tell ya, he comforted me for at least an hour—well, it seemed that long to a kid—before he told me to go fetch Mom." Kenny touched his fist to his chin as he gazed beyond Rosalie toward a broad cedar standing watch over the busy city street.

"That's a wonderful story."

"There are so many more stories like that," Kenny almost whispered. The memories brought comfort, but also dread.

Rosalie pulled Kenny's hand into hers and ran a thumb over his palm.

"All I ever wanted was to make him proud."

"He's a good man, isn't he? Like you."

Kenny's heart sank as frustration and disappointment in himself caused a heaviness to fill his chest. "Not like me," he muttered. "I haven't done anything but let him down."

Out in the bay, Kenny spotted the *Kalakala* forging its metal hull back toward Bremerton, and he wished he were on it, dressed in a sharp army uniform, ready to serve his country in a real way. No more writing meaningless articles. Kenny stood and tramped to the curb, leaving Rosalie on the bench.

She followed, grasping his arm. "How did you let him down, Kenny? He seemed so proud of you."

Kenny searched down the street. "Why's the bus so late?"

"Kenny?" Rosalie's tender voice now irritated him. Couldn't she see he didn't want to talk about this?

She waited silently.

Fine. If she had to know. "Haven't you wondered why I'm not off fighting, Rosalie?" He held his gaze straight ahead. "It's because I promised my father I'd use writing to fight the Nazis." He laughed too loudly. "But now all I get is lame local stories." He turned his gaze in her direction. "And I can't even nab a story about a local girl who won the riveting contest."

The words were barely out of Kenny's mouth when a bus turned the corner, approaching the bus stop. Two older women, with shopping bags in hand, approached the curb, preparing to board. Kenny looked to Rosalie. He didn't want to go, especially to follow a dumb story, but he knew he had no choice.

Kenny blew out a slow breath when he realized it wasn't his bus that rumbled to the curb. The women boarded, then it rumbled away, its exhaust clouding his thoughtless words as if suspending them in air.

Why did I say that to her? Kenny's hand rushed to his forehead, shame seeping into his chest. He pivoted to Rosalie. Her eyes appeared moist—saddened but not angry. "I'm sorry."

Soaking in her wounded gaze, Kenny longed to enwrap her in his arms and beg forgiveness. Protect her from his own frustration, his unkindness.

But before he could reach out to her, she lifted her hand and smoothed her fingers through his hair. "It's okay, Kenny." The corners of her lips rounded upward as her hand cascaded to his neck, shoulder, arm, then back to her side. Kenny's shoulders relaxed. "He is proud of you, you know."

Kenny didn't know his father really was proud. Couldn't. Because he hadn't been completely honest with him. His dad assumed Kenny printed stories that actually helped people. Now he'd know the truth.

"I tell my men that my son's fighting the war with a typewriter instead of a gun," Dad wrote in one of his letters.

And Kenny had let these statements ride, uncorrected. How could he tell his father his outpouring of pride was misplaced? Kenny tried to avoid the subject of his career. He could do this in letters, but face to face? His dad would know everything now.

And he knew Dad would *say* he was proud of Kenny anyway. But Kenny knew that, inside, more than anything else on this earth, Reverend Davenport wanted a son who rose above the average man and soared in excellence. Whether it be as a reporter, a soldier, a doctor didn't matter to his father. What mattered was the magnitude of help to humanity. God created each of us to serve, to give—his father had made sure he'd known this. Each man's role in life was to follow in the footsteps of Christ. And writing macaroni stories did not reach that mark.

Kenny eyed the girl standing next to him, supporting him. He knew Rosalie couldn't understand all this, but she seemed to care, and if she did, he would let her in. He'd tell her what was really going on in his heart. But not today. Now he had the macaroni man's story to write, and then, he'd visit his father. And beneath all his trepidation, a trace of joy over seeing his dad stirred.

Finally, Kenny's bus wrangled to the curb, its brakes screeching. "Thank you, Rosalie. Thank you for telling me he's here. And thank you for—being a friend. I'll see you soon, I hope?"

"Yes. I'd like that. And Kenny." She gripped his sleeve, hindering him from stepping away. "Your father *is* proud of you. It wasn't hard to tell. You need to know that." She released her grip, and Kenny advanced toward the bus.

Passengers boarded as Kenny stole one last moment with Rosalie. "See you soon?"

She nodded, then perked up. "I almost forgot. He's at the naval hospital in Lake City."

"You comin', mister?" the bus driver called.

"Coming." Kenny stepped toward the door. "I'll visit him tonight. I'll be seeing you!" He climbed the stairs as the door squeaked closed.

"Kenny!" Rosalie's voice sounded from the street, and Kenny raced to an open window, peering down at her at the curb.

"What is it?"

"He said to give you two more messages!" The bus began to move, and Rosalie ran alongside. "The first one is, he loves you!"

The bus gained speed, and Rosalie lagged a bit behind.

"What's the second message?" Kenny shouted.

"Meet me at the plant for an interview tomorrow at one o'clock, and I'll tell you!"

* * * *

Kenny's steps had been light as he left his interview with Mr. Merlino. Writing a softball macaroni story didn't seem to matter anymore. Rosalie was willing to be interviewed, which meant he'd be able to write bigger, better stories soon. More than that, she cared for him.

Yet Kenny's buoyancy sank as he strode up the sidewalk toward the military hospital. A hint of breeze ruffled his hair, and a misty rain fell. Wiping away water droplets from his forehead, he hurried up the front steps. He stepped inside the doorway and paused. The hall was nearly empty. Only a few nurses bustled around with dinner trays. His stomach growled, but he ignored it. He removed his hat as he approached the nurses' desk.

"Can I help you?" The middle-aged nurse lifted tired eyes, brushing a strand of graying hair back under her white nurse's cap.

"Andrew Davenport's room, please."

"Are you family, sir?" she asked, eyeing his camera bag. "Only family is permitted."

"Yes, I'm his son." Kenny patted his bag. "Just came from work. Is he doing okay?"

"As good as could be expected. It was a hard journey, and the injury—it's not something one could recover from overnight." Sympathy laced her eyes, and Kenny also saw questions. He imagined anxious parents normally came to check on their sons, not a son to check on a father.

"He was sleeping last time I peeked in." She pushed back her chair from the desk and rose. "We're keeping his dinner tray in the kitchen, but if you'd like us to wake him…maybe we can make you a sandwich too."

"No, no. Don't wake him." Kenny's fingers balled tightly. "He probably needs his rest."

She nodded and then turned and hurried down the hall, pausing at the last door on the left. Then she looked back over her shoulder. "Oh, it makes sense now," she whispered. "You must work for the *Tribune*. The first thing Mr. Davenport did when he arrived was ask us to find all the old papers we could. We had a large stack, saving them for the paper drive, you know."

Kenny forced a small smile, but inside he felt as if he'd been sucker-punched in the gut. Even though he wrote his father nearly every day, he rarely sent clippings. He'd wait to write a real story before he did that. He struggled to swallow down the emotion rising in his throat. Now Dad knew what Kenny's stories consisted of—celebrity visitors to Seattle and cute local stories. Dad saw that his hopes for a son who would fight for victory with the pen were nothing but misplaced ideas. Kenny's writing hadn't helped the war effort one bit.

"Feel free to wait around until he wakes up, if you like." The nurse's voice was soft.

Kenny quietly stepped into the room, purposefully focusing on his father's face. His hair looked grayer than Kenny remembered. His face paler. His cheekbones more prominent. Did their country realize it had taken the last of his father's good years? Taken his...

Kenny's gaze moved down his dad's body to his legs. His right leg looked the same as it always had, but the left...ended just below the knee. Kenny sucked in a breath and leaned back against the wall. A stream of tears pushed past the rims of Kenny's eyes, and he quickly wiped them away. Sad tears. Angry tears. Ashamed tears.

He moved to the chair, but it was occupied with a stack of newspapers open to his articles—every one. Victory Square, with the photograph of Rosalie and Kenny on stage with Lana Turner, topped the stack. It only made sense since his dad had already met Rosalie. He wondered if Dad liked her, approved. She was so different from the church girls back home.

His dad stirred slightly, a low moan escaping his lips. A heavy weight, confusing and arduous, settled on Kenny's chest. His dad lay before him, softly snoring, unlike the wild roars he used to unleash to the rafters—and neighbors—at home. A part of Kenny wanted to wake him, look in his eyes, and see the acceptance and love he so longed for. And then spend the afternoon playing checkers, laughing about old stories, and sharing their dreams for the future. He'd missed his father so deeply over the last two years.

But the weight restrained Kenny from acting on his desire, because he dreaded a disappointed gaze even more. Holding his position, he waited, but Dad didn't wake.

After a moment, Kenny pulled his notebook from his shirt pocket. *I'll leave a note, so he'll know I was here. He obviously needs to sleep.*

> *Dad,*
>
> *I came by but you were sleeping. I'll stop in again tomorrow or maybe the day after. It's good to know you're here—safe on American soil. I'll call Mom and let her know. I can picture her excitement. I'll tell her you've already met my girl too. That'll really get her excited.*
>
> *I love you, Dad, and I know you'll be up and around in no time. I'm proud of you.*
>
> *Your son,*
> *Kenny*

Kenny glanced over his words, wondering if he should say more. He padded to the bed and gently touched his father's strong hand. Memories of those hands flooded his mind.

"And I'll work to make *you* proud," Kenny whispered.

* * * *

The next day Rosalie's paintbrush swished a coat of white paint over the dining room wall at Tilly's house. Beyond the room, many of her soon-to-be housemates' voices echoed across the wood-paneled hallway. A crew of them had gathered in the kitchen, wrenches in hand, to replace a rusty pipe. If they could pound out B-17 bombers in record time, surely a rusty pipe wouldn't defeat them.

As brilliant white covered over dingy yellow paint, Lanie hustled into the room from the front living room, her hair tied up in a yellow bandanna. "There you are."

From the look of her pristine work getup, Lanie wasn't planning on getting her hands dirty. Rosalie glanced across the room at the grandfather clock, its face the only part uncovered by sheets. She'd need to leave in fifteen minutes to catch the bus.

"Yes, here I am. Busy at work. Trying to get the house all ready for us to move in." Rosalie forced a grin, reminding herself this house was a gift, and it didn't really matter that some people put in more work than others. Rosalie gave one last stroke and then placed the paintbrush in the tray next to the can.

"I've been wantin' to talk to you." Lanie leaned on a chair, her manicured finger accidentally plunging into a plop of paint. She wiped it on the sheet covering the table, then tilted her head. "I heard from my brother stationed on the same base as Iris's husband, Jake. I was talking to him, and it seems Jake has a girl down there. I just don't know how to tell Iris."

Knowing Iris was a few feet across the hall in the kitchen, Rosalie shook her head and waved her hands. But it was too late. A loud clang sounded from the kitchen, like a pipe dropping to linoleum. Rosalie's heart fell.

Rosalie left Lanie and raced to the kitchen. Confusion lurked in Iris's eyes—along with disbelief. Birdie stood next to her like a protective pit bull.

Footsteps approached, and Lanie peered in. She moved to Iris and took her hands. "I'm so sorry," she said, her Southern accent dripping with remorse. "I didn't know you were here. I never would've—"

"Lanie! How could you repeat such things?" The words spurt from Birdie's mouth.

Lanie's head jerked away from Iris toward Birdie. "I just wanted to figure out how to talk to her about it." She stood taller, her voice firm but not harsh. "I was hopin' Rosalie could help."

Iris pushed away from Lanie, her hand rubbing her forehead. "What did you hear, exactly?"

Everyone looked at Lanie, whose shoulders slumped. "My brother said he saw Jake keepin' company with a beautiful English lady. I didn't even know it was your husband, until he told me the fellow's last name, and that he was married to a motorcyclin' parts carrier in Seattle. I'm sorry. I can't imagine how you must feel."

"Hold on a second." Stepping forward, Rosalie eyed Lanie. "You say your brother *saw* Jake with this woman?"

Lanie's eyes flit upward, and she coiled a strand of hair around a finger. "I think so. Or was it his friend who saw him?" She scrunched her lips together. "Does it really matter?"

Rosalie knew Iris and Jake had struggled in the past. This kind of rumor would kindle doubts Iris already had about her marriage. And for Lanie to even bring it up when the evidence was so weak was another example of Lanie's lack of common sense—or was it sheer spitefulness?

Placing a hand on Iris's back, Rosalie kept her gaze on Lanie. "You should've been more careful, talking about this kind of thing." Lanie's eyes drooped, and she looked at her hands, so Rosalie softened her voice. "I suppose you didn't mean to hurt Iris."

With a quick turn, Rosalie focused on Iris. "Listen." She grasped her friend's shoulders. "It's only a rumor. Lanie doesn't even know who exactly saw them. Maybe she was someone he worked with, or a friend's wife. There could be a hundred reasons he was seen with her, if he even was. You know how rumors are."

"I know, but—" Iris's chin quivered, and she lowered her head. "I guess I'm not surprised. I mean, the way things have been lately. It could be true, Rosalie."

"No. There's no reason to think it's true until you know for sure." Rosalie thumbed away a tear on Iris's cheek. "Keep your chin up, hon.

Keep smiling. Be the strong woman I know you are. We'll find out the truth, and then we'll work it out."

Birdie sidled up next to her. "That's right. We'll be with you whatever happens. But I don't think it's true."

Clara joined in the hug. "We're on your side."

"Miss Madison?" A male voice broke the girls from their moment and caused Rosalie to jump. She looked up to spot Phil from the lumberyard standing in the doorway where Lanie had stood a moment before. Lanie was nowhere to be seen.

The man cleared his throat, removed his cap, and twisted it in his hands. "I'm sorry to interrupt, but can you spare a few minutes?"

"Of course." She gave Iris's shoulder one last squeeze.

Rosalie hurried toward the waiting man. She led him through the dining room, where Lanie had picked up the painting where Rosalie had left off.

"I need to talk to ya about the roof," the man said as they moseyed through the living room. "Wanna follow me outside?"

Reaching the front yard, they swiveled and gazed at the house. "You've been doing a swell job cleaning up the inside, but there's a bigger problem." He pointed toward the roof. "You're going to have to replace it."

"Replace the roof?" Rosalie shook her head.

"Yep, and the attic. Too much dry rot up there."

Rosalie's hand moved to her chest, remembering the time she'd dangled from a hole in the attic. Thank goodness Kenny'd saved her. "I tried to clean up the attic and almost broke my neck. There's no way I'm going up there again—and especially not to the roof. How can I ask my friends to?"

"We have folks who can do that. Skilled carpenters a little too old to join the military."

"But we have no money. Almost all of our materials have been donated, and we've been doing all the work ourselves."

"That's a problem." The man crossed his arms and rocked back on his heels. "Don't know what to tell you. But I wouldn't live in that place with that roof. "

"Well, thank you, I'll have to talk to the others and the owner." Even as she said the words the idea of them coming up with any amount of cash seemed impossible. She looked up to see Birdie striding out of the house.

"Hey, sweets," Birdie said, struggling to sound chipper, but obviously still upset by the incident with Iris and Lanie.

"Don't worry. I'll catch up. I just need to talk to Tilly. I need to ask her to pray."

Birdie gave Rosalie a quick hug. "Nothing is impossible with God," she said, and Rosalie wondered how she knew.

Rosalie thanked the man, then headed around the house to find Tilly, who was trying to tame the weeds in her victory garden. As Rosalie approached, she saw that Iris was already there, pouring out her heart.

"C'mon, Rosalie." Tilly patted the patch of dirt beside her. "I can see from your face you've received some not-so-good news as well."

Rosalie ambled toward them. "Oh, Tilly, I'm afraid after all the work we've done, it's not going to be good enough." She sank to her knees, not caring that she'd be a mess when she got to work. "But I can't stay. Kenny'll be waiting at the plant. Today's the day we're doing the interview."

"Don't worry, Rosalie. I'll give you a ride." Iris attempted to offer a smile.

"See, an answer to your first problem." Miss Tilly patted her hand. "Now with that matter taken care of, let's talk to God and tell Him about the rest...all of it."

Chapter Twenty-three

Rosalie's thighs clung to the worn leather motorcycle seat, and she loosely gripped Iris's waist as her friend zoomed up one of Seattle's many hills. Cool splashes of late-morning air enlivened Rosalie's cheeks, forehead, chin. Summiting the hill, Rosalie felt the metal horse's engine wind down.

Even though the scene was beautiful and peaceful, nothing could settle down her heart. Today was the day she told Kenny she'd do the story.

"Nothing like the view from here," Iris said as she pulled to the stop sign. Iris put her feet down, taking a moment to appreciate the view. Rosalie did the same.

Rosalie scanned the vast valley below. Houses and businesses created color splotches amidst the tapestry of green. "No wonder they call it the emerald city." She allowed a smile. "Oh look, there's the Boeing plant."

"Where?" Iris took off her leather helmet and shook out her brown hair. "I can't see it."

"You know about the camouflage, right?" With a hand on Iris's shoulder, Rosalie inclined her head next to her cheek and pointed. "Right over there. See those houses and roads? They're all fake. That's the airplane plant underneath. They camouflaged the top to make it look like any other Seattle neighborhood."

It was still amazing to her. From the hill—and from the air—no one would guess they were looking at the roof of the Boeing plant. She wondered how long it had taken to build those houses, to create roads and trees, and even place automobiles up there.

Today, Rosalie could relate to the desire to be hidden. On the outside, she appeared her normal strong, all-sufficient self—like the Rosie the Riveter in the posters. But underneath she felt more panicked than when her legs dangled from the attic. In the last day she'd confessed to Kenny that she liked him. He liked her too. More than that, she agreed to the articles. She did it to help him save his job, and she wanted to, but her thoughts kept roaming to unmapped territory—and the more she dreamed about Kenny, the more she longed for a future with him.

So how am I supposed to stay focused during the interview? Like Birdie said, take the time to get to know him. Rosalie's palms began to sweat thinking about spending this week with him. *I really can't dwell on this.* She commanded her thoughts to change course. *I'll be material for the loony bin before we do the first interview.*

"Oh, wow, I still can't tell it's the plant," Iris commented, pulling Rosalie back to the moment. Iris squinted; then a slight smile of recognition emerged. "I've never noticed it from this far away before. Those trees and yards are part of it too?"

"Yep."

"Looks so real. The Japs could never see it from the air."

Iris tried to act like her heart wasn't surging pain and frustration, but Rosalie knew her strong friend's facade was like so many others hurting during this season of national loss. The strong demeanor arose from not wanting to worry those around her, knowing that, for the sake of victory, she must quell her own pain and forge ahead. Iris's heart cries left her like a desert, needing water. Now was the time for prayers, encouragement, hugs.

But Rosalie didn't push. Instead, she spent the ride waiting for Iris's lead. Until she wanted to talk, Rosalie would pray.

Rosalie pointed over Iris's shoulder. "If the Japs did figure it out, those barrage balloons wouldn't let them maneuver close enough to bomb anyway." Rosalie pointed to the large gray balloons in the distance, near the harbor, and she couldn't help but relate to them too. Part of her was filled with hope, which lifted her. But another part wanted to keep herself protected from anything, or rather, anyone who could hurt her.

Iris's situation reminded Rosalie of how quickly something good could turn around.

And keeping herself protected would be harder to do once her name and face were splashed all over the papers.

"Is it true FBI agents live in those little houses?" Iris returned the helmet to her head, tucking her hair up inside.

Rosalie laughed. "I can't imagine they'd let anyone make their digs in a fake town designed to disguise our famous Plant 2 from enemy fire. And I can't imagine *wanting* to live there. Probably just a tall tale someone thought up."

"Oh." Iris's voice softened as if slowed by a hot, oppressive wind. "Just another rumor." Her forefinger found an angry tear and quickly wiped it away. "I'm sorry. You must think I'm such a crybaby." She heaved in a deep breath, palmed her cheeks, and emerged with a brave smile. "Hey, maybe we can move in there if the Victory Heights house doesn't work out."

Iris had meant it as a joke, but a sinking feeling hit Rosalie's gut as she was reminded again of the overwhelming obstacles of getting into the house by the rapidly approaching due date of its scheduled demise. They'd all worked so hard, but would their efforts be enough?

"Ready to go?"

Rosalie nodded and clasped her arms around Iris's waist once more.

Then Iris let out a deep sigh. "If only the enemy flying overhead was the only thing we had to worry about these days."

Rosalie's palm edged across Iris's back as if it were an open wound she didn't want to agitate. Her leather coat felt smooth under her touch. "I can only tell you about the one who dove into the flooding river of my darkness and breathed new life into me. Jesus, my friend. Only Jesus can help us."

The motorcycle growled as Iris shifted it into gear. "I don't have much else to turn to right now." Her eyes zeroed in on the road as the motorcycle tipped to a balanced center, then set off down the hill.

"You can come to church with me tomorrow," Rosalie hollered over the rushing wind and whirring motor. "Since I've asked God to help guide my life, it's not perfect, but I've discovered I can turn to Him. Tilly says church is the best place to learn about God. I'm going with Miss Tilly. You can join me."

"Yeah, I'll consider it," Iris hollered back.

Rosalie prayed her friend would accept the invitation. This morning wasn't the only time Rosalie had walked alongside her friend through marriage heartaches. Seeing how hard Iris and Jake struggled to keep their relationship strong gave Rosalie a real-life education on the difficult journey. And war just made things harder. Maybe Rosalie should take note of that. Maybe she shouldn't hurry things along with Kenny.

Fifteen minutes later, Iris zipped the motorcycle to a swift stop in front of the Boeing gate. Rosalie climbed off the back, then turned to thank her friend.

Before Rosalie got the words out, Iris pointed. "There's that word slinger of yours."

Rosalie turned and followed Iris's gaze, freezing in place when she saw him.

"It's Kenny, isn't it? He's quite the bee's knees in his suit coat and hat," Iris snickered. "Don't see that kind of get-up at the plant every day, I bet."

Rosalie inspected Kenny's back as he stood alongside the queue of bandanna-clad women waiting to show their IDs and pocketbooks to the check-in guard.

"Yep, that's Kenny." Her stomach churned as an overwhelming fright claimed her. They hadn't talked since yesterday at the bus stop, when their attraction and care for each other had been so evident.

Iris waited, a tease growing in her smile.

"I'd recognize him anywhere." Rosalie forced a chuckle. "Even his back."

"I bet you would." Iris's lips nipped together, and her eyes grinned. "Well, I'm off to work."

Thank you for not teasing me, Iris. Rosalie heaved in a breath. "I'll be praying for you today." She gave her friend a quick hug.

"Thanks." Iris revved the engines, then zoomed away.

Gazing at Kenny, excitement embraced Rosalie. *Kenny's here. It's going to be a good day.*

But following those thoughts rushed in a blitz of doubts. *I'll be in the paper. People will recognize me in public. They'll want to talk to me.* Worries whipped at her heart.

She placed a hand on her stomach, attempted to breathe in her Rosie the Riveter courage, and then marched forward to where Kenny stood. The laughter and chatter of ladies lining up for work filled her ears.

"Maybe the articles will encourage more women to join our ranks." Birdie and Iris had both mentioned that. By letting Kenny into her own little world, she'd also be informing King County residents of the struggle of women workers. Tens of thousands of people would better understand the hard work women put in, their struggle with housing, and the other numerous issues they faced on a daily basis.

She approached Kenny and eyed the white collar of his work shirt. *My hands felt that fabric. I breathed in his musky scent.* The memory of his cologne ushered in yesterday's flowering emotions like a waterfall, washing over her. There was too much going on inside to understand. She didn't try. Instead, she kept her eyes on his broad shoulders.

In her mind's eye, she drifted next to him and slipped her hand in his, like she was his gal. But as soon as that picture emerged, she shook her head and shooed it away.

Instead, she brushed her palms on her pants, then folded her arms over her chest. *No, Rosalie, he's here to interview you—not so you can make beautiful music together.*

She took in a deep breath, preparing to greet him, when she saw that he was already engaged in conversation.

Rosalie's eyes flitted past him to Lanie, whose eyelashes fluttered as she maneuvered herself nearer to him, giggling. Even worse was the smile on Kenny's face as he seemed enthralled by her story.

Jealousy nipped at Rosalie's heart.

Why would she flirt with Kenny, both now and at the diner, but show interest in Nick as well? Rosalie eyed the girl's innocent features. She couldn't possibly intend to cause pain, but she needed to be more careful.

Birdie caught sight of Rosalie first. Her pretty head popped up as she waved. "Hiya, Rosalie!"

A skipping breeze whisked Kenny's light-brown hair across his forehead as he swung his gaze over his shoulder. Catching sight of her, his dimple appeared. His eyes took her in as she ambled toward him. "Hi, doll."

Doll? Birdie's and Lanie's eyes rounded, and Rosalie's neck heated up. She rubbed her palms together and flashed an equally playful grin his direction. "Hi, dear. Sort of dressed wrong for a day like today—all prettied up and such." She playfully walloped his arm. "Are you ready for the hardest workday of your life?"

He opened his mouth and then closed it, as if unsure what to say. Then he merely nodded. Lanie may try to flirt, but Rosalie could clearly see Kenny only had eyes for her.

* * * *

Kenny passed through the gate, and his heartbeat quickened as the sounds of women at work filled the large building. Women talking. Machines making all types of racket. Huge rows of plane parts lined up. The scents of metal, and the heat of iron joining iron.

Kenny followed Rosalie to her boss's office.

"Do you promise not to expose any manufacturing secrets in your articles or photos?" Mr. Hawkins growled in a surprisingly quiet voice.

"Yes, sir, I promise. My father—well, he just returned home after losing a leg to the Japanese. I'm not going to give those Japs one smattering of information to help their cause."

"You're a good boy. I normally don't let reporters in, but your boss Bixby was convincing. He promised you'd provide good publicity—and the prospect of new recruits."

"Yes, sir, of course."

"And I can't let you be with Rosalie here, as she works—much too dangerous for the likes of you—but she can give you a tour."

Kenny noted the glimmer of amusement in Rosalie's eye. She liked the idea that Mr. Hawkins thought her work too dangerous for a soft reporter.

"Of course, I understand."

He walked out of Mr. Hawkins' office with a guest pass in hand and followed Rosalie down the hall. He eyed the other women who walked alongside her. Pride and respect were clear on their faces. He could see they felt Rosalie wasn't just one of them. She was tops in their book. Kenny pulled the small notebook from his shirt pocket and jotted down notes.

The truth was, if he'd been attracted to her before, it was nothing like the feelings that surged through him now. Kenny had always thought he'd marry a sweet church girl someday—the kind who wore pastel dresses and wide-brimmed hats. That type of girl no longer interested him. He'd take a hard-bodied riveter any day. He placed a soft hand on Rosalie's lower back as they walked together. More than anything he had to suppress his longing to pull her aside and kiss those delicious lips. Boeing Airplane Company seemed like the perfect place for a first kiss.

The previous night, as he lay in bed, he'd convinced himself that to make his boss happy, he'd have to go slow. To make sure he didn't mix business with pleasure.

But now that he saw her slim form again and felt the tenderness of her presence, the idea he'd settled on of going slow in their relationship bugged out the escape hatch. Yet, he'd have to tug it back, at least for now, while *on* the job.

Rosalie paused at the door to the locker room. "Wait here, okay? I have to go powder my nose."

"Uh, sure."

She scampered inside and Kenny scrutinized the immense room. The plant's thunderous hum amazed him the most. And he figured the noises would pierce even louder when distinguished from each other in the various work areas. But from his spot at the entrance, the clashing sounds combined into a deep rumbling that vibrated his gut.

A herd of weary workers, peppered with both men and women, slogged toward the time clock. Kenny figured it was the end of their shift. A burly man with a bulging middle along with a skinny, younger fellow straggled behind the crowd.

"I don't know if we'll ever live it down, Pop," the younger one, apparently the other man's son, said. "At least ten ladies who weren't here the day we gave the official apology demanded payment from me today. Are we going to have to keep apologizing forever?"

The older man shrugged. "I know how you feel, George."

A couple women, one with short red hair and the other donning a flower-patterned bandanna, apparently overheard and tramped back toward the men.

"Hey, Bill, hey, George," the redhead said. "I can answer that question for you. You'll apologize until you've spoken to every woman on every shift. That's what you promised our Rosalie and Birdie." She glanced at her friend. "Isn't that right, Em?"

Her friend nodded. "That's right, and hey, I didn't get my apology yet. Did you?"

The redhead shook her head. "Nope."

Both the men's shoulders slumped, their eyes rolled, and exasperated sighs flowed.

"Fine," Bill said. "We're very sorry we treated you women like you weren't as good at working here as the men."

George repeated his father's words in the same rote tone. Then they moved toward the time clock.

Kenny, watching it all, swelled with an unexpected pride. Those women spoke so highly of his Rosalie. He already thought of her as his girl, but seeing her respected and admired strengthened his connection.

Just then he noticed Rosalie, who'd been hidden by the other workers. She sauntered to Bill and George.

"Hey, you two." Her eyes held their feistiness but also displayed sincerity. "I hope if you say that enough times it might actually sink in."

Bill and George rolled their eyes and stomped past her.

Rosalie's eyes searched, and when they landed on Kenny, she smiled and pointed toward the time clock.

Walking amidst the other workers, Rosalie smiled and laughed as they praised her, then a couple began pointing his direction. Kenny relished the pink that rose to her cheeks, the sparkle in her eyes.

Kenny approached, taking a photo as she lined up with the others, preparing to clock in. "Well, this is where it begins," she said.

"How many times have I seen this building from the outside? A thousand. But it feels so much bigger in here." He looked up. All the way up. The height of the ceiling alone made him feel like an ant in a sandbox.

"I don't think about it much anymore, but when I first started…" She eyed the huge room and let out a big breath. "Wow."

He again pulled out his notepad and took notes. "Who works up there?" he asked, pointing to the scaffolding.

Instead of answering him, Rosalie eyed the notepad. Her eyes tittered with nervousness.

He guessed he knew the problem but tried to play it off, sidling up to her. "What's eatin' you, doll?" He smiled and then shrugged. "I must really appear like a reporter today, huh?"

She nodded.

A childlike trepidation lingered there, and he longed to comfort and reassure her. "Can I tell you something before we get started?"

Rosalie glanced at the clock. "We have five minutes." Her fingers jostled the timecard, and she granted him a weak smile.

"You seem to know your onions about reporters. I'm not sure what your particular beef is, but I'd guess shady word jockeys populate every newspaper in every burg in the country."

Rosalie slanted to the side, her shoulder resting against the wall.

Kenny propped an elbow on the time clock. "I've met fellows who'll publish a story for their own gain, not caring one iota about the masses they leave bloodied along the way. But doll," he saturated his gaze with as much sincerity as he could, "I'm an honorable man."

He remained silent for a breath, hoping his words would sink into her heart, her being. "I'm a skilled reporter, yes. But I wouldn't hurt, or use, anyone for a scoop." He retained his steady gaze but also curved his lips in a smile meant to console. "I hope you can trust me as a friend and as a reporter."

Rosalie's shoulders visibly relaxed. "I know you're an honorable man, Kenny. It's not that. I should have told you this before, but part of the reason I have a problem being in the paper is that when people approach me, I'm not sure how to act or what to say. More than that." She lowered her voice. "I want to trust you—and I'm learning to—but my father, you see, is a reporter…somewhere. And, well, he's not a very good man."

A mouthful of air fled Kenny's lips. No wonder she hesitated to be interviewed, to trust him. But she did it anyway, despite a valid, deep soul ache. "You're wonderful, Rosalie Madison. Thank you for doing this article. I'm sorry I pushed you."

Rosalie shook her head. "No. You were very patient. I'm nervous about this, for many reasons, but—" Her eyes glimmered. "I want to help encourage women to join our bandanna brigade so we can pound out the Flying Fortresses." She paused and looked at the poster hanging on the wall. Kenny followed her gaze. One side of it said 1778 and showed early patriots marching in line with muskets in hand. The other side said 1943 and showed today's modern soldiers in their dark brown wool uniforms. The caption at the bottom of the poster read: AMERICANS WILL *ALWAYS* FIGHT FOR LIBERTY.

"I want to do it to help the fight. So our boys can come home. Plus, you never know how God could use your articles, Kenny." She grinned. "That's what Birdie said, so it must be true."

"Must be." He didn't want to argue, but he hoped from now on—because of her—that would be the case.

Rosalie moved back to the clock and clicked in her timecard. "C'mon. What're you waiting for?" She threw a nod toward the tool shop.

"Waiting for nothing. I'm ready to be taken through a day in Rosalie's life."

"Don't you mean 'Seattle's Own Rosie the Riveter'?" She cringed as she said the words—or at least most of her did—but he also noticed a glint in her eyes he hadn't seen before.

"I wasn't going to use that term. You're a little sensitive." Kenny squeezed her arm. "By the way, you never told me the other message from my dad."

An embarrassed flood of red rushed to Rosalie's face. She seemed to lose her words, but then a playful defiance danced over her eyes. She lifted her head with pride. "He said to tell you he likes your new girl."

Kenny shook his head. "Well, doll, why wouldn't he?"

Chapter Twenty-four

....

Rosalie and Kenny laughed as they walked, and with each step Kenny's reassurances about being an honorable man solidified in Rosalie's heart, like clay forming up into a beautiful vase, ready for use.

After yesterday's mutual confessions of affection, Rosalie's overwhelming, almost giddy hope had become tangled with an irksome fear. Trusting a reporter meant breaking free of chains that tied her to her past, and even though she knew Kenny wasn't like her father, the memories still restrained her, slowed her readiness. Despite her burgeoning trust in—and formidable attraction to—the handsome reporter, she still had reason to clamp back her feelings. At least until she told him about Vic. Told him everything.

Her guilt for betraying Vic, not loving him, and postponing their wedding no longer enslaved her. But like an unwelcome visitor, it sometimes wormed its way into the rooms of her soul. Praying, reading the Bible with Tilly or Birdie, and receiving the Word at church chased the waves of guilt away. But still, she needed to come clean with Kenny about her errant past. She couldn't be sure if his feelings were based on a true understanding of who she was until she did. And now that she relished every moment his eyes searched hers, she really had no choice. Her stomach churned with a preview of how it might feel if he couldn't accept what she'd done. She'd be disappointed, certainly, but it was better to know—and hiding it from him was not an option.

She glanced at him strolling beside her. Soon they'd have that talk, but now she'd delight in the moments together. Her pulse kicked up its pace in anticipation, happy to share her passion with him—her awesome privilege to help construct the world's greatest airplane, the Flying Fortress.

Kenny walked beside her, jotting notes in his reporter's pad. "This place really hops." His gaze shot around the massive floor, gathering facts and filing them away.

Reaching the tool shop, Rosalie's gaze arced around her scope of vision. The plant was too vast to view one end to the other, but at every angle her eyes accessed, people were hard at work. Middle-aged and young, men and women—all worked with speed, focus, and precision.

"Yeah," Rosalie agreed as she received her riveting gun from Ralph and pivoted back to Kenny. "That's how we get it done. A lot of hard workers here. Patriotic workers."

A transport car zipped by, its miniature engine whirring like a child's rendition of a race car.

"What's that?" Kenny asked. "Looks like one of those motorized carts they used on the golf courses before the war." His pencil was poised to jot down the answer.

"That's a transport car. They use it to carry supplies, tools, and workers around the plant. There's a whole fleet of them."

Kenny silently scribbled, and Rosalie clutched his arm to jostle his attention. "All right, Mr. Reporterman, my assignment for today is the fuselages, which is actually great, because it's all the way on the other side of the plant. We can take one of the transports, but I thought if we walked you could see more."

"Certainly, ma'am, whatever you think." Kenny's businesslike tone rattled her but also ignited a new level of respect. She'd looked forward to flaunting her skills—just a smidge—but as she watched him, she wondered if she would be the one who'd be impressed.

They advanced over the shining concrete floor. "These floors are glazed every night to prevent dust from clogging the precise parts in the airplanes." As they paced by the different areas of the plant, she continued to bat her gums as fast as a propeller, unleashing a flood of facts.

"When we get to the row of airplane bodies, I'll point out where Helen Keller stood." The sounds of the machinery were so loud she almost had to yell in his ear for him to hear her.

"Helen Keller?"

"Yeah, they helped her climb a ladder and she fingered the rivets."

"I didn't know she came here." He whistled, impressed. "You, my dear, are full of information."

"Hey." Rosalie's heart pranced with the fun of sharing this with him. "This is my thing."

Kenny chuckled.

Rosalie grabbed his arm. "Okay, and get a loada this. Even more nifty than Helen Keller. In that very room over there—where they're sticking skins onto steel—President Roosevelt visited." She crossed her arms and tilted her head proudly.

Kenny's eyebrows raised and his left eye squinted. "I guess that's impressive. Did you meet him?"

"Well, no," Rosalie protested. "But he was here. And I even worked on the plane he touched."

Cheekiness twinkled from his eyes. "But did you ever talk to the Macaroni Man of Capital Hill? You're nobody until you rub shoulders with Mr. Merlino."

Rosalie quieted her voice. "Oh, you're right. That's big noodles there." Her shoulders squeezed to her ears and she threw him an "Aren't I funny?" grin.

"You silly girl." Kenny shook his head and smiled. "I think I'm gonna keep you around." Then, abruptly, his eyes flitted from hers as if trying to decipher a sound. "Is that music I hear?"

Rosalie nodded. She'd looked forward to surprising Kenny with this. "Before we go to the airplane bodies—" She strode to the meeting room and stole a look inside, then called Kenny to the door.

She opened it just an inch and put her ear to the opening. "*When der Führer says we is de master race, we heil, heil right in der Führer's face,*" voices inside sang. Rosalie recognized the song from the Donald Duck cartoon she'd recently seen at the pictures, and a giggle bubbled up from inside her.

"I wanted to show you this. Boeing brings in musicians from all around Puget Sound, and beyond. Once we had Dizzy Gillespie to entertain us—keep us happy little riveters," she explained. "They come play for us on our lunch hour." She opened the door wider. Take a peek."

They shuffled closer and heard a sizzling bass line booming the song's undercurrent. Kenny glanced inside, and his eyes lit up with recognition.

"Nick!"

Nick threw a grin as he and the band jammed a new tune.

Kenny shifted to Rosalie. "Even though we're roommates, I haven't talked to him in days. He's always asleep when I leave—or gone to The Golden Nugget—and then he works nights at the clubs. Never thought I'd see him here."

"Well, I'm glad I could surprise you. We'll have to come back at lunchtime. I think Lanie's going to sing. She's in the Flying Fortress Quartet. Did you hear her on the radio?"

At Lanie's name, Kenny's forehead furrowed, but he kept his smile. "Uh, no, but I heard she was going to be on. She came by the paper the other day."

Rosalie threw a glare. "She did?" How much was that girl going to flirt with Kenny? Especially now that she was engaged to Nick?

A pleased glint passed through Kenny's gaze. "Apparently her uncle works at the *Tribune*. She was visiting him."

Nick winged a swinging lick on his bass, and Kenny eyed Rosalie. "Did you know they're engaged?"

"I heard—can you believe it? What I'd like to know is why's she always flirting with you—" She stopped herself, but sadly too late.

Kenny grinned way too big. "Are you jealous, doll?"

"Well," she whined, "I don't like it when she does that. She shouldn't be flirting with anyone if she's engaged." She didn't wait for an answer but marched away from the meeting room with Kenny padding behind.

They finally came to the rows of airplane bodies where hordes of women and men crawled like worker bees. Rivet guns, pounding like hail on a metal roof, deposited thousands of rivets into the skins of tails, bomb bays, and fuselages.

Rosalie'd spent many hours with Birdie and her rivet gun in this room. Four hundred sixty-five Flying Fortresses that she worked on patrolled the skies over Europe and Asia. She told herself not to forget to tell Kenny later how the long hours together had bonded these workers. Even though the repeated pounding of rivet guns prevented them from talking, they'd learned to communicate. And had become tighter than the Seattle Rainiers, or any other big league team.

She eyed Pierre, a French immigrant whose flat feet kept him on the homefront but didn't stop him from working for freedom—for his new country and the old—in the factory. Most men respected Rosalie and the other women. *Most*. Rosalie thought of Bill and George. *But not all*. Rosalie grinned to herself, remembering their embarrassed faces when they had to wander through the plant apologizing. She thought of the incident at the time clock this morning. Their lesson in respect for women continued.

Kenny furiously wrote on his pad, and Rosalie waited till he paused to tap his shoulder. She pointed toward a plane with a section where the skin hadn't been riveted on yet. Through the "window" this created, she spotted a woman riveting supports inside the tail section. The riveter's partner, the bunker, worked on the other side.

Rosalie pointed to the riveter and then to herself. "That's what I do," she mouthed.

He nodded, an impressed smile forming. "Can I see you?" he mouthed, then acted like he was riveting—badly, though.

You don't hold a rivet gun like that.

"I wish you could." She shrugged. "The boss's rules."

After giving Kenny enough time to get a feel for the workings, Rosalie motioned him to the side. "Sorry to leave ya. We'll have to catch up at lunch. Birdie's been waiting for me, and Bullhorn won't let you on the line."

"Bullhorn?"

"I mean, Mr. Hawkins. He—"

The view of two supervisors walking onto the floor halted her words. They walked with their hats in hand toward the line of nose-less gleaming aluminum airplanes. As they passed, the workers halted their riveting guns, their eyes wide with trepidation.

The supervisors sidled up to the bottom of a step ladder, and Rosalie's heart dropped to her gut. Her friend Doris perched on the top rung, working as a bucker.

Doris was oblivious to the many eyes on her as she tucked a light brown lock beneath her floral bandanna, then grasped the metal plate for her partner on the other side of the plane's tail.

Her partner spied the men first, and Doris continued holding the plate, waiting. She finally peered at her riveter, whose eyes must've held an unwelcome message. It was then Doris's gaze shaded. She glanced behind her, and her face immediately registered fear. The supervisor steadied her back as she lowered herself, climbing down the ladder with trembling steps.

Like a silent movie, Rosalie couldn't understand the men's words, but she watched the scene unfold.

Rosalie could see her mouth form the word "No" and her shoulders tremble.

The man wouldn't tell her here on the floor but would take her to the back office.

Motioning to Kenny, Rosalie led him back toward a side hall, where it was quieter. Finally, away from the chaotic noise, Rosalie answered his unspoken question. "That's how they tell you if your man's hurt or—"

Kenny's eyes closed as he nodded his understanding.

"It's not always bad news, but we all dread it."

"Do you know her?"

Rosalie pinched her bottom lip. "Yeah, we work together, and her husband was friends with Vic."

She paused and moved steepled fingers to her lips. She hadn't meant to mention Vic. But now she recognized the uncertainty in Kenny's gaze.

His eyebrows squeezed toward center. "Vic?"

Rosalie's hands dropped to her waist. "My fiancé," Rosalie said, simply, "who passed away. I'll tell you about him. I have a lot to tell, actually." Shedding the Rosie the Riveter strength for a moment, she let her gaze linger on his eyes, imploring him to trust her, like he'd asked her to trust him.

"Engaged?" His voice was drenched with questions, but he didn't ask. Instead, he became the reporter again. He pointed to a section where a dozen women wired radios. "Tell me, uh, about them."

Rosalie understood, as he did, that this wasn't the time to delve into their fledgling relationship.

"It's incredible, actually," she started, speaking slowly, inspecting his reaction. "Many of those women are deaf mutes. Since they use their hands to speak sign language, they have amazing dexterity to work with the intricate wires. Their pastor got them jobs here, and he comes with each one when she's first hired to help her find her way around and get adjusted."

"Interesting." Kenny's gaze was directed at his notebook, but Rosalie knew his mind pondered something else.

His confused disquiet caused panic to rise within her. She thought about explaining it all. More than anything, she wanted to dispel the tension between them, but Birdie was waiting.

Her stomach ached, and she placed a hand over it. The last thing she wanted to think about was rolling up her sleeves and getting to work.

Would her past sins change the way Kenny thought of her? He cared about her, she knew that, but what if this dampened his attraction? What if he was waiting for someone pure, untainted by previous relationships? *Oh, Lord, give us a chance to talk, soon. In the meantime, please help Kenny to trust me.*

Rosalie pressed her fingers against his hand. "I'm sorry I didn't tell you. I promise I'll tell you about Vic. I want you to know."

"Rosalie Madison," a voice behind Rosalie rasped, startling her. She dropped Kenny's hand and swiveled around. Her supervisor's tall frame loomed. He was glowering. Next to him stood another man she'd only seen once before—her boss's boss, Mr. Sterling.

"You've been playing show-and-tell," Hawkins growled. "You need to come to the office."

Rosalie's stomach clenched. Mr. Hawkins had given her permission to show Kenny around. Had she taken longer than she was supposed to? She glanced at Kenny, whose eyes darted between Mr. Hawkins and Mr. Sterling.

The ache in her gut grew as she remembered that she'd been late to work twice in the last few weeks. First, because of Victory Square, and then yesterday, because of lingering at the bus stop to talk to Kenny. Had Hawkins had enough?

"Follow me," Bullhorn said, turning and stomping down the hall with Mr. Sterling by his side. "You may as well come too, Reporter," he called over his shoulder.

Chapter Twenty-five

....

Oh, Lord, she was engaged? Kenny's mind reeled as he followed Rosalie and the two men up the metal stairs racketing under their movement. Did she still brood over a love stolen away before the long years of life allowed it to blossom? Was he just an attempt to fill the gap left open when her fiancé died? Did she even care for him the way he was beginning to care for her? How could he ever compare with a dead war hero that she'd promised to commit her life to?

She said there was "a lot to tell." What did that mean? He needed answers to these and countless more questions. An ache coiled its way through his veins, poisoning his thoughts. Kenny's hand crept to the back of his neck. Tension turned his muscles into stone.

With so many women deeming it their patriotic duty to give the GIs someone to come home to, Kenny should've guessed Rosalie had a past relationship. Perhaps she just wanted to do her part. After all, Rosalie was the most patriotic woman he'd ever met. Peering through Kenny's clouded vision came the image of Rosalie at the USO Club slinging eggs to the hungry GIs.

Maybe she'd just wanted to give Vic the will to survive. Kenny was surprised they hadn't married before he left. Many couples did. Kenny had written one of his "enthralling" articles about the flurry of war brides. The county had even run out of marriage licenses for a while.

Rosalie's deep brown eyes glanced back, full of concern, remorse. And Kenny read in them that she longed to explain her relationship. But even if she did, Kenny still wrestled with the ultimate question: *can I trust her?* He'd just learned about her dad being a reporter today. And then, added to that, she finally clued him in on Vic. Was there anything else she was trying to hide?

A rush of doubts rumbled as echoes from his past. He thought about Alicia. He considered the many ways he'd been lied to before.

But also stirring inside were the memories of how Rosalie was different. He remembered Rosalie's red face as she swallowed air after racing to tell him his dad was here. He considered her patience when he snapped at her. He remembered the pride of her friends as they'd gazed at her this morning.

Alicia didn't possess half of Rosalie's strength, courage, heart. None of the reasons Kenny esteemed Rosalie had changed because she'd once given her hand to another.

As he whiffed in the lingering rose scent that trailed behind Rosalie and viewed the dark curls that sneaked from beneath her bandanna, Kenny's coiling doubts ebbed. *Who am I to judge Rosalie's past relationships?*

She cared about Kenny. He didn't doubt that. But would his love always be compared to that of a guy long gone?

He hoped not.

* * * *

Rosalie's heartbeat drummed against her chest. Bullhorn stomped up the stairs in front of her, and Kenny skulking behind—questions unanswered—made her feel like the steel waiting in between Birdie's bucker and her own rivet gun. For now she'd focus on Mr. Hawkins.

Supervisors escorted workers to the offices for many reasons—mostly to give demerits or bad news, like with poor Doris. Rosalie didn't have any loved ones overseas—anymore—so she assumed she'd done something wrong.

But what? Was it her recent rash of tardiness? Rosalie grasped the cold railing as she hiked up the steps. *Surely Mr. Hawkins is not giving me another demerit for taking too long with Kenny today.* She examined her memory as if she were inspecting her riveting job.

Did I do anything wrong? Nothing. She couldn't think of anything.

She sighed and followed Mr. Hawkins and Mr. Sterling, but rather than lead her to the supervisor's office, he passed it, entering the conference room instead. Rosalie stole a glance through the window on the door of the office as she passed. Doris sat curled in a chair, shoulders trembling, pink hands covering her face. A sob rose in Rosalie's throat. *Dear Lord,* she started to pray, but everything she wanted to say felt trite. *Help her...help her.*

Shifting her gaze back to Mr. Hawkins's bald head, another question gushed to mind. Why'd he let Kenny come? She gripped her hands into fists and grimaced at her palms' chilly sweat. If she was reprimanded, she doubted that Kenny would write about it, but just knowing that he knew was bad enough.

Yet all that was nothing compared to her desperation to smooth things over with Kenny. The room faded slightly, and she told herself to stay strong.

Lumbering into the conference room, chin held high to camouflage her fear, Rosalie gasped out loud when she saw two other bigwigs waiting in the room. They stood as she entered, and Mr. Hawkins joined them on the other side of the table. She recognized one—a stout, gray-haired man with bushy eyebrows—as Mr. Sterling's boss, Mr. Stafford. She didn't recognize the other man. His long fingers twirled an unlit cigarette. He reminded her of the actor Edward G. Robertson, shifty with his hair combed back. Rosalie snuck a gander at Kenny, but he looked as confused as she felt.

"Sit down." Mr. Sterling pointed to two seats opposite the suits.

Rosalie sank into the hard chair, and the men sat down. She palmed over the nicks in the wooden table, then moved her hands, still damp with cold perspiration, to her lap.

Kenny sat next to her, his chair screeching as it pushed in. She sent him a quick non-verbal plea: *Oh, Kenny, please don't be mad at me. Not now.*

Rosalie felt a soft, warm presence on her arm. Kenny's hand. A river of stress, pent up as if blocked by the Grand Coulee Dam, slowly seeped out. Her shoulders loosened as Kenny's hand moved to hers, interlocking fingers and not seeming to care about their clammy state. Feeling his support, Rosalie bustled up her confidence and gazed at the muckamucks gaping at her.

"So." She slid an elbow onto the table. "Are you fellas gonna tell me why you made us hotfoot it up here? My bucker Birdie's waiting for me."

"Well, Miss Madison," Mr. Stafford said, his deep voice echoing around the room. But his bushy eyebrows rose, and his eyes smiled.

"Yes, sir?"

Kenny squeezed her hand, and she sat up straighter. Rosalie's gaze scoped to Mr. Hawkins, and surprisingly, the side of his mouth curled in a grin as well. Then Mr. Hawkins produced a black velvet box.

"We called you here—and we wanted you to see this too, Mr. Davenport—to tell you how proud we are of you." Mr. Stafford's thick fingers folded together as he inclined forward.

Relief warmed her. Rosalie blinked. "What did you say?" They didn't march workers up here to say they were proud of them. She zeroed her stare on Mr. Stafford.

"Not only did you break the national record for most rivets, you've been a model employee since you started. We appreciate that, Miss Madison. You encourage other workers—men and women— and we've noticed how you help with recruitment. Some ladies told us that you even helped them find housing in Victory Heights."

Mr. Stafford's fingers, still folded together, tapped against his hand. "Because of your faithful service to Boeing and your country, we want to give you this." He fired a glance to Mr. Hawkins, who opened the black box, revealing a silver pin.

Rosalie's hand flew to her mouth. The Outstanding Service award was the highest honor a plant worker could receive. She shifted in her chair as a grateful stream of tears lined her face, defying her tough demeanor. She glanced at Kenny.

His lips formed a tight smile, accentuating his dimple. "That's great, Rosa—uh, Miss Madison." Kenny tilted toward her as if he wanted to embrace her but held back.

"Thank you, Mr. Hawkins. Mr. Sterling, Mr. Stafford." She nodded at the fourth man.

For the past year and a half—even before Vic left—her life had centered on supporting the war effort at the plant and everywhere. Then, after Vic died, she'd cast her whole heart, mind, and riveter's biceps into it. For her efforts to be acknowledged was more than she'd ever expected.

Though appreciative for the award, another thankfulness whispered through her mind. One she didn't expect—the realization that the award didn't really matter. *Lord, I'm so grateful this honor doesn't define me.* Six months ago she would've clung to it as absolution for her guilt—though temporary. *Now I know even the most hoity-toity award could never make me worthy of Your love. I'm not worthy, but You love me anyway.*

"You're welcome, Miss Madison. But it's Boeing who wants to thank you." Mr. Stafford nodded. "Right, Mr. Hawkins?"

"Yes, sir." Mr. Hawkins' eyes peered out from beneath his long forehead. "There is that other thing," the Bullhorn's voice rasped.

Mr. Stafford clapped. "Yes, well, this is where you come in, Mr. Davenport. We're hoping the Rosie the Riveter articles will also help with recruitment and promotion of the plant. We want to take advantage of the publicity." He smiled expectantly at Rosalie.

Rosalie's stomach lunged.

"You'll be our proverbial poster girl, Miss Madison." Mr. Stafford's smile deepened, and Rosalie's nausea did too. "Our publicist here, Mr. Burrows, will work with you—"

Kenny edged forward.

"What do you have in mind, Mr. Burrows?" Kenny asked.

"Ho daddy! I'll tell you what we've got up our sleeves." The Edward G. Robertson look-alike next to Mr. Stafford shoved up his white shirt-sleeves as if to illustrate. "I'm talkin' radio, print ads, rallies, and even—" His beady eyes twitched side to side, then back to Rosalie. "A short film," he continued, slapping the table, "to be shown across these United States." His hand swept across the table as if he expected applause to follow.

Rosalie felt cold all over. Not only was she upset by what they were asking, she was horrified that Kenny was going along with it.

She frowned at Kenny, jutting out her lower lip, but he didn't seem to notice.

"We'll take your articles nationwide," Mr. Burrows continued. "Your stories will be read all over the States."

Kenny's nod reminded her that she *decided* to let him write the articles, knowing they would reach many people. She just had no idea it was more than she thought—and this was just the start. A *newsreel? Really?*

"You're a real asset to Boeing, Miss Madison." Mr. Stafford's bulky eyebrows then aimed at Kenny. "And we're expecting you to write a stellar article."

"I will, sir."

All sets of eyes again turned to her, excitement filling their faces.

"Miss Madison," Mr. Stafford said, "do you have anything to say?"

"Thank you, Mr. Stafford," Rosalie managed to choke out, fingering the silver pin. "I'll, uh, be happy to do whatever I can to help."

* * * *

Kenny let out a breath as his black shoe stepped off the stairs onto the plant floor and into the rumbling noise. Then, glancing at Rosalie's forlorn face, he sucked his breath back in. "I'm sorry, doll," he said as they strode back toward the meeting room on the way to the fuselages. "I know a bit of attention is not what you want."

"A *bit* of attention? Didn't you hear them? It's more like an oceanful of attention."

Kenny tipped his head with sympathy. "But you're going to receive a nifty award. That's kind of hipper dipper, isn't it?"

Rosalie's eyes closed, and she heaved in a mighty breath. "Yes, it is. I'm very grateful to receive such an honor. I'll show up at the B-17 rally next week to receive it in front of *all* the thousands of Boeing workers." She opened her eyes wide. "I'll do all the stuff they tell me to do, but—"

"C'mon." Kenny stretched out his palm. "Don't you think it'll be a little fun?"

They reached the entrance to the meeting room.

Rosalie paused and faced him. "I'm going to try my best to enjoy it." Her gaze softened. "And as long as you're with me, I *know* I'll be okay. But"—Rosalie's lips closed, her chest rose and fell—"Vic."

Kenny felt his heart fall as she said the guy's name. Her eyes studied his, and he knew that if he didn't play this right, her attempts to be positive would quickly sink. He'd worry about that later. For now he needed to keep her emotions moving in a positive direction.

"You're worried about that?" Kenny waved a hand in the air. "I'll listen to whatever you want to share with me about Vic, or any of your previous boyfriends—John, Art, Sylvester."

"There weren't *that* many."

"Glad to hear it, but even if there was, doll, you're my girl now." He offered a toothy grin, hoping she'd buy it.

A tiny gasp slipped from Rosalie's lips, and Kenny relished the pink that flushed her face. "Oh, I'm your girl, am I?"

"Of course, and if I could, I'd plant a big ol' kiss on those smackers of yours right now, just to show you."

Rosalie's face turned as red as the stripes on the flag hanging across the wall.

"C'mon, let's have lunch. It's gotta be time." He started walking.

Rosalie skipped to catch up. "What makes you think I'd want to have lunch with a cad like you? Seriously though, *darling*, I don't think I should take a lunch today. I've been off the line all morning. You go grab a bite. The Igloo has a stand inside the canteen. Then watch Lanie and Nick, and I'll find you later. Maybe I can convince Mr. Bixby to let you watch me build the plane that will wipe out the Nazis."

"And the Japanese."

"Of course."

"Okay, but first I need to ask you something." Kenny paused, turning to her.

Rosalie folded her arms. "What?"

"Well, I've been thinking that it's been too long since I've held you in my arms."

Rosalie's jaw dropped. "You never...we never..."

He slapped his leg. "Ha, got you. All I'm asking, doll, is if you'd like to go dancing with me tonight after our shift? I was thinking we could go to Playland. Ride a few rides. Do a little jitterbuggin' in their dance hall." He bopped a rock step. "I've won a few dance contests there myself."

Rosalie's eyes brightened, but then she frowned. "Hmm, should I be stepping out with a scoundrel like you?"

"What? I'm not a scoundrel. C'mon, doll. Say yes."

Rosalie's head tilted back as she laughed. "Of course. I'd love to."

"Great!" Kenny said as he be-bopped to the meeting room.

Chapter Twenty-six

....

"Cotton candy! Thank you." Rosalie's finger brushed against Kenny's as she reached out and received his offer. Kenny settled on the bench of the picnic table next to her, his presence blunting the chilliness that crept up Rosalie's arms. After Rosalie's shift ended, Kenny had borrowed Miss Tilly's Model A and driven Rosalie to Playland, Seattle's amusement park where Fun for All reigned in the boondocks of the city.

The sky's smeared shades, nearly matching the cotton candy's pink hue, now drizzled away into a deep navy. Only the horizon still whispered with the muted light of the earlier colorfest.

Breaking off a bit of the grainy delight, Rosalie plopped it in her mouth, then aimed the puff-topped cone toward Kenny as her morsel dissolved on her tongue.

"How many rides do you think we hit?" Kenny's eyes scanned the park's nightline, which arced around a manmade lake.

"Well, you protected me from plunging to my death on that thing." Rosalie pointed to the rotating Ferris wheel, its lights waltzing on the glassy lake waters. Her head sloped back as she eyed the top. "It's really high."

Kenny's chest puffed out. "Happy to be of service, miss. And I must say, you were very brave on the Dipper. It's even higher than the Ferris wheel."

"Ah, but it goes so fast over the drops and rises I didn't have time to be afraid."

"Not scared, huh?" Kenny's eyebrows crumpled. "You let out a pretty good howl on that wicked turn."

"Screaming's a hoot. It's gobs more fun if you scream. You should try it," she said. "But what I didn't like was that Laff Factory. Walking in through the clown's mouth gives me the heebie-jeebies."

"You looked cute warped in those mirrors."

Rosalie batted her eyelashes. "Gee, thanks. I think the only ride we missed was the Shoot the Chutes. See." She pointed to a ride where pretend logs carried daring patrons down a watery hill, landing with a splash. No logs seemed to be moving at the moment, though. "I guess it's closed. If it opens, we should. It's my favorite."

Rosalie breathed in the blended scents of popcorn, hot dogs, cotton candy, and all the other amusement park treats. A coming-home feeling embraced her. "Did I tell you I worked here in high school? But only during the three weeks when I came to stay at my grandma's place."

"Whata ya know? I worked on my parents' farm, lugging rocks."

Rosalie chuckled. "I doubt that."

"I'm on the level. But the rock lugging—that was only when I needed a punishment. It was effective."

"I can't imagine you ever needing a punishment." She tossed him a sarcastic grin.

Kenny's eyes gleamed. "Oh, I was a handful. Always up to mischief." He reached his arm behind her. Rosalie's shoulder blades quivered when his bicep brushed against them. His warm hand curled around her cool shoulder, and she leaned next to his firm chest.

Another bite of cotton candy melted in Rosalie's mouth.

"I'm glad I'm here." Rosalie caressed his hand on her shoulder. "With you." Over the last few hours their conversation had wound down paths as they each shared about their lives. Often their paths merged. They both liked swimming in lakes, riding bikes on country roads, and, of course, a rip-roaring political discussion.

But sometimes the roads veered apart. Kenny'd traveled to Europe before the war. He majored in literature at the University of Washington. He'd grown up in a Christian family.

As knowledge of him filtered in, Rosalie evaluated each bit.

Would all these pieces fit together to reveal a man she could care about? She nudged closer, her cheek touching his musk-scented shirt. Someone she could love?

Rosalie exhaled. *Love.* Her very essence longed for that. She wanted to go for the ride, racing down it—getting caught up in it—like an avalanche on Mt. Rainier.

Vic had offered his love, yet she hadn't opened it, embraced it. This was different. Kenny was different.

Her attraction to him vastly surpassed anything she'd ever felt for Vic. Her draw wasn't just to his handsome form, but to his honest, kind, godly character. Their conversations—fun or serious, full of friendly disagreement—never lacked vitality.

Rosalie's chest mounded as she hauled in a breath. *Is this what I've always longed for, Lord?* She swallowed. *Am I falling in love?*

But she still needed to tell him about Vic.

Rosalie moved from the warmth of Kenny's embrace and scooted back. She crossed her legs and faced him. "I need to tell you—"

Kenny's strong hands cupped over hers. "About Vic?"

"Yeah. That, and everything." Rosalie slowly blinked her eyes closed. When she looked back up, Kenny's accepting gaze swelled her attraction to him, solidifying her decision to risk spilling out her heart. If he rejected her now, she could accept it, but many more romantic moments like tonight and a rejection would leave her heart in splinters.

"You don't have to." He touched her face with the back of his hand. "But if you want to, I'll listen."

And as the throngs of people revolved around them like the carousel, Rosalie unbolted her heart, releasing all its messiness. Kenny didn't probe or push, just waited as she exposed everything about Vic, how she betrayed him, deceived her friends, the nasty details about her father.

But just like he promised at the plant, Kenny didn't condemn or judge. In fact, he held her hand as she spoke, thumbed away a tear, embraced her.

A breath, like water over a brittle rose, smoothed over Rosalie's heart as Kenny's smile enveloped her. She'd known he promised to accept her. When rational thought won over her wispy emotions, she grasped that his commitment to the unconditional giver of love would prevent him from judging her, rejecting her.

But she hadn't believed it. Not really. Her quiet fears rasped that if he understood the mire of her past, saw every part of it in its raw ugliness, he'd turn his face from her. The loving gaze in his eyes would harden. The admiring grin would straighten. His gentle hands would pull back. And she'd be alone in her self-made morass, blaming herself.

Kenny's warm lips grazed her forehead as she finished, and a grateful, awe-filled joy rushed through Rosalie.

"Thank you for being honest with me," he said. "It makes me like you even more, you know."

So unbelievable. "Really? Why?"

"Because it takes courage to expose our mistakes to the light, but when we do, our Father transforms us, laden by the shambles of our sin, into His beautiful children—like a deserted street child adopted into a king's family. That's why." He enfolded her into a tight embrace, and Rosalie felt as if the burden she carried suddenly lightened under his strong care.

The soft warmth of Kenny's hand roamed over Rosalie's neck, then trailed over her jawline. Rosalie's hands slinked around his waist as her body inched closer, his heat emanating to her chest.

"Is this what love is like?" she dared to ask.

"Yes," he whispered. "It is." Then he cleared his throat. "And Rosalie, I have a surprise for you."

Kenny's head leaned in, and Rosalie closed her eyes. His soft lips pressed against hers, as his fingers raked through her hair. Their lips pulsed in a tender rhythm, and Rosalie's hands traced the muscles of his back. Lost in a fog of desire, Rosalie felt his lips pull away, then heard his voice speak softly.

"That wasn't the surprise."

Rosalie blinked. "What?"

Kenny shifted and straightened his back. His dimple surfaced, along with the grin that melted her. "I have something for you." Swinging his arm from around her, he leaned back against the table and reached into his shirt pocket.

"But I thought the cotton candy was the surprise," she teased, snuggling against him, her hands on her lap, waiting to be held.

"What kind of surprise would cotton candy be? You used to work here. Probably ate it all the time."

"Well, that doesn't mean it's not a killer-diller surprise." She scrunched her shoulders and grinned. "I don't need anything else." She lowered her eyes. "Only you."

Kenny snatched her gaze as he lifted a silver bracelet from his pocket. "Well, you've already got me. But I wanted to give you this." He rested his hand on her thigh, then strung the bracelet across his palm. Three charms dangled from it.

Rosalie eyed his satisfied gaze. "What's this?"

Fast-paced swing music echoing from the dance hall slowed as if in response to Rosalie's contented heart. A familiar woman's voice lilted, "Someone to Watch Over Me," and a double meaning rang to mind. *You're watching over me, aren't You, Lord? And now so is Kenny.* She'd always felt she needed to watch over herself. *It's much richer to let others do it for me.*

"I could get used to this, you know. Letting you care for me."

A child, up past bedtime, squealed with glee as he scurried near them, but Rosalie's gaze continued to dwell on Kenny.

He tucked a stray curl behind her ear, his face still dripping antic-ipation. "I know how worried you are about the publicity mumbo-jumbo for the Rosie the Riveter story. So I got you something to help." He pointed to the first charm.

"A *K* from a typewriter key?"

"That's right. I figured you'll be doing a lot of speaking to people, interviews for magazines and radio, speeches—"

Rosalie sucked in a shaky breath, and Kenny patted her back. "This is a key from my typewriter at work. All my words are created on that typewriter, so I gave you a little bit of it to inspire you. When you get nervous, just tap a finger on the K, and the words'll come."

"Really? Just like that?"

"Yep."

"I wonder why it's a K, hmm?" Rosalie scratched her temple like Abbott. Or was it Costello?

Kenny played along. "It's so you'll think of me, silly."

Nuzzling in, Rosalie returned her focus to the second charm. "Praying hands. I like that one."

Kenny smoothed Rosalie's hair. "My grandma Gerty gave me this when I moved to Seattle. She wanted me to remember that I was in her prayers."

Padding a finger over the beveled charm, Rosalie shook her head. "Kenny, you can't give it to me. Grandma Gerty meant it for you."

"Yes I can." Kenny's bottom lip protruded defiantly. "I called and asked. She said I could give it to you, then asked all about my new girl. If I give it to you, she said, it has to mean that not only am I praying for you, but my sweet grandma is too."

"Okay then, I'll gratefully accept your offer to pray for me." She patted his hand. "I can definitely use it."

"You know, you've encouraged me in the Lord, Rosalie."

"I have?"

"Yes, your openness, your simple trust in Christ's forgiveness. Those of us who've been Christians a long time need to remember the simplicity of Christ's love."

"I don't know what I'd do without it. And I'm learning more every day."

"I can tell." Kenny's gaze fell on the third charm. "Don't you want to know about this one?"

"Of course I do."

* * * *

"Rosalie, there you are!" Birdie's voice split the air, and Rosalie shifted her gaze behind her to the sidewalk, where a half dozen women strolled along with her friend. "We've been looking all over for you. Nick mentioned you might be out here."

Rosalie glanced at Kenny and pouted, saddened that their magical moment was interrupted.

"This better be an emergency," she mumbled. Kenny squeezed her shoulder as if reminding her he wasn't going anywhere.

"Well, it could be." Birdie pulled a folded piece of yellow paper from her slacks pocket. "The telegram arrived a few hours ago. It took some convincing for the delivery boy to let me bring it to you."

"A telegram?"

Mostly bad news was delivered by telegram. Could something have happened to her mother, one of her sisters?

She took it from Birdie and opened it with shaky fingers.

THANK YOU FOR YOUR LETTER STOP
I AM GLAD YOU'RE DOING WELL STOP
I HAVE REMARRIED AND HAVE NO NEED FOR A CAR STOP
PLEASE KEEP IT OR SELL IT STOP
IT IS WHAT VIC WOULD HAVE WANTED STOP
FOR YOU TO BE TAKEN CARE OF STOP

Vic's mom. Rosalie closed her eyes, her heart overflowing with gratitude. She'd never expected Vic's mom to offer such a gift. And the way the dear woman had written the letter, it was like Vic himself offered the car. Well, that's how Vic was—always giving. And for the first time, Rosalie's gratitude for him outweighed her shame over not deserving his kindness. God had guided her through those years, even though she didn't understand it. But Vic knew. He always trusted God's guidance.

Rosalie touched Kenny's hand, which still rested on her shoulder. No guilt over Vic pierced her anymore, not even over falling for another man. Vic would've wanted her to be taken care of—like his mom said.

Skimming the women's questioning faces around her, Rosalie smiled. "Vic's mom is giving me his car."

Birdie clapped. "Oh! That awesome Ford? You'll have so much fun with it."

As Birdie spoke, Rosalie suddenly realized the prayers she'd raised in the Victory Heights garden with Miss Tilly and Iris had been answered. "If we sell the car, we'll have money for the roof."

"Really?" Iris asked, her excitement echoed by a splash from the log ride zooming into the lake. "Do you think we'll be able to finish the house in time after all?"

"I don't know why not."

"Oh!" Birdie did a wiggly jump. "I know someone who wants a car," she spouted. "One of the new welders Clara met."

"That's perfect." Rosalie nodded in agreement, but inside a tiny doubt stirred. She'd have to sell the car, her last tie to Vic. Music from the dance hall grew louder as someone opened the door. Rosalie leaned her head into Kenny's chest. Letting go of the car was okay now. Right. She fingered the bracelet on her wrist.

Iris linked arms with Birdie. "Do you two want to join us at the dance hall to celebrate?" she asked, the two of them rocking into a Lindy twirl.

Rosalie stood, then stretched her hand to Kenny. "What do you think, sir? Would you like this dance?"

He nodded and smiled. "You bet I would."

Chapter Twenty-seven

Rosalie yawned as she slumped into a chair at the wobbly table in the kitchen. She broke off a chunk of an apple-cinnamon muffin left over from Betty's breakfast. Plopping it into her mouth, she savored the taste she'd been waiting for since the sweet aroma greeted her.

Aside from a few creaks upstairs from the two or three ladies still at home, Tilly's Place—the now official name for the home she shared with seven other ladies and two children—rested under a quilt of silence.

Birdie and the others on the swing shift had caught the bus to work, but Rosalie stayed behind. Since the Rosie the Riveter articles had come out, her assignments had changed, and she no longer worked the line.

No more losing myself in the rhythm of my rivet gun. She craved the weary satisfaction after she finished a shift. She missed the camaraderie of not only the girls closest to her, but the smiles, nods, and "you can do it" while walking through the plant. She even missed the smell of the plant—that heated oil scent mixed with metallic and rubber. Rosalie breathed in, sensing it in her memory. It had been like home.

Now interviews, photoshoots, meetings, and public appearances marked the hours of her day. Each step challenged her to press past her insecurities, and downright fears, to put on a "Rosie the Riveter" determined look and press on. Seeing her picture in the *Tribune* or a magazine triggered the most nausea, and she dreaded watching her promo film. She enclosed her fingers around her teacup, warming her hands. Parts of her new position were fun, and the goal of influencing other ladies to join the war effort spurred her to press on.

Eyeballing a pile of eight-by-ten glossies of her far-from-glamorous form dressed in her blue shirt, denims, and bandanna, Rosalie flipped through them.

Ugh, these are so awful. She cringed with each one. *My face looks fat—like Shirley Temple. It's cute on her, but not on a grown woman.* Her stomach burbled at the thought of her image plastered on billboards throughout Seattle—and now they were talking about the whole Northwest.

She still had an hour before the film crew would be there to prep for her commercial to be filmed next week—here at Tilly's Place. She sipped her tea, seizing the chance to let her thoughts unwind. Two weeks had passed since Kenny finished his week-long interview with her. He'd joined her at the plant the whole week, learning more, interviewing other ladies with different jobs—welders, mechanics, electricians. And in the evenings they played. Either hitting the dance spots, but more so, just sipping Cokes and talking.

Rosalie breathed in air, then exhaled. Many more Kenny kisses had joined her collection during that week, along with handholds and gentle embraces. How she'd reveled in his touch and presence. And not just the attention he gave her, but the fact that she longed to give love back. She'd always thought she couldn't feel love—but during that week, with Kenny, she had.

She took another sip of tea, but it was cold. Since he'd finished the interview, Rosalie had barely seen Kenny.

Not a moment slipped by without thoughts of him—more vivid than the photographs on the table. Memories of their good times together caused those butterflies to perform loop-de-loops and nosedives in her stomach. Their sometimes witty, sometimes intense, phone conversations intensified Rosalie's craving to share her moments with him. Fingering the charm bracelet that decorated her wrist, she dreamt of a future wedding. More than that, of waking up next to him every morning, breathing their days and nights together in a happy rhythm.

Before Kenny could explain the third charm, a heart—giggles from a tittering troop of ladies had vibrated the air behind them. They'd pleaded that she and Kenny join them in the dance hall, where Nick's band played.

I thought that voice sounded familiar. Apparently Lanie was now the full-time lead singer. Rosalie wondered what had happened to Nora.

Kenny had clasped the bracelet around her hand and stood. "Since dancing was the original reason we came here," he had jigged a rock step into a spin, then stretched out his hand to her, "do you wanna cut a rug with me, doll?"

Rosalie had placed her hand in his but paused before rising. "I will, but you have to promise to explain the third charm to me—tonight." She touched the cool silver heart.

Kenny gazed into her eyes. "I promise," he had spoken solemnly. "Tonight."

But that had never happened. And even in the week of time together, she somehow never remembered to ask about it. After only a few minutes of dancing, everything changed.

Rosalie closed her eyes and was back there again. She'd been in Kenny's arms in a slow dance, when out of the corner of her eye she'd seen Nick collapse, landing on top of his bass with a reverberating clang. The wound on his thigh had become infected, causing a fever.

They'd only learned later—after the doctor's report—that it had been throbbing, incredibly painful, for the past week. Since the VA wouldn't cover it, Nick had put on a brave face and had kept going.

Her stomach turned as she pushed the muffin away, remembering the sight of Nick's wound as Kenny lifted his pant leg. Rosalie acted as Kenny's nurse as he struggled to bring Nick back to consciousness and clean the oozing wound. Lanie had slouched on the other side, holding Nick's hand, whispering encouraging words to him. Maybe Lanie was sincere in her feelings toward her fiancé Nick after all. With Lanie's help, Kenny finally managed to get Nick to the car. Then Kenny left to drive him to the hospital.

Rosalie had leaned next to the open window of the Model A before he left.

"I'll tell you all about that heart—my heart—soon." Kenny's hand gently traced the shape of her face.

Rosalie closed her eyes, relishing one last touch. "Take care of your friend," she said, blanketing his hand. "The girls will give me a ride home, and I'm sure I'll be seeing you soon enough. Will you call?"

"I promise. I'll call you soon."

After he left, Rosalie had fun with just the girls, but her thoughts always veered back to Kenny—and when she'd see him again.

Well, I did see him a lot that week, but now it's been two weeks, and I've seen him how many times? Twice. Once for a rushed Saturday morning breakfast at The Golden Nugget. And then for a backyard afternoon baseball game with every stray kid in the neighborhood. Rosalie smiled to herself recalling the littlest VanderLey boy scampering around the field—mostly in the wrong direction. Kenny had delighted in the little Dutch boy, grasping his towhead with his large hand and pointing him in the correct direction. Kenny also encouraged the older kids to help the young ones. *He's like a coach to them,* Rosalie thought. *A father.*

On both occasions, with the Rosie the Riveter stories all researched and coming out weekly, Kenny had to leave early to chase after a story. Rosalie understood his work drove him. He'd craved opportunities to army-crawl his way to the top his whole life. He seemed even more driven now that his dad was around, taking it all in with pride. Plus, his visits to his father included touching base with Nick, who was also at the Naval Hospital. Kenny's dad had reined in a favor to get him there, but Kenny didn't know how Nick would be able to pay for the hospital bills.

Rosalie got up to start another pot boiling. Standing at the stove, the warmth of the gas flame radiated to her.

I'm grateful for the time I spent with him, Lord. The kettle whistled, and she replenished her tea. *But I long for more.* She blew on her tea and snickered at herself. *I'm seeing him today.* She smiled as the anticipation of time with him percolated. Later after the film crew left, he'd promised to help her write her speech for the awards ceremony.

"Well, hey." Lanie meandered into the kitchen, jarring Rosalie from her ponderings, and sat down at the chair next to her. Scraping the chair against the hardwood floor, Lanie fingered one of the photographs. "Landsakes, you're gettin' a bushel of attention these days, aren't you?"

"Good morning," Rosalie said with a welcoming grin. Over the last couple weeks, her opinion of Lanie had shifted from suspicion to appreciation. While the other girls slept, she and Lanie passed the midnight hours laughing, talking, and sharing heartfelt feelings—mostly about their men, Kenny and Nick. Rosalie unloaded her heart about feeling neglected by Kenny, and Lanie shared her concern over Nick's health and need for medical care.

Rosalie and Birdie still prayed together before the others woke up, sometimes taking walks around Victory Heights and ending up sitting on the cedar-lined edge of the ravine. She confided in her best friend during these brief morning wanderings, but with Rosalie's new schedule, the rest of their days were spent apart. At the plant, Birdie was partnered with Lanie now.

"Lots of attention I never asked for." Rosalie circled back to the topic. "I suppose I don't mind, though. It's for a good cause, right?"

The sun angling in through the paned windows of the old house gleamed against the glossies on the table.

"Yeah, for your man." Lanie grasped a strand of her shiny hair and twirled it between her fingers.

Rosalie shared her teabag with Lanie, then padded to the stove, returning with the kettle. "For my man?" She filled Lanie's cup. "I like Kenny a lot, but I'm not doing it for him. I'm enduring all this humiliation to help recruit more lady workers to the plant. Get them involved." She sighed as she sank back into her chair. "I hope it's working."

The richness in the colors of the brown wood, Lanie's blue blouse, even the red in her bandanna in the photographs darkened as a cloud swept in front of the sun. Rosalie shivered.

"Well, it's sure helping him." Lanie flared a smile, then scooted her chair back, moseyed to the icebox, and lifted out a bottle of milk, fresh from the Smith Brothers Dairy. "You must be so happy for him. My uncle says since the Rosie the Riveter articles came out, the paper's sales have doubled. Doubled! And Kenny's getting all the big scoops now."

Rosalie rubbed her arms. She wanted to be happy for Kenny, and she really was, but these "big scoops" made up part of the reason he hadn't explained the heart on her bracelet—or shared any more intimate moments with her. She closed her eyes as the memory of his kiss wrapped around her.

Lanie plunked milk into her tea, then poured some into Rosalie's without asking.

"I'm very proud of him." Rosalie took a sip, despite her concern that the milk should be saved for the children. "He's a good writer."

Lanie sipped the daintiest taste, then sat back and twirled her hair again. "Do you think he'll hang around after your articles are done?" She lifted an emery board from her pocket and filed her nails. "I mean, with all these great assignments, once you're no longer the talk of the town," she chuckled dismissively, "he won't have an excuse to talk to you anymore. I know my uncle doesn't want his reporters fraternizing—franchising as he says—with his sources." She puffed dust from her nails and glanced up. "It'll probably put an end to your little fling. Oh, well, right? It's basically over anyway. I mean, when's the last time you saw him?"

Rosalie placed the mug on the table and swallowed. She looked to Lanie's sweet face and suddenly understood. Her father's face filled her mind, but she quickly pushed it away.

Chapter Twenty-eight

Rosalie's stomach sank. The platinum blond's words caused her father's broken promises and abandonment to scratch through her mind, leaving aching wounds along the way.

Would Kenny break her heart like her father had? She picked at a thumbnail. *No,* she told herself. *He's nothing like Pops.* But then, Kenny had broken promises—more than one.

"I promise," he'd said. "I'll tell you about the heart soon." When he backed out, he cited valid excuses—power outage, a factory fire, even a Jap sub spotted in the Columbia River down by the Oregon border.

Pops also had weaved the most convincing excuses. He was good at inventing stories. After all, he was a reporter. *Maybe I shouldn't have trusted Kenny. Oh, Lord, why'd I let myself trust...*

Rosalie strained to push away the doubts, but they still roiled, causing her stomach to ache. Kenny had the best intentions to keep that promise. *He still will. I know he will.*

Lanie must've read Rosalie's struggle because she returned the emery board to her pocket, then reached her arm across Rosalie's photos and lightly gripped her hand.

"Oh dear." Her eyes dripped sympathy. "What was I thinkin'? I shouldn't have said those things. My brain's not kickin' on all cylinders, like my daddy used to say." She made a quirky face. "Of course Kenny will hang around after the stories are done, no matter what my uncle says. Kenny wouldn't leave you high and dry. I can be so insensitive sometimes. I've been prayin' about that."

Rosalie patted Lanie's hand, which was covering hers. "It's okay, Lanie. I know you didn't mean to hurt me, but you should know

Kenny's not like that. He wouldn't hurt me for all the salmon in Puget Sound." Rosalie forced her voice to portray strength, confidence, hoping not only to dispel Lanie's doubts, but also her father's voice gnawing at the borders of her mind. *Not all reporters are like my father.* And, no matter what, Rosalie needed to cling to that truth.

Lanie finished the last swallow of her tea, then ambled to the sink. "I know you're right, Rosalie. I've never seen Kenny behave in any less than an honorable way. He wouldn't hurt you. I'm sure you'll be together again soon." She moved back to Rosalie and rubbed her tense shoulders. Rosalie tried to believe Lanie's words. Tried to relax and let the knots be rubbed away.

After a few minutes, Lanie returned to the chair next to Rosalie. "Will you forgive your thoughtless friend?" Her pink lips curved in a sweet smile.

Returning the smile, Rosalie touched her friend's arm. "Of course."

As if signaling the end of their conversation, the front door groaned open, and footfalls approached the kitchen.

"Thank you, Rosalie. I really am sorry." Perking to an upright posture, Lanie moved to the pegged rack where the housemates hung their bandannas. Removing her pink one, Lanie flipped her head upside down to get her hands on her hair. "I've got to take off. Don't want to be late for work, you know." Winding her hair into a ball, she then secured the bandanna.

Rosalie cocked her head. "All the other girls already left. You probably missed the bus." She grimaced empathetically.

Then her eyes fell on the source of the sounds from the other room. A splash of giddiness slapped Rosalie. "Good morning, Miss Tilly." She rose and gave her favorite mentor a big hug. "How wonderful to see you."

"I'm off!" Lanie patted Rosalie's back. "My uncle let me borrow his car indefinitely." She tilted her head and grinned like a spoiled schoolgirl. "That ol' bus takes so much longer. I'll still make it on time."

Miss Tilly peered around the room. "Well, who's gonna be ridin' with you?"

"Oh, I'm just headin' out for a solo flight today."

Miss Tilly's lips turned downward. "Young lady, you don't mean to say you're drivin' from here all the way to the plant all by yourself in that car, do you?"

Lanie shook her head innocently and shrugged. "Why not?"

Rosalie's heartbeat pulsed. She knew what Miss Tilly was thinking. The same thoughts had darted through her mind as well.

Brandishing a finger like a sword, Miss Tilly began the onslaught. "Haven't you seen those posters of a young man ridin' alone in a car—but really Adolf Hitler himself is sittin' next to him? If you ride alone, missy, you're stealin' gasoline right out of one of our boys' airplanes."

Lanie's already fair cheeks grew even more pallid. "Why I never," she muttered before being rescued by Kenny, who was entering the room.

"What's going on with you chickens?" he asked, a chipper grin filling his face. "You birds engaged in a good bout of chitter-chatter?"

Without a word, Lanie slipped her keys from a nail near the doorway and slunk out of the kitchen, hustling to the front door.

Kenny wagged his head after her, then looked back at Rosalie and Miss Tilly. "What's wrong with her?"

Miss Tilly tsked her tongue. "Irresponsible girl. Young people these days." She exhaled as if expelling any trace of Lanie from the room, then sandwiched Rosalie's hand between hers. "I know you'd never think of doing that, darlin'. Such a waste." Her wrinkled hand tapped against Rosalie's. "Now, how's my girl?"

"I'm well, Miss Tilly. Busy, but it's for a good cause."

A cloud like the one that had draped the sun dampened Miss Tilly's twinkling eyes. "I hope you're not *too* busy, darlin'. It's not healthy for you—or your new relationship." Her gaze flicked to Kenny. "You're takin' good care of my girl, aren't you, Kenneth? Don't let her wear herself out, ya hear."

Kenny patted Miss Tilly's back. "Yes, Aunt Tilly." His gaze landed on Rosalie. "I'll cherish her with all my heart."

Warmth seeped up her arms, and she hugged them to her. Rosalie wondered if his loving words and infiltrating gazes would ever cease to make her swoon.

"Okay, I'm countin' on you." Miss Tilly spoke over her shoulder, then shifted back to Rosalie. "Let's talk later. I've been prayin' for your new position. Some people crave that kind of attention, but I have a feelin' it's not your thing." Her eyes squinted, defining her crow's feet. "We can talk about that"—she flitted a glance toward Kenny—"and a few other things later."

Bobbing her head up, Miss Tilly peeked out the window at the backyard, then stretched out her long, brown hands. "These old hands could use some time in the Good Lord's soil. I'm thinkin' that victory garden could use a bit of tendin'. Will you two be all right in here?" She chuckled, not waiting for an answer, as she lumbered out the kitchen door to the yard and their new garden plot.

"Hey, doll." Kenny grabbed Rosalie's hands and pulled her to her feet. "I've been missing you." He wrapped his arms around her in a deep embrace, and Rosalie's doubts from a moment before evaporated like steam on a damp road after a rainfall.

Relishing his kiss on her forehead as they pulled apart, Rosalie traced his hairline over his ear and to his neck. "You're early. I thought—"

He closed his eyes, as if savoring her touch. "I couldn't wait to be with you. I actually have a morning off, Rosalie." His hand slipped down, interlocking with hers. He led her to the kitchen door. "It's a gorgeous day. What say we take a walk together? I can show you all the fun stuff in Victory Heights."

Rosalie tilted her head. "Fun stuff? I thought this was just another subdivision."

Kenny opened the back door, and they stepped out. Miss Tilly was already on her knees in the dirt.

"Oh, no, there's lots of fun stuff. I can show you the water tower. It's a windmill."

"Ooh, exciting." Rosalie caressed his arm with her other hand.

"I know." Kenny tilted his hat forward and raised his eyebrows. "And there's more. There's an air-raid siren, and"—he paused, looking in either direction—"a tire swing."

Rosalie leaned her head against him. "Now you're talking." She grabbed a post next to the porch swing and angled in front of him. "Some folks from the film crew are coming, though, to set up for my commercial that's being filmed next week."

"You'll be wonderful. Then everyone'll get to see my girl."

"Yeah, isn't that *wonderful*," Rosalie said sarcastically but threw Kenny a grin so he'd know she was teasing. "Maybe we could go for a short walk, then come back. Are you still going to help me with my speech? I can't even think straight when I try to figure out what to say."

"I'm planning on it." He touched her arm, then slid his hand down to her wrist, stopping at the bracelet. "And I still haven't told you about that heart." He caressed her hair, and the loving look in his eyes melted her.

"Kenny?" Rosalie edged back. "You've gotten a lot of good scoops since the Rosie the Riveter articles came out, haven't you?"

Kenny's chin tilted up. His shoulders straightened. "Yes. It's been amazing. I'm getting more stories than Charlie Hudson."

Rosalie's heart pounded. "After the articles about me are done, you won't—"

Fear halted the query, *You won't leave me, will you?* What if his answer stung her, left her crippled like after Vic died? Or worse, what if his words rang with comfort, but the wrenching truth emanated from his eyes?

From inside the house, two distractions saved her from the question's unforeseen consequences—the telephone jingled and the doorbell rang.

Kenny kept his gaze on Rosalie. "What is it, doll? You look worried or something."

Rosalie shook away his inquiry. "It's nothing." She dressed herself in a smile. "I'll get the door. Would you answer the phone?"

"Phone!" Miss Tilly called from the garden.

Within minutes, the creaky old house buzzed with commotion—its normal state over the past few weeks. The three fellows in the film crew arrived early, misjudging the traffic.

"How do ya do? You must be Rosie? Heacock, Stanley Heacock." He thrust out his hand for Rosalie to shake. "You don't mind if I look around a bit; find the spot to film you ladies."

"Ladies? I thought it was just me."

Mr. Heacock apparently didn't register her question, because his eyes peered past her, and he began strutting through the house.

"Don't mind him," one of Heacock's lackeys explained. "He does this every time."

"Okay, well, let me know if you need anything." Rosalie observed Mr. Heacock pace over the rugs in the living room, out the back door, back in, out the front door, down the street. The other two fellows meandered to the back door, and Rosalie eyed Kenny finishing his phone call.

Kenny replaced the black receiver onto the wall phone box, then walked to her, standing next to the sofa. She slid onto the arm and inspected Kenny. The carefree glimmer that shone when he arrived was overshadowed by a distracted concern.

"Was that call for you?" Rosalie asked, knowing the answer. "You sure talked awhile."

Kenny's lip stuck out in an exaggerated frown. "Yeah, it was."

"How did they know where to reach you?"

"Well, now that I'm Bixby's first call for a scoop, he needs to know where I am. I left him your number. Don't have much choice about it, if I want to keep getting the bigger pieces."

Rosalie stood still, like a statue, but her mind roiled. Her heart thumped. Always, everywhere they ever went together, the paper's far-reaching grasp would pull him away from her.

"Kenny, I don't know if I can—" *Handle this.* Again she failed to finish her thought. Gazing at his handsome form, remembering the sincere words of affection, verging on love, and fingering the bracelet, she couldn't let go of him. She'd continue to try to trust.

"I'm so sorry, dollybird." He rubbed her arms, and Rosalie's gut ached. "Bixby called me to another story. He's sending a car. Three downtown banks were just robbed—simultaneously. The police don't know how they did it, and they haven't caught the thieves yet. If I get down there, I could be the first to nab the story." He glanced beyond her out the front window. "The car's already here."

A dissonant honk blared from the street. Kenny rushed to the front door and waved him off, then turned back to Rosalie, still standing across the room. He slowly paced to her. "I can see you're upset." Reaching her, he gently grasped her hands.

But Rosalie didn't move, her body refusing to obey her mind's decision to trust him. "I'm not upset," she lied. "I understand how busy a reporter's life can be." Her words crackled over her throat and past her lips.

Kenny tangled his fingers through her hair. "Doll, I promise this craziness won't last forever."

He promises.

"Hey." He grinned his heartwarming smile, and Rosalie longed to revel in it. "Your awards ceremony is Saturday, right? What say I come and pick you up? You can arrive to the field in style—well, in Aunt Tilly's Model A."

The horn honked again. Kenny's gaze flitted out the door, then back to Rosalie, who struggled to form a smile.

"Well, I'll be seeing you." She shrugged.

Rosalie waited for his next words, followed by a door closing and a car zooming away. She longed to get it all over with so she could skulk to her room and cry before facing the film crew again.

But rather than racing away, leaving her in the dark state, Kenny gripped her shoulder, softly seating her on the sofa. Then he joined her.

"You know what?" He wrapped his arm around her. "I don't have to take this story." He lowered his head and gazed into her eyes, that loving look deeper than ever. "You're more important to me, Rosalie, than any story. I'll call Mr. Bixby and tell him I can't."

Rosalie felt swathed in the admiring look she'd learned to trust, to love.

"I'll stay, Rosalie. I'll stay."

Bricks from the fortress of fear that had sprung up around her heart began to crumble, letting in the light of truth. *What am I thinking? This is Kenny. He won't hurt me.* She brushed the pads of her fingers over his cheek and he leaned into it.

"Let me call Bixby," he said, his eyes still focused on her. "And then we'll go for that walk." He glanced at the production crew. "Well, once these blokes fly the coop." He started to stand, but Rosalie tugged him back.

She grasped his hands tightly in hers. "Thank you, Kenny, for offering to stay." She smiled. "It means so much to me, I really can't express. But you should go. This is a huge story—three banks?" She chuckled. "I don't know what's wrong with me. You really should get the scoop. I'll see you Saturday."

Kenny rubbed her arm. "Are you sure?"

"Yes, I'm sure. Now, c'mon." Rosalie stood and hoisted him to his feet. "Hurry, or some other namby-pamby reporter's gonna nab it first."

The horn screamed again, and Rosalie shoved Kenny toward the door and outside.

He turned back and drew her into a hug. "You're amazing, you know."

Rosalie breathed in his musky scent as his arms embraced her. "Yes, I know. I'm amazing." She let go. "Now go."

Kenny waved as he hoofed it to the beeping car. "I'll see you Saturday."

"Saturday! One o'clock!"

"I'll be here. And be sure to tell Aunt Tilly I'm sorry I can't drive her home. And tell her to drive carefully!"

Chapter Twenty-nine

While many pleasures delighted Kenny during this period of his life, none satisfied quite as well as typing four pound signs after a block of type, alerting the editor of the article's end. Those four little tic-tac-toes represented hours of interviews, hoofing it up and down Seattle's hilly streets, and clacking the typewriter till his fingers numbed. Kenny scanned the keyboard, his gaze snagging on the makeshift letter K he'd glued on to replace the one he'd given to Rosalie. Though he was extremely grateful for the waterfall of assignments, the busy rush did soak up his hours, causing him to neglect the pretty riveter. But thankfully she was the most understanding woman in the world.

The missed moments with Rosalie caused a deep loneliness in the rare occasions he paused to ponder her. He opened his drawer and removed a cutout photo of Rosalie from that day in Victory Square. The camera caught her a second after his wink flushed her face for the first time. The pink didn't appear on the black-and-white photograph, but Kenny's mind flashed her rosy cheeks before him.

Each night they'd talked on the telephone—Kenny in the squalid hallway of his tenement, whispering to prevent the Italians from listening, and Rosalie at Tilly's Place. He visualized her leaning against the wood-paneled walls, maybe settled down on the stairs.

In a way, Kenny was grateful his assignments prevented him from seeing her in person. Phone conversations eliminated the distraction of her attractiveness—those curls, her bright eyes, the rosy aroma—and accentuated beauty that outshined the rest. Her kind, funny, talented, genuine heart.

Kenny blew out a breath as a tinge of uneasiness pricked him. Most of their conversations had revolved around his latest scoop or his adventures while grabbing the perfect interview.

Perhaps I've been insensitive, he thought. But she hadn't mentioned feeling looked over. In fact, she'd been more supportive than he could've imagined. Just the kind of wife a reporter needed. *Still, I should be careful to support her too. Today'll be the day, Rosalie. It's all about you.*

Returning to the matter at hand, Kenny heaved in a contented breath, pressed down the shift key, and dive-bombed the number 3—once, twice, three, and four times—creating four pound signs at the bottom of his paper. "I'm done!" He yanked the page from the typewriter. Its *zip* created the sense of a powerful victory.

And how many powerful victories had Kenny completed in the last week? He'd lost count. The bank robbery had been Wednesday. The police apprehended six out of the ten robbers, one who was a fourteen-year-old, Daniel. Interviewing him, Kenny felt the kid would've rather been playing baseball than robbing banks, but his uncles and father had forced him into it. Kenny paused his rapidly firing thoughts and prayed for Daniel. He'd promised to visit the boy after his sentencing. There wasn't much Kenny could do for him except offer friendship and his prayers. *Lord, it's people like Daniel whom I've been wanting to help with my writing. Thank You for giving me these opportunities.*

After the bank robbery story, Kenny had taken the bus down to Tacoma to write a piece about German and Japanese prisoners of war being housed in Washington. Then, on Friday, he'd even interviewed one of the Doolittle Raiders, the boys who'd bombed Tokyo after Pearl Harbor. Major Everett Holstrom was visiting his home in Tacoma, and Kenny got the exclusive scoop about how he and his surviving crewmates escaped Japan, with help from local guerrillas, into India, where, the Major said, "we gorged ourselves with ice cream."

That was the piece he now held in his hand. "I've gotta scoot," Kenny said to himself. "Don't wanna be late."

Kenny grabbed his hat and coat from the rack and pulled them on as he hurried to Mr. Bixby's office. Seeing he was on the phone, Kenny knocked softly, then opened the door. "I'll just put this on your desk." Kenny pointed to the story in his hand, then laid it on top of the pile of papers.

Mr. Bixby's eyes broadened and he waved his hand, signaling Kenny to come in. He pointed to the chair.

"Oh no, sir, I have to go cover the Flying Fortress that's landing at Boeing today." *And see my sweet Rosalie.* "It's coming all the way from overseas to honor the workers who built it."

Mr. Bixby lifted his hands as if to say, "What do I care?" Then he pointed more adamantly to the chair.

Kenny plopped down, his backside only barely hanging on the edge.

"Okay, Russ. Thank you. Yes, I'll tell him. He's actually sitting in my office right now." Mr. Bixby clamped down the phone, then bolted to his feet and came around the desk with the speed of Flash Gordon.

Kenny clasped his hands together. "I really have to fly, Chief. I don't want to miss that B-17—"

Bixby's pupils twinkled. "Well, now, son, just settle your head on down. I won't keep you long, but you'll want to hear this."

Kenny tried to focus on his boss's words. "Okay, sir, I'll listen."

"First of all, I want to tell you what a fantasmic job you've been doing on these assignments. Nice work. My only complaint is that you didn't assert yourself earlier. Why were you holding out, son?"

Kenny's eyes revolved at least once around the circumference of his sockets. *Because you wouldn't let me.* But he didn't say it. "I don't know, sir. Just needed your guidance, I suppose."

A wide grin spread across Bixby's face. "Well, now. You are like a son to me, you know. I'm glad to be your guide. Those Rosie the Riveter stories, they've done more than sell papers; they've brought the community together."

Kenny eyed the clock on Bixby's desk. "Sir, thank you, but I really need to go." He pointed at the clock. 1:15.

"Oh, yes, sorry. Well then, young man, I'll get to the point. I was just on the phone with Mr. Young, and he's approved your trip overseas."

Kenny bolted to his feet. "What?"

"You heard me. Tomorrow morning one of the new C-47 Skytrains will take you to the South Pacific to cover the subcontractors there. It's all set up. You'll follow the paramedic group around for three days. You couldn't do that if they were military, you know. Are you up for it?"

Kenny's heart slammed against his chest. He felt like hugging Mr. Bixby but shook his hand instead. "Thank you, sir. Thank you! I don't know what to say. I have so much to do before tomorrow."

"Yes, you do, son. You have to cover that Flying Fortress story." Bixby ambled back to behind his desk and opened a side drawer.

"That's right!" Kenny straightened his fedora.

"But before you go—" Bixby pulled a cigar box out from his desk, opened it, and offered one to Kenny. "I was going to partake of it with you, but since you're in a hurry, enjoy it on your own time."

Kenny lifted one of the brown Cuban cigars and inhaled its sweet scent. "Oh, sir, I could never enjoy this on my own." He slid it back into the box. "When I get back, we'll celebrate."

Mr. Bixby's bottom lip poked out approvingly as he shut the box. "All right then, son. That's a steal."

He meant *deal.* Kenny stepped out, then paused. "Thank you again, Mr. Bixby."

Closing the door behind him, Kenny re-entered the newsroom, buzzing with his fellow reporters, most of whom had been in meetings all morning.

"Hey, Kenny." An upstart named Chuck strode toward the beveled glass door. "Love your latest Rosie piece." He doffed his black felt hat, revealing flat brown hair, plastered to his head. "It's a doozy." He pressed the hat against his heart.

"Uh, thank you." Kenny had been so enthralled with finishing the Doolittle story, he hadn't even glanced at the morning edition. "Glad it turned out okay."

"Oh yeah." Hank, a squat, seasoned feature writer, swayed his porkish shoulders like Dorothy Lamour. "Real sweet piece, dollybird."

Kenny's forehead wrinkled. "What on earth are you talking about?" He glared at the two mocking men, then shook it off. "Never mind. You two should be committed or something, but I've gotta run."

He faced the newsroom's young clerk, Rodney. "I'll be at that place in Victory Heights for a bit; then I'll be at Boeing Field if anyone needs me." Kenny reached for the door handle, then opened it, stepping backwards as he waited for Rodney's acknowledgment.

Rodney's freckled face blushed. "Yes, sir, Mr. Davenport."

"I *bet* you'll be at that place in Victory Heights, lover." Chuck framed his babyish face with his hands pretending to be a forlorn girl.

Other reporters gathered round as Hank joined Chuck. "Oh, Rosie the Riveter, you're my sweet dollybird," Hank teased in an overly deep voice.

Chuck lifted his handkerchief from his trouser pocket and donned it over his head like a bandanna. "I'm a riveter, Kenny, but I think I can love a reporter like you, only if you take me on a roller coaster and give me a bracelet."

A mad chill howled up Kenny's back. He marched to the two juvenile men and grasped their shirts, then shoved them against the wall. "Tell me what you're talking about. How do you know these things?"

The men's shocked faces didn't move Kenny.

Hank wiggled to get out of Kenny's grasp, his jowls jiggling. "No one can take a joke around here."

"Gee, Kenny," Chuck whined like a schoolboy, "it was your article. We're just having a little fun with it."

Kenny dropped his hands, and Chuck and Hank scurried to their desks. "What do you mean it was my article?"

Rodney shuffled to him and handed him the morning edition. RIVETER AND REPORTER FIND LOVE AT LAST was the front-page headline. And the byline? WRITTEN AND LIVED BY KENNY DAVENPORT. He shook the paper and eyeballed each reporter in the room. "Is this a joke? I didn't write this story. Tell me who did."

No one answered, and Kenny eyed the clock. 1:25. *Shoot! I'm going to be late.* Without another word to his so-called colleagues, Kenny dashed out the door and down the stairs. He reached for the doorknob but was stalled by Rodney tramping down the stairs.

"Mr. Davenport, you have a call. It's your father."

"Tell him I'll call him back later," Kenny grumbled.

The lines in Rodney's freckled forehead angled up. "I'm sorry, sir. I wouldn't have bothered you, but he says it's important. You can take it down here." He pointed to the unmanned reception desk.

Kenny rubbed his brow. "It's okay, Rodney, I'll take it."

Rodney barreled back up the stairs, and Kenny picked up the receiver, blowing out a long breath.

Chapter Thirty

....

"Lord, please strengthen Rosalie with Your might, according to Your glorious power, unto all patience and longsuffering and joy. Help her remember that You have delivered her from the power of darkness and transferred her to the kingdom of Your dear Son."

Rosalie breathed Birdie's Scripture-filled prayer in deeply. The two had scoured Victory Heights and finally found the windmill water tower that Kenny had mentioned but not been able to show her. The misty morning fog chilled Rosalie's arms as she sat atop an old army blanket they'd spread out. A stone's hard edge, hardly softened by the itchy blanket, pushed into Rosalie's backside and she shifted.

Birdie continued praying. "Give her peace about her speech and about Kenny. Amen." Birdie's hands released Rosalie's, and she peered up at her.

Sending her friend a grateful smile, Rosalie flicked an ant from the blanket. "Thanks, Birdie. I hope someday I'll know the Scriptures well enough to pray them freely, like you do."

"It helps when you don't know what else to pray." Birdie tilted her head and grinned. "You can pray Scriptures with the Bible sitting in front of you, you know. You don't have to have it memorized."

Rosalie gaped at her friend. "But then I'd have to pray with my eyes open."

"Do you think God can't hear you when your eyes are open?"

"I don't know." She brushed a pine needle from Birdie's shoulder. "I just never imagined praying any way but with my lids clamped shut. I'm new at this, remember."

"Yes, sweets, but just remember, God can hear your prayers

anywhere you are." Birdie rubbed Rosalie's back. "C'mon, we should be getting back."

Rosalie stretched as she stood up. She peered out over the landscape from their spot next to the water tower. Though blurred by the light covering of fog, the view rambled beyond the acres of fir trees down to Victory Highway and beyond. Rosalie picked at her thumbnail. She was supposed to experience this view with Kenny.

She wondered if she'd ever spend real time with him again. The nightly phone calls were wonderful, and she strove to be as supportive as she could, but in her gut, she knew that if he really cared, he would find a way to be with her. She wanted to be pursued. She threw these feelings into the mist.

Today everything will be different. The old Kenny who couldn't wait to be with me will show up again—on time.

"If it weren't for the fog, I bet we could see Lake Washington from here. Don't you think, Birdie?"

Birdie picked up the blanket and shook it. "Definitely." She ambled across the small grassy field toward the narrow path leading home. "But this is Seattle, sweets. I think we've been spoiled with all this sunshine so far this summer."

Rosalie strolled beside her. "Well, maybe, but what you Midwestern folks don't know is that Seattle has the brightest, most sparkling, perfect summers in the world. We just say it rains all the time—to keep the riffraff out."

"Good to know," Birdie said with a snicker.

Dew-dappled ferns lined their footpath as Rosalie and Birdie edged through the woods. Rosalie breathed in the earthy, living scent, but her own zest for life lagged today.

Unspeakably grateful for Birdie's prayers—and the peace that came with them—Rosalie's nerves nevertheless wrenched into a tight bolt. *The speech. In front of all those people. No, don't think about it.*

"I'm so proud of you, sweets." Birdie seemed to sense Rosalie's wave of nervousness. "I can't even tell you how proud." She twisted a thin branch off a tree bending over the path. "I'm just sorry I haven't been much support to you these last few weeks."

"Oh, don't worry. You had a lot going on. I'm so glad they found John."

She sighed. "I don't know if I slept more than a few hours a night after hearing his plane had been shot down. I don't know what I'd do without my sweet darlin'." She giggled and her blond tresses bounced as she strolled ahead of Rosalie. "Hey, when John returns home on furlough, we should all go out together. Maybe hit The Jolly Roger for dinner, then dance at the Lake City Dance Hall."

"That would be fun."

"But then again, I don't know if I really want to bebop around you two serious jitterbugs." Her giggle sounded through the foggy woods.

"Well, I'd really like to meet John, and go dancing with my Kenny again."

"Oh, sweets, he is *your* Kenny, isn't he?"

Rosalie sighed. The overwhelming nerves about giving a speech in front of 100,000 Boeing workers paled in comparison to her nerves over Kenny. But as much as she'd spun her doubts around like a record on a phonograph, it always ended up playing the same tune: "Trust him."

So Rosalie continued to try to trust Kenny, and with prayer and reading her Bible, she felt more at peace about their relationship than ever. A surge of joy tingled though her. "I get to see him today."

"I know! He's picking you up." Birdie grinned. "And he'll probably plant a few smoochies on you too."

"Birdie!" Rosalie walloped her friend's arm, but she was thinking—hoping—the same thing.

An hour later it was 1:00, and Birdie and the other Boeing girls, dressed for work—because an awards assembly certainly didn't mean Boeing could lose a whole day off the line—scurried out the door. Rosalie watched them titter and tease as they pranced down the street toward the bus stop.

"Kinda wish you were going along with them?" Iris clopped down the stairs, hung an arm on Rosalie's shoulder, and nuzzled against her head.

Rosalie leaned in, her forehead tickled by a wisp of Iris's hair. "Yeah. Sometimes I really wish someone else could be Seattle's Own Rosie the Riveter, and I could just be Rosalie, Birdie's partner and Iris's friend."

"Y'know, if it were me, I think I'd kinda like all the attention." She tilted her head and rested it on Rosalie's shoulder. "Wanna trade places?"

"Now you're talkin'!"

Iris stepped over to the hat rack and grabbed her leather helmet. "Nothin' doin'! Then you'd have to deal with my headache of a man. Did you hear he didn't have an affair after all? Guess Lanie was mistaken."

"I'm so glad."

"Me too." Iris smiled pensively. "You know, he's not so bad. It's just the pressure of being apart that rattles us. So, anyway, we're not trading places. I need to work it out with Jake, and you'll be keeping company with that handsome reporter of yours."

Her gaze flitted to the grandfather clock. Rosalie's followed. 1:05.

"He's late."

"Do you need me to drive you, hon?"

Rosalie smoothed her hands over her jeans, nervousness over the speech crawling through her. "Are you coming to the assembly?"

"Wouldn't miss seeing my Rosie get that amazing medal. You worked hard for it."

"Thank you, Iris." Rosalie grinned. "I don't need a ride. Lanie's upstairs if Kenny doesn't make it. I'll see you there."

As Iris whirlwinded out the door, the phone rang. Rosalie's stomach lurched. *It's probably Kenny, canceling again.* She lumbered past the coffee table and picked up the receiver from the phone on the wall.

"Tilly's Place."

"Yes, hello," a woman's voice responded, vaguely familiar. Rosalie detected an almost angry edge. "Is there a Rosalie Madison there?"

Rosalie's gut sank, as if predicting something was wrong, but she didn't know what. "I'm Rosalie Madison."

The line was silent a moment, then Rosalie heard the woman inhale. "This is Flora, Rosalie, remember me?"

Rosalie did remember her. One of Vic's sisters. The other one was Marie. She hadn't talked to anyone from Vic's family for months—not counting the telegram she'd received from Vic's mom about keeping his car. She gripped the railing to the stairs next to the phone.

"Vic's sister. Or don't you remember my brother, either, seeing as you never loved him?"

Rosalie gasped audibly. "What? Flora, what are you talking about? Of course I—"

"See, you can't even speak the word *love* concerning my brother, can you? I wonder how many times you lied to him over the years. I probably couldn't even count. Not to mention all the oodles of other people you lied to. And then to finally reveal the truth to some reporter? Besmirch my brother's good name in print? How could you?"

"In print? What do you mean?"

"As if you don't know. Take a look at the front page. It's all there."

Silently, Rosalie picked up the paper from the coffee table. Her eyes scanned the words describing the deepest, ugliest details of her past. She gasped, struggling for breath. Kenny wrote this?

"Well," Flora continued. "Are you proud of the pain you caused?"

A full array of flak from enemy fighters couldn't compare with the devastating power of Flora's words. An intense desire to fix the situation emerged, to soothe Flora's anger, explain. But how could she? Everything Flora said was true.

Rosalie leaned against the wall, silent, emotions like whistling winds drowning out clear thoughts. "I'm sorry, Flora," was all she could think to say. "I'm so sorry." A surging gale of sobs rippled from her chest to her throat, but she forced her cries back so she could speak. "I didn't talk to the reporter about these things—well, I did. But I swear I never dreamed he would print them."

"You were not worthy of my brother, and you deserve any pain that comes your way. I hope it's a lot." The line fell silent a moment, and Rosalie heard Flora sniff. *How I've hurt her.*

"Never, ever be in touch with me or my family, especially my mother, again. And to think—to think what she did for you. I hope you'll remember her unselfish gift every time you walk through the door of that house." Flora's voice trembled, and Rosalie ached for Vic's sister's pain. Pain Rosalie caused by her years of lies and deception.

The phone clicked silent, and Rosalie crumbled to the ground in sobs.

Chapter Thirty-one

....

"Rosalie, are you okay?" Lanie rushed down the steps to where Rosalie sat on the sofa, her hands trembling as she read the article.

Wrapping her arms around her, Lanie held her in silence for just a few minutes, then gently lifted the paper from Rosalie's hand. She left and returned with a handkerchief, then wiped Rosalie's face. "Darlin', I don't know what's wrong, but I do know that Miss Tilly's grandfather clock says twelve forty. That ceremony starts at one o'clock, and both you and I need to be there. Now I don't mean to be coldhearted, but I think the best thing I can do for you is to get you cleaned up and out of here as fast as possible. Is Kenny comin' to pick you up?"

Rosalie heaved in a breath, grateful for the hanky to wipe her face. "No."

"Then I'll take you."

Lanie kindly helped the still-breathless Rosalie get up and ready for the assembly. Rosalie's heaving cries kept her from talking, but her mind spiraled into the darkness of pain and heartbreak.

Vic. Yes, she'd been forgiven for hurting him, but oh, the pain the consequences of her sins brought. Her body itself ached at the thought of Flora—and Vic's mother—weeping over something Rosalie had done. *She was always kind, loving, motherly to me. She must feel like her own daughter betrayed her.*

Betrayal. Kenny. Rosalie was angrier at herself than him. *I knew not to trust a reporter. I knew.*

But she had anyway, despite the dark memories of her father. She fell for Kenny's grins and winks and sincere words. How wonderful it felt to not be alone, even for the short time they were together. But now that was over. And even before the article came out, Rosalie had known. She should've believed her doubts instead of forcing herself to trust him. Ended it a week ago, before he could trash her heart. She took off the bracelet and threw it on top of the paper on the table where Kenny would find them, if he showed up at all.

Never again, she promised herself. *I knew when he didn't come around, he was done with me.* And then she crumbled in tears again. *But I didn't know his cruelty would be so far-reaching—affecting not just me but Vic's family.*

After a quick freshening up, Rosalie and Lanie hopped into her car, and soon, thanks to not much traffic, the two women sat next to each other in a tent set up as a dressing room for the performers. A Korean woman, Mrs. Lee, attempted to smooth Rosalie's tear-splotched skin and camouflage her bloodshot eyes with makeup.

"Do you want to tell me what happened now?" Lanie touched Rosalie's arm. "It's okay if you don't want to. I've been prayin' all the way here. I didn't want to push."

"Thanks, I appreciate that." Rosalie pulled the *Tribune* from a pile of newspapers lying on the table next to them and pointed to the cover. "Here, read this. Kenny betrayed me by spilling all our private moments onto the front page of the paper. He even must've had a photographer spying on us when we"—her throat stopped up like a clogged sink— "when we kissed."

Rosalie eyed Lanie's face in the mirror. All the color drained from it, and her eyes glossed.

"I wrote that article, Rosalie. Not Kenny."

Rosalie pivoted in her chair toward Lanie, causing Mrs. Lee to grumble. "I need finish. Your one eye not done. Lopsided."

Ignoring the makeup artist, Rosalie gaped at Lanie. "But it has his name on it."

"It's called ghostwritin'." She turned back to the mirror and smiled, as if letting Rosalie in on an private joke. "My uncle had such a great idea," she bubbled. "You know how popular Kenny's articles about you are. Well, Uncle Bixby knew that if it had a romance twist, they'd sell even more. I guess he offered the idea to Kenny, but Kenny refused to do it. I don't know why."

"Because he's an honorable man who wouldn't want to hurt me or all the people that article affected. I can't believe you—you would do that."

Lanie scooted sideways toward Rosalie but still only gazed at her reflection. "No, you don't understand. It was just a trick. I was supposed to get as much inside information from you as I could, then write the article. My uncle told me to be sneaky about it. Don't you see how fun that was?"

"Fun?" Rosalie stood up, seething frustration and disgust from her pores. Then she opened her mouth and roared like a lion. "So then your uncle had you spy on us at Playland? You snapped a picture of us kissing? Can't you see what an invasion of privacy that is?"

"Of course not. And the photograph was my idea. It's the only way to secure a front page." Lanie focused on the perfect reflection that smiled back at her. "I really don't know why you're mad. If I were you, I'd be revelin' in the attention."

"I bet you would, you selfish beast."

Lanie's lips twisted in a smirk, then she shook her head. "You're just upset right now. I know you'll feel bad tomorrow for sayin' all those mean things." She huffed. "I only told you because I didn't want you to be mad at Kenny. Is that selfish?"

Rosalie drew in a breath. In less than ten minutes she had to wave, smile, and give a speech as Rosie the Riveter. "It doesn't matter, Lanie. It's over with Kenny and me anyway."

* * * *

Pushing open the whining front door to Tilly's Place, Kenny poked his head in. "Rosalie, are you here?" He paced through the entryway and gazed around the empty living room. In the silence, the wind whistled through the attic, and Kenny remembered the simple days of college when he'd slept in one of the drafty bedrooms.

He meandered toward the staircase, meaning to call upstairs for her, but as he passed the old nicked-up coffee table, his eyes stalled. This morning's edition of the *Tribune* lay unfolded. The bracelet sat atop it, bunched in a pile. Kenny's throat thickened with harsh pain as he lifted the bracelet and laid it out neatly on the table.

He called for her one more time, but he knew she'd left without him. How could he blame her? That article had his name on it—even though he didn't write it. And the story was much more devastating than the headlines had depicted. It detailed everything about their relationship: from the Coke spilling at Victory Square, to her blowing a gasket at the diner, to their confessions at the bus stop. Even the intimate moments they shared at Playland.

But worse, so much worse, were all the secrets the article exposed. Tender, private feelings and fears. Rosalie's relationship with Vic. His own fears about his father's health. All of it was spewed across the front page, along with a photograph of their kiss at Playland.

These were things he hadn't told a soul. Who wrote it? How did the person get the information?

All Kenny could hope for was that Rosalie trusted him enough to know he wouldn't betray her like that. *Lord, please let her know it wasn't me.*

Kenny glanced at the grandfather clock. 1:45. He was so late. Rosalie must've found another way to the ceremony. It started at 2:00, but the Flying Fortress would have to land and the pilot and his crew give their speeches. There'd be music, and probably a comedy act or two.

Kenny glanced at the phone as an idea formed.

He'd miss the Flying Fortress landing anyway, but he could still make it on time to hear Rosalie's speech, to talk to her, to calm her worried heart. Explain that he didn't know who wrote the article, but it wasn't him. He imagined her sad eyes softening, accepting him again. He should have time for all of that, so perhaps a few extra minutes wouldn't hurt. He picked up the receiver and called the naval hospital.

"Mr. Davenport's room, please."

* * * *

Forty minutes after leaving Tilly's Place, Kenny, Dad, Nick, and Aunt Tilly were traipsing along the path bordering the original Boeing plant in Renton. Kenny remembered visiting Aunt Tilly before the war, and the Boeing Airplane Company was just a large building across from the Cedar River. He glanced next to him at the river swaying by. Now the plant reached all the way across the valley.

When Dad had called before Kenny left the office, asking if he would come pick him up for a drive—*real important*—Kenny told him he couldn't. But as he drove to Rosalie's his conscience niggled him. He'd only visited Dad three times since he'd arrived at the hospital—and the first didn't count because he hadn't even been awake. They'd had some good talks, but the best was on the way here. Kenny relished the proud look in his father's eyes when he told him about his assignment overseas.

He'd been surprised when he'd arrived at the hospital and had found Aunt Tilly and Nick there also. Nick for a checkup, which he only received because Dad pulled in some favors—not only from the VA, but also from some Christian charity groups in town, willing to help. Ultimately, Kenny knew, it was the contracting company that needed to work out the situation with the VA, but he'd delve into that more on his trip overseas.

The two unexpected visitors had wanted to watch Rosalie's speech as well—Nick mostly wanted to see Lanie sing—so Kenny agreed to drive them.

"Why'd you have to park so far away?" Aunt Tilly asked as she slowly ambled on the pavement, clinging to Kenny's arm as he pushed Dad in the wheelchair.

Nick hobbled with his cane. "That's what I was thinking."

"I'm sorry. There was nowhere closer left. We're late!"

Kenny's dad chuckled. "We must look like quite a motley crew—two cripples and an old lady."

"You watch your mouth, mister." Aunt Tilly's finger wagged at him.

"I'm just saying," Dad continued, "it's a good thing you're with us, Ken, or we might just get stuck out here. I could see Nick wobbling into my chair, sending me tumbling into the river. They'd have to dispatch a rescue unit to get me out."

Kenny felt Tilly's arms tremble because of the cool, drizzly Northwest day. He took off his coat and draped it around her shoulders.

"Now, Andrew, you have a nice boy here." Tilly patted Kenny's arm.

They approached the mechanic's hangar, where crews worked on airplanes that didn't pass their test flight. Three B-17s waited, but only two gangly fellows were there, lollygagging at a table playing cards. Kenny figured everyone else was out watching the activities.

He glanced at Aunt Tilly as they walked. "Thank you, Aunt Tilly. I do try to be a 'nice boy,' but I doubt Rosalie thinks so now."

His dad looked toward him. "You know, son. She will probably be upset about that article, but if she cares about you, she'll understand you didn't write it."

Kenny knew Dad was right, but something still nagged at him. Something about the way Rosalie looked at him the other day before he left for the bank robbery story. "I have this feeling something else is wrong, but she hasn't said anything."

Nick patted his back. "Listen to your engaged friend, Kenny. Women don't always tell you what they're upset about."

"I know what she's upset about," Aunt Tilly blurted out. "You've been spending too much time at work. No woman likes that. She needs to feel like a priority."

Kenny rubbed the back of his head. "I just don't think that's it. I offered to skip a big story just to go for a walk with her"—he patted his father's shoulder—"the one about the triple bank robberies. Passing on that one could've nixed Mr. Bixby's confidence in me. Then I'd be back to writing Macaroni Man stories."

Dad reached behind and pressed Kenny's hand on the chair. "Son, have you ever thought that the Lord may want you to write lighter stories—'as unto him'?"

Kenny coughed, the absurdity of Dad's comment prickling his throat. "What are you saying? How on earth could writing softball stories help anyone?"

"We don't always understand God's purposes, but son, I'd be proud of you no matter what you wrote."

"Well, thanks, Dad, but you'll be even prouder once you read the story I'm leaving tomorrow to write."

Dad lowered his hands and folded them on his lap. "Saipan. That's pretty impressive, and I am proud of you for getting that piece. It'll help a lot of people, I hope. But I'm just as proud of the Macaroni Man story."

Kenny nodded as he listened, but he didn't believe it.

"I'll be praying for you every moment, son."

"As will I," Tilly added.

"Me too, pal."

Kenny eyed Nick suspiciously.

A grin spread across Nick's face. "Now, don't look at me like that. My sweet Lanie's been teaching me a thing or two about spiritual things. We even went to church together last Sunday."

"Lanie? I didn't know she was a believer."

"Me either, but she sure is. Reads her Bible every day, she tells me. Always wanting to help people."

They finally reached the wide open parking lot where everyone was gathered—thousands upon thousands of people. The B-17 Flying Fortress had already landed and was parked behind a stage decorated with red, white, and blue banners, flying like the Fourth of July.

"Hey," Kenny said, pointing, "isn't that Lanie there on the stage?"

"Shoot, I'm missing it." Nick peered at the stage. "It's the Flying Fortress Quartet. They call it a quartet, but the other girls are really just Lanie's backup singers." Nick rolled his eyes. "I better get over there before she's done." He trotted ahead, teetering as he balanced between his cane and a bum leg.

"We'd better make our way too. I want to be there when Rosalie gives her speech."

"Onward and upward!" Dad said, thrusting out his arm like a general.

Tilly tightened her grip on Kenny's arm. "But not too fast, honey."

Kenny led the other two through the crowd, arriving a few feet back from the bannered stage just as Lanie and her backup singers began the last verse of "Praise the Lord and Pass the Ammunition."

To the side of the stage, Kenny spotted a folding chair where he thought poor, worn-out Aunt Tilly could sit. They meandered to the chair, and Kenny situated Aunt Tilly and Dad in a spot with a clear view. Then he lifted his camera from his bag strapped around his shoulder, and pinned his press pass onto his coat.

Before he jaunted to the stage to click some photographs, he knelt in between their chairs and held their hands. "Say a prayer for my girl." Nerves eddied in Kenny's stomach as he gazed at his father and aunt. He cherished their support and love. He depended on them as much as his lungs depended on air. He glanced up at the stage, knowing Rosalie would stand before the silver microphone soon. His heart ached to think of her waiting to go on, probably trembling with anxiety, alone.

"We will, son."

Making his way next to the stage, past the cordoned-off line, Kenny aimed his camera at the microphone, judging the best angle. Then, through his lens, he saw Rosalie waiting in the wings. She wore her work outfit, but for some reason, she looked more beautiful than he'd ever seen her. Perhaps it was because it'd been so long since he'd really looked at her, appreciated her.

Yet he knew she must be aching inside. Not only because of the slanderous article but also because she was moments away from facing her greatest fear.

I bet her hands are sweaty. If I could, I'd hold them anyway, as long as she needed. He nearly succumbed to the urge to jump onto the stage and rush over to her. Pray with her, hold her, and whisper encouraging words. He lowered the camera and tried to catch her gaze, but her eyes were focused on the microphone, where Lanie sang the last note.

If he couldn't hold her, at least he could pray for her. *Lord, give Rosalie peace.*

Chapter Thirty-two

....

The crowd howled as the Flying Fortress Quartet, led by the veritable movie-star Lanie, in her tight blouse and perky red lips, finished their set. Rosalie waited in the wings, not a veritable anything, just a real-live riveter wearing a yellow-checkered work top and denims and calloused hands. She was only doing this for one reason, to help the war effort. She released a dull sigh. *I've got to focus on that, or I'm not going to make it.*

Mr. Stafford stood next to Rosalie. Perhaps because she bit her thumbnail and wiped her hands on her jeans, the tall balding man must've noticed her nerves and awkwardly patted her head from time to time. Sweet, but not that effective.

Lanie peacocked off the stage, pausing to give her adoring fans one last wave, then scampered off stage, directly toward Rosalie. Rosalie didn't clap, or even smile, but glared straight ahead as Lanie traipsed toward her, face glowing. When Lanie spied Rosalie, her eyes wilted, the corners of her lips dipped.

Rosalie shifted her shoulders, showing mostly her back to Lanie—to give her the hint to stay away. But Lanie stopped in front of Rosalie anyway. Before the Southerner spoke, Rosalie narrowed her eyes. "I don't want to deal with you right now. I have to give my speech."

Lanie's lips formed a pretty frown. "I'm sorry, Rosalie. Please don't be angry with me."

Rosalie's old friend, rage, burbled inside like a simmering tea-pot, ready to boil. *Does she really expect me not to be furious?* "Lanie, you didn't just hurt me. You hurt others too. Now go away and let me concentrate on my speech."

Lanie's eyes, glittering a moment before, reddened. "Okay, fine. Be mad at me, even though I didn't mean any harm. But don't blame Kenny."

"I don't blame Kenny, but that doesn't mean it's going to work out. What do you care anyway?"

One of the other singers grasped Lanie's arm before she could answer. "We have to get changed for our second song!" The girl giggled, and Lanie's face hinted excitement.

"I'll talk to you later, okay? I really didn't mean to hurt you; please believe me," Lanie pleaded as she was dragged away by the girl.

Rosalie didn't say anything as Lanie disappeared. She didn't care about Lanie anyway, or her aching, shattered heart. In a moment, she'd step onto that stage, smile, wave, shout out a "We're in it, let's win it!" and give her speech. She needed to center her thoughts. *Think about the war effort. This will help people. Put your own troubles aside.*

She breathed in, practicing the tricks her advisors taught her. Exhaling, she focused on the words she'd labored over—alone, despite Kenny's promise to help. *Nope.* She warned herself. *Can't think about him.* Right now, none of that mattered. *Concentrate on the words.* Just the first sentence, then the rest would follow. *How does it start again?* Cold moisture oozed from the pores in her palms. *Oh no, I can't remember!* She sucked in air. *This is supposed to help, right?* It only made her heart slam faster.

Mr. Stafford patted her head again, and Rosalie attempted to reassure him with a smile, but it only came out as a louder wheeze. His eyes looked worried.

Then as if to magnify her terror, the emcee, Ann Miller, grasped the long metal microphone. "Let's hear it one more time for the Flying Fortress Quartet!"

When the crowd settled down, words coming out of Miss Miller's mouth slurred into Rosalie's ear canal, sticky like oatmeal glopping from a serving bowl. "And now for a special treat. You've read about our very own Rosie the Riveter?"

The throngs of humanity cheered and clapped, like a summer thunderstorm echoing off the hills. A gag plugged Rosalie's throat. She wanted to scream, *Wait! I've changed my mind. I can't do it!* But not even a whisper shook past her lips. She closed her eyes and willed her fear to be quiet. Willed time to stop. But the emcee's radio voice forged ahead.

"Give a warm Seattle welcome to Rosalie Madison, Seattle's Own Rosie the Riveter!"

Again, the thunderous clapping blended with hollers and whistles.

"Okay, Rosalie, let's go." Mr. Stafford offered his elbow, and Rosalie slipped her hand through. "Don't worry, Rosalie," he said as their feet clomped across the never-ending wooden stage.

Rosalie didn't answer. She just focused on not tripping. Right foot. Left foot.

"Hey, Rosie!" a man's gravelly voice called from the crowd. "Where's that reporter boyfriend?"

Rosalie face burned in contrast to her icy hands. She didn't dare peek at the heckler but focused ahead. Just a few more steps.

"I love you, Rosie!" another man hollered. "When you're done with that reporter, give me a call, baby."

Rosalie's throat thickened, and then the thickness lurched to her nauseated stomach. *Lanie, why'd you write that article? Kenny, if you weren't in my life, it wouldn't have happened.* She wanted to run away, but she focused ahead. *A few more steps, girl. In twenty minutes, you'll be done.*

Mr. Stafford patted her hand as they reached the microphone. "Don't worry," he whispered, cupping his mouth. "They'll settle down once you get started."

The next few moments blurred by as Mr. Stafford spoke about Rosalie's accomplishments at the plant and her great efforts to help with the war effort. "And because of all these outstanding achievements, we're delighted to give you, on behalf of the Army-Navy awards committee, this card with a personal note from President Roosevelt and this E-award for Excellence in War Production. Congratulations, Rosie."

Rosalie grasped the award with her fingertips and shook Mr. Stafford's hand. "Thank you," she mumbled. Then fright gripped her. His next words would be asking her to give her speech. Her tongue felt numb.

"You're an example for us all. And now, Rosie, would you like to say a few words?"

She was supposed to say, "I'd love to. Thank you, Mr. Stafford." But no words came.

Mr. Stafford lightly stroked her arm, compassion curving his lips. "You can do this, Rosalie," he whispered. Then his eyes brightened, and he shuffled in his pocket. "Listen, I heard Mrs. Roosevelt say something the other day. Oh yes, here it is." He lifted a folded paper. Opening it, he read: 'You gain strength, courage, and confidence by every experience in which you really stop to look fear in the face. You must do the thing you think you cannot do.'" He tapped Rosalie's arm. "You can do anything, Rosalie Madison. Remember, we're proud of you. Everyone here loves you. And don't forget to smile."

As he marched off the stage, Rosalie felt the tension lessen. *"You must do the thing you think you cannot do."*

Okay, Mrs. Roosevelt, here goes. Rosie hauled in a breath, then straightened her stance in front of the microphone.

"Thank you, Mr. Stafford. I'd love to say a few things," she said, gaining momentum. She then shooed him the rest of the way off the stage with a playful wave—all part of the script. "And now that the big boss isn't hanging around, we can really talk." She peered over the crowd, careful not to catch anyone's gaze. To her surprise, a laugh rippled.

A smidge more comfortable, Rosalie exhaled and began her speech. She broke all the rules—too many "ums," she giggled, lost her place a few times, but overall, the crowd laughed, cheered, and fell silent at the right moments.

But then her momentum was interrupted by a camera flash. Her eyes flitted to the source. Another flash blinded her, and even though she knew the speech by heart, she stumbled to find her place. She glanced at her hand where she'd written cues, but all she could see were the ricocheting splotches. When she looked up again, a flash hit. The crowd started to murmur, waiting for her to continue.

She'd been too focused on not forgetting her words, on avoiding looking at anyone. But now, as she struggled to regain her vision, she spotted them. A row of reporters lining the edge of the stage.

Kenny was there.

When Kenny spotted Rosalie looking at him, he moved his camera aside and grinned, that grin Rosalie had trusted, almost loved.

The gates to an army of invading emotions swung open—loneliness, frustration, disappointment. And in that moment Rosalie was again tempted to revert to anger. She wanted to call him out, bring him on stage and announce to everyone that the "reporter" they thought was so great actually broke her heart by breaking promises. She pictured herself bombarding him with the truth that he used articles as an excuse to not see her. That he wasn't man enough to tell her he didn't want her to be his girl anymore. Rosalie's chin quivered. Her eyes stung.

But the surge of wrath that used to satisfy left her feeling empty. And she knew the anger was only a dishonest veil for her pain. So she squelched it, and the true state of her heart rushed into anger's place.

Sadness. Over losing the hope she'd allowed herself to embrace. Over losing a man she thought she could trust.

She gazed at Kenny, standing there with his camera, and sent him a small smile. A good-bye smile.

Then, choking back tears, she continued on with her speech.

Chapter Thirty-three
....

Only those who stood next to the stage could see the tears. But Kenny not only saw them trickling down Rosalie's face, dripping off her chin and onto the platform, he felt the weight of her pain. *Doll, just finish your speech and then I'll hold you. Explain, and everything will be all right.*

Moments later the crowd cheered. She delivered her speech perfectly, with energy, enthusiasm, humor. She only stopped a few times to clear her throat, grasp a breath, but from the moment she spotted him, tears seeped down her face, echoing the Seattle drizzle.

Kenny knew what a sacrifice it was for her to end the speech with, "We can do it!" She raised her hand triumphantly. But then her shoulders slumped as she walked off, and he guessed relief must be rushing through her.

Fastening on his lens cap, Kenny moved to the canopied backstage area where painted white folding chairs and food tables were set up for the performers.

The miserable mist solidified into a drizzle, and a cold wind whooshed through the covered area. Kenny's gaze hovered on the steps leading down from the stage.

A shiver rippled over Kenny's arms as Rosalie finally slogged down as the Roosevelt High School Band jogged up to the wings. Crossing the damp pavement, the bright smile from her performance was now replaced with evidence of the feelings that inspired the tears. Her eyes were red and swollen, her mouth never curved so deeply downward.

"The Battle Hymn of the Republic" played from the stage, and Kenny's heart ached with an almost panicked urge to battle against

Rosalie's tears. Not until now did he suspect the depths of pain that article caused her.

She paced, slowly, deliberately, then silently stood before him.

Kenny reached for her hand, but Rosalie shook her head. "No, Kenny." She pulled her hand back and folded her arms.

"I didn't write the article," Kenny blurted out, desperately yearning to splash fresh water on her arid heart. He clasped his hands in front of him awkwardly, longing to hold her but respecting her wishes.

"I know, Kenny. I know."

He blinked. "You know? But how?"

"Lanie wrote it. Her uncle put her up to it. She says she didn't mean any harm, but—" She shook her head, her eyes staring blankly. Band members were lining up, preparing to go out for another number. "I don't know. It doesn't matter, I suppose."

Kenny pulled her to the side as two caterers in white aprons tramped behind her toward the food table carrying hot pans. Knowing who wrote the article sent a wave of relief through Kenny. The article presented the biggest obstacle. Whatever else bothered Rosalie, he was sure they could settle it, pray over it, come to a compromise, if needed.

"But if you know I didn't write it, why the tears?" He fingered away a teardrop, but Rosalie's eyes remained cold.

A heavy sigh loaded with a weight Kenny didn't understand flowed from Rosalie's depths. "I can't do this, Kenny. I mean," her lip quivered, "I can't do—us." Her chest trembled under labored breaths.

Kenny stepped closer, searching her face for a clue of understanding. "What do you mean?"

"I don't want to see you anymore. I can't."

Unable to restrain his concern, Kenny gently gripped her arm, but his touch sent fear into her eyes, so he released it. "Why? If you know I didn't write the article?"

"Kenny, that article hurt more than just me. I received a call from Flora, Vic's sister, today. She and Vic's family were devastated to know that I didn't love Vic." She closed her eyes, and pooled tears spilled out. "I know you didn't write it, but the world of scoops and stories, probing questions and reporters—don't you see, Kenny, just being near that world caused indescribable hurt to good, loving people. I grew up in that world, Kenny, with my father. I saw how it destroyed my mother...and me. I won't live there again."

Were these words really coming from Rosalie's lips? She was ending their relationship because of an article he didn't even write? "I'm so sorry the article hurt Vic's family, but that doesn't mean pain and heartache automatically comes with being a reporter. I want to help people, not hurt them. I'll protect you from the negative side."

As if by some dark irony, a reporter from the *Herald*, the *Tribune*'s rival, hurried toward them, the stench of cigarette smoke emanating from his clothes. Intruding on their conversation, he asked for a picture of the two lovebirds of Seattle. Without waiting for an answer, the reporter snapped his shot, then left. Rosalie's eyes ovaled; her forehead creased.

"It's not only that." Rosalie folded her arms, obviously chilled. "I won't be a reporter's wife, if that's where our relationship was leading. I need a husband who will chase me, Kenny. I can't wait around for you to come by when you're done with a story. I can't have a man leaving in the middle of a date."

"Rosalie, I'm sorry. I thought you understood."

Her eyes held firm, hard. "You've broken promises. I'd rather die an old maid than live like that."

Kenny's hand shaded his face as a sob threatened to show through. *How can I lose her?* Rosalie brought encouragement, conversation, laughter. He admired the way she strove for excellence, yet befriended everyone. Her hunger for her new faith and her zeal to grow and change in Christ. He relished the times she allowed him to take care of her. He longed to do that for the rest of his life. Was all that gone? Forever stalled?

"There must be something I can say to change your mind."

Rosalie's eyes glistened as her hands trembled. She pinched her eyes closed and leaned almost imperceptibly toward him.

Is she softening? Please, Lord.

She shook her head. "I respect you, Kenny." She faced him but avoided his eyes. "You're an honorable man. Being a reporter is *who* you are. I can't expect you to change." A lone tear dripped from her chin. "But I can't live that way."

Kenny gazed at her beautiful face. Her eyes so sad, her shoulders slouching. He wanted to hold her, comfort her, but it was his very presence that was causing her pain. He wouldn't prolong her heartache. He heaved in a breath and stepped back. Searching her eyes, a realization hit him, something he had always known but never consciously pondered.

He grazed his fingers over her cheek, then let them drop to her stiff shoulders.

Her head leaned into his hand. Her eyes pleaded. "Kenny." Her voice was almost a whisper. "Please, this isn't easy for me."

Kenny longed to pull her to him, grasp her against his chest and let her cry out her pain, but he couldn't. She made that clear.

"I know you're frightened," he said, "but I don't think you're afraid of my job as a reporter. You're afraid of loving me...and of being loved. We could figure out my work schedule. I'd be willing to try harder to be with you, but you didn't even ask me to."

Rosalie broke from his gaze. Her eyes focused on her hands.

"Well, Rosalie, I have fallen in love with you, and that won't stop just because you ask me to stay away." He lifted her chin, forcing her to look him in the eyes. "I'll let you go. I won't bother you, but if you decide you love me, as I love you—"

Kenny leaned closer, his palm brushing over her hair. For a moment Rosalie's body relaxed, and he thought she might succumb to his waiting arms—let him love her. But then she stiffened, stepped back.

Beads of tears slipped from the corners of her eyes. "No, Kenny. No. I won't be calling you. Please don't think I will."

A photographer approached them, cracking the bond of emotion between them. "I'm sorry, Miss Madison. We need a few shots of you with the B-17."

Rosalie wiped away the tears. "Yes, of course."

And without another word, she turned her back and followed the photographer into the misty afternoon.

Chapter Thirty-four

. . . .

"Rosalie! Someone's at the door!" Iris called to her as Rosalie rushed through the living room, hugging silk stockings in a bundle. She stooped to pick up one that had fallen behind her. "I've left a trail of stockings, haven't I?" She scrambled back, more sneaking out as she went.

"It can't be the film crew. They're not due for another thirty minutes." She glanced around the room at Birdie, Iris, Betty and her son, Danny, Bonnie and little Buddy, and other gals who were scrambling to clean up before the crew came to film Rosalie's big sponsorship commercial spot.

"Thanks for your help, ladies."

"Sure thing, sweets. We're all excited for you!" Birdie called as she jogged up the stairs.

Since the Awards Ceremony a month ago, Rosalie's schedule had grown even more overwhelming than before, but not only with media demands. It seemed every war effort organization in the city sought after her help. To them Rosie the Riveter embodied working together for victory, so of course Rosalie would be willing to take on any drive they put together.

Rosalie sighed as she stepped over piles of salvaged clothes, string, wire, even rubber bands. *I guess I asked for this.*

Rosalie said yes to the organizations' requests, figuring the crazy pace would keep her mind off Kenny. And in some ways it worked. She had no time to slouch around and wallow in her lone-liness and doubts. But her thoughts still always returned to him, when she sorted donated socks, or washed out hubcaps, or wound string into balls.

"Penny for your thoughts," Birdie asked many times in the last weeks. Iris, Bonnie, even little Buddy, noticed her gaze floating away. Conversations, events passed her by, unnoticed.

Fortunately for Rosalie the ladies were more than willing to help—thus Iris's bundle of silk stockings. Rosalie figured the house probably suffered the most from her own propensity to help. Finally finished with renovation, its broad old rooms now looked like a dump truck had unloaded the communities' throwaways into them.

And Rosalie couldn't deny that the long hours of sorting through salvaged materials, struggling to keep the charities' donations separated and labeled, not to mention the massive energy depleted by going to meetings, interviews, and press conferences, made her more exhausted than a twelve-hour day pounding rivets ever had. She inhaled a deep breath, but the oxygen didn't rejuvenate.

Even though Rosalie could barely eke out a moment alone, she'd never felt so isolated. She'd exchanged the overwhelming support of ladies at the plant—and the encouraging appreciation of Kenny—for demands thrown at her every minute. For individuals wanting her only for her image and message, not for friendship or love.

A sob welled in her chest, but she smothered it. The urge to cry had become her attendant, like a sinister bucker, taunting her to crumble under the pressure.

The only shining moments since that day—and since Kenny's assignment took him out of the country, validating her fears—were her quiet prayer times with Birdie. *Lord, if it weren't for You, I don't know how I could've survived these last few weeks.*

Rosalie reached the door, her stomach coiling into its now-familiar knot. It didn't matter how many times she spoke at Victory Square or was interviewed on the radio or handed out awards, the knot always formed. The more Rosalie struggled to force the tangled mess away, the larger it grew, so she'd learned to accept its presence. It would unravel when the event finished.

She pressed a hand to her stomach. Today's event was by far the most terrifying yet. Not just the thousands of Boeing workers would watch her, not just the city of Seattle at Victory Square, but possibly millions of moviegoers all across the country. The knot spun larger. *Millions, ugh.*

And it wasn't just that she would be displayed larger than life on the silver screen, although she didn't particularly rejoice in that part. But Boeing counted on her to inspire thousands of women to get off their duffs and grab some coveralls.

Lord, I want to do a good job, but I'm so glad it'll soon be over.

As far as Rosalie knew, this was her last major engagement as Rosie the Riveter. She'd tried to persevere until the end, and hopefully today would be the last. Not that today would be easy. The production crew had dropped another bomb on Rosalie just two days ago.

Lana Turner would be doing the commercial with her.

The muckamucks had clamored to nail down a commitment from her people for weeks. When they finally grabbed the yes, they'd scheduled the taping quickly, hoping she wouldn't change her mind.

Rosalie remembered how starstruck she was when she met the famous actress. She'd surprised herself at being tongue-tied and nervous around her. Now, through her role as Rosie, she'd met Bob Hope, Ginger Rogers, and even Jimmy Durante. Seeing Lana Turner again would probably feel like greeting an old friend. *I hope.*

Opening the door, Rosalie was bombarded by a crew of men holding metal contraptions—lights, cameras, a fan, a bullhorn. The director's lackey whom she met last time stood like a captain in front of them all, his suspenders neatly lining his striped shirt. He held a notebook in his hand, and a pencil peeked from behind his ear. He eyeballed Rosalie briefly, then pivoted to the group waiting behind him.

"Harry, did you bring the extra reels? What if we run out?"

"Got it, boss."

Shifting back around, the lackey's forehead furrowed when he glanced over at Rosalie. "Is that what you're wearing?"

* * * *

"Ah, Mr. Davenport, you not so great surfer!"

Kenny grabbed the long, fat surfboard from the foaming waves, which slapped at his ankles as he trudged toward the beach. Shaking the water from his hair, Kenny paced over to his critical Samoan friend, who was holding his belly and laughing. As he walked, Kenny's feet left footprints on the soggy smooth sand.

"You're right, Akamu, I'm 'not so great surfer,' but I did get up for a few moments. Didn't you see me?"

"I saw you wipe out." Akamu howled, his mouth wide. "Crazy *haole*."

Kenny sauntered next to him on their way back to the Moana Hotel on Waikiki Beach brightly settled against the blue Hawaiian sky.

As he walked, he scanned the scores of sunbathers. Kenny spotted a dark-haired GI with a long, narrow face lounging next to his girl. He stretched onto his elbow to talk to her, then twisted her brown curls through his fingers. She smiled, adoring eyes gazing at him.

Akamu must've caught his pensive stare. "You have girlfriend, Mr. Davenport?"

Kenny gaped at his Samoan friend. "How'd you know what I was thinking?"

Akamu shrugged. "I dunno. Lots of soldiers miss their girls when here."

Brushing sand from his arm, Kenny felt the heartrending yet tender wave return. The longing for a love he couldn't have traveled with him everywhere. Sometimes he prayed it would pass soon, but mostly he prayed it wouldn't—that Rosalie would change her mind.

"I do miss someone," he finally answered. "But she's not my girl anymore."

"Ah, sorry. You come to Hawaii. You meet someone. It a good place to fall in love." Akamu hugged himself and grinned. Then his brown eyes widened. "I know. My sister, Alioli. She's the cat's meow."

"You must be listening to too much radio." Kenny chuckled at Akamu's earnest attempt to help. "Thanks, *aikane*. You'll have to introduce me, but," he slumped his shoulders, "fiddlesticks, I'm leaving today."

Akamu shook his head. "Too bad."

They trekked on toward the hotel, and as Kenny dried, he soaked in the tropical warmth. It was so comforting here on protected U.S. soil. In contrast, the heat had scorched like a moveable torture while Kenny was attached to the American Field Service Ambulance Core for two weeks.

The AFS crew he followed stuck by troops through the jungles of Saipan. Kenny had read countless reports from foreign correspondents, had watched the newsreels, but not until he was immersed into the war himself did he begin to understand. Not just the heat, but the mosquitoes, which always threatened to carry malaria, the filth of slogging through rain-drenched fields, and the palpable stench that slapped his senses faster than he could take it in, or write it down.

But even more than exhausting conditions, the determined expressions of ambulance drivers, doctors, and medics pierced him. At one point, the Japs, with their full array of weapons—everything from tanks to swords—had closed in around the Americans.

Soldiers on the front lines were being slammed by enemy fire. Some guys were so young Kenny couldn't help but visualize them sipping soda at the corner pharmacy after school. At the sound of a retreat, they grasped their guns and ran.

The *crumpff!* of mortar fire grew louder, but a retreat for the soldiers did not mean the ambulances would withdraw. Instead, it was their cue to rev the motors of the brown ambulances with red crosses and canvass the still-hot-with-firepower field for wounded men, whom the AFS crew determined would not be left behind.

Sitting next to Sam, the ambulance driver assigned to him, Kenny had jumped in to help. Sam seemed glad to have another pair of strong arms to lift wounded men from the dirt. Kenny had never seen such pain in men's eyes. And he had never felt so proud. Of himself, the soldiers, Nick, and his country.

During these missions, the men in Kenny's crew seemed to act on instinct, their skills rising to meet the demands of the moment. He searched for signs of fear or panic but never uncovered any. He asked Sam about this later. "I'm terrified," he'd said, simply.

For two weeks Kenny's pen couldn't write fast enough. These AFS men deserved to be honored by their country, but because they were not in the military, they received none of the benefits—not the GI bill benefits, the VA care, the medals. Kenny wasn't sure of the exact solution, but he knew, if nothing else, AFS needed to become their employees' advocate.

Men on the front lines, whether soldiers or ambulance drivers, got wounded, and when they did, they needed to be cared for.

Kenny had left the island a week ago, by transport plane, and arrived in Hawaii a few days later. He'd spent hours at the desk in his hotel room pounding his passion for what he'd seen on his portable typewriter.

He tried to write through the evenings until he fell asleep, but at times, when he couldn't think anymore, he'd pause.

In the top desk drawer, Kenny kept his photo of Rosalie. Often in these moments, although still pained by the ache of missing her, he prayed for her. The praying hands on the bracelet were a promise, and whether the Lord meant for her to be his wife someday or not, he'd pray.

The hours in the room blazed by, but since he'd finished and wired it to Mr. Bixby, a stark emptiness had rattled through him. He knew this article would help people like Nick. He was certain his father would finally have a real reason to be proud of him. He finally felt justified for not serving in the war. But as the exhilaration of these things wore off, his mind began to search for the next way to prove himself.

Ideas sprang to mind, but if this story—traveling across the world, being entrenched with ambulance drivers, helping heroes get what they deserve—didn't make him worthy, what would?

And he kept thinking about Rosalie—would these kinds of stories make her proud? He sniffed. No. But what else could he do?

In the meantime, his new friend Akamu, the hotel's junior concierge, had been pestering him to try surfing. Kenny thought it might be a good way to get his mind off the heaviness. So he tried it. But even with a local friend of Akamu's skilled instruction, Kenny tasted the sand of the ocean floor more than the thrill of riding a perfect curl.

"You know airplane leave today, right? Four o'clock. Don't miss shuttle."

"I know," Kenny said as they approached the large, curved *lanai* that served as the hotel's restaurant. "I'll be there."

"Back to Seattle today," Kenny mumbled as he opened the door to his room. "Guess I better start packing."

He changed out of his wet clothes, then spread his suitcase on the bed. By the time he had everything lined up to put inside, he heard a knock on the door.

"Mr. Davenport, sorry to interrupt. It's Akamu."

Kenny opened the door to let the always grinning Samoan inside. "What can I do for you, Akamu? Didn't get enough digs in about my surfing fiasco?"

"Ha ha! That funny. No, Mr. Davenport, this came for you." He handed Kenny a telegram. "And this. It's a letter."

Kenny took the letter from his hand. "It's from my father." He put it in his pocket to read later.

"Good thing they come before you go."

Kenny nodded and eyed the telegram. It was from Bixby. His heart raced. "Could be good news. Could be bad." He held it up for Akamu to see.

"Won't know till you open."

Nerves constricted Kenny's chest as he ripped open the thin envelope. His eyes scanned Mr. Bixby's note.

"Well?"

"He liked it!"

"That great, Mr. Davenport." Akamu grasped his hands together. "What'd he like?"

"My article." Kenny sucked in a breath, trying to fathom the next line. "He wants me to be a permanent foreign correspondent, stationed here." A gleeful satisfaction swelled through Kenny. He'd done what he set out to do, and Mr. Bixby saw it.

"I happy for you, Mr. Davenport."

Kenny sank into his desk chair, thinking about what to write back. Of course he'd take the job. What would keep him from it? Nothing in Seattle waited.

Chapter Thirty-five
....

The lackey practically shoved Rosalie up the stairs to change out of her "completely inappropriate" outfit into a more camera-friendly one—just a plain blue shirt instead of her checkered one. As she changed she heard Stanley Heacock come in, his loud voice shouting demands at his crew—and the ladies trying to clean up.

Rosalie returned downstairs just as the director completed his rant about the house being an unholy mess. She leaned on the railing, waiting to be told what to do.

"You ladies'll have to step out now," the director hollered, beads of sweat emerging from his forehead. "We are on a tight schedule." Mr. Heacock eyed his lackey, who immediately shooed the ladies.

"You heard him. Out you go."

Buddy, Bonnie's little guy, zoomed up to her with baseball mitt in his hand. "Can we play, Mom? The kid from next door's been teaching me to throw a spit ball."

Bonnie's back was to the front door so she didn't see Lana Turner enter through just in time to hear the boy's comment. Eyes sparkling with electricity, the striking actress strutted into the living room. Her heels clacked on the wood floor, and her navy dress's shoulder pads funneled the eye toward her slim waist. She threw Rosalie a smile.

Bonnie's forehead furrowed as her gaze remained on her son. "A spit ball?" She twisted her lips skeptically, then patted her son's mop of hair. "Well, I don't know about that, but I think baseball would be a great way to spend the afternoon."

Miss Turner turned to talk to the director as Birdie pranced down the stairs. She sidled up to Bonnie and clapped. "Did you say baseball? Fun! Count me in."

Both women caught sight of Miss Turner at the same moment. Their lips, upturned with baseball excitement a moment before, wilted into gawking circles.

"Miss, um, Miss, um, Miss, um," Bonnie rambled, and then Birdie giggled and giggled, her shoulders shaking uncontrollably. She may never have stopped if the director hadn't blown a fuse.

"No!" He shook his fist, and his scraggly hair trembled. "We can't have screaming kids in the backyard." He whipped his head toward Rosalie. "Didn't I tell you we needed a quiet house?" His red nose grew crimson.

Rosalie winced at Birdie, Bonnie, and Buddy apologetically, then squatted next to the boy. "I'm so sorry. Maybe you can play baseball tomorrow."

"Aw, sassafras." He snapped his fingers.

"I'm real sorry, pal." She stretched out her hand. "You and I'll toss the ball around, okay?"

He slapped her hand. "Okay. I can always go worm hunting. You know, if you break one in half, then you have two!" He formed a two with his fingers and grinned.

Rosalie cringed as he scrambled out the back door.

The girls and kids gone, Mr. Heacock then banished Rosalie and Miss Turner to the kitchen where they'd use the breakfast table as a makeup station.

Before Birdie had obeyed the director's orders to skedaddle, she'd brewed a pitcher of iced tea for the visitors. "But it's mostly for you, sweets," she'd said. "You're nervous about the filming, but God is with you." Grateful for her friend, Rosalie lifted a bouquet of freshly cut white daisies from the table—also gifted from Birdie— and moved them to the counter.

After pouring two tall glasses of iced tea, she placed them both on the table and sat down next to Miss Turner. Slouching into the chair, weariness settled over her. The lingering September heat, broken only by a slight breeze coming in through the open window, sapped her even more. As Mrs. Lee tickled her face with a blush brush, Rosalie's weary eyelids sagged. She would've fallen asleep if Miss Turner hadn't chattered.

Rosalie's guess that seeing Miss Turner would feel like greeting an old friend was right. After trying to soothe the loopy Bonnie and Birdie, Miss Turner had hugged Rosalie with a "hi de ho" and a big smile.

Gazing at the mirror set up on the table, Rosalie sighed. "There I am again," she said as the two makeup artists set up their trays of colors. "Miss Turner, I don't know how you actresses ever get used to spending so much time in front of a mirror."

"Sister, you're one in a million." Miss Turner patted Rosalie's arm with her candy-apple-red fingertips. "There's nothing actresses like to do more than look in a mirror." She laughed. "And please, call me Lana for heaven's sake. I'm not that old."

Rosalie smiled. "Of course not. I just—"

Lana closed her eyes as her gal, another Asian lady who seemed to know Mrs. Lee, puffed powder over her face. "So, whatever happened to that fella you were so furious with that day? I thought for sure you two were a match."

Rosalie gulped a drink. "Would you like some more tea?"

The puffing completed, Lana's eyes squinted toward Rosalie. "You didn't answer my question. Trying to divert me with cold beverages, are you?" Lana tilted her head toward Rosalie, her long brown hair cascading over her shoulders, her perfect blue eyes waiting.

Mrs. Lee indicated that Rosalie close her eyes. While the sweet woman skillfully applied eyeshadow, liner, and mascara, Rosalie unwound the events of her and Kenny's relationship. She left out as much about her feelings as she could, afraid tears would pour out like they had every night since Kenny had left.

"And so you can see why I had to end it," she finished.

Lana's girl finished painting the actress's face. "You like?" she asked.

Stunning before a drop of makeup was applied, now Lana's face glowed with even more starlike beauty. Rosalie glanced at her own image. Sad in comparison, but at least she wasn't a complete wallflower. "My eyes look pretty good, don't they?"

"As my pal Humphrey would say, 'Gorgeous, sweetheart.'"

The makeup artists switched hats and now moved to work on Rosalie's and Lana's hair. Mrs. Lee grabbed a strand, pulled it high, then backcombed it all the way down.

Lana tapped a finger to her lips. "Hmm, from what you said, this Kenny sounds like a stand-up guy, and he was definitely a hunk of a heartbreak." Her expertly plucked eyebrows arched. "Ah, that must be it. Was he a big-time operator? Fresh with the ladies?"

"No, of course not. He was wonderful. I just couldn't handle him being a reporter."

"But he treated you good?"

"I suppose, I mean, the first thing I noticed about him was what a good listener he is—well, that's actually the second thing. First, that boy could really cut a rug."

"Now that's what I'm talking about."

Rosalie snickered. *Ah, what a relief to laugh.* "He had me jumpin' jive, sister."

Lana clapped excitedly, then gazed at Rosalie in the mirror. "But I suppose dancing's not everything. Was he too strict, want a woman to stay in her place?"

Rosalie shook her head. "He treated me like a lady—opened doors, carried my bag, stood when I entered a room." Rosalie's butterflies returned for the first time since Kenny left as she remembered his kindness to her. "He said I was pretty." Warmth rose to her neck. "He was definitely a gentleman, but he never kept me from speaking my mind. Rather, he encouraged me to delve deeper into my views, all the while respecting my opinions."

"Wow." Lana's eyebrows crinkled together as if formulating a question. "So you broke up with him because—"

Peeping out the back door window, Rosalie spied the swing where Kenny freely forgave her. "And Lana," Rosalie continued, delaying Lana's question, "the best part was that he accepted me with all my flaws. Even forgave me for being horrible to him at first. You saw how angry I was."

"You were! Like a snorting bull."

Rosalie cringed. "I know, but he let that go. He prayed for me, and when I told him about all the ugly junk from my past, he said he only cared about who I am today." She folded and unfolded her hands, the loss of Kenny renewing its pensiveness on her. *He really is a remarkable man. Why did I break it off?*

"So what happened?" Lana repeated Rosalie's unspoken question.

The ladies were done with their hair, and now Rosalie and Lana waited alone in the kitchen. Outside the open window, two hummingbirds flittered about the flower boxes overflowing with color. Rosalie cupped her iced tea glass.

"He stopped coming around."

Lana leaned forward. "Really? But he seemed so interested. Did he just get bored or something?"

"I don't think so. Maybe. His work got really busy. He's a"—Rosalie picked at her thumbnail—"reporter. He was gone all the time."

"Not a reporter!" Lana gaped at her, confused. "But I bet the creep probably didn't call you either, huh."

"We talked every night, but—"

"Still, if you told him you needed him to come around more, and he didn't—"

Rosalie's heart, which had been draped in depressing fog for the past month, fluttered, just a smidgen. "I didn't actually tell him it bothered me. In fact, I kind of told him I didn't mind." A grin was working its way up toward her waiting lips. *Maybe we could've worked it out.* Could they get back together? Rosalie had been so sure she couldn't handle his job—not because of Kenny, but because of her own challenging past—maybe. *Just maybe I was wrong.*

"Okay, ladies!" The lackey entered, his voice much louder than it needed to be. "We're ready for you."

Lana flashed a scowl. "Well, I'm not ready. Just tell Stanley Heacock he's going to have to wait."

The lackey scampered off like a scared puppy.

Lana twisted her lips to the side. "Being a world-class movie star comes in handy sometimes." She snickered, then shifted to Rosalie and grasped her hands. "So, Miss Rosie the Riveter, tell me if I'm understanding you."

Rosalie's heart thumped harder.

"This handsome reporter treated you like a lady, yet let you speak your mind?"

Rosalie nodded.

"When he did something that bothered you, you never talked to him about it. Just dumped him like a yesterday's trash?"

An ill realization clamped Rosalie's gut. "Yeah, I suppose I did."

"And even though he forgave you for being a royal pain in the derrière, you didn't even try to forgive him?"

Rosalie stood and moved to a drawer. She tugged it open and pulled out an envelope, then sat back down. "He gave me this." She ripped open the envelope and removed the bracelet with Kenny's three charms.

Rosalie felt the charms on the bracelet, one by one, letting them dangle between her fingers. The K, to give her words. The praying hands—*is he still praying for me*? Rosalie's eyes pinched closed. Her palm pressed against her forehead. *Oh, Lord, I know he is. How could I have been so foolish?*

She eyed the simple silver heart, then felt its smooth surface beneath the pad of her thumb. She held it up for Lana to see.

"He gave you his heart." Lana spoke softly, awe-filled. "Girl, that boy loves you, and if I were you, I wouldn't let go of him if my life depended on it. In fact, I'm in between husbands at the moment. Give me his number, and I'll call him up." She winked, then leaned back and folded her arms.

"There's a story behind this heart, but Kenny was so busy he never explained it to me." Her lips tightened. "But I knew what it meant. I just chose to fixate on a broken promise. Rather than giving grace, I condemned him. Despite everything—"

"Well, sister, there's only one more reason that you'd give up a fella like that. You must not love him. All that other stuff doesn't make sense." Her lips pushed forward, and her eyes glinted. "So you have to ask yourself, do you love him?"

A joy she hadn't felt in a month welled inside Rosalie's chest, and a broad smile moved across her face. She looked Lana right in the eyes. "Well, of course I love him."

"Honey!" Lana slapped Rosalie's thigh. "Then you've got to tell him."

"I know." Rosalie stood up, then sat back down again. "I have to! I mean, I must." She grabbed Lana into a tight embrace. "Thank you for helping me see it. I'm going to tell him." She released the suffocated actress, her heart speeding like the *Kalakala* through Puget Sound. "But, Lana, what can I do? He's not here." She stood up again, unable to sit still. "Do I have his phone number? No, of course not. I can't call overseas."

"Applesauce, girl. Calm down and think. Where is he?"

"He's in Hawaii right now. A girl who lives here—her uncle is

Kenny's boss—is always telling me where he is. He was on Saipan, but now he's in Hawaii for some reason."

"That's where the press wait to be told where they can go next."

Rosalie slumped back down in the chair, her excitement zapped by the realization that she'd have to wait. "He won't be home for another month, my friend says. Oh, Lana, how can I possibly wait that long?"

Lana's eyebrows twitched up, and a sly gleam shone in her eyes. "Girl." She stood and grabbed Rosalie's shoulders. "I've got the best idea! I'm leaving for a USO tour to Hong Kong on Wednesday. Our plane stops in Hawaii, sister. Why don't you come with me?" She clapped, and giggles poured out.

Rosalie gasped out loud. "Really? But I couldn't impose."

"No imposition. I'll just tell them that Hawaii needs a Rosie the Riveter too."

Swirling thoughts and feelings shimmied through Rosalie's mind. "Yes, of course, I'd love to come." Suddenly a speck of doubt seeped in. "But what if he doesn't love me anymore? I broke his heart."

Lana smiled gently. "Well, sis, you'll never know unless you tell him. Now c'mon, we've got a commercial to film and then you need to start packing for Hawaii."

Chapter Thirty-six

....

"So you stay, Mr. Davenport?" Akamu's broad shoulders shifted toward the bed where the suitcase lay open. "Do you want me to put away your suitcase?"

"Sure, thanks." Kenny opened his desk drawer to grab a pen and his eyes fell on Rosalie's photograph.

Akamu walked toward the bed. "That your girl you were talking about?"

Kenny took in Rosalie's eyes, the silhouette of her face. "Yeah." He pushed the longing away. *At some point, I have to get over this.*

"She broke your heart?"

"You could say that, but it's all in the past now."

He ambled to the bed and picked up the suitcase. "This thing's dusty, Mr. Davenport. I'll wipe it down for you. So you fought for her, right?"

"Of course. You've got to fight for love." Kenny appreciated the kid's hopeful outlook—even if it wouldn't help Rosalie and him. "She just didn't want to work it out."

"Ah." Akamu moved to a closet. Returning with a rag, he wiped out the suitcase. "Then you fight harder." He closed it with a *snap*.

Kenny jotted down his response to Mr. Bixby on a small paper as Akamu joined him at the desk. He rose and patted the boy's shoulder. "Y'know, Akamu, as much as I still care for her, maybe it's good that we broke up." Kenny's pulse jabbed at the slight untruth. He didn't think it was good, but he couldn't pine for her forever. It was time to think rationally.

"If hopping around Seattle bothered her, she'd never get used to life as a foreign correspondent's wife." He handed the paper to his young Samoan counselor. "Will you send this wire? Gotta let the boss know I'm taking the position." He forced himself to sound excited, but inside it felt like the end of hope.

Akamu left, and Kenny decided to take a walk along the ocean. Seattle, although surrounded by Puget Sound and Lake Washington, was a five-hour drive from the ocean, and Kenny hadn't visited in years.

He locked the door and wandered down the steps to the lobby of the largest hotel on Waikiki Beach. A bellboy sweeping up sand—probably a full-time job—greeted him with a smile. Kenny appreciated the friendly island attitude. He wouldn't mind living in a place like this—not only paradise-beautiful, but also teeming with lovely people.

The thought of moving here, living anywhere besides Seattle—away from his family and Rosalie—caused Kenny's stomach to ripple with doubts. *Lord, I don't know what else to do. I want to make Dad proud... and You.* He opened the door and the warm, fragrant breeze splashed his face, even as unpleasant realities squashed his dreams. *Rosalie doesn't want a relationship, Lord. I can't go back to Seattle for her.*

Kenny passed the column of palm trees, their waving arms welcoming visitors from across the sea. Soon he was strolling barefoot along the shoreline with his pant legs rolled up to his knees.

Thoughts about his new life as a foreign correspondent thrummed through Kenny's mind like the pulsating waves. Woven in with them, doubts knocked, disturbing the rhythm, yet urging him to return to an uncertain future in Seattle. The foamy remnants of mighty waves splashed his feet as he took in the aqua blue offshore waters slowly melding with the deep.

Still unsettled, Kenny strolled at least a mile along the seemingly endless shore until he finally found a piece of driftwood in a shady spot. He slumped down and lifted his father's missive from his pocket. As he unfolded the letter, he sensed this wasn't an ordinary correspondence. He hoped in the midst of his confusion, he'd read the words he'd longed to hear for so long. That his father was proud of him.

Not that Dad didn't verbalize those words in the past, but Kenny could never believe his father meant it. How could a man like Andrew Davenport, always willing to lay down his life for others, strong in every way, be proud of a macaroni-writing son who didn't go to war?

But now. Now that he'd written a real story—and was even offered a job as a foreign correspondent—these were things a father could be proud of.

Kenny scanned the page and smiled, recognizing his father's handwriting. But then he frowned. Oddly, there was no greeting or small talk.

> *Son, I tried to tell you this at Boeing Field, but you wouldn't listen to your old man. Mom suggested writing it in a letter. You know, since you're a writer, maybe you'll grasp it easier this way. Mom always knew what to do.*
>
> *I know you want me to be proud of you, but son, you've let me down.*

Kenny read the words again, and a thickness throttled his throat. His fears about disappointing Dad flooded over him. His whole life, all he wanted to do was make his bigger-than-life father proud. He even flew across the world to cover a story, hoping Dad would finally have something to brag about. If Dad would only wait till the article came out, he'd see Kenny's success. The difference his pen could make. Kenny's hands gripped the wafer-thin paper.

> *My disappointment in you has nothing to do with your writing assignments, son. I don't care what you write—at least not in the way you think I do.*

Kenny rubbed the back of his head and gazed at the undulating ocean. With each wave crashing, more confusion pounded him. What did Dad mean? If it wasn't his ineptitude at helping people through his writing that disappointed Dad, what could it be?

> *I know you love Christ, Kenny. You want to please Him, but you've been chasing after the world's success. Maybe you're trying to prove you are doing something of value during this time of war. Maybe it's to please me.*
>
> *What will please me is if you seek Christ first.*
>
> *I love you, Ken.*
>
> *Stop.*
>
> *Did you do it?*
>
> *I know you want to keep reading, but read these words again: I love you.*
>
> *It doesn't matter what story you write or don't write. You don't have to change the world or do anything other than be faithful in all that Christ calls you to do, and when you fail at that, I'll still love you.*
>
> *Whatever you do in life, your mother and I will support you, whether you write a world-changing story like the one you're on now, or a simple article about a macaroni man.*
>
> *Love, Dad*

Kenny shifted in his spot on the driftwood. A tropical bird landed next to him and looked at him as if confused that a human would be sitting there, then fluttered to a branch on the tree behind him. Kenny was also confused. He closed his eyes. As he sat there, the sun shifted in the gleaming blue sky, sending shafts of bright lights upon him. He wiped his forehead.

I let Dad down, but not because I didn't write big stories that helped lots of people. He slowly worked through it. *Actually, striving to get the big stories is how I let him down.*

Kenny took in a breath of the humid, hot air and released it. Then, as if to surprise him, a gust of cool wind scurried off the waters, soothing his hot face. *Is he accusing me of trying to be some Dick Tracy reporter who uses his pen for the righteous good of the entire world?*

"I think so!" he said out loud.

He's saying I don't have to strive to please him. Kenny's chest coursed as his breaths quickened. A lifetime of his father's words spun through his memory. *"I'm proud of you, son."* The first story he made up as a five-year-old boy, his sixth-grade art project, his first date, his college graduation. *"I'm proud of you, son."*

Why didn't I believe you, Dad?

His hand moved to his mouth as years of striving threatened to depart—if Kenny could grasp the truth. A tall wave crashed, and the breeze carried its light mist to Kenny's face. *I couldn't believe him, because I never trusted that I was truly good enough.* But that was the point. He scanned the page.

Even when you fail, I'll still love you.

Kenny sat up and took in the ocean's relentless rhythms. *I need to do my best, even in the small stories, and that's enough. Enough to please my dad, and God.*

And then, as the tree's shade again blocked the sun's hot yoke, the burden Kenny carried his whole life—striving to live up to an unreachable standard—released. And joy rushed in its place. *Why didn't I give this burden to You a long time ago, Lord? Thank You, thank You for Your patience with me.* He lifted the letter and gazed at his father's handwriting. "And thank you, Dad."

The confusion that had sent him on his stroll along the beach seemed clear now. *I want to go home.* He longed to hold his mother's face in his hands and hear his father say those words—"I'm proud of you"—and finally believe them. And whatever story Mr. Bixby gave him, he'd write faithfully for God's glory and not to earn anybody's love. *I want to go home.*

As he glimpsed his father's letter one last time, his eyes snagged on a postscript that was hidden under a fold.

> *P.S. I have one more bone to pick with you, son. It's about that Rosalie you treated so badly. I don't know what she told you, but I think she broke things off with you because you neglected her and put your work before family—well, almost family.*
>
> *You have a responsibility to make it right with her. I'm talking a real apology. And maybe she'd even take you back if you said it real nice. I liked that girl. Would've loved to have her for a daughter-in-law.*

No more confusion roiled in Kenny's mind. Dad's words about Rosalie rang true immediately. Kenny slapped the letter with the back of his hand.

"Dad, you're right! And you know what? There's a plane leaving for home today."

Kenny sprinted across the sand, back to the hotel, and to his room. He glanced at a bamboo clock on the wall. *Uh-oh, I missed the shuttle. Still have time to make the flight though, if I can catch a ride.*

In minutes Kenny reopened his suitcase and shoved everything inside. He rushed down the stairs to the concierge desk where Akamu talked with his coworkers, mostly girls.

Kenny smacked his hand on the counter. "Akamu, my friend, I need to get to the airport, and I think you're my man."

"But Mr. Davenport, I thought you weren't going. You had me send that wire to your boss."

Kenny frowned. He'd forgotten about that. "Did you send it?"

Akamu nodded, his forehead crinkled. Then he reached under the desk and retrieved the note. "Just kidding, Mr. Davenport. Ha ha! I knew you shouldn't take that job."

Kenny patted Akamu's arm. "That's a good man. You were sure right, my friend. I'm fighting for love." He grabbed Akamu's hand and tugged him around the counter. "Fighting for love!"

Chapter Thirty-seven

....

White clouds, like puffed pastry, skimmed across the dazzling blue sky, and a dragonfly skittered past Rosalie's view as she soaked in the warm afternoon sunshine. The backyard at Tilly's place swirled with a host of friends—all gathered for the same reason. To support her.

Rosalie gripped Kenny's mom's hand. "It was so nice of you to come, Mrs. Davenport."

The middle-aged woman, hair neatly coiffed, eyes emanating the same kindness as Kenny's, returned Rosalie's smile. "I wouldn't have missed it. I just hope my son uses the sense God gave him." Rosalie answered with a grin, and Mrs. Davenport meandered to Kenny's dad and two sisters, Bernice and Catherine, in the shade under the white gazebo.

A soothing breeze danced through the white leaves of the plum tree Rosalie stood under, and she placed a hand on an intricate iron-work chair parked next to the food table. Most of the guests had finished eating their hot dogs, hamburgers, and barbecue—supplied by Lanie—and now were gathering around her. Rosalie held on to each encouraging word. She'd need it, if her trip to Hawaii was to go as she hoped.

"Speech! Speech!" a man's voice called.

Rosalie rubbed the K on her bracelet, which never left her wrist, as Birdie and her pilot husband John weaved through the crowd to her.

"Sorry, sweets." Birdie patted Rosalie's arm. "John's the one who shouted that." Birdie cuffed her returning hero's arm. "Now, you leave my girl alone. She's not too keen on speeches." Birdie wrapped an arm around John's waist, and he pulled her closer. Rosalie's eyes welled, sharing her friend's joy.

"Have I told you how happy we are that you're here, safe and sound? We're so proud of you, and all our boys fighting for us."

John's hands fidgeted. "Just doing my job." He massaged Birdie's shoulder. "Thanks for taking care of my wife for me."

Watching John and Birdie the last few days had created an even greater desire to reconcile with Kenny. Their lives intertwined naturally, blending intimate friendship with deep love and protection. She longed for a relationship like that, yet one molded especially around Kenny and her, unique to only them. Glancing back at John and Birdie, she squeezed Birdie's hand.

"She's the one who took care of me." She smiled, hoping Birdie caught the sincerity she felt.

"Aren't you going to say something?" Nick piped in.

Rosalie situated her shoulders toward the group. "What Birdie said was true. I don't think there's much in this world I despise more than giving a speech." She hopped up on the chair. "But I think I can handle saying a few words to friends." Then when the group quieted—all but little Buddy and Danny, who were throwing plums at the neighbor girl—Rosalie spoke.

"I want to thank you, my dear friends, for your encouragement and love during these crazy weeks. First when Kenny and I broke up, you were so supportive—even though I was incredibly irrational."

Soft chuckles rumbled through the crowd.

"And now with my plans to leave for Hawaii, I couldn't be more grateful for each one of you."

A burst of thankfulness soared in Rosalie's heart for each person there: the neighbors, her girls from the plant, Kenny's family. Scanning the yard, Rosalie's eyes stalled on Miss Tilly, who squatted to snatch up an "evil" dandelion.

Lord, thank You for sending Miss Tilly to tell me about You. And the dear woman didn't just introduce Rosalie to the Lord, she continued to support her with simple phone calls, notes, Scripture-filled words, like a true mother in the Lord. *I'm blessed to know her.*

"I'm blessed to know all of you." Rosalie lifted her chin. "And thank you for throwing this amazing going-away party. You guys thought of everything—a gourmet spread—hey, hot dogs are gourmet to some folks—croquet, even music." She glanced at Nick's band waiting under a tent. Scrunching her shoulders and opening her hands, Rosalie eyed the group. "You people know I'm coming back, right?"

The crowd murmured, then a voice sliced through the chatter.

"Hopefully, you'll come back with a man." Iris sauntered into the backyard, just getting off work. "That's what I heard this party was about. Your quest for that reporter!"

"Iris! What a thing to say." Rosalie shook her head. "I mean, of course—"

"What's this about a quest?" a man's voice interrupted.

She knew that voice. Rosalie's hand flew to her chest. Her gaze flicked over the yard toward where the voice originated. Her hands trembled, and her heart had never kicked so hard.

And then she saw him, hands slipped into his pockets, charming grin. He tilted his head and gazed at her as if viewing a beloved treasure. Rosalie's knees felt as mushy as Lanie's sweet potato pie as she stood frozen on the chair. Her eyes stuck on him in the dreamlike moment, and she watched as a familiar glint passed over his eyes, and he winked.

Rosalie teetered, grabbing the back of the chair. *He's so mean to me,* she thought happily. *I love it.*

Those gathered faded as she hopped down and walked to him. Pats on the back and well-wishes lined Rosalie's path like petals on a wedding aisle. He also padded toward her until finally they met.

Standing before him, Rosalie longed for him to touch her face, slip his hands down over her shoulders, and pull her into a tender embrace, but he hesitated. And Rosalie understood why. She also felt timid, unsure. The initial rush of seeing him was replaced by uncertainty. He was here. He winked at her. But did that mean he still wanted her? She had so much to apologize for, to explain.

She opened her mouth to speak, but Kenny went first. "I think I owe you a walk."

"Perfect."

He pointed across the yard toward the woods. "I've got a spot to show you." He moved forward across the grass, and Rosalie cautiously slipped her arm through his. He immediately caressed her hand. Gazing toward him, she caught his eyes landing on the bracelet on her wrist. He explored her eyes and smiled.

"So does this mean you're not going to Hawaii, Rosalie?" Iris hollered.

Rosalie turned around. "I'll tell you when I get back."

* * * *

Kenny led Rosalie through the fragrant woods. In moments, Tilly's Place disappeared behind them, and they were surrounded by ancient cedars towering over them as if guiding them along their way. Kenny grinned to himself. After all the waiting, the uncertainty, the whole trip here had happened in a flash. Ever since reading Dad's letter, Kenny'd felt like an unseen hand had steered him. Akamu's rusty old truck huffed and seized up, but somehow they'd made it to the plane on time. Then once he'd arrived in Seattle, he'd somehow bumped into an old friend. Well, not so much a friend, but someone who could help. Lana Turner, of all people. And who would've thought that her driver would be on the way to pick up Rosalie. So he rode to Victory Heights in a limousine.

God's providence always amazed him. *Thank You, Lord.* And nothing could describe the awe of seeing Rosalie after so much time. But did she still fear his job as a reporter? Would she forgive him for breaking promises and not pursuing her like a suitor should? She seemed happy, but he didn't know. He caressed her arm with his fingertips. *Lord, please give me words to show her my heart. Help her to trust me.*

"So, what are they all doing there?" Kenny asked, scooting over a fallen log as high as his waist, then reaching a hand to Rosalie.

Hopping back to the rich soil, Rosalie smirked playfully. "I'll tell you that if you'll tell me what you're doing here. I thought you were in Hawaii."

Kenny grabbed her hand as they continued walking. "Oh, ho! You're good. You know what, look. There's what I wanted to show you."

The woods opened up to a circular grassy field. Beds of dandelions and their baby sisters, the delicate white-tipped seedlings, danced in the summer breeze. The field sloped downward to a narrow stream, and a brown-paneled footbridge arched over it.

Kenny angled his head toward Rosalie. "Do you like it?"

"I love it." Rosalie sighed, her gaze skimming over the circumference. "What a tranquil place."

Kenny walked her across the soft grass, where tiny white daisies poked their heads past the blades toward the sun. "I used to come here in college, when I lived at Tilly's. The peacefulness readied me for my hectic day in classes."

Rosalie bent down to pick one of the daisies, her white cotton dress rippling in the breeze. Kenny imagined her laughing and racing through fields, perhaps even this field, with little girls tagging along. He saw her picking daisies and weaving them into their girls' hair, yet in the same afternoon teaching them how to use a hammer and nails to mend the bridge. Those two qualities, among others, drew Kenny.

Rosalie's strength didn't hinder her gentle beauty. Her loveliness never subdued her strength. Kenny's heart almost out-paced his chest as he pondered these things about the woman strolling next to him.

Stepping to the center of the bridge, Kenny paused and faced her. "Rosalie, I don't think I can take another step until I know." She inched closer, her head angled toward him. He gained confidence. "I want to tell you, Rosalie, that—"

Then, suddenly, the words wouldn't come. Not the words he longed to say. Instead, he stepped back, then shifted and gripped the railing. "Well, I came back from Hawaii because I got offered a job as a foreign correspondent, you see, and—"

Splashing water sang over stones in the brook, and Kenny twisted his head back to Rosalie, whose hopeful gaze had darkened.

"But I won't take the job if—"

She leaned next to him, and he shifted to gaze at her. Resting an arm on the railing, he reached out his other hand and moved a tress of hair out of her eyes. Rosalie's chest rose as she drew in a breath. His hand lingered on her head, and she leaned into his touch.

"I need to say I'm sorry...doll." He eyed her. Was it okay to call her that? Her eyes flickered and the corners of her lips slanted up. He dropped his hand to her shoulder, softly padding behind her, pulling her closer. "I neglected you, broke promises." He tipped up her chin so she could see the honesty he hoped showed in his eyes.

"Kenny. I understand. You don't have to—"

"You are more important than any story. I was wrong to neglect you. I promise—if you can believe a promise from me—you'll always be the most important person in my life. Can you forgive me?" He gazed at her, waiting, hoping.

Tears glistened in her eyes. "Of course I forgive you, Kenny." She moved her hands to Kenny's neck, then raked her fingers through his hair.

"Rosalie."

"But I need to ask you to forgive me. You showered me with more appreciation and care than I ever dreamed possible. When I was feeling hurt, I should've worked it out with you, not just given up. I'm sorry."

Kenny wrapped his arms around her waist as she fell against his chest. "I forgive you, doll." Slipping his hands back to her sides, he pulled back. "Well, we should get started right away." He threw her a grin.

She squinted her eyes warily. "Get started with what?"

"Keeping promises. C'mon."

* * * *

More than butterflies fluttered in Rosalie's stomach as Kenny led her to the other side of the bridge where a bench waited. After they settled next to each other, Kenny slunk his fingers over her hand to the bracelet and unfastened it.

"Do you want to hear the story of the heart?"

Rosalie rested her head against his shoulder, relishing his scent and the warmth of his presence. "I didn't know if I'd ever sit like this with you again, Kenny."

Rosalie felt Kenny's chest rise and fall. "I know," he said. "Let's never be apart again."

"Deal," she said softly, wondering if that was a proposal.

Kenny held the heart charm between his thumb and forefinger. "My father gave this heart to my mother years ago before he left for the Great War. He was a pilot. Did you know that?"

"No."

"He told her that if she would take care of this small silver heart while he was gone, when he came home, he'd give her his own."

Rosalie stroked Kenny's shoulder. "That's so sweet, and now you're giving it to me?"

"But there's more. When he came home, he asked for the heart back. Said he wanted to trade it for something. Do you know what it was?"

A robin plopped off a blackberry bush and hopped through the grass. Soon a friend joined it. "His heart, like he said?"

Kenny nodded. "Yes, but he wouldn't take the heart charm away and give her nothing tangible in return. He gave her his heart as well as—" His eyes embraced Rosalie's as he slipped off the bench and knelt.

Rosalie gasped. Tears shot to her eyes, but she fought them back.

With that melting grin, Kenny slipped his hand into his pocket and pulled out a gold, antique-looking diamond ring.

"Kenny?" *Lord, is this really happening?* Rosalie felt a smile seize her face. She couldn't force it away if she wanted to.

Kenny reached up and touched her cheek. "My father gave her a ring instead."

Kenny held Rosalie's trembling left hand. "I love you, Rosalie Madison. And I want to spend the rest of my life showing you. Will you be my wife?"

All her life she never thought she'd love a man, not with the passionate commitment she loved Kenny with. And now, the one thing she dared not dream of came to her like an unexpected gift. She told him yes with her eyes before her words passed her lips. "Yes, Kenny. Of course I will. I love you too."

Kenny slid the ring on her finger then straightened. He paused, gazing at her. "I always want to remember the look in your eyes at this moment." Then he moved his hands over her cheeks and into her hair. "I do love you, doll," he said and pressed his lips against hers.

Rosalie melted into the love she'd always suspected he felt for her but now knew for sure.

As they pulled apart, Rosalie cupped Kenny's cheek. "And I love you."

Kenny tilted his head. "Even though I'm a reporter?"

Rosalie smiled. "Yes, even though you're a reporter—I'll be proud to be your wife."

Kenny drew her into another kiss before the quietness of the moment was interrupted by the rhythmic rumbling of a bass.

"They must've started the music," Rosalie murmured.

"Well then, that's our cue. Wanna cut a rug with me?"

Rosalie grasped his hand as they stood. "You bet I do!"

Epilogue

....

THE SEATTLE TRIBUNE
LOVEBIRDS FINALLY TIE THE KNOT
BY LANIE THOMAS, STAFF WRITER, WOMEN'S PAGE

Lana Turner was right! About a year ago, you may remember, the *Tribune's* own Kenny Davenport wrote a story about himself and a certain hotsy-totsy brunette who would soon be dubbed *Seattle's Own Rosie the Riveter.*

Lana Turner said the two should be a couple, and this past Saturday, a warm June afternoon, I was privileged to walk the aisle—not for my own wedding, but as a bridesmaid of my dear friend Rosalie Madison, now Davenport. The two finally proved Lana Turner's prediction to be true.

(For those of you following my own road to nuptial bliss: Our wedding has been postponed so my Nick and I can learn about what the Bible has to say about marriage.)

And where was the wedding held, you ask? Where else? Victory Square, of course. On Thomas Jefferson's porch, the beautifully adorned bride—like a riveter princess—gazed into her reporter prince's eyes as he took her hand and promised to love her forever, through the happy days and the hard ones. When the blissful pair sealed their hearts to each other with the traditional kiss, the thousands of Rosie the Riveter supporters in the crowd cheered so loudly I expect our boys across the Pacific could hear the boom.

Kenny's father, Reverend Andrew Davenport, married the happy couple from his wheelchair. The Reverend, a navy chaplain, lost his leg while valiantly serving his country and returned home last year. He, his wife, and Kenny Davenport's two sisters now reside in Seattle, where the Reverend has found a new calling as minister of Victory Heights Presbyterian Church.

After the ceremony, the two led the crowd in Lindy swing dancing, backed by my Nick's band, with him bopping on his bass, and me on lead vocals. My guy's leg is much better. Kenny's story about contracted workers (you may have read it) started the ball rolling to get them the medical care they need. Thank you, Kenny!

As for the future for Mr. and Mrs. Davenport? Don't worry. They're sticking around Seattle—at least for a while. Kenny's been promoted to lead local reporter here at the *Tribune*, and Rosalie? Here's what she had to say: "I'll just be happy to return to the plant."

Rosalie's too modest to admit that, because of her publicity blitz, new women recruits have flooded into the Boeing Plant 2, and Rosalie's been promoted to supervisor to help train them. Guess the big bosses want lots more like her.

But for now, Rosalie and Kenny are looking forward to enjoying their honeymoon. If you're wondering where they're going, ask Lana Turner. She arranged a trip to Hawaii for them! Wish I had a friend like that.

Something tells me the lovely riveter and her handsome reporter are going make it to their golden anniversary and beyond. With a story like theirs, how could they do anything less?

About the Authors

....

TRICIA GOYER is an award-winning author of fourteen novels, many of them set during the World War II era. She has interviewed more than one hundred war veterans to make her stories come alive for her readers. Among her published historical novels are *Night Song*, which was awarded ACFW's 2005 Book of the Year for Long Historical Romance, and *Dawn of a Thousand Nights*, which won the same award in 2006. She has also authored nine nonfiction books and more than three hundred articles for national publications. In 2003, Tricia was one of two authors named "Writer of the Year" at the Mount Hermon Christian Writer's Conference, and she has been interviewed by *Focus on the Family*, *Moody Mid-Day Connection*, *The Harvest Show*, *NBC's Monday Today*, *Aspiring Women*, and hundreds of other radio and television stations. Tricia and her husband, John, have four children and live in Arkansas.

OCIEANNA FLEISS has co-written one historical novel, *Love Finds You in Lonesome Prairie, Montana*, with Tricia Goyer. She has written for several publications including *CBA Marketplace* and *Guideposts* and contributes a bi-monthly column to the *Northwest Christian Author*. Ocieanna Fleiss has edited six of Tricia Goyer's World War II novels and two of her non-fiction titles. An avid historian, she teaches home-schooled junior high students intense history classes involving considerable research and creative methods of bringing history to life. A resident of the Seattle area, Ocieanna had easy access to the key settings in this book. She interviewed several "Rosies" personally and was able to conduct a great deal of research on life on the home front. Ocieanna lives with her husband, Michael, and their four children.

Want a peek into local American life—past and present?
The *Love Finds You*™ series published by Summerside Press
features real towns and combines travel, romance,
and faith in one irresistible package!

The novels in the series—uniquely titled after American towns with unusual but intriguing names—inspire romance and fun. Each fictional story draws on the compelling history or the unique character of a real place. Stories center on romances kindled in small towns, old loves lost and found again on the high plains, and new loves discovered at exciting vacation getaways. Summerside Press plans to publish at least one novel set in each of the 50 states. Be sure to catch them all!

NOW AVAILABLE IN STORES

Love Finds You in Miracle, Kentucky
by Andrea Boeshaar
ISBN: 978-1-934770-37-5

*Love Finds You in
Snowball, Arkansas*
by Sandra D. Bricker
ISBN: 978-1-934770-45-0

Love Finds You in Romeo, Colorado
by Gwen Ford Faulkenberry
ISBN: 978-1-934770-46-7

*Love Finds You in
Valentine, Nebraska*
by Irene Brand
ISBN: 978-1-934770-38-2

Love Finds You in Humble, Texas
by Anita Higman
ISBN: 978-1-934770-61-0

*Love Finds You in
Last Chance, California*
by Miralee Ferrell
ISBN: 978-1-934770-39-9

*Love Finds You in
Maiden, North Carolina*
by Tamela Hancock Murray
ISBN: 978-1-934770-65-8

*Love Finds You in
Paradise, Pennsylvania*
by Loree Lough
ISBN: 978-1-934770-66-5

*Love Finds You in
Treasure Island, Florida*
by Debby Mayne
ISBN: 978-1-934770-80-1

Love Finds You in Liberty, Indiana
by Melanie Dobson
ISBN: 978-1-934770-74-0

Love Finds You in Revenge, Ohio
by Lisa Harris
ISBN: 978-1-934770-81-8

Love Finds You in Poetry, Texas
by Janice Hanna
ISBN: 978-1-935416-16-6

Love Finds You in Sisters, Oregon
by Melody Carlson
ISBN: 978-1-935416-18-0

Love Finds You in Charm, Ohio
by Annalisa Daughety
ISBN: 978-1-935416-17-3

Love Finds You in Bethlehem, New Hampshire
by Lauralee Bliss
ISBN: 978-1-935416-20-3

Love Finds You in North Pole, Alaska
by Loree Lough
ISBN: 978-1-935416-19-7

Love Finds You in Holiday, Florida
by Sandra D. Bricker
ISBN: 978-1-935416-25-8

Love Finds You in Lonesome Prairie, Montana
by Tricia Goyer and Ocieanna Fleiss
ISBN: 978-1-935416-29-6

Love Finds You in Bridal Veil, Oregon
by Miralee Ferrell
ISBN: 978-1-935416-63-0

Love Finds You in Hershey, Pennsylvania
by Cerella D. Sechrist
ISBN: 978-1-935416-64-7

Love Finds You in Homestead, Iowa
by Melanie Dobson
ISBN: 978-1-935416-66-1

Love Finds You in Pendleton, Oregon
by Melody Carlson
ISBN: 978-1-935416-84-5

Love Finds You in Golden, New Mexico
by Lena Nelson Dooley
ISBN: 978-1-935416-74-6

Love Finds You in Lahaina, Hawaii
by Bodie Thoene
ISBN: 978-1-935416-78-4

Love Finds You in Calico, California
by Elizabeth Ludwig
ISBN: 978-1-60936-001-6

COMING SOON

Love Finds You in Sugarcreek, Ohio
by Serena B. Miller
ISBN: 978-1-60936-002-3

Love Finds You in Deadwood, South Dakota
by Tracey Cross
ISBN: 978-1-60936-003-0

Love Finds You in Silver City, Idaho
by Janelle Mowery
ISBN: 978-1-60936-005-4

Love Finds You in Carmel-by-the-Sea, California
by Sandra D. Bricker
ISBN: 978-1-60936-027-6

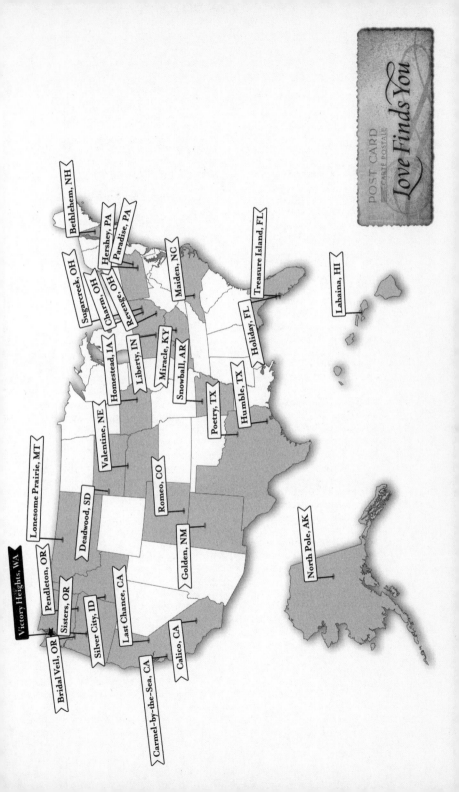